PRAISE FOR *IF IT RAINS*

"Reminiscent of the striking narrative of Delia Owens and with the poetic grace of Julie Cantrell, Wright exhibits an inimitable voice and pitch-perfect historical acumen. Wholly immersive and gorgeously spun, there is a classic resonance to this treatise on belonging and family with a wonderful homage to L. Frank Baum as two sisters find themselves and each other against seemingly insurmountable odds. One of the freshest debuts I have read in an age by a uniquely talented author to watch!"

RACHEL MCMILLAN, author of *The London Restoration* and *The Mozart Code*

"Set against the suffocating cloud of the Oklahoma Dust Bowl, *If It Rains* is an unforgettable debut. Wright's evocative descriptions of grief and grace will echo with readers long after the last page has been turned."

NAOMI STEPHENS, Carol Award–winning author of *Shadow among Sheaves*

"*If It Rains* transports you so fully, you catch yourself gasping for breath and praying for rain alongside the characters. And the characters! Each one is multilayered and intriguing; sisters Kathryn and Melissa are loyal but complicated, sincere but imperfect—and fiercely lovable. As they cling to courage and fight for faith, you find yourself doing the same. Their story stays with you long after you reach 'The End.'"

ELIZABETH LAING THOMPSON, author of *All the Feels* and the When God Says series

IF IT RAINS

IF
IT
RAINS

A NOVEL

JENNIFER L.
WRIGHT

Tyndale House Publishers
Carol Stream, Illinois

Visit Tyndale online at tyndale.com.

Visit Jennifer L. Wright's website at jennwrightwrites.com.

TYNDALE and Tyndale's quill logo are registered trademarks of Tyndale House Ministries.

If It Rains

Designed by Jennifer Phelps

Edited by Sarah Mason Rische

Published in association with the literary agency of Martin Literary & Media Management, 914 164th Street SE, Suite B12, #307, Mill Creek, WA 98012.

Unless otherwise indicated, all Scripture quotations are taken from the *Holy Bible*, King James Version.

Scripture in the dedication taken from the Holy Bible, *New International Version*,® *NIV*.® Copyright © 1973, 1978, 1984 by Biblica, Inc.® Used by permission. All rights reserved worldwide.

For information about special discounts for bulk purchases, please contact Tyndale House Publishers at csresponse@tyndale.com, or call 1-855-277-9400.

Library of Congress Cataloging-in-Publication Data

Names: Wright, Jennifer L., author.
Title: If it rains / Jennifer L. Wright.
Description: Carol Stream, Illinois : Tyndale House Publishers, [2021]
Identifiers: LCCN 2021006457 (print) | LCCN 2021006458 (ebook) | ISBN
  9781496456847 (hardcover) | ISBN 9781496449306 (trade paperback) | ISBN
  9781496449313 (kindle edition) | ISBN 9781496449320 (epub) | ISBN
  9781496449337 (epub)
Subjects: LCSH: Dust Bowl Era, 1931-1939--Fiction. | Sisters--Fiction. |
  GSAFD: Historical fiction. | Christian fiction.
Classification: LCC PS3623.R5396 I37 2021 (print) | LCC PS3623.R5396
  (ebook) | DDC 813/.6--dc23
LC record available at https://lccn.loc.gov/2021006457
LC ebook record available at https://lccn.loc.gov/2021006458

Printed in the United States of America

27   26   25   24   23   22   21
 7   6   5   4   3   2   1

For Jesus, who changed everything

———————

"And now I bring the firstfruits of the soil
that you, O LORD, have given me."

DEUTERONOMY 26:10

CHAPTER ONE

KATHRYN

Helen lost her third baby on the day of my sister's wedding.

I'd tried to tell Melissa. Told her Helen was too pregnant, the late-April sky was too ripe, and—most of all—that getting married was a stupid idea anyway. She told me to stop being hateful and help her with her dress. Her *dress*. All this dirt and dead crops, and what she cared about was looking pretty for Henry.

Sure enough, the sky turned black by midafternoon. But not from rain. It was never from rain anymore. The wedding party scattered before they so much as cut that ridiculous white cake. A few escaped to their cars; the luckiest were able to start them before static cut the ignition. Even then, not many would make it home. Most would pass the storm stuck in a

1

sand drift. At least the wedding would give them something to talk about while they waited. Rubberneckers, all of 'em.

We didn't even have it that good. We would have to walk. Pa's truck hadn't started for weeks. Too much dust or not enough gas. Or both. Sure, we could have stayed at the Mayfields'. Waited it out like the other sheep. But I would rather chance a duster than spend another second with the new Mr. and Mrs. Mayfield. So I left. Pa and Helen followed.

A cloud of earth swallowed me when I stepped out the front door. Melissa had tried to make her old pink dress look new for me, but the fabric was still thin. Nothing she could do about that. I pulled it up over my mouth and nose, gagging on the cheap perfume Helen had doused me in that morning. "I won't have you smelling like a pig even if you insist on looking like one," she'd said. "Not today." Like it even mattered.

Helen slowed us. Her stomach threw off her balance in the wind, making the two-mile walk home seem longer. If not for Pa, I would have trudged ahead. Forget her. But I couldn't leave Pa. He was all I had left now. And since he insisted on helping his wife, I knew I had to be the one to count fence posts or we'd miss the house completely.

House. We hadn't had a house since Ma died. Sometimes the blood won't come out, Pa said, even when you can't see it no more. But the dugout was good enough. Cool in the summer, warm in the winter. And at least it kept the wind out.

"Get that sheet under the door."

I did as I was told, eyes stinging, trying not to listen to Helen's moans and wheezes. Did she have to make all that *noise*? The whistling, the scratching, the rattling—I could take the storm. But *this*? It was her own fault for making us go to that circus wedding. A woman in her condition weren't in no fit state to be walking. Come to think of it, it was Melissa's fault, too, for having a wedding in the first place.

Helen's voice, desperate in the darkness. "James."

I felt around until I found the cabinet door, pulling a rumpled sheet from within. Two steps over was the water bucket; then it was eleven steps back to the door. Listening to Pa fumble for the lantern, I punched at the wet sheet, willing it into the cracks. The sooner it was in there, the sooner I could plug my ears. The door popped and creaked like a monster was seeping into the very boards. I missed Melissa already.

The stench of kerosene and a sudden flare of light. Helen stood at the table, clutching her swollen belly. Her eyes were shut, hair matted to her forehead. "James—" she started again but broke off as if strangled. At her feet, water began to pool, thick and shiny in the flickering light. The soft dripping was louder than the storm raging just outside our walls.

I squeezed the sheet in my hand, feeling my fingernails penetrate the thin fabric. It wasn't the baby. It couldn't be the baby. It was too early.

But it was always too early.

Dirt lay in the creases of Pa's face and coated his thinning hair. His eyes were red with grit. Yes, grit. There was no way he was crying. Helen just had an accident, that's all. She couldn't make it to the outhouse in all this dust.

We stood silent, staring, unable or unwilling to accept the injustice of truth, as if remaining where we were would change it somehow. For minutes or for hours. It was impossible to tell. And then, with the faintest of sobs, Helen made it real.

Pa pushed past me, grabbing her arm to steady her as another pain twisted her face. "I have to go get Emmalou." His voice betrayed none of the panic twitching his eye. "Kath, you'll need to stay—"

"No!" The word slipped from my lips before I could stop it. Loudly. Urgently. "I'll get Mrs. Patton. You stay."

Outside, the wind roared, but my plea hung heavy and immovable in the airless dugout. Pa cleared his throat. Helen shifted where she stood, one hand gripping the table, the other rubbing the sweat-caked dust on her brow. She very purposefully didn't look at me. She didn't need to. I already knew.

The only thing stronger than her aversion to my help was her memory.

"She won't make it," she said finally, defeat souring the edge of her words. "Please . . . not again, James." The last part softer. But not soft enough.

The midwife lived in a small house about three-quarters of a mile south of here, across a stunted wheat field plagued with plow ruts and rabbit holes. Last time it had been clear, not a cloud in the sky, and I'd still failed. And although it wasn't my fault the barbed wire had been covered in dirt, it *was* my fault my brace had gotten tangled and the midwife didn't make it in time. Helen made that perfectly clear. I had killed her baby. She told me so right after we buried her. In a voice low enough Pa couldn't hear but loud enough I would never forget.

"James . . . ," Helen whimpered.

There wasn't time to argue about what I could or couldn't do. Not now. I stuffed my pride into the window with another wet blanket and nodded without looking at him. The dust was making my eyes water, too. A scream of wind, a blast of dirt, and he was gone into the storm.

Helen wailed and coughed. Like she was the only one scared.

I rewet the sheet and shoved it beneath the crack of the door again. *This* I could do. Maybe if I kept wetting sheets, she wouldn't ask me to do anything else.

"I need to lay down."

Helen's dress was saturated with sweat, leaving muddy stains under her arms and across her chest. I could see her belly button through the fabric. It was hard and knotted, heaving with each shallow breath.

A sudden gust of wind knocked a spray of dirt against the window, startling us both.

I could make it to the barn. I knew the way, even in a duster. Helen didn't want me here, and Pa would be back soon with the midwife. It was better for everyone if I stayed out of the way. And still I found myself saying, "What . . . what do you want me to do?"

"Water. I need water."

I hobbled to the kitchen area, gasping as a sharp pain shot through my leg. I'd pushed too hard today. The traveling, the wedding . . . I needed to sit down. But I couldn't. Not when Helen was staring at me like that.

Our water bucket was only half-full. Pa would be mad. The last duster had clogged the well, and I was supposed to pump through it this morning. All this wedding stuff had me distracted. I pulled up a cupful, watching particles float to the bottom. How much water did one need to have a baby?

I returned just as Helen let out another scream. Startled, I dropped the cup. The water bounced against the dirt floor, too hard and dry to soak it in.

"Kathryn."

The water puddled at my feet, nudging against my shoes.

"Something's wrong."

"What—?"

"Come over here. You need to check."

Check? No. No, no, no. She didn't mean . . . ? "Water. I was gonna get you more."

Tears rolled down Helen's gray cheeks. "Kathryn, please. I need you to check. Which way is the baby facing?"

"Facing?"

The water was mud now, holding my feet in place. I wasn't a midwife or a doctor. And she wasn't even really family. Just a stepmother. Not that either one of us would ever call her that.

"Please." She moaned as another pain erupted. It was an eternity before she could speak again. "Something's wrong."

Of course something was wrong. Everything about this was wrong. I needed Melissa. She'd helped with the others. I wasn't supposed to be doing this. I was only fourteen. I knew where babies came from. I'd helped with the cows and pigs before most of them had starved. But this . . .

Was this what it had been like for my mother? Had I made her scream like this before I killed her?

"Please . . ." Helen's voice was barely above a whisper.

The window rattled. I couldn't look at her; instead I counted my fingers. Right now she needed me. My new brother or sister . . . he or she needed me, too. Needed me to help. Needed me to look. And I just couldn't.

"Kathryn, what do you see? Can you see the head?"

I backed away. I shouldn't be here. I'd only make it worse. Where was Pa? Where was Melissa?

"Kath—" Helen's words choked as another pain gripped her.

I closed my eyes and stumbled backward, smashing into something that hadn't been there just minutes before.

Pa. Pa was back. He grabbed my arms and shook me. "Kathryn, what's happening? What's wrong?"

I couldn't speak. My foot throbbed. Bile pooled in my mouth.

The midwife rushed past us, bag in hand.

Helen shrieked again.

My father dropped my arms, forgetting about me. He ran toward the bed.

Ignoring the protests from my foot, I pushed out the front door, coughing as dirt filled my lungs. But I could breathe out here. Somehow, in the dirt, I could breathe. I felt around blindly until I found the rope leading from our house to the barn. Pulling my dress over my nose and mouth once again, I stumbled through sand drifts until I felt the worn wood of the barn door beneath my fingers and pushed.

The chickens scattered. Our one remaining cow glared.

The lantern gave a comforting glow as I pulled my book from its hiding spot in the rafters. My mother's book, my real mother, the only thing I had to remember a woman I'd never met. *The Wonderful Wizard of Oz.* The book from before Helen. Before the babies. Before the drought.

Melissa's face floated before me in the dark.

"Now, Kath, listen. You can't talk and listen at the same time."

"But I know *it already," I said. "I don't even need the book anymore."*

She sighed and closed the cover, like we hadn't done this a million times before. "Well, if you already know the story, I guess we don't need to read it no more. I'll be going."

I'd known she wouldn't really leave. She never left. But still I would cry out, beg her to stay, read a few more pages. I'd be quiet and listen, I'd promise. If only she'd stay and read just a little more.

But this time she hadn't stayed. She'd really left. And all I had was my mother's book and this barn, where I could get away from the nightmare she'd left me in.

Dorothy lived in the midst of the great Kansas
prairies with Uncle Henry, who was a farmer, and
Aunt Em, who was the farmer's wife. Their house
was small, for the lumber to build it had to be
carried by wagon many miles. . . .

Helen's screams outlasted the wind. By sunrise, the storm had finally passed, leaving dust and death hanging in the air. The house quiet, I retreated from Oz to dig yet another hole in the parched earth near the fence line.

CHAPTER TWO

MELISSA

"I hope they made it home all right."

The wind whistled around the window frame, sending a blast of sand against the glass and causing me to jump.

I knew Kathryn hadn't caused the duster. But it sure felt like it. The way she'd sulked and moped and cursed under her breath during the ceremony, it wouldn't have surprised me one bit if she was praying for a storm. And not the kind we usually prayed for.

Whether she'd meant for it to happen or not, it had worked: it was my wedding night, and all I could think about was my grumpy little sister.

"Of course they did. Your pa's a smart one."

"But Helen—"

"They're fine," Henry said, closing the curtains. His perfect face softened at my concern. "Anyways, this is your home now. This house . . . and me." He raised my chin slightly and kissed me.

Heat rose in my cheeks as his chest pressed against mine. My first instinct was to push him away. But I didn't want to. And now I didn't have to. My body tingled beneath my white-lace dress. This was proper now. This man in front of me—a man with hair the color of summer wheat and skin as soft as a sunrise—was my husband. Henry Mayfield had finally chosen a wife, and he had chosen me.

My father always told me I was beautiful. *You look just like your ma.* Always said with a twinkle in his eyes and a smile on his lips. I never believed him. My hair was too red, my skin too pale. I was nothing like her, I thought. And beauty didn't mean much in Boise City, anyway. Yet still I couldn't help but notice the stares and whispers from the boys in school, though my shyness stalled any pursuit beyond the initial "hello" phase.

Except for Henry Mayfield.

Folks around town said it was no surprise I had caught his eye. It was a surprise, however, when our courtship began in earnest. Because he was Henry Mayfield. And I was Melissa Baile. And those two names had never been together on anyone's tongue.

Until now.

Our wedding was the event of the year in Boise City. The drought hadn't given us much to celebrate lately, but a wedding was something to behold in the prairie, especially when it involved the Mayfields. Everyone had come, rich and poor, old and young, like the royal weddings in my childhood storybooks. The church had been filled with flowers, something I knew I'd remember for years to come. After months of brown and gray, my wedding was overflowing with greens, reds, and pinks. Henry had brought color back into my world. It was a perfect day. Even Kathryn's scowls and the duster's abrupt interruption couldn't spoil my mood. Too much.

Those same flowers now filled Henry's home. Our home. Our big, beautiful home full of beautiful furniture and fancy china. Two stories tall and almost a dozen rooms, with walls not made of dirt, and no snakes or centipedes hiding in their depths. The air inside smelled of tobacco and leather, not sweat and dung. The bathroom was bright and white and indoors. I wondered if I'd ever get used to hearing my shoes click on the wooden floors.

"I have something for you," Henry murmured, brushing a hand across my cheek.

I closed my eyes and smiled, Kathryn and Helen and Pa forgotten. "More?"

"You're a Mayfield now. There's always more." From behind his back, he pulled a small parcel wrapped in tissue. "Open it."

I unwrapped it slowly, savoring the moment. Fire crackled behind us. The wind outside howled, but in here I was safe and warm and married. Beneath folds of white paper lay a blue- and white-checked handkerchief. The letters *MM* were embroidered with red thread.

"Oh, Henry," I breathed. "It's beautiful."

He tucked a strand of hair behind my ear. His hands weren't scratchy like Pa's or dirty like Kathryn's. They weren't even cracked like Helen's. "I can't stop the dust, but I can protect my wife's face from its sting."

"It's too much."

"Nothing is too much for you."

I held it over my mouth and nose, batting my eyelashes. "How does it look?"

"Perfect."

"Thank you, Henry. I love it."

"I knew you would." He gave a quick wink, his eyes sparkling. His eyes. They were what first attracted me. So pale blue they were almost transparent. Oozing with confidence and charm. He nuzzled my neck, his breath sprouting goose bumps across my arms. "You're finally mine." His lips brushed my earlobe. "Mrs. Mayfield."

The name sounded foreign, as if spoken to a stranger. And yet his gaze remained fixed on me.

He ran a hand down my back and gestured to the stairs. "And now, my beautiful bride . . ."

The butterflies in my stomach turned to moths. I knew this was coming. And I wanted it to come. I did. I was a wife now, and I had to do what wives did, although I wasn't quite sure what that was. It was improper to ask my friends, and I'd been too embarrassed to ask Helen.

The worst of the storm had passed, leaving a stillness even louder than the wind. Or maybe that was just the sound of my own heart as I allowed myself to be led to his bedroom.

No, *our* bedroom. With its white walls and squishy rug and fluffy bed big enough for two people.

Henry let go of my hand and lit a bedside lamp, causing me to wince. The usual soft, comforting glow was too bright in here. Like a spotlight, trained directly on me. It was hot and glaring and yet somehow I shivered.

My husband sat down on the bed and loosened his tie. The bedspread crinkled beneath him. I moved to sit next to him, but he pushed me back, gentle but firm.

"Get undressed."

There was a smile on his lips. One I'd never seen before.

I fiddled with the folds of my wedding dress. Lace and satin—two fabrics I'd never thought I'd wear, let alone own. But Henry had insisted on this gown because it was the best. He'd had it brought in all the way from Dallas. I wasn't ready to take it off, and not just because it was beautiful. "Henry, I—"

"I want to see you."

My modesty swelled. I'd never allowed anyone to see me unclothed, not even Kathryn, and we'd shared a room since the day she was born. Still, I wanted this to happen. I wanted to be his in every sense of the word. Just not in this light. Something softer. Dimmer. "Maybe we could light a fire?"

"No." His voice was soft but impatient. The faint smile faded.

Unexpected tears formed in my eyes as I tugged at my dress. *Grow up,* I scolded myself. *You are his* wife. *This is what married people do. In the light, in the dark, it doesn't matter. So stop it.*

My dress fell to the floor silently. I crossed my arms over my chest.

"Put your arms down."

Henry's gaze washed over me. Hungry. No, not hungry. Hunger could be ignored. I'd done it countless nights before. This . . . this was like the crops when the heavens opened. Insatiable. Ravenous. He inspected every inch of my exposed flesh steadily, deliberately, and when his eyes finally met mine, I did not recognize what they were trying to tell me.

Heat rushed through my cheeks but still I trembled. Henry sat on the edge of the bed, his back to the light, his face hidden in shadow. The clock ticked loudly in the hallway. Seconds. Minutes. How long was he going to make me stand here like this? I'd never felt so cold.

Finally he moved. Slowly. Confidently. His hands traced circles along my back and twirled a strand of hair around his finger. "You are so beautiful."

I melted into his touch. He loved me. He wanted me. And I wanted him, more than I could say.

He unclasped the silver cross at my neck. My mother's necklace. A relic of her faith, a faith she'd passed on to me during our few short years together. A faith I'd clung to when she'd slipped away and Pa had retreated into himself, leaving me with an inconsolable newborn and a tarnished cross. I never took it off. I grasped for it, but Henry covered my hand with his. "I need all of you," he whispered. "Nothing between us." Running a hand down my arm, he kissed me, a kiss I felt in every nerve in my body. The necklace was forgotten.

It was rougher than I expected. Henry's hands were urgent, his actions fevered. Initial pleasure faded into pain. I cried out, but he covered it with a kiss. He did not ask if I was okay. Tears flooded my eyes and still he continued. His eyes remained on my body but avoided my own, no matter how much I tried to meet his gaze.

And then it was over. I waited for his panting to cease, for some kind of sign he was happy. Was I supposed to feel something afterward? Did he? Had I done it right? I hadn't expected the physical act of love to be so . . . physical.

After several minutes, he kissed my forehead and rolled onto his back. Wrapping the sheet around me, I excused myself to the bathroom. My legs were wobbly, and my back was tender from the scratch of the bedspread. My hands shook as I cleaned myself.

I opened the door to find Henry fully dressed. His eyes were once again soft, a playful smile dancing on his lips. "Up for a nightcap?"

Later that night, I lay next to my husband. My body ached. My mind refused to settle, and I found myself unable even to pray. I wished I were listening to Kathryn read, her slow, meticulous intonation as she sounded out unfamiliar words. I pictured her curious brown eyes peering over the top of the book, seeking my approval at her pronunciation. She was six years my junior, and I'd taught her everything I knew. Starting with reading.

I wondered what she was doing now. Perhaps she was reading, just like I pictured. If I listened hard enough, maybe I could hear. But that was ridiculous. Kathryn was miles away. And she was probably sleeping. Or sitting in bed, still stewing at me.

For the second time that day, a tear rolled down my cheek. Frustrated, I wiped it away. I hadn't been a child for a very long time, since my mother died. So why was I acting like one now?

The house creaked in ways our dugout did not. Henry snored and snorted in ways Kathryn never did. I couldn't get used to sleeping on a pillow. Even the smell in here was wrong—like flowers and aftershave and clean air, above the ground and not below it. Everything was different. I was different. Or I would be. One of these days.

This beautiful house was my home now. Henry Mayfield was my family now. I rolled over and watched him breathe. My husband. His golden hair fell perfectly across his forehead, even in his sleep. His chest rose and fell as his mouth, those two perfect lips, twitched. I wondered if he was dreaming. After several minutes, I grabbed the necklace from my nightstand and refastened it around my neck. The warmth of the silver cross soothed me, and I finally fell asleep.

CHAPTER THREE

KATHRYN

"Kath, we need to talk."

Light streamed from the rafters, landing on tired eyes that stared up at me from the cracks at my feet.

I threw another mound of wheat to the floor, ignoring Pa. I had too much work to do. Trapped in the loft, the grain was starting to rot in the summer heat. We couldn't even sell good wheat; letting it go bad was more than I could bear.

It had been just over six weeks since the baby but things hadn't gotten back to normal. Well, as normal as things could be now, with Melissa gone. Helen spent most of her time in the dugout, cleaning stuff that would just get dirty again and moping or else snapping at me for tracking in dust, for touching the clean sheets, for chewing my stew too loudly. For being here. Like it was my fault it wouldn't rain and the wind wouldn't stop blowing. Like it was my fault another baby died.

But the change in Pa was worse. It wasn't that he was quiet. He'd always been quiet. But this was a different kind. It was the kind of quiet you hear in the middle of a twister. Melissa says there's no way I remember the tornado of 1925, the one that went right over the cellar and doggone near took everything. But I do, whether she believes me or not. And what I remember is when the wind is angry and roaring and hell-bent on destroying you, there's a thin layer of quiet that covers you after you stop fighting and decide to let it. That was the kind of quiet filling my pa.

So when he came to me in the barn, I already knew what he was going to say. But I wasn't going to make it easy. "'Bout what?"

"Just get down here."

"I'm busy."

"You watch your sass, young lady."

Helen. I hadn't seen her come in behind him. Her face showed no signs of tears, which meant today was the other Helen—the angry one. Fantastic.

I lowered myself down the ladder. My brace used to slow me down, but I'd gotten to be an expert at swinging my legs just so. The metal didn't even scratch against the wooden rungs anymore.

"Come inside. Get some water."

"I'm fine right here."

Helen clasped her hands tightly in front of her, knuckles turning white. After all these years, she still looked out of place in our barn. Too pretty. Features too delicate and hair too blonde. Even though three dead babies and two years of drought had put a twitch in her lip and wrinkles under her eyes, it still couldn't make her fit.

"As you wish."

My father stepped out from behind her, picking flecks of mud from his weathered hat. Willfully not looking at me. "Kath, Helen and I have decided—"

"Jackrabbit."

"Huh?"

I pointed out the barn door. "Jackrabbit. In the garden again."

The rabbit turned and looked, challenging us, his small mouth twisting with each bite of our precious crop. They'd gotten stupider over the past few months. Or more desperate. Either way, we weren't looking to feed all of God's creation, not when we were barely getting fed ourselves.

Pa cursed under his breath and retreated into the blinding sunlight.

I smirked.

Helen's lips disappeared under her irritation. "Stall all you want, Kathryn. We're leaving."

"Says who?"

"Says me and your pa. We're going to Indianapolis to stay with my family until this drought is over."

"Over my dead body."

"Don't talk like that." My father reappeared suddenly, a grimace lingering on his face long enough for me to feel a stab of guilt.

Death weren't nothing to toss out like that. Not anymore. But seeing the hardness in Helen's face stifled any remorse before it ever really began. "Is she making you do this?"

"Kathryn, enough."

But it wasn't enough. I was just getting started. "What about the Last Man's Club?"

"Kathryn—"

"When they signed that charter in Dalhart, you said you'da signed it if you could've. Bunch of pussyfooted quitters, those suitcase farmers. But we're *real*. The last men of Boise City, you said. We'd never leave."

Pa averted his eyes. "Things are different now."

I glared at Helen. "Yes, they are."

"Now you stop that." His tone was sharper than he ever took with me. "It ain't about Helen. It's about all of us. There ain't no money coming in, and there won't be any money coming in until God decides our punishment has been enough. People are starvin' and gettin' sick. This ain't no way to live. And I won't let it be how I die, neither."

"But if we just—"

"We're doing this for you, too."

I spat out a laugh I did not recognize. "For me?"

"My father can help you, Kathryn," Helen said quietly.

If Pa hadn't been standing so close, I would have slapped her. Or maybe even worse.

When I was born, the doctor said it was clubfoot. *"Poor thing,"* he'd said. *"Life will be so hard."* And he was right. My childhood *was* difficult. But not because my foot was misshapen. Because I was ill-mannered and bullheaded, always getting into trouble, according to Pa, though he said it with a smile on his face. When I got older and started asking questions, Melissa told me it was how God made me special. She'd helped me learn to walk, stuffed cotton in the places my brace pinched, and never let me use it as an excuse to get out of doing chores. I learned to make do.

Until Helen came along.

The first day I'd met her, she wouldn't look at my foot. After that, she wouldn't stop. And she wasn't as sneaky as she thought. I always caught her.

Then I started to catch other people looking too. The kids at school. Mr. Clark down at the sundry. The lady who played the organ at church. But it wasn't just the look. It was the *thing* in their eyes I couldn't place. Pity? Shame? Curiosity? Whatever it was, for the first time, I realized something was wrong with me. I wasn't normal. And where once there had been nothing, there were suddenly a bunch of things I couldn't do. Like help Pa plow. Like get to school on my own after Melissa had finished. Like do *anything* right for Helen.

She made me realize the truth: my foot didn't make me special; it made me a problem.

"There's a surgery he could do," Pa was saying. "We could get rid of that brace altogether."

Helen smiled like a rattler. She knew exactly what she was doing, getting Pa to say what I wanted to hear. Pa wouldn't leave without me. She knew that. And the only way to get me to go—willingly—was to give me the only thing in the world I wanted more than to stay. I hated her for knowing dreams I hardly dared admit even to myself.

"I don't want the stupid surgery," I lied. "If you want to go, go. I'll stay here."

"Kathryn—"

"You might be a quitter, but I ain't."

"There's no way you could live here by yourself. Not in your condition."

In that minute, I prayed. But not in the way Melissa always told me to. In that minute, I prayed for the strength not to punch Helen in the face. Of course I couldn't work the farm on my own. Didn't mean she had to say it out loud. "I'll get a job in town."

"Doing what?"

Smugness dripped from her words. Jobs were scarce for everyone, but especially for a cripple. No one would hire me. No one would marry me. No one would want me. I was a burden. *Her* burden. "You just want to leave because Oklahoma is killin' your babies."

It was as if the whole earth froze. I swear even the grasshoppers stopped their cursed chirping. And they don't stop for nothing. Ever.

"Kathryn!"

Pa's voice was a million miles away. I could see nothing but Helen. Soft, perfect, horrible Helen. "It knows you don't belong here. You're weak. And you make weak babies."

I knew the words were wrong as soon as I said them. I felt it in the thickness of my throat, the tremble in my lip. But that ridiculous, ugly smile finally left her face.

Helen let out a soft cry and fled to the house.

Satisfied and disgusted with myself at the same time, I

turned to Pa, ready to brawl. He would scold me and tsk-tsk me and tell me I was being mean and heartless and "Why can't you just be nice to her? She's *trying,* Kathryn."

But he wasn't looking at me. He was studying the holes in the roof. It took a few moments to even realize what I was seeing. He was crying. A lone tear rolled down his leathery face, getting tangled in his black stubble.

Dang it.

I tried to remind myself I was mad at him, too. For bringing her here. For giving in. For always giving in. I didn't want to feel bad for him. But *this* . . . this wasn't Helen. She could make him say her words, but these tears were his own. And I'd caused them.

"Pa—"

"We've got to give Helen a chance, Kath. She ain't like us. She don't have prairie in her blood. And she never will if she only knows the pain of this place. She—" His sentence collapsed under his cough, wet and mucus-y, the sound of too much dirt inside his lungs.

This place was killing him too. It wasn't just the pain and the dead babies. It was the very earth itself. He needed to leave just as much as Helen did. And maybe just as much as I did. I was mean and ugly, getting meaner and uglier with each day the sky held its breath. But how could that be? How could home possibly be the place we didn't belong anymore?

"Don't make this harder than it already is. This ain't only about Helen, and you know it."

I did know. But I didn't have to say it.

"You've wanted surgery for a long time, Kathryn. I've seen it in your eyes. Don't act like you don't just to spite me."

I wasn't trying to spite him. I was trying to spite *her*.

"This surgery will change your life. Make things better. Make at least one thing in this whole miserable world better. No more brace. No more pain. Ain't that what you been wishing for?"

Yes. But . . .

"We'll come back, right, Pa?" I don't know why those were the first words out of my mouth. It had nothing to do with his question. And everything.

He stared at his hands, calloused and brown, covered with a permanent layer of dust. "Maybe next year. After the surgery. If this drought lets up."

His boots cracked on the dry grass as he walked away. He didn't look back.

"Ain't that what you been wishing for?" If only Pa knew all the things I'd been wishing for. I wished I hadn't been born with a crippled foot in the first place. I wished Ma hadn't died. Wished Melissa hadn't gone and married that Mayfield. I wished Helen's father's traveling charity clinic had never pulled into Boise City, that Pa had never broken his arm and that the regular doc hadn't been tending to a flu outbreak in Guymon. I wished she'd followed her father right on out of town instead of finding her way to our house, and I wished they'd both realized how stupid it was to think they were in love.

Most of all, though, I wished it would rain.

* * *

We waited two more weeks until Pa's truck was fixed and the last of the farmwork was done, not that there was much to finish. Most of the wheat rotted; even for pennies on the dollar, it was impossible to sell. The livestock was even worse. Practically had to beg someone to take 'em. The chickens could still lay, Pa insisted, though I noticed he left out the part about just how few eggs we were actually pulling from the coop. And that cow—milk as sandy as a bowlful of grits. I doubted she'd make it to the fall before being slaughtered for meat. What meat she had left anyway.

The night before we left, I saw Melissa for the first time since her wedding. She'd come to visit Helen after the baby, but I'd been in town, lollygagging after buying the nails Pa had sent me for; the longer I could stay out of the house, the better. When I'd returned and discovered I'd missed her, I'd made for the door, planning on a visit of my own, but was stopped cold by Helen. "Don't you dare go knocking on that door," she'd spat. "I shooed her out just as soon as she arrived. Newlyweds need time alone, and it wasn't right for her to be here fawning over me with a new husband at home. She's a Mayfield now and her place is with the Mayfields—and she don't need you over there, making her feel otherwise."

So I stayed. But not because Helen said to. It was because her words—though cruel—carried truth: Melissa wasn't mine anymore. She was Henry's, and I had to get used to it. I stayed away, even when I needed her help fixing the grasshopper muslin, even when Helen tried to make me wash the windows for no good reason, even when Pa started packing up our stuff like we were fleeing a sinking ship. I wondered if she knew we were leaving. Or if she even cared. Which was stupid because of course she cared. It was just easier to leave her—even a her that wasn't her anymore—if I was mad.

It was the longest I'd ever gone without talking to her. But then it was the end of June and our dugout was bare, the truck was loaded, and Pa announced we were having dinner at the Mayfields whether I liked it or not. The next thing I knew I was standing on the porch I didn't want to be standing on, getting ready to have dinner with people I didn't want to have dinner with, and when Melissa opened the door to the Mayfields' house—excuse me, her *father-in-law's* house—I found myself face-to-face with a stranger.

"Oh, Kath." Delicate arms wrapped around my neck. The smell of lavender overpowered everything. It felt like hours before she broke away, though it could have only been seconds. But even then she refused to let go of my hands. Tears glistened in the corners of her eyes. "I was hoping I'd get to see you before—"

"Are you wearing makeup?"

Melissa's cheeks turned a deep shade of crimson. At least I thought they did. Hard to tell under all that goop.

"I've never seen your face look like that before." Makeup in Boise City was almost unheard of. And yet here stood my sister: Irish skin rosy, green eyes smoldering beneath honey-colored shadow, and shimmery red lipstick on her pout. Even her eyelashes seemed longer.

She dropped my hands and averted her gaze. "Henry likes it."

I pulled at my dress. Melissa had sewn it for me last year out of a leftover flour sack. It was covered in small, faded strawberries. My favorite. The prettiest thing I owned suddenly looked hideous. And suddenly I cared.

"Come in. Please."

The front parlor was bright and clean. Spotless. I'd bathed before I'd come—no way I was letting Helen douse me in her disgusting perfume again—but I still felt dirty. You couldn't wash Oklahoma off you anymore. It hung in the air, stuck to your skin, invaded every single nook of your house no matter how much you swept. Unless you were a Mayfield, apparently.

Melissa embraced Helen and gave Pa a kiss on the cheek. "I'm so glad you came. It's right through here."

I'd been in the dining room before. For the wedding, they'd decked it out in ridiculous flowers and silver that probably cost more than Pa made in two years. Somehow, the whole room had smelled like cinnamon. I'd told myself it was just because of the wedding. Even regular folks liked to get a little fancy when it came to a wedding. But as Melissa led us inside, I realized that wasn't the case. The room still smelled of cinnamon. The silver was still everywhere. And while the flowers were less, they were still there.

It was the most absurd thing I'd ever seen in my life.

Mr. Mayfield Sr. sat at the end of a long table but rose when we entered. "James!" His voice was too big, even for a room this size. "So glad you could make it! Come! Sit! Sit!"

My father looked dark against the brilliant lights as he let his hand be enveloped inside Mr. Mayfield's. Henry, appearing from the kitchen, patted his back. All three men smiled and laughed like our presence in this home was the most natural thing in the world.

Helen pushed me forward. I wanted to push her back. My brace squeaked as I made my way toward my father. Loudly. Everyone turned to look at me.

"Ah, and there she is. The lovely Miss Kathryn." Mr. Mayfield was old and fat and smelled like tobacco and Ivory Soap. He held out his arms like he was expecting a hug.

No way was I going near that starched white shirt with this dress on. I grabbed his hand awkwardly.

He chuckled and adjusted his grip, giving me a firm handshake. Winking, he turned his eye to Helen. "Mrs. Baile, how are you this evening?"

"Fine, Mr. Mayfield, thank you."

Did she really just curtsy? Good grief, Helen. Why don't you shine his shoes while you're at it?

"Shall we all have a seat?" Henry put his arm around Melissa's waist and guided her to the table.

Good. Enough small talk. We could get to the table and I would finally be able to talk to Melissa. Maybe my sister was still in there somewhere under all that makeup and fancy hair.

But Melissa did not sit by me. She let herself be led to a seat on the opposite side of the table. Next to Henry. Across from Helen. I sat at the end by myself like a leper. Or a cripple.

Dinner was served by a servant—a *servant*. Pork chops and

green beans and new potatoes and water without even a hint of dirt in it. I wasn't going to eat it, I decided. I didn't need the Mayfields' fancy food, thank you very much. No sir. Let the rest of them stuff their faces with their shiny forks. Kathryn Marie Baile was perfectly fine with rabbit stew and lentils.

I lasted three minutes. But I protested inside my head with each delicious bite.

Mr. Mayfield coughed and spat into his hankie. "Excuse me. Doggone dust is everywhere!"

I stifled the urge to roll my eyes. Like he knew anything about the dust.

"So," he continued, voice once again light, "are you all packed up?"

"Yes, sir," my father said, wiping his mouth with a napkin. "Ain't too much to take, of course. Just some essentials. Helen's folks have a real nice place in Indianapolis with plenty of room. Don't make no sense to take much farmin' stuff to the city."

When Mr. Mayfield nodded, his entire belly shook. "Very true. Well, I meant what I said about holding on to your land until you return. We own the deed now, but that doesn't mean it isn't still yours."

"Own the deed?" The words fell from my lips, surprising even me. All eyes turned to look at me. All, that was, except Melissa's. She stared at her hands as if they were the most fascinating things in the room, as if I hadn't spoken at all.

Pa cleared his throat. "Kathryn."

I could read my father's tone. It was a request—no, a

plea—to let it drop, to talk about it later. But my stomach was at my feet, my heart in my throat. There was no going back from here. "What's he mean 'own the deed'?"

Mr. Mayfield laughed again, though whether he did it to break the tension or because he thought I was funny, I wasn't sure. "It's just a piece of paper, dear. Family members helping family members. Because that's what we are now, Kathryn. We're family."

My breath came forth in quick bursts. "But what—?"

"Gentlemen, shall we not discuss business at the dinner table?" Helen's voice dripped with honey, but her eyes, narrowed in my direction, crackled with electricity.

Mr. Mayfield laughed—again—and raised his glass. "Agreed, agreed! Polite conversation in polite company, Mrs. Baile."

I wanted to scream. Something was happening between my father and Mr. Mayfield. Some secret they were keeping. But not from Helen. Probably not from Henry or Melissa, either. A secret they were keeping just from me.

I'd known that after the wedding, Melissa would start siding with the Mayfields. I had even started expecting Pa to side with Helen. But I'd never expected all of them to be on the *same* side . . . with me on the other.

I shifted in my seat, causing my brace to squeak again.

"Heard we might be getting some rain soon," Henry said, clearing his throat.

"Is that so?" Helen's voice was tight.

"Boys up in Campo said a storm blew through last night with more rain than they'd seen in a year. Streams flooded and old man Follett's grainery washed clean away." He chuckled. I wasn't sure what was so funny about someone losing their entire livelihood in one night. "Lost about eighty bushels of wheat along with it. But it's a small price to pay if it means the rains are coming back."

The table all murmured in agreement.

Of course. One man's entire crop was worth sacrificing if it meant the Mayfields would soon be making money again. Who cared? I chewed my fingernails, fretting. I could still taste the last of the pork chop's juices, the dark-brown broth having soaked into the dry skin on my fingertips. I sucked at it, ashamed of the neediness of my body, letting out one accidental slurp in the process.

All eyes turned to me.

I lowered my hands.

"So," Mr. Mayfield said, smiling. The shine off his silver hair made me squint. "Kathryn, Helen tells me her father is a surgeon."

I nodded, glancing at my father's wife. Her smile was tight.

"And he's offered to fix that foot of yours."

Everyone's eyes flickered toward the table, like they could see through the cloth and wood to the monstrosity I was hiding beneath it. I tucked it behind my other leg and nodded again, feeling my cheeks flush.

How dare she tell him about the surgery? And how dare this man ask me about it like he knew me?

Mr. Mayfield blinked twice, his smile frozen on his face. "Well, aren't you excited?"

Everyone stared.

I pushed my lips together, the pork chops curdling inside my stomach. I knew what I was supposed to say. I was supposed to say yes, to ooze praise for Helen and her father and the magical city of Indianapolis. But I wouldn't. I couldn't.

Mr. Mayfield waggled his eyebrows. Playfully. Expectantly. He had no idea the weight of his question, the sheer impossibility of an answer. No one at that table did.

Except Melissa.

"Kathryn," she said quietly. So quietly, the word sounded like a scream. It was the first she'd spoken all evening.

And that was all it took to break me. I stood suddenly, causing my chair to topple backward. I didn't say sorry. I didn't pick it up. Instead, I walked out. I didn't know where I was going. Home, maybe. Well, home for one more night at least. Or maybe I'd find a room in this house and just hide until Pa and Helen came back from Indianapolis. It was so big there were bound to be rooms they didn't even use. It didn't really matter. I just knew I had to get out of that room.

I pushed open a door. The Mayfields' library—good gracious, they even had their own library—was the size of our dugout. The wooden floors shone beneath a red-and-white rug. A massive brick fireplace nestled into the far wall, with shelves of books lining the others. A piano sat in the corner. I wondered if Henry could play.

Melissa swept in behind me, her blue heels clicking loudly on the hardwood. Her navy dress—new by the look of it— swung like a bell. "Kathryn."

"What did Mr. Mayfield mean when he said he owned the deed?"

"Kathryn—"

"I know you know."

She sighed, crossing her arms over her chest and rubbing her shoulders. She didn't look at me. "It's not that we were keeping it from you. I honestly thought Pa would have told you by now."

"Told me what?"

"Pa sold the land to Mr. Mayfield." She flinched as if expecting me to lash out.

But I only stared. Numb. Dumb. "He did what?"

"He sold the land to Mr. Mayfield," she repeated. Then, quicker: "Money was tight, Kathryn. You know how bad things have been. Don't act like you don't."

I looked down at the ground. There was a dust bunny on the rug, gray against the stark white. So the Mayfields weren't immune to the dirt, after all.

"He needed the money. For food, for clothes, for . . . travel." She spoke the last word quieter, like a burden. "And selling it to Mr. Mayfield means it stays in the family. Means the land will still be here when the drought is over. When the surgery is over. When you all come back."

When you all come back. Somehow she still had it—that irrational faith. I believed in God, sure. But He was distant, judgmental, maybe even just a little bit mean. I didn't understand Melissa's God. To her, He was Someone bigger, Someone there in the room with us, Someone not contained in words on a page or the walls of a church, awesome and powerful and loving. Someone in whom she had enough faith to say words like *when you all come back*.

I wanted to believe her, to feel it too. But the truth of the situation—our land gone, swallowed up inside the Mayfield name like so many other farms—welled up inside me, bigger than my floundering faith.

"Kathryn, please sit down."

"I'm fine right here."

"Kath, please—"

"Henry read all these books?"

Melissa stopped, the ball of her thumb twisting her wedding ring around her finger. Like if she stopped touching it, it would disappear. "What?"

I ran my fingers over the faded spines on the shelves. "All these books on the walls. Henry read 'em?"

"I . . . I don't know."

"Kinda wasteful, don'tcha think?"

"What?"

"All these people got nothing to read," I managed, fighting my tight throat and lips that were beginning to quiver. The concrete slab was sliding from my heart, the sight of all these beautiful, unread books pulling me from my numbness. "And the Mayfields have walls of 'em, just going to waste."

"I don't think—"

"I'm scared, Em." The words fell out before I could stop them, grief rushing forth out of the darkness inside. I used her nickname desperately, hoping to find my sister beneath the new Mrs. Mayfield. "I don't know if we're coming back."

"Of course you're coming back—"

"Pa's giving up. Selling the land, running away."

"That doesn't mean he's giving up. If anything, he's trying to save it."

"But if it doesn't rain soon—"

"It will rain."

"How do you know?"

"Because I just know. God is good, Kathryn, and this drought will not last forever." There it was again. That faith she'd tried so hard to make me understand. But something else, too. Just below the surface her face spoke the doubt her words refused to acknowledge.

And that grieved me more than anything.

"Em—" I was not a crier. But somehow tears formed behind my eyes.

"Please don't cry."

For a moment, I forgot about her dress, her makeup, her too-tall shoes. I ignored the expensive furniture and dirt-free floor. And I didn't even care about the phonies in the next room or the drought lurking just outside the door. For this one moment, it was just us two, clinging to one another yet again in a land of never-ending wind and want. Our sobs echoed in the massive room.

"You *will* be back," Melissa hiccuped, smoothing my stringy hair. It was chin-length and greasy, not quite blonde and not quite red, but some hideous shade in between. Melissa had even gotten the prettier hair. "Henry is a good man, and he promised that old dugout ain't going nowhere. It will still be here *when* you get back. *When.* And I'll be here to keep an eye on it for you. So don't you say another word about it."

I wanted to believe her. Or even just to pretend to believe her. For one minute more.

"You know," she said after a moment, "you don't have to have this surgery if you don't want to."

I pulled away, irritated once more. "Who said I didn't want to?"

Mascara smudged her cheeks. "There's nothing wrong with your foot, Kath."

"Stop it." The brace on my leg was even more grotesque in this artificial light. Scratched. Rusted. Monstrous. "I want this. You know I want this."

"But why?"

I scowled. "Maybe I want to be normal for a change. Do normal stuff."

"You are normal."

"You don't know what it's like."

"Kath—"

"You'll never know. You're beautiful. And kind. And smart. And everyone's favorite. Even Pa's."

"Kathryn."

"And you're a Mayfield now."

The words hung over us like a storm cloud refusing to break. I sat back and stuck my chin out, daring her to respond, pleading with her to have an answer. Instead, she bit the inside of her cheek and said nothing.

I picked at my dress, trying not to let my disappointment show. "This is how it's gotta be. I'll go and get that surgery, and I'll come back. And I won't be a burden no more."

"You've never been a burden."

And she'd never been a good liar. She'd had to carry me for years. And not just with her arms. She'd miss school sometimes to care for me. Because I couldn't care for myself. I'd seen the way people around town looked at her. Poor, pretty girl with her crippled sister. No wonder she'd gone running off to that swine Henry Mayfield. He'd given her an out. A big, fancy out.

"But how can you be Dorothy without the Silver Shoes?"

I bit down on a smile. My loafers looked nothing like Dorothy's magic sparklers. Even the metal on my brace had lost its shine. But I liked when Melissa called them that anyhow. "I'll just have to find another way."

Her eyes crinkled, leaving faint smudges of eyeliner below her brows.

"What?"

"I have something that might help." From her pocket, she produced a beautiful blue-and-white handkerchief and pushed it into my hand. "I want you to take it with you."

The material was soft and smooth like Ma's old curtains . . . before Helen hung them out to dry one day and the grasshoppers ate them. I held on to it loosely, afraid my dirty fingers would ruin the colors. "But where did you—?"

"Never mind that. It's mine, and I'm free to do with it as I choose. And I choose to give it to you."

"Em—"

She folded my hands over it. "Take it. Please."

I wanted to hit her. Or hug her. She was being stupid, giving me something so beautiful. My heart swelled with feelings I couldn't put into words. I had nothing to give her in return. Nothing . . . except everything. I pulled a worn book from the fraying pocket on my dress. With all the packing, I'd been too scared to let it out of my sight; Helen would have found a way to leave it behind. "You should take this."

Melissa's hands ran delicately over the cover, tracing the gold lettering with her finger. She shook her head, causing a red curl to fall loose over her forehead. "I can't. It's your favorite. And besides, Pa gave it to you . . . from Ma."

I shrugged. "Yeah, but I'm going with Pa. You're not." The words came out meaner than I meant them. "I just mean I know it by heart. And I'm guessing Henry doesn't have a copy of *The Wonderful Wizard of Oz*. With all these books around, you might need something to read."

Tears welled in her eyes again, and suddenly I knew. I knew I had to do this. I had to go; I had to get better. Melissa had wasted so much of her life worrying about me. And unless I learned to stand on my own two feet—literally—she would waste years more. She had a husband now, and soon, babies. And she would be their mother. It was time to stop treating her like she was mine. I needed to let her be happy, even if that meant letting her be a Mayfield. Even if that meant leaving.

I let her hold me as she sobbed, but this time I didn't join her. I had to be strong for the both of us. I had to be strong enough to go so I could be strong enough to come back. Strong enough to let Melissa be who she was—my sister. Not my caretaker, not my crutch, but my sister. Just my sister.

When she kissed my forehead and led me back to the dining room, I pretended not to notice the dusty footprints I left in my wake.

CHAPTER FOUR

MELISSA

They were gone.

I didn't see them leave. There wasn't really any point. We'd already said our goodbyes. No, not goodbyes, I'd assured Kathryn. See-you-laters. Anything more would have been overkill. And probably would have broken me. Still, Pa had told me they were leaving at seven this morning, trying to make the most of the daylight. And it was now 7:03. They were gone.

Not that I needed the clock.

I could feel every mile Kathryn got farther away from me. My heart was cleaved; with every second, my sister faded a little more. How I wished I could have seen her face one more time. Her stoic gaze, her brave reassurances that everything would be okay, even if neither of us believed it. For years I'd cared for her as a mother to a child, preaching to her about the hope she could never truly seem to grasp; how was it that now her faith seemed so much stronger than my own?

But it was a good thing. It was. Henry was now the only family I had in hundreds of miles. I was his and he was mine. Home was no longer that little dugout on that dried-up piece of land. And without Kathryn in it, maybe I could stop thinking of it that way.

Home was the Mayfields' farm, three miles outside Boise City and several thousand dollars outside what anyone else could ever dream of affording. There was money in oil, and the Mayfields had been lucky enough to find it first. They owned nearly all of Cimarron County because of it and rented out plots of land to farmers. What was left of the farmers, anyway.

The main house where Mr. Mayfield lived—I mean, William; he insisted I call him William—sat at the front of the property. Less than a mile down the jutted and cracked drive, on the other side of the windswept grass field, was our house, smaller but just as showy. White with blue trim, thick columns all along the front. Straight shutters, a porch swing, painted steps. And in the yard, a lifeless pecan tree and a flower bed long since abandoned. It was kind of funny, actually. The large, wooden houses were ornate and well-kept; the land surrounding them was just as dry and barren as everyone else's.

The main house had servants, the senior Mrs. Mayfield having passed several years ago, and William had insisted on sending one to our house. It was the one and only time I'd put my foot down in front of my new father-in-law. I could accept the cotton sheets and braided rugs and indoor plumbing. But I could not accept being waited on and served to and cleaned up after, especially when it was just the two of us. Mayfield or not, I wanted to care for my home and my family. I'd done it my whole life. And I intended to keep on doing it without assistance, thank you very much.

William had laughed. Henry had found my resolve adorable. But they'd relented. And so, the first morning of my new Kathryn-less world, I found myself as I always did: with a broom and rag in my hand. With too much change happening too quickly, there was solace in the familiar. Even if the familiar was sweeping and scrubbing.

I was no stranger to hard work, but keeping a two-story house in pristine condition in the middle of a dry Oklahoma summer was a bigger challenge than I had imagined. By the time I finished wiping down one room, the previous one was already coated with a fine layer of brown. Closing the windows didn't help. The dirt was determined to find its way inside. After six hours of rigorous cleaning, my hands were chafed, my back ached, and still the dust lingered. Convinced I'd done all I could do, I retreated to the backyard to find some wildflowers for the dining room table. A little color would take the sting out of my imperfect undertaking.

Henry's old coon dogs lounged in the shade beneath the oak tree. Try as I had to win them over, they still cared about no one but Henry. They raised their heads as I emerged, watching as I made my way out of the house. Realizing I was alone, they settled back down. It was just me. And it was too hot to care.

The heavens were pale. Not even a hint of clouds blemished the sky. The morning had been still, but a breeze had begun to trickle in from the north, gaining steam as it reached the open expanse of the prairie. In the distance, clouds of dirt detached themselves from the ground and spiraled upward, blending the earth and sky into an indistinguishable haze.

What little grass remained crunched beneath my feet. It was no longer green. It hadn't been green in years. But every so often, a small yellow bloom—a weed, really, but the only source of color for miles—poked its way through the parched soil, stubbornly refusing to believe the drought. I gathered a handful in the folds of my dress.

The flowers reminded me of my mother. Picking them with her and later making circles of daisies that I draped around her belly, Ma insisting my baby sister would need a crown. She knew it was going to be a girl. Somehow she knew. And she loved her. This child she only knew through the bulge of her stomach, through the kicks that would cause her to jump and laugh. She loved her.

Even when those giggles turned to pain, those smiles to grimaces. When Pa tried to shoo me from the house and I'd hidden beneath the window anyway. The whispers of the midwife, the panic in her voice clear even if my six-year-old mind didn't quite understand the words.

And my mother's insistence, her plea steadfast through her agony. Kathryn would be born, one way or another.

I'm sure hours passed. But in my memory, it happened quickly, Pa pulling me back inside, telling me to hug my mother, to kiss her pale cheek. I remember the sweat and the smile, the love on her face as she placed my baby sister in my arms for the first time.

And then she was gone.

Everything was different after that, and yet somehow still the same. The land still sang when the wind blew, soft and sweet, like the grass itself. The rains still fell. I remembered the smell the most—clean and earthy, fluffy clouds collecting overhead, looking as supple and billowy as goose down. The soil was brown as chocolate when the rains came, and the wheat doubled in size overnight, covering the land like a blanket as far as the eye could see. Pa would whistle in the fields and Kathryn would ride the plow and I would shell peas in the sunshine. In the evenings, tummies full and bodies tired, we would read or play cards. In the midst of tragedy, Oklahoma continued on, a reminder of what was lost—but more importantly, what remained.

Until now. Kathryn says everything changed when Helen arrived. Perhaps. It changed more when the rains stopped, though.

I was just returning to the house when I heard Henry's truck rumble down the driveway. Surrounded by prairie hills and my own memories, I'd lost track of time. My heart fluttered.

"Melissa?"

I shoved the flowers into a jar hastily and smoothed down my dress. "In here!"

My husband swept into the kitchen and wrapped me in a hug.

I breathed him in deeply. He smelled of hay and dry air, only the faintest trace of his aftershave still lingering on his skin. "How was your day?"

"It was fi—good grief, Melissa. What happened to you?" His lip rolled up over his teeth.

My hand went to my face. "What?"

"You're filthy."

I glanced down. There was a raw spot in the knee of my new dress. Dried grass clung to the fabric at my chest. And my nails—goodness, they looked like Kathryn's. Grimy and broken. "I didn't have a chance to freshen up. I've been cleaning all day, and—"

"You've been cleaning all day?" His eyes surveyed the kitchen. A small pile of dust had collected in the corner.

"Well," I stammered, "I tried but—"

Henry held up a hand.

I collapsed into silence, ready to cry. I'd worked all day, and I'd failed. I'd tried to not think about my sister and my father and our dugout, and I'd failed at that, too.

"Honey?" Henry's hand was on my chin. "Are you crying? I'm teasing."

"No," I whispered, refusing to open my eyes. I didn't want to fail at not crying, too.

I felt his lips on mine, soft with a slight hint of tobacco. I couldn't help it. I needed to see him. I opened my eyes.

His lips were puckered into a tight smile. "There you are." He kissed me again. There were no tears this time. There was just him. And us. And this.

I didn't want him to pull away, but he did. I leaned my

head into his chest, savoring the feel of it rising and falling beneath my touch.

"You haven't started dinner? I'm hungry."

His tone was still light—joking, I reminded myself—but the words settled on me like an indictment. "I was . . . I was getting ready to. I didn't realize you'd be home so soon. I was . . ." I gestured limply to the flowers on the table.

His face softened. "You were just trying to make it nice."

I nodded.

"Sometimes I forget how different we really are." He smiled. "I'm sure you had to use a lot of flowers inside that old dugout to bring in some color, didn't you?"

He was trying to be kind, but his words stung. It was the first time he'd ever mentioned the difference in our upbringings. Not that it wasn't always there. But saying it made it bigger. I suddenly felt filthy, and it had nothing to do with a day's worth of dirt staining my face.

"It's sweet, really," he said, breathing softly in my ear. "I appreciate the effort. I like that you want to please me. A beautiful house, a beautiful wife . . . I am the luckiest man in Oklahoma."

My body relaxed. I managed a slight smile.

"We'll go into town for dinner tonight. Something real special." He flashed me one of his million-dollar smiles. "Why don't you go get cleaned up?"

I ascended the stairs on wobbly knees.

"Oh, Melissa?"

"Yes, darling?"

"Let's try a little harder tomorrow, okay?"

* * *

People stared when I went out in public now.

And not like before. Not the shy glances. Not the gentle looks I got when I was with Kathryn. These stares were different, invisible. Stares that weren't stares. Stares that meant something I couldn't yet figure out. It was one more thing I would have to get used to. I was a Mayfield now, and people looked at the Mayfields.

The Oklahoma Club had been little more than a hole-in-the-wall before the boom days of the 1920s, much like the town of Boise City itself. Built as a prop to appeal to eastern sophisticates, it graced the cover of the town's brochures, showcasing the tree-lined streets, artesian wells, and thriving businesses. Truth was, behind its beautiful brick exterior, the Oklahoma Club was nothing more than a dirt-floored speakeasy, the centerpiece of our founders' deception. There was nothing sophisticated about Boise City. In fact, it was barely even habitable.

Maybe that's what made the town so special. The original settlers—men like William Mayfield—refused to believe they'd been duped. Call it stubbornness, call it arrogance, call it whatever you will. Arriving here and finding no amenities and no culture, they could have left. Cimarron County wasn't exactly welcoming. But they dug in, stuck it out, and created something out of nothing. Like the Oklahoma Club, whose cozy interior now matched the elegance of its once-phony front.

True, the drought had reduced its menu and minimized

its customers, but it was still the nicest, most extravagant place in town. I had only been there twice in my entire life: when Pa had married Helen and the night Henry proposed. The former had been quiet and small, just family and a few friends in the back corner with dinner and drinks. The latter had been boisterous: a center table, a serenade from a visiting mariachi, all eyes on me as Henry asked for my hand in front of what felt like the entire town with a ring he'd had made especially for me in Amarillo. Even tonight, months later, I still found myself staring at my finger. I'd gotten used to the weight of it, but even under lights as soft as these, its glare was conspicuous.

I wore a green dress, one I knew he liked, since he was the one who bought it for me. He said it matched my eyes. Aside from my ring, it was the brightest thing inside the dim restaurant, with its dark wood, wine-colored tablecloths, and smoldering fire. I had hoped for an intimate affair, but it wouldn't be possible with this dress. Or with Henry Mayfield.

We'd been seated exactly two minutes before the first intrusion.

"Mr. Mayfield! Good to see you!"

Henry rose and shook the newcomer's hand. "Mr. Egan, how are you?"

The bank manager was a fat man with perpetually red cheeks. His teeth were a sickly shade of gray, the stub of a cigar always hanging from his cracked lips. Kathryn asked me once how he kept from choking on it in his sleep. I smiled, remembering it.

Mr. Egan took my smile as his cue to kiss my hand. His

lips were as dry as they looked. But he at least removed his cigar first. I would have to tell Kathryn next time I talked to her. Whenever that might be.

"I've been trying to get ahold of your father, Henry. There's some business to attend to regarding the Avery estate. Hemorrhaging money, it is. I think your best bet is to sell it now before the drought gets any worse. Fine time to—"

"Surely, Mr. Egan, you're not insisting on talking business in front of the lady, are you?"

Henry's tone was peaceful, controlled, but distress flickered across Mr. Egan's face. He licked his lips, somehow keeping his cigar in place, and tugged at his jacket.

"Of course not, Hen—Mr. Mayfield. I merely . . . merely stopped by to wish you both a pleasant evening."

"And to you, Mr. Egan."

The banker made an exaggerated bow and nodded in my direction, causing a bead of sweat to fall onto his shiny black shoes.

After Mr. Egan, there were others. The sheriff and his wife. Mr. Bonnifeld, the owner of the last department store in town. Mr. Clark, the Oklahoma Club's owner and head chef. An endless parade of Boise City's who's who all come to pay their respects to the new Mr. and Mrs. Mayfield. It was flattering. And overwhelming. And exhausting. After a while, the chitchat and toadying grew old. My cheeks hurt from smiling. And my husband and I still had not shared a single word alone.

My gaze floated to the picture window at the front of

the club. Outside, the rest of Boise City drifted by with fake busyness, stealing glances at a place they would probably never set foot inside. The adults who passed kept their heads down, too proud to admit longing. But the kids—the kids stopped and stared. And they stared right at me without shame. Only hunger.

I picked at my fingers under the table, pretending I didn't see them. But nothing I did could keep me from feeling their eyes on me. Henry, meanwhile, didn't seem to notice.

The visitors abated only when our food arrived, balanced on a large tray by a boy not much younger than me. It took a few moments to place the dark hair and freckles.

"Lucas?"

The boy paused as he set a plate in front of Henry.

"Lucas McCarty? It's me, Melissa Bai . . . Melissa Mayfield. James Baile's daughter."

Lucas smiled, revealing a row of crooked teeth. "Yes, ma'am. I know who you are."

Ma'am. Never in my life had I been called ma'am. Especially not by Lucas McCarty, the boy who used to bring Pa feed from his father's general store every Friday. That was, before the store, like so many others in town, went under.

"How is your—?"

"Everything to your liking, Mr. Mayfield?" Lucas remained by Henry's side, his face turned firmly away from my own.

Henry waved him away without ever once meeting his eye. His gaze, instead, narrowed at me. "Fine. That will be all for now."

Lucas nodded once. "Of course, Mr. Mayfield. Thank you."

I smiled and tilted my head, trying to catch his eye. "Thank you, Lucas. And tell your father I said hello, please."

The corner of his mouth curled up slightly but he looked over my head instead of at me as he backed away, turning heel only after reaching the door to the kitchen.

On the table before us lay an assortment of bread and vegetables and meat. Corn and potatoes and collard greens. Bread as thick as a book and steak—real steak, not the rabbit fillets Pa'd been trying to fool us with for months—steak as big as Helen's fine china, before she'd sold it. It was enough to feed my family—my old family, I reminded myself—for a week, more food than we'd had even at Pa's wedding. All of this for a regular evening meal.

And yet Henry was not eating it. He was still looking at me.

"Honey?"

He smiled with his mouth but his eyes remained neutral, distant. Drumming his fingers on the burgundy tablecloth, the still-new gold band making a loud clicking sound against the hard wood beneath, he studied my face as his tongue explored the inside of his cheek.

"Henry?" I ventured again, quieter.

The drumming stopped. In its absence, the air in the room rushed forward to surround us, muting the noise of the other patrons. It pressed on every inch of my body, squeezing my lungs and forcing my heart into my throat.

And still Henry stared.

The other customers had stopped eating, the clinking

of silverware ceasing as utensils hovered over plates. Food cooled, and glasses froze in midtoast. Every eye was on us, on me. At least it seemed that way.

And then it was over. Henry blinked and his hand was on mine, his pale-blue eyes once again lively. "A feast worthy of a king . . . and his queen."

The air rushed out, releasing the pressure and forcing the blood back into my arms and legs. All around us, people laughed and talked, crunching their salads and cutting their steaks, indulging as if nothing had happened. And maybe it hadn't. I nodded shakily, pleading my pulse back to normal.

Henry winked and squeezed my hand. "But first, my dear, we pray."

The food was delicious. I think. Every bite was ash in my mouth, soured by the unrest in my heart. I had done something wrong. But I had no idea what it was.

By the time we'd finished, the early evening breeze had given way to an angry gale. Outside the window, the sky was the color of earth, and the sand dunes collecting around the boardwalk were starting to shift. The earlier stragglers were gone.

"Do you think the truck will start?" I asked, clutching Henry's arm as we made our way to the foyer.

Henry pulled his hat from the rack and scowled. "Of course it'll start. It ain't no jalopy."

But his eyes flickered to the window anyway. Dust swirled in the twilight, scratching against the door. Even a truck as nice as Henry's could only do so much in the face of ten-foot drifts.

He yanked his brim down low and tugged on the collar of his shirt. "Well, let's get going. You best cover up. Where's your hankie?"

The steak in my stomach lurched. My hankie. My beautiful new hankie was in Kathryn's pocket. Right where I wanted it to be. But judging from Henry's face, not where it was needed most.

The wind whistled through the rafters.

"Melissa?" Henry glanced at me sideways. "The hankie."

"I . . . I gave it to Kathryn."

"You what?"

"I gave it to Kathryn. For the journey. She was sad, you see, and I wanted her to have something of mine. To comfort her." I waited for Henry to say something, to nod, to blink. Anything to signify he heard what I was saying and understood. But he did nothing. "She just . . . she was scared, is all. And you know how bad the dust gets on the road. She—"

"You gave your sister your hankie."

It was not a question, but I answered anyway. "Yes."

"That hankie was your wedding present. A gift. From me to you."

I swallowed, my shoulders drooping. "I'm sorry, Henry. I know. And it was such a lovely gift. But Kathryn needed it more than I did." I moved to put my hand on his arm. "And besides, the real wedding present is you, right? Us."

He flinched under my touch, pulling away so quickly it made me jump. "Do you know how much that hankie cost?" he whispered, though his voice was anything but soft. "That fabric came all the way from Dalhart. The stitching was done by one of the top embroiderers in the state of Texas."

"I didn't—"

"I bought it for *you*. For my wife." The words came out hushed but firm. "That hankie was not yours to give away."

Behind us, the voices of the other patrons rose and ebbed in the dining room, but Henry's displeasure built a wall around us, muting them. No one even glanced in our direction. We were alone. I was alone.

I pressed a hand to my collar, trying to rub away the tightness slowly spreading through my chest. Yes, I'd disappointed my husband, created strife within our marriage. But as sorrowful as I felt for grieving him, giving Kathryn that hankie still didn't *feel* wrong. I'd been sacrificing for my sister my entire life, putting her needs first, trying to model a life of a faith and selflessness the way our mother had done for me. What was mine was hers. Always. Loving my sister wasn't a sin.

And yet, in this new world, this other one in which I now lived, somehow it was.

Henry looked at the ceiling and let out a deep breath. "You should have asked, Melissa. You should have asked. You're my wife and you don't just go throwing away my money without asking."

"I'm sorry."

Henry shifted a toothpick with his tongue, staring at me with that look again. The same one from dinner, the one that had stolen my air and iced my heart. The wood clicked against his teeth, somehow echoing in the small foyer.

"Well," he said finally, "let's go, then. Before this duster gets any worse." He grabbed my elbow roughly. I didn't dare cry out.

The storm was a welcome companion during the ride home, commanding my husband's attention. His eyes strained, knuckles white on the steering wheel. The darkness turned the ten-minute drive into thirty; the tension made it seem even longer.

When we arrived home, Henry didn't open my door. He didn't help me inside. He didn't even say a word. But the sound of that slap. Of skin on skin. I would never forget it, even after the bruise faded. It burned into the walls of our kitchen, echoed like his footsteps as he climbed the stairs without giving me a second look.

When I finally collected myself enough to join him, he roused from his slumber to kiss me good night.

It was our two-month anniversary.

CHAPTER FIVE

KATHRYN

I regretted giving Melissa that book twenty minutes into our trip.

Pa and Helen rode up front, and there was no room for me. Not that I would have sat up there anyway. Helen was doggone near dancing when we left, and it was only Pa's sad eyes that kept my mouth shut. I sat in the back, on top of the few trunks Helen allowed us to take, trying not to watch home slip away. My foot, Helen's babies, the drought—I knew all the reasons we were leaving. But none of them seemed good enough when Oklahoma looked at me like that.

I fingered Melissa's handkerchief inside my pocket. I wanted to take it out, hold it against my face, breathe in her scent—her new scent, of course, but hers just the same.

But I didn't dare let Pa or Helen see it. They'd make me give it back for sure. It was the only piece of home I had left; I wouldn't let them take it away too. I traced her initials with sweaty fingers. If she were here, she'd make up games for us to play. Or sing to me. Or read. But she wasn't here. And I didn't know if I'd ever see her or Boise City again. I wondered what she was doing now. Not that it really mattered.

We headed east, our truck bouncing over narrow jutted pathways barely visible between barbed fences half-covered in dunes. The road was straight, but the journey was twisted, as Pa maneuvered our truck around drifts and clots of tumbleweeds. At the end of the first day, we'd only made it to Pa's cousin's farm just on the other side of Sturgis. It felt like God Himself was trying to keep us from leaving Oklahoma. If only Pa would listen to Him instead of Helen.

On our second day, we passed into Kansas. I leaned over the side of the truck as Pa called out, feeling something other than bitterness for the first time since the truck had groaned to life beneath me. Kansas was where Dorothy lived. She'd given up Oz for it. Surely it was something special. Pa honked his horn as we crossed the state line, but the earth remained brown, crunchy, and flat. I settled back into the truck, scowling. Kansas was just as dead as Oklahoma, only worse. Because it wasn't Oklahoma.

It was the farthest away from home I'd ever been. My stomach turned in a way that had nothing to do with Pa's driving. The land was the same, but the air was different. Less friendly. There was nothing familiar about these fields, these roads, these barren trees. They were imposters. The dust from our wheels floated southwest with the breeze. Even it was trying to get back across the state line.

We drove three days straight and then another, stopping only when the sky behind us faded to orange. Seeing as how there was no one within a hundred miles who knew us and how we barely had enough money for gas, a hotel wasn't an option. Camping was fine the first three nights. It felt good to stop, at least, give the rattling in my bones a chance to still. But by the fourth night, not even the prospect of stretching my cramped legs could raise my spirits. Not when Helen's were mixing with the very clouds.

"James, did I tell you about the garden?"

Pa was busy making a small fire under the only cove of trees we could find. He paused just long enough to shake his head.

Helen pushed a strand of hair from her eyes as she rummaged through our small supply of food. "As big as our dugout! With every kind of vegetable you could imagine. Just wait until you taste the tomatoes. Oh, how long has it been since I've had a tomato?"

I slammed a pile of firewood at Pa's feet. He glanced at me, eyebrows raised.

Helen continued to rummage with her back to us. "And the soil! As dark as your hair and so rich I half expect it to sprout money." She giggled at her own stupid joke. "My father hires a man to tend to it, but I expect he'll allow you to care for it once we arrive, if you want. He understands a farmer's need to be out in the dirt."

I snapped a branch under my foot, hoping it would ease my irritation. It didn't. "And what about you, Helen?"

The tone of my voice finally shut her up.

"What's that?"

"Do you understand a farmer's need?"

She turned around slowly, tattered basket in her hand, face tight.

I smiled, meanly but the first one in days, and took a step toward her. "Seems like common sense that a person attuned to a farmer's need would understand the last thing you should do is take him away from his land. Maybe city folks like you and your pa ain't quite smart enough to—"

"That's enough, Kathryn." Pa was behind me suddenly, a hand on my shoulder. Firm.

"I'm just sayin'—"

His grip tightened. "I said *enough*. Jibber-jabberin' ain't gonna get food into the pot, and we've got another long day tomorrow. Make yourself useful and help Helen with those vegetables."

I opened my mouth but closed it as he squeezed my shoulder tighter, pinching the flesh beneath. Glowering, I wrenched free from his grasp and shuffled over to Helen, yanking the vegetable basket from her hand. Pa retreated to the fire once more.

Beside me, Helen pulled a can of beans from a burlap sack and studied the label. From the side of her mouth, her words came out as a hiss. "You can be as ugly as you want, Kathryn Marie Baile, but nothing is going to stop us from getting to Indianapolis. And I mean nothing."

I grabbed a shriveled carrot and snapped it in two. "We'll see about that."

She grabbed my wrist suddenly, her nails digging into my skin with more strength than her weak frame revealed.

Behind us, Pa's back was turned, the first wisps of smoke rising from the pile of tinder. I bit my tongue, not wanting to give her the satisfaction of a yelp.

"Yes," she breathed, the vein in her forehead bulging. "We will."

Dinner was quiet, the only noise coming from the crackling fire and the constant chirruping of grasshoppers. The stew was thin and bitter, the few vegetables I'd salvaged from our garden having already begun to spoil. I ate it anyway. Who knew when I'd taste Oklahoma again?

Afterward, Helen fell asleep quickly, sprawled across the seat of the truck. Pa and I were expected to sleep outside. She did share a couple blankets, at least, though I'm sure if she could have gotten away with it, she would have made sure both went to Pa and not me. I was lucky she wasn't that bold. Yet.

I settled myself at the base of a tree, staring up through the gnarled branches to the darkening sky above. They might have been pretty once. Now they were nearly naked and gloomy, just like the rest of the countryside. The air smelled like manure, probably from some shriveled-up herd of cows nearby. Even the sunset was ugly here.

My body ached from the jarring ride, my foot especially. It felt as if I'd walked a hundred miles, which was funny since I hadn't walked at all. I wanted to take my brace off. But Pa was watching. So I lay down instead, rolling my leg slightly to relieve the pressure. Inside its cage, my foot cramped and throbbed and screamed, but taking off my brace right now would be like admitting I wanted the surgery. That I needed it. And I wasn't willing to give anyone that kind of satisfaction.

The ground was hard, packed, and riddled with pebbles my thin blanket couldn't hide. But the sky was clear and, before long, filled with thousands of stars. The fire smoldered nearby, popping every so often and sending sparks dancing into the air. I tried to pretend I was camping with Pa and Melissa on our farm in Oklahoma. We'd done it lots of times when it was too hot to sleep in the dugout. Before Helen.

"Kath?"

I rolled over.

Pa's face stared at me from across the fire. "You okay?"

I looked back up at the sky. "Fine."

"You lie."

I turned my back. He could call me a liar all he wanted. It wouldn't change where we were. And where we weren't.

A long, wet sigh. "Did I ever tell you about your *maimeó* and *daideó*? 'Bout their trip across the ocean?"

I still didn't look at him.

"They was young. Not much older than you are now. Your *daideó* was kicked out of Ireland for—"

"Selling a bull on a Sunday," I huffed, pulling my blanket over my head. I'd heard this story about my grandparents before. I loved it. But I didn't want to hear it right now.

"Right, right." My father paused. "But do you know *why* he sold that bull?"

I stilled. I'd never thought to ask. Melissa would have. Probably did when I wasn't around. She was good like that.

"He never had a ma, and his daddy died young. Left my

da a copy of the Good Book, a pair of strong arms, and a parcel of fertile land. But Da never quite got over the loss. And a broken heart will kill you if you don't let it mend."

I scowled. My heart wasn't broken over Ma or Melissa or Oklahoma. It was angry.

Pa coughed and spat. When he continued, his breathing was uneven. "He was a fool. Lived his life tryin' to run from death and threw his inheritance away on gamblin' and drinkin'. Soon he had nothing but a large debt, an unworked farm, and one scrawny bull."

I pretended to be asleep. He kept talking anyway.

"One night, after a particularly rough fight with a bottle of whiskey, my da found himself laying in a field, staring at the sky. Now, the sky in Ireland is a lot like the sky in Oklahoma. Big. Beautiful. And he found he couldn't look away from the stars. See, the stars make no noise. Yet you notice 'em anyway. Your eyes are always drawn up. Why do you think that is?"

Without realizing it, I had rolled onto my back. The stars blinked at me from between the dried leaves.

"Because even against all that blackness, they're there. The darkness doesn't scare 'em. In fact, you notice 'em precisely because of the dark. Because they keep going. In a dark, scary, noisy world, they shine out bright, quiet, and brave."

I bit the inside of my lip, swallowing a lump. I wanted him to stop. And keep going.

"That's when my da decided he'd had enough of the dark, had enough of bein' scared and hidin' behind the bottle. Had enough quittin'. He got up right that second, grabbed that scrawny bull by the horns, and dragged him into town. Sold him to the first person he saw. Problem was it was Sunday morning, and doing business on the Sabbath was against God's law and man's." Pa chuckled. "Found himself on a boat to America not long after."

So that's what it was. He was trying to tell me to have courage, to do the right thing. Because leaving Oklahoma, fixing my foot, caring for Helen was the right thing to do. But I wasn't no star. I'd never be a star. I was the darkness.

I blinked away the burning at the corners of my eyes. "Why didn't he just wait one more day?"

Pa looked over at me, his eyes orange in the dying firelight.

"If he'd just waited one more day to sell that bull, he could have stayed in Ireland. Could have stayed *home*." I spat the last word.

Across the flames, Pa sighed and pulled his hat over his eyes. "I don't know, Kath. I just don't know."

I'd wanted to disappoint him. And I had. But I still hated myself for it.

A sudden breeze rustled the branches, dropping several dead leaves onto my stomach and revealing the North Star directly above my head. The directional star.

Leading me nowhere.

* * *

We drove three more days. I didn't see any more stars. The nights were overcast and gloomy, though no rain fell. I knew I was being punished for being ugly to Helen and to Pa. I almost apologized. But only almost.

And maybe that's why it happened. On that fourth day, the sun was too hot, even for July. The clouds broke, and the air was white; the drought had sucked even the blue from the sky. Pa and Helen didn't notice from inside the cab. But in the back, I did. My skin prickled with static. The birds were silent, hiding. They could feel it too.

The truck shuddered to a stop. I knew before I saw it. Before the word came out of Pa's mouth.

"Duster!"

In front of us, the pale sky had turned black. A mountain of dirt rushed toward us. From here, its jagged peaks looked like teeth, giving the appearance of a beast, feeding on the very ground it prowled. The smell of spoiled earth hit first. All around us, the ground trembled, sending particles of dirt rolling for cover. There was nowhere to hide.

Pa jumped from his seat. "Kath! Get up here! Quick!" He struggled to roll up the truck's window. "Helen—get those blankets across the dash. We gotta keep that dust out best we can."

My foot cried out as I tried to stand. My leg twisted, frozen in place. I couldn't move. My brace was caught on the frayed rope holding Helen's trunk in place. I pulled at the snag with numb fingers.

The sand beneath our truck started to tumble. Waves of dirt washed across the road, an ocean in the middle of the prairie. The first layer of dust coated my arm. It was getting closer now.

"Kath! Let's go!" Pa moved to Helen's side, securing her window.

I tried to call out that I was stuck, but the words wouldn't come. I pulled on my foot. The rope held tight, its fiber twisting around rusted metal.

"Kathryn!"

The truck began to rock. The outline of the storm faded into a blur, too close now to make out its distinct shape. It was in my nose, on my tongue. I could taste Kansas. It was here, upon us.

I pulled again. Still nothing.

The wind slammed into me with a violent scream. Dust scraped across my bare arms like a nail file. Sand rolled beneath my eyelids. It hurt to breathe. It hurt not to breathe. My cry for help collapsed inside the cloud.

And then Pa was beside me. Grabbing my foot, ripping the strands that bound it in place. With surprising ease, he lifted me from my spot and set me on the ground. One hand covering his mouth, he yelled something that sounded like "Get in the truck!"

I took a step forward and reached for Melissa's handkerchief. Before I could bring it to my face, the wind ripped it from my sweaty fingers, dangling it in front of me like an insult before whisking it away. I lunged for it, the blue-and-white pattern barely visible in the swirling dirt. It danced forward along the cracked earth. I stumbled after it blindly, my eyes burning.

"Kathryn!" My father's voice. Desperate. Distant.

But I couldn't stop now. A flash of blue and white. I was so close. I cried out as my body crashed into a hidden fence post. A tangle of barbed wire tore at my dress, slashing the skin beneath. It would not stop me. I pulled until I felt it give and stumbled forward. The handkerchief. Flashes of color in the angry air. If I could just reach it . . . And suddenly it was in my hand. I pressed it to my mouth, hoping for a clean breath, and turned to retreat to the truck.

But the truck was gone.

"Pa!"

The wind whipped around me, trying to force me to the ground. The air was black, thick, angry.

"Pa!" My scream was cut short by the sudden need to retch. I could feel the dirt inside me, filling my lungs, my stomach, my veins. I had to find shelter. Somewhere. Anywhere.

I stumbled in the direction of the truck. Or did I? I didn't know which way was which anymore. Air and ground blended together all around me. I couldn't see. I couldn't hear. I couldn't breathe. And then I was falling. I cried out as sharp rocks tore my flesh. A bed of rocks. The wind was lighter down here. I eased my eyes open. A dry creek bed. And there—up there. A hollow embankment.

I crawled toward it, curling myself beneath the root-covered overhang. The wind shrieked. Midnight reigned in the middle of the day. I tried to cry, but all that came out was dust. This was the end. I was going to die out here. And maybe I deserved to.

CHAPTER SIX

MELISSA

I'd been embarrassed when Henry first bought me makeup. I'd never owned any, never worn it, never seen the need. It seemed like such frivolity. But the first time I brushed the rouge across my cheeks, I felt like Katharine Hepburn in *Morning Glory*. My freckles disappeared. *I* disappeared. Melissa Baile was pretty, but Melissa Mayfield was beautiful. I felt glamorous. I felt *loved*.

It was different when I put it on the morning after our first fight.

The powder did little to hide the swelling, but at least it muted the bruise. Perhaps it could pass as a new shade of blush. Or as if I'd gotten too much sun. I played up my eyes with liner and mascara. Maybe people would look at them instead.

Henry was gone by the time I awoke, his truck absent from beneath its usual spot under the oak tree. I busied myself making breakfast, tensing at each creak in the house, unsure how to act when I saw him or even who to expect when he reappeared. That man last night, the one with my husband's beautiful face but malevolent hand was a stranger. I hadn't known he was going to hit me, of course. He'd never done it before. But his eyes across the dinner table . . . the new set of rules I hadn't known I'd broken, the guilt and the shame I hadn't known I was supposed to feel. That was what unnerved me most of all.

"Good morning."

I jumped as Henry's arms wrapped around my waist from behind. I'd been so far inside my own head, I hadn't heard him return.

He nuzzled into me, his stubble irritating my already-tender cheek, before spinning me around and kissing me deeply. The force of his need reopened a small cut on my lip. The taste of blood mixed with the Oklahoma air on his skin. When he finally pulled away, he studied me, his eyes lingering on my bruise. Or did it just feel that way?

I looked down, grasping my apron with shaking hands.

He pulled one of them into his own. "I got you something." Uncurling my fingers, he pressed a warm, solid object into my palm.

It was a brooch. A beautiful silver-and-turquoise brooch. Gasping, I ran my finger over the colored stone.

"I had to drive all the way out to that Indian trading post near Guymon. Doggone near wanted my scalp for it. I told him I'd pay him anything but that." He chuckled at his own joke. "Because it was a gift for my wife." He leaned in close, sending a shiver down my spine. "A new gift. *For. My. Wife.*" He paused after each word, his breath heavy on my skin.

"Thank you," I whispered, keeping my eyes on the brooch. "It's . . . it's stunning."

Henry lifted my chin, forcing my eyes to his. He ran a thumb over my swollen cheek before kissing me softly. "You're welcome."

It was a reset, I knew. A do-over. A chance to choose better this time around. And it was what I wanted, for sure. I wanted things to go back to before. Before I'd messed up, when there was only one set of truths in this world, when I knew exactly what was wrong and what was right.

Before he'd hurt me.

He could do that. If anyone had the power to turn back time, make everything right again, it was Henry Mayfield. But how could I tell him that it wasn't a gift I needed? It was his words. His apologies and reassurances, his whispers of love and approval. As I stared into his eyes—once again as clear and beautiful as the prairie sky—my heart pleaded with him to say something that would heal the wounds makeup would never cover.

But he merely turned and settled himself at the table. "What's for breakfast? We need to hurry or we're gonna be late for church."

* * *

The gleaming stained-glass windows and cheerful red brick of St. Paul's Methodist Church seemed out of place next to its sun-bleached neighbors and scorched-earth lawn. The land withered away all around, but somehow the church remained untouched. Perhaps that's why it was the most popular place to be Sunday morning. For a few short hours, we could pretend we weren't in hell.

When Pa arrived in Cimarron County in 1908, there wasn't much here. But there was Ma. And Ma went to St. Paul's. So Pa, despite being raised devoutly Irish Catholic, went to St. Paul's too. He struggled with it—I once heard him tell Ma that my *maimeó* and *daideó* were rolling in their graves—but his love for Ma trumped all. Plus, he said, it's all the same God, right?

When I was a Baile, we sat in the back. After Ma's death, it was during these times I felt her absence the most—and somehow her presence, too, a strange contrast that had never truly faded. Inside these walls, I could still hear her voice, soft but sturdy, rising and falling with the thrum of hymns, could still feel the rustle of her dress, starched and ironed, beside me and hear the crinkle of pages as she flipped through her weathered Bible. But on those first dark Sundays after she passed, Ma's seat was just empty. Beside it, Pa, here in body but spiritually a million miles away, wrestled with the Lord and his overwhelming grief. In those black days, our family pew, once so comforting and joyful, contained only myself, an empty seat, a faraway Pa . . . and Kathryn.

As a baby, she would fuss and squirm, making the wooden pews creak. Pa—the shadow of Pa—was deaf to her cries, and though members of the congregation often tried to help by asking to hold her, I refused. She was my sister, a part of my mother, a part of *me*, and she would stay with us in our pew. I soothed her with whispered prayers and familiar songs, rocking her in my small arms. As she grew older, I tried my best to keep her entertained, drawing silly pictures on the bulletin or folding it into boats or birds or planes. I'm not sure she ever listened to a single word during the sermon. But at least she was there. And her being there made me feel a little less alone.

Her favorite thing to do during church was turn around and stare at the mosaic of St. Paul in the window behind us. Flanked by a cross on either side, he welcomed worshipers every Sunday with his outstretched glass hand. Most passed by without a sideways glance. Kathryn, however, was mesmerized. The shifting colors, the sparkling light. It was like nothing else in Boise City. Maybe that's why she liked it so much. Because everything else in her life and in this town was bland.

I glanced at the window now as we stepped into the sanctuary. It looked duller today. Probably because of the dust. The pew was still right in front of it. Our pew. But there was no Baile in that pew this morning. The worn wooden seat was empty, waiting for worshipers who would never come. Not that it was any of my concern anymore. The Mayfields sat up front.

I had worn the blue dress at Henry's suggestion. The one that made my hair look like copper. Brooch attached firmly at the collar, with a tight bodice and long skirt that rustled when I moved. Walking down the aisle to the Mayfield pew, the fabric was so loud it drowned out most of the whispers. But it couldn't save me from the stares.

I'd put on another layer of powder before we left the house, but I knew the bruise was still visible. Or maybe it was more than that. Here was Melissa Baile, parading around like a Mayfield. Who did she think she was? I kept one hand firmly on Henry's arm; the other shook in the folds of my dress. I'd never been more relieved to hear the preacher's command to grab our hymnals. Losing myself in the gentle singing made me forget everything else . . . at least for a time.

The sermon was short. Something about the fruits of the Spirit. It seemed longer when I sat in the back. But before I knew it, I was standing again, ready to make the long march back down the aisle and into the stares of the congregation. This walk was slower, though. Everyone wanted a piece of Henry Mayfield. And he was only too happy to oblige.

"Mr. Mayfield, happy Sunday to you!" Mr. Taylor, the town councilman, shook my husband's hand, flashing a gold watch in the process. He didn't push it back under his sleeve.

"And to you. Where's your wife this morning?"

"Bah," he said, waving his arm. The watch flashed again. "Home resting her feet. Due any day now, you remember?"

Henry nodded in a way that indicated he did *not* remember. "Of course, of course."

"Where's your father this morning?"

"Laid up in bed with a head cold. Been pushing himself too hard, like he always does."

"This dust makes every little sniffle a big deal. Better safe than sorry, I say. Please, give him—"

"Mr. Mayfield! Lovely to see you this fine morning!"

Another man—balding, bearded, with skin way too pale for the Oklahoma sun—pushed his way into our circle. "I was just telling Pastor Brownstone how great it was . . ."

I held Henry's arm and smiled, playing my part. But whatever it was the newcomer had found so great about Pastor Brownstone got lost in the noise. It was so hot in this dress, and there were so many people. Had there always been this many people at St. Paul's? And why didn't I recognize any of them? The Bailes left and a whole new town moved in, all of them strangers. Except for . . .

"Doris!"

Henry's arm tensed beneath my hand.

Mr. Taylor stopped in midsentence.

I'd interrupted him. It was bad enough I hadn't been listening, but now I'd interrupted him. The town councilman.

My face flushed. "I am so sorry, Mr. Taylor, Henry . . ." My voice trailed off as I looked at the other man. The newcomer. The one whose name I hadn't bothered to learn. "Um, gentlemen. Forgive my manners, but there's a . . . ladies' matter I simply must attend to."

Mr. Taylor waved his hand dismissively. "Of course, Mrs. Mayfield. Our business is of no interest to women anyway."

I tried to release my grip on Henry's arm. Instead, he pulled me back toward him. His kiss on my cheek was filled with every word he didn't say. I was to hurry.

I rushed over to Doris McIntosh. Her family had lived down the road from mine for years. Our fathers shared a tractor. Our mothers shared everything else. Or at least they had before. Mrs. McIntosh had not been keen on Helen.

But Doris and I had not let that stop us from being friends. I embraced her, breathing in the scent of old towels.

As I pulled away, her gaze washed over my cheeks but did not linger. In fact, she did not look at me at all, preferring instead the frayed carpet beneath our feet.

"You seem well," she said flatly.

"And you."

"How's married life? Ain't seen you around town much." There was a hint of accusation behind her words.

"I . . . I try to stay busy at home." A drop of sweat rolled down my back.

She nodded, revealing a smudge of dirt under her chin. She still did not look at me.

"Where's your mother? I don't believe I saw her this morning. I'd love to say hello."

She shrugged. "Ain't feeling well. Coughing. Fever. You know her. It's a sin to miss church, she says. But she just couldn't do it today. Can't keep the dust out of the house long enough to get her better."

"I'm sorry," I said, frowning. "I know how it is."

Doris raised her chin, meeting my eyes for the first time. Did she think I'd forgotten already? The dust, the sand, the never-ending dirt. Did she think the Mayfields somehow lived in a sterile bubble? "Well, please send her my well-wishes," I said quickly. "I pray she feels better soon."

She smoothed her dress. It was obviously an old one of her mother's she'd tried to make new again. She was practically swimming in it. Patches of skin were visible through the worn material.

I crossed my arms over my own dress, ashamed. I never used to notice her clothes.

"Well, you better go," she said quietly. "Looks like he's waiting."

"Right," I stammered. "Of course. Well . . . it was lovely to see you, Doris. Please, stop by the house. Anytime. I'd love to catch up."

Behind her nod, I saw the truth. She'd never stop by. And even though a part of me wanted her to, I was relieved. I didn't want to think of what Henry would say if he found a McIntosh in his kitchen. And I didn't want to think of what she'd say if she saw my new house. My new life.

She squeezed me tightly before she walked away. We both knew it would be the last time we would ever speak.

I returned to Henry, but his attention remained on the group of men in front of him, none of whom I recognized. Judging by their suits, I gathered they were important. I stood behind him silently, clasping and unclasping my hands.

"Mrs. Mayfield?"

I flicked a speck of dirt from my dress. I wondered if it had gotten there from hugging Doris.

"Mrs. Mayfield?"

I looked up.

The preacher's wife, Mrs. Brownstone, stood in front of me, smiling. "Mrs. Mayfield," she said again.

Mrs. Mayfield. *I* was Mrs. Mayfield. She was talking to me. "Oh," I stuttered. "Yes?"

"May I have a word?"

I glanced past her at my husband. Henry was still deep in conversation. "Yes, of course."

She pulled me to the side, where a group of ladies stood in a circle. "Mrs. Mayfield, this is Mrs. Egan—" the banker's wife—"Mrs. Bonnifeld—" Bonnifeld . . . like the department store—"Mrs. Marimen—" must be the sheriff's wife—"and Mrs. Willis—" I recognized her from church bake sales; her cherry pie was a bestseller.

I nodded at each one. "How do you do?"

"Mrs. Mayfield, we are the chairs of the Ladies Auxiliary Club."

I cringed. So they were the ones. For each of Helen's pregnancies, someone from the Ladies Auxiliary had dropped off a basket of baby gifts—diapers, blankets, and such. I'd had to return them twice. I wondered if Kathryn had taken the latest one back before they left.

Mrs. Brownstone's eyes crinkled at the corners. "We'd like to extend an invitation for you to join. We meet once a week here at the church."

The ladies all murmured their agreement.

"Oh, I don't know . . ." I glanced in Henry's direction. He laughed loudly and patted the man next to him on the back.

"Oh, but you must!" Mrs. Brownstone exclaimed. "I remember your mother being a part before . . ." Her voice faded as her eyes flickered downward.

Before she died, she was going to say. My mother had been a member before she died. Or maybe she meant before the drought, when regular women had the time and energy to do such things. Before being a part of the Ladies Auxiliary was a luxury only the luckiest could afford. Before Helen, who'd struggled just to keep our homelife afloat as it was, who'd needed far more from these ladies than she could ever give back in return. Before life itself had simply gotten too hard.

"We're here to help the community," Mrs. Willis popped in, trying to cheer away all the unspoken sorrow. Sweat glistened on the rolls under her chin and she fanned herself with her bulletin. "We knit blankets, collect food, whatever we can. We strive to be Jesus' hands and feet. The good Lord knows our town needs it."

The women all *amen*ed in agreement.

"Please consider it, dear." Mrs. Brownstone squeezed my hand, her silver bracelet scraping my skin. "What with your legacy of faith and your newfound resources, you could do so much good. We'd just love to have you on board."

Newfound resources. Yes, the town did need help. My family had needed their help. But now these women saw me as a giver, not a receiver. I was no longer a charity case; I was the charity. All because I'd changed my last name.

"Yes," I said weakly. "I will. Thank you."

This seemed to satisfy the group. They returned to their chatter.

Mrs. Bonnifeld, however, led me a few steps away. "I hope you'll join us," she said, leaning toward me. Her long blonde hair, which was pulled back in a sensible bun, smelled of honeysuckle. "It's important for women like us to give back."

Women like us. I was part of the *us* now.

"And," she continued, lowering her voice, "sometimes we need a reason to get out of the house. We have to do what we can to . . . keep the peace." Her eyes flitted over the cut on my lip.

I sucked it in, feeling the wound reopen beneath the pressure.

And then she was gone, swallowed back into the crowd of worshipers. Most would go home, change out of their one set of Sunday clothes, and work their farms, praying for the rain that would surely come tomorrow. Others, like my husband, would retreat to their houses, to their elaborate Sunday dinners, to their books and brandy.

As I sat next to my husband on the drive home, I wondered if I'd ever understand why the world was full of such disparity. And if I could ever truly make the leap from one side to the other.

CHAPTER SEVEN

KATHRYN

I was dead. The sudden stillness in the air, the earsplitting silence, the rapid shift from darkness to light—that didn't happen on earth. There was a gradualness to things. I had to be dead.

And yet there was a sharp rock at my back. A layer of dust on my skin. Fuzziness on my tongue. Stinging in my eyes. And my aching, deformed foot was still in that cursed boot. If I was dead, then I must not have made it to heaven.

I pulled Melissa's handkerchief from my face. The blue-and-white checks were brown. Everything was brown. I coughed and hacked and spat, then coughed and hacked and spat some more. The dirt was coming from inside me. I'd never get it all out. I crawled from my hiding spot and shook my head, watching a cloud of dust float to the ground. I rubbed the handkerchief across my face, even though it wouldn't do much good.

I shoved it in my pocket and stretched, making my brace creak. Dust in the joints. It would make it that much harder to walk. Fantastic. My arms were crisscrossed with dirty blood and fresh bruises. I tried to spit on the worst, but even my saliva was mud. I needed water. Surely Pa had some in the truck.

The truck.

My eyes scanned the prairie. Which way would the truck be from here? I took a step away from the trees to get a better look.

Nothing but parched earth.

No. Something had to look familiar. It *had* to. But I was hundreds of miles from familiarity, in a different land that looked completely the same. Shifting dunes and dry grass and hilly fields that should have been covered in wheat but weren't. Every single direction was brown, empty nothingness.

Panic rose in my throat. Or was that vomit? Both. I heaved into a cluster of tall grass, retching bile, dirt, and what little water remained in my body. Mud ran from my nostrils, making me gag again. I wiped my face and was surprised to find tears.

"Stop it." The words fell to the ground. "Stop it," I repeated, more forcefully. These words seemed to linger in the air a bit longer. Satisfied, I spun around, squinting against the light. There had to be something, *something* I would recognize. If only I'd stop being so weak.

I closed my eyes and held my breath. It was a trick Melissa taught me. When Helen was being Helen, it made my insides spin like a twister. But if I held my breath long enough, there wouldn't be enough wind to fuel that twister and it would die down. Then I could think straight again and not get in trouble.

I counted to ten and opened my eyes. The hills rose and fell for miles around me. Sand dunes broken by clumps of grass. Behind me was the dry creek bed I'd taken shelter in. The only trees in sight sat on its banks.

And then there it was. A fence post. Half-hidden by sand, but still it was there. I limped toward it, my brace squeaking with every step. Never mind there were probably dozens of fence posts scattered across these fields. This was the same fence post I'd run into during the storm. It had to be.

A small tangle of barbed wire hung from its side, barely visible beneath the dirt. I began to dig, feverishly, desperately. I knew I was the last person God probably wanted to hear from, and yet I prayed anyway, hoping to feel Him the way Melissa did. But all I felt was the sand growing thick under my fingernails. Finally, miraculously, after what felt like ages, I found it: hidden under several inches of soil was a piece of my dress, still clinging to the rusted wire.

I ripped it free and held it to my face. "Thank You!" I breathed. "Thank You!" This was it. This *was* the same fence post. Which meant the road was right behind me.

I spun around. Sure enough, yes, the road was there. You'd have to be looking right at it to find it, seeing as how it was all but covered in fresh dunes, but it was there.

The truck wasn't.

I rushed forward, tripping over a pile of knotted tumble-weeds.

Most of the sand had blown against the ditches. There were no dunes big enough to cover a truck. Not on the road. The tallest was about half my height, slumping to the north as if tired from its journey.

Maybe the wind had tipped the truck on its side. Yes, that's probably what happened. That's how it got buried. I didn't even let myself consider how stupid that was. I was going to cry again if I didn't start digging. And there wasn't enough water left in the world to fuel tears.

So I dug. First one hole, then another, then another. Praying again, this time to feel metal, rubber, wood, anything besides dirt. I dug until I felt gravel, until my fingertips bled. And still I dug. It had to be here. Trucks didn't just blow away, not even in a duster like that. No, it was here. It was here. It was here. I just had to find it.

It was after the fourth dune that I saw them. Tire marks. Old ones would have blown away in the storm. These were new. Fresh.

They'd left me.

I folded onto the ground, sinking into the dune I'd been fighting. There was no truck. And there weren't even any footprints. Not on the road, not in the field, not in the ditch that lay filled with half-covered tumbleweeds.

Only tire marks headed eastward. Not just toward India-napolis . . . but also away from me.

The dirt shifted beneath me, covering my legs. I didn't

try to push it away. They'd driven away. Left me behind. They'd gotten their chance to finally be rid of me, and they'd taken it. A chance to finally be free from their mean, ugly, deformed daughter. The one who'd been a curse since the day she was born. Who'd killed her mother. Who refused to let anything good come into their lives.

I bit the inside of my cheek as hard as I could, ripping the tender flesh and tasting blood. But the pain wasn't enough to stop the tears. With nothing but wasteland in front of them, my screams raced across the open prairie, carrying my despair for miles before drying out in the stale Kansas air. The earth seized my tears, pulling them into the depths before the sun had a chance to snatch them away. I wailed and thrashed until my throat was raw and my face stiff, until the ground around me covered my body like a death shroud. I closed my eyes and let it.

The setting sun left orange spots behind my eyelids. I watched the dots shrink and expand, wondering how long it would take for me to die. Hours? Days? Maybe if I was lucky, I would just sleep. Sleep and never wake up.

The sudden caw of a crow made me jump. I opened my eyes to see him circling overhead, watching me. Waiting. I'd heard rumors about crows scavenging dead livestock lately, eating whatever they could find since the plants dried up. Eyeballs and noses, Matthew Warren had said. Those were the first things to go on the goats after the crows landed on his daddy's farm.

I put a hand to my brow, instinctively protecting my eyes. This bird was waiting for me to die. He was waiting for dinner.

Digging my fist into the dirt, my hand curled around a rock. Even in my wretchedness, I would not allow myself to be reduced to bird chow. With a scream, I hurled it toward him, missing by miles but sending him away squawking curses. I followed his silhouette until it disappeared in the rapidly setting sun. West. Toward Oklahoma.

I could go. Nothing was stopping me. Return to Boise City. The dugout was still there. Melissa was still there.

The cramp in my leg spread to my chest. No. Melissa Mayfield was there. Melissa Baile was not. I pulled the hankie from my pocket and wiped the sweat from my lip, trying to force a breath into knotted lungs. The material was frayed and filthy, a shadow of its previous state. I'd ruined it already.

I couldn't go home.

But even if I deserved it, dying didn't seem like much fun either. Not with those doggone crows around.

I could continue east. Find Pa. My heart was cleaved as I pictured him behind the wheel, tires rolling over the dunes. How could he have done such a thing? He loved me. No matter how mean and ugly I got, he loved me.

I think.

No, he did. I had to believe he did. He'd never have left me if it wasn't for Helen. It had to have been Helen, pushing him onward, convincing him I was gone.

But I could go after him. Find him, get the surgery, and wait for the rain. Because the rain *would* come. And then Pa and I could come back, with or without Helen. If I quit now, she'd win. Pa'd never return to Boise City if I wasn't there to make him. To keep those city-slicker nails from digging in too far. I could get the surgery, and I'd finally be strong, inside as well as out. Strong enough to fight for Pa and for Oklahoma.

And if I was wrong? If it was true he did want to be rid of me? Then so be it. My leg would be fixed and I'd return to Oklahoma without him.

That would show 'em.

I watched the sky fade from orange to purple to black. Then I pocketed the hankie, pushed the sand off my legs, and limped back toward the creek bed. Settling myself at the base of a dead tree, I removed my brace. There was no one I had to impress anymore. I was free. I massaged my foot. It was stiff, achy, and cramped. But I'd need it to cooperate tomorrow. Because tomorrow I was heading for Indianapolis. On my own.

*　　*　　*

It was a restless night. The sky was clear but moonless, and the air felt heavy on my skin. Like the duster had left an invisible blanket over the land. The absence of wind made every rustle echo. Although I knew it was probably nothing more than jackrabbits and crickets, my mind drifted to darker things. I wished I'd grabbed Pa's gun from the truck. I wished a lot of things.

"The stars make no noise," Pa had said. But tonight—tonight they were screaming.

I began my walk before the sun came up. I was hungry, but I was used to being hungry. It was the thirst I couldn't stand. I needed to find water. My throat ached from the lingering dust and my earlier screams. I could barely swallow. There simply wasn't enough moisture to do it anymore. If I was to have any hope, I had to find water first. The creek bed I'd slept in followed the road, so I followed the creek bed. Maybe there'd be a puddle the drought had forgotten.

But the drought had forgotten nothing. That much was clear within the hour. The ground was cracked and the grass disintegrated under my steps. Even the rocks looked parched and desperate. There was no water here. And there hadn't been in a very long time. I gave up and retreated to the road. Maybe I'd see a house I could beg from.

My foot ached. My head pounded. My mouth was as dry as cotton. I could feel what little moisture I had left being sucked from my skin. The sun was so hot. It wasn't this hot in Oklahoma, I didn't think. The heat was starting to make me forget. There was no shade. No streams. No houses. And nothing but dust on the horizon.

What was I thinking? Did I really think someone like me—barely capable of making the two-mile journey to school each day on her own—could *walk* to Indianapolis? My mind was as crippled as my foot. It hadn't even been half a day, I figured I was less than ten miles from where I'd started, and I was dangerously close to fading away in the noon sun. I'd be dead before nightfall. I couldn't do things normal people could do. And not just because of my foot.

The heat made my head spin. I collapsed in a drift and vomited. Or tried to vomit. My stomach had nothing left to give. Not even any spit to wet my lips after the attempt. I didn't bother to get up. There was no point. I lay on the side of the road, feeling my skin sizzle. I wanted to cry. But I was too dry.

I reached down and yanked off my brace. My foot was swollen. Several new areas were rubbed raw. I closed my eyes and pushed against them, wanting to feel the pain. Anything other than barrenness.

"Ya dead?"

I blinked. A shadow blocked the sun above my face.

"Nah, you ain't dead. Whatcha doing down there?"

I blinked again. From the sound of his voice, the shadow was a man. But I couldn't see his face. I struggled to get upright.

The figure stepped back, allowing me some space. He was tall and gangly, dressed in a navy-blue suit two sizes too small, patches on his elbows, drooping socks around his ankles. A dusty bowler hat perched crookedly on his head. His skin was greasy and red from the sun, his hair and mustache the color of straw.

"Whatcha doing down there?" he repeated.

I opened my mouth to speak but my lips cracked at the attempt.

The man snapped his fingers. "Ah, right!" He took a few steps backward, and I noticed, for the first time, a car parked several paces up the road. He jogged toward it, then jogged back, his long legs reaching me before the rest of him. "Here," he said, thrusting a canteen at me. "Drink."

I was too thirsty to be wary. Greedily, I did as he said, feeling life return to my body, then sour just as quickly. I vomited between my legs.

"Whoa, whoa," the man said. "Slowly now. Slowly."

I took another sip, letting it slide into my stomach before allowing another.

"Better?"

"Yes," I said, my voice muddy. "Thank you."

He shrugged, his suit straining with the movement. "Now maybe you'll tell me what you're doing down there, laying on the side of the road?"

"I'm going to Indianapolis." I didn't mean to say it, but my tongue had a mind of its own, excited it could move again.

"Indianapolis?" The man brayed like a donkey, smacking his knees and causing his hat to topple from his head. His hair was thinning and stringy. "You're a long way from Indianapolis."

"I know that," I snapped, standing and wiping the dirt and bile from my legs. I turned my back to him, lacing my brace with stiff fingers. My foot screamed, but I stuffed it inside anyway. When I turned back around, the man was staring. "What?" I asked, puffing out my chest.

He scooped up his hat and looked at the sky, suddenly interested in the absolute nothing above us. "Nuttin'."

"Well, thanks for the water. But as you have already pointed out, I have a long journey ahead. So goodbye."

"You really think you're gonna walk to Indianapolis? In your condition?"

"And just what is my condition?'

He pulled his hat down lower over his already-red face and kicked at the ground with his shoe.

I curled my lip and let out a short burst of air through my nose.

He put his hands on his hips, yellowed fingernails scraping against shabby fabric. "How old are you anyway? Why are you out here by yourself?"

I straightened my body as best I could, trying not wince as the brace rubbed my swollen ankle. I did not answer his questions.

He stared at me.

I stared back.

Finally he sighed, shrugging his bony shoulders. "Well, keep the canteen then. You'll need it."

I nodded once. "Good day, sir."

I started back eastward down the dusty road, trying my best to keep my gait steady. I could feel the stranger's eyes at my back. But now that my body was no longer concerned with finding water, the pain in my foot grew more intense. I was less than twenty paces away before I started limping.

"Aw, come on. Get back here."

I kept going forward.

"I can't leave you out here. Not like this. Let me give you a ride into town."

"No thank you," I whispered through clenched teeth. He couldn't hear me. I didn't care.

The next sound I heard was the car engine starting. I moved to the side of the road to allow him to pass.

He did not. "Sweetie, get in the car."

I kept my face forward, the stabbing in my calf seizing my breath. But still I walked.

"Don't make me force ya. I'm trying to do the right thing here. I ain't a smart man, but I know enough not to leave a young woman out here in the middle of nowhere."

I shifted my eyes just enough to look at him.

"The next guy who comes along might not be so nice. It ain't safe for a girl out here." Inside the car, his face looked different. Creepy. Shadows wrapped around his temples, darkening his eyes. "I'll take ya to Pratt. Next town up. 'Bout fifteen miles. I got me some business there, and we'll get you some food. Figure out what to do with you after that."

My skin prickled. *Run, Kathryn. Just run.*

The man's car sputtered and grumbled, waiting.

I took a step back. And then a fleeting shadow forced my gaze skyward. The crow was back, swooping and circling, threatening me with his shrill caws. And this time he had brought a friend.

The man smiled at me with gray teeth. "So you coming?"

Maybe Pa had stopped in Pratt. Maybe he was still there. And I could get there a lot faster in a car than on foot.

I slid inside, keeping my body pressed to the door and one hand on the handle. The interior smelled of tobacco and sweat.

"Good girl. Now what did you say your name was?"

CHAPTER EIGHT

MELISSA

The Ladies Auxiliary Club met in the church basement every Wednesday morning from nine to noon. A three-hour, once-a-week commitment seemed excessive, especially when there was so much to do at home. I'd been prepared for Henry to say no.

And truth be told, I wanted him to. Those women . . . I'd said nothing, and yet they already seemed to know everything. Who knows what Henry would say—or do—if our dirty laundry was aired all through Boise City because I couldn't keep my tears where they belonged.

But to my dismay, he had agreed wholeheartedly. I needed friends, he'd said, in a tone that conveyed quite plainly he did not mean Doris McIntosh. All the wives were part of the

Ladies Auxiliary. Which in Henry's world was true, though it hadn't been in my own. Not that I mentioned this. I was no longer a part of that old world. The Ladies Auxiliary was for the wives of the *important* men in town, which now included me.

The following Wednesday, Henry and I took the ten-minute drive to Boise City together. I'd planned to ride my bike. It was one of the few things I'd brought with me from my previous life; I'd ridden it everywhere, usually with Kathryn balancing on the handlebars. Nonsense, he'd said when I suggested it. I couldn't ride properly in those clothes. He wanted to take me. Or wanted to make sure I actually went. Henry was very good at saying things without actually saying them. He dropped me off in front of St. Paul's with a lingering kiss and a promise to return promptly at noon.

I hadn't been in the church basement since my mother's funeral. I was six. Kathryn was just a newborn. I don't remember a lot about that day, but I do remember it was hot. Too hot for October. Sweat dripped inside my black dress, Kathryn's small body pressed against mine, doubling the heat. Pa had held her all through the night Ma died, but he wouldn't hold her that day. I thought maybe it was because it was so hot. Now I knew better.

She wiggled and cried through the preacher's eulogy. I tried swaying with her, rocking her, whispering and pleading. Still she whined. And still the preacher droned on. My eyes scanned the room, desperate to make contact with someone, anyone, who could rescue me. All eyes pointed at the ground, unable or unwilling to help. Perhaps grief made people deaf, too.

After the preacher finished, the crowd moved to the basement, where the Auxiliary Club had prepared a meal for the mourners. It was even hotter down there. The meat was lukewarm and sticky. The cheese was like rubber. Everything smelled like dead flowers. And Kathryn continued to cry.

I shifted her to my other arm, perspiration trickling down my back, wetting the top of my underpants and making me itch. People milled around, knocking into me and murmuring muted apologies. They didn't really look at me. Or maybe they did. But looking back now, all I can remember is one mass of black, sweaty stink.

Kathryn erupted into a full-blown wail.

Nervous glances flitted in my direction. Sympathetic maybe, but to me every look said, *There's the baby that killed Lynette Baile. The deformed baby. She killed her, and now she won't even let us mourn in peace.*

Another wave of heat washed over me, this time from the inside out. I couldn't breathe. Even my lungs were too hot. I clutched Kathryn to my chest and fled up the stairs, bursting through the church door. Collapsing under the nearest tree, I laid my sister on the ground and clawed the buttons on my collar.

She continued to scream.

I grabbed the mass of blankets surrounding her and tore them back, exposing her pink flesh to the air.

Instantly she quieted. Her dark eyes studied my face as her arms and limbs flailed with sudden freedom. The toes on her clubfoot stretched and twisted. Everyone who visited talked about her deformity in hushed voices, like it was some kind of monstrosity with a mind of its own. But seeing it now, laid bare in the bright sun, it was just a foot. Soft, wrinkled skin. Five toes. Tiny nails. Perfectly normal but turned inward, as if an invisible magnet drew it toward the other foot. I traced my finger along the top, watching goose bumps sprout on her leg.

And then she smiled at me.

I know they say babies that small can't smile. But Kathryn did. She smiled at me. And I smiled back. We were going to be okay, me and her. Because all my sister needed was freedom. And fresh Oklahoma air. And me.

Creeping down the church basement stairs all these years later, I was struck by how much everything—and nothing—had changed since then. The carpet was still ugly and brown, but my dress was no longer old and black and itchy. It was pink and cotton and new. The walls were still papered with faded flowers, but my face wasn't gritty with sweat and dirt. It was clean and powdered, enhanced with lipstick and blush. And the air still smelled old down here, like books and mothballs, but I no longer clutched my baby sister. No, Kathryn was gone and my hands were empty, save for the diamond on my finger.

Mrs. Brownstone rushed to greet me. "Oh, honey. You came!" She embraced me with thin arms, her lavender dress stiff against my body.

"Yes, I came."

Her eyes swept over my face but didn't linger. The bruise was faded now, practically invisible beneath the rouge. "Well, come here, come here." She grabbed my hand and led me to the corner where a group of women gathered around a table, mugs in hand. Some of them I recognized from the meeting at church a few days ago; many more I did not. They quieted as I approached. "Ladies, as some of you may already know, this is Mrs. Mayfield."

The women nodded and smiled their hellos.

"Well, Melissa—may we call you Melissa?"

I nodded. *Yes, please. Please call me Melissa.*

"Melissa is here for the first time, and we are so excited she's decided to join us. The body of Christ can always use the extra hands and feet."

The women murmured *amen*s. Mrs. Willis raised her chubby hands toward heaven.

"Now, dear, for the past few meetings, we've been doing some sewing and mending for local widows." Mrs. Brownstone gestured to a pile of clothes on a nearby table. "We distribute used clothing to them but also collect discarded fabric to make new dresses and pants for their children. Most of them are so busy trying to make ends meet, they have little time for such matters. So we do it for them."

I didn't tell her I knew all of this already. Before Helen came along, when I was still too young to mend, we'd received several donations of clothes from the Ladies Auxiliary. Did they remember? Or did all the needful faces of the past blend together?

Mrs. Brownstone led me to the table. "Do you know how to sew, dear?"

"Yes."

She winked. "I figured you did."

So she did remember.

She rummaged through a pile of fabric, pulling out various pieces of brown and gray. "So how are things at home? Settling into married life okay?"

I twisted the ring on my finger, swallowing much too loudly. "I—"

"Learning to be a servant wife takes time, dear." Her hand on my arm, a look in her eyes I couldn't quite place. "Before, you were a child with childish ideas and childish dreams. But the time has come to put those away. You are a woman now, and a woman's job is as a helpmate to her husband. You remember the story of Creation, don't you?"

Not a question. A rebuke. Gentle, but a rebuke nonetheless.

"God designed us to be helpers, taken from Adam's rib. Not an easy role, of course, but necessary. And *blessed*." The last word sharp and pointed. "Why, take Mrs. Marimen over there." She nodded her head ever so slightly at the table behind us and lowered her voice. "You think it's easy being the sheriff's wife with things the way they are? It's enough to drive a man to drink . . . and his wife to pick up the bottles."

The muscles in my legs seized, causing a shuffle in my step, which I tried quickly to shake off. Sheriff Marimen, a drunk? Surely not. I'd never seen the man with anything stronger than a lemonade.

Mrs. Brownstone cleared her throat as she pulled a small dress from the pile, holding it up to judge the size. "It's our job as wives to meet the needs of our husbands and help them in whatever way we can. Quietness, obedience, and respect should be your defining qualities. Practice those things, and I promise your marriage will be a happy one. A peaceful one." She folded the dress and put it in a pile with several others. Lowering her voice, her hazel eyes met mine for the first time. They were the eyes of a mother—stern but tinged with a sorrow too deep to voice. "And in these things we find our strength, Melissa. You must practice them even when it hurts. Do you understand me?"

I nodded, putting one hand on my chest to silence my heart. I did understand. Even these women, for all their love and faith, for all their respect within the community, were still just pawns in the game, powerless to change the rules, so intent on enforcing them instead. Their motives might have been pure but theirs was a prudent love, care shown in the constrained way that was appropriate for women of our station.

I would find sympathy here, but little else.

Mrs. Brownstone clapped her hands, causing me to jump. "Good!" She gathered the folded clothes in her arms. "How about for now you take this pile here to Mrs. Gale?"

"Mrs. Gale?"

Her face contorted into a sympathetic pucker. "Annie Gale? Do you know her? Poor thing. Five kids underfoot and her husband done succumbed to the dust pneumonia last fall. She had to sell the farm—oh, but I'm sure you know that."

Heat rose in my cheeks. Of course. The farm was one of Henry's now. One of ours. I gripped the sides of my dress with sweaty hands, unsure what to say. Or feel.

"Anyway, she moved to a place over on Murray Avenue. She does some cleaning for people to earn a little money. When she can get those little ones to school, that is. It isn't easy to keep five kids healthy in a time like this."

She pressed a basket into my hands and filled it with clothes. "I believe we have a few canned goods in the pantry over there too. Let me grab some for you. We usually pass out food at the beginning of the month, but I can't send you over there with nothing. Who knows if those kids have eaten anything this week."

So it was that I found myself walking with rubbery legs westward from St. Paul's, searching for Annie Gale's house on Murray Avenue. Most of the sidewalks were so drifted over, I had to walk on the road. I could remember as a child walking these same streets to Norma's Cafe for a Green River after church. Pa'd be hankering for some chicken-fried steak, and I'd wolf down my lunch—usually pancakes and sausage, a special treat—just so I could get that lemon-lime sweetness. But Norma's was closed now, the paint on the windows advertising her specialties—old-fashioned meat loaf and green chile stew—long since chipped away. I noticed a small pile of sand gathered in front of the door as I passed, crisscrossed with small footprints and claw marks. Jackrabbits most likely. They could find crumbs and scraps quicker than a hound dog nowadays. Desperation does that to an animal.

The houses were no different. Beaten near to death with sun and wind, it was amazing most of them were still standing. You could tell they'd been nice at one time—picket fences, trimmed lawns, trees planted with the hope of shade.

Most of them weren't yet forty years old. Neat little squares of land divided up for neat little homesteads, all planned to grow into a tidy little town full of promise. But Oklahoma is not a place for the neat and tidy. And all the planning in the world couldn't make up for the drought.

The basket grew heavier as I approached, my footsteps louder. Less than two blocks, and yet I felt faint by the time I arrived at the base of her sagging porch. I could leave the package on her doorstep and run. Tell the ladies back at church no one was home. I didn't imagine they'd care. I eased up the steps, wincing as the rotting boards creaked under my weight.

Through the ripped screen door, a child wearing only a diaper stared at me. I was caught.

"Hi," I ventured, taking a step forward. "Is, um, is your momma home?"

I couldn't even tell if the child was a boy or a girl. Its brown hair was short and tangled and looked as if it hadn't been washed in weeks. Dirt colored his—her?—cheeks, and dried snot collected beneath the nose.

"Can, um, can you get her for me? I'm from the Ladies Auxiliary over at St. Paul's. I have something for her." I held up the basket.

The child didn't even blink.

I crouched down. From here, I could tell the diaper needed to be changed. "Can you get your momma for me? Please?"

"Mary Beth!"

A figure emerged from the interior of the house. I stood

up and straightened my dress, then immediately felt foolish. The woman who materialized out of the shadows did not care about my dress. From the look on her face, she did not care about—or for—me at all.

"What do you want?" She grabbed the child and swept her into her arms. Her face was plain and weathered, brown and cracked from too much time in the sun. Stringy red hair was pulled back into a bun nearly as tight as her mouth.

The resemblance was striking. Green eyes, red hair, though all of it muted, tired, aged beyond the years she held over me. No one would call her beautiful, yet I could still see it. It lay just below the surface, hidden beneath layers of dust and grief.

I touched a hand to my throat, willing out my breath. It was as if I were looking in a mirror, though not the ornate and impossibly clear one that hung over the sink in Henry's tiled bathroom. No, this mirror was like the small one Helen had kept in the dugout, a relic of her previous life. The glass was scratched and warped, twisting our reflections into unrecognizable ghosts.

The woman was me. Me several years in the future. Me without this new dress and my new last name. Me in another life, another world, another twist of fate.

"What do you want?"

Her words pulled me out of my spiral. "You, uh, you must be Mrs. Gale," I stumbled. "I'm from the Ladies Auxiliary. Mrs. Brownstone—from the church—asked me to bring this to you." I held the basket out in front of me.

The door did not open. Annie Gale did not speak. Or

move. Or even look at me. Instead, she stared at my shoes. They were bright and white against her gray porch. Annie's shoes were ordinary. Brown and sturdy, worn through at the toes. I used to have the same pair.

I tucked one foot behind my calf. "It's, um, some clothes for you and the kids. I believe there's some mending in there too, as well as—"

"What's your name?"

"I'm sorry?"

"Your name. What's your name?" She shifted the child on her hip. The girl picked at a piece of lint on the frayed fabric.

"Melissa Mayfield." The answer came out like a swear word. Hushed. Timid.

Annie's face remained neutral. "That's what I thought."

My mouth suddenly had too much saliva.

With a rude creak, the door swung open. When she grabbed the basket, she was careful to avoid touching my hands. The entire house shuddered when the screen slammed shut.

"You tell the ladies at St. Paul's I said thank you. But I'd appreciate if they'd send someone else over next time."

Then she turned and disappeared back into the shadows.

Shaken and wounded, I fled down her steps, not stopping to catch my breath until I reached the corner, out of view of the house's accusing glare. It was only then that I noticed dirt on the bottom of my dress. No matter how much I rubbed it, the black smudge refused to fade.

CHAPTER NINE

KATHRYN

Frank Fleming's car was full of dynamite. Dynamite and something he called "so-lid-o-fied nitroglycerin."

I immediately regretted getting inside.

"Relax." He laughed and leaned back in his tattered seat, like there was nothing but kittens sitting behind him. "They ain't gonna blow up all by themselves. Trust me, you're perfectly safe."

This man had shown me kindness, saved me from probable death . . . and yet something about him gave me the willies. And that was before I knew the car was full of dynamite.

He waggled his eyebrows, a dry smile playing under his sweaty mustache. "So you gonna tell me your name or not?"

Not. But I found myself saying, "Kathryn Baile."

"Well, Miss Baile. You mind telling me how you ended

up in the middle of Kansas all by yourself?" He alternated glances between the road and me, one clown-size hand draped lazily on the steering wheel.

I crossed my arms over my chest. "You mind telling me what you're doing with explosives in your back seat?"

He slowed to maneuver around a drift. In the back seat, boxes shifted.

I hunched my shoulders, waiting for a bang. None came.

"I told ya they ain't gonna go off. No need to be scared."

"I'm not scared."

He clicked his tongue behind his ugly teeth. "Alright, Miss Baile."

I stuck out my chin. "And it don't matter how I got here. All that matters is where I'm going."

"And just what exactly is it you're hoping to do in Indianapolis?"

"I'm going to find my pa. He . . ."

He left me.

"We got separated," I said instead, swallowing the shame bubbling in my throat. I turned to watch a pheasant scurry out from under our wheels. "In a duster. He might even be in Pratt, waiting for me."

"Lucky for you I came along then, isn't it?"

Being in the car with Frank Fleming was a lot of things. Lucky was not one of them. "Your turn. Why you got all those explosives?"

"Because I'm fixing this here drought."

Well, that explained it. He was crazy. Fantastic. "Oh? And how you planning on doing that?"

"With science!" His voice deepened. His posture straightened. This was obviously not the first time he had given this speech. "Rain follows military battles. Plutarch knew it, Napoleon knew it—do you know who they are?"

I stuck out my tongue.

He laughed, the grating hee-haw echoing off the roof of the car. "Alright, alright. I was just making sure. But I digress! Yes, rain follows battles! Even Civil War soldiers knew it to be true! And why does it rain after military battles? Why?"

"I don't—"

"My dear, it's called the concussion theory. Explosions disturb the atmosphere's equilibrium, making rain fall from the sky. Now, the good Lord has blessed us with a time of peace in this country—" he made an exaggerated sign of the cross on his chest—"but we are still in a time of hardship. And in times of hardship, we must turn to lessons we learned during times of war." He bowed his head respectfully.

"What in Sam Hill are you talking about?"

He stared at me so long I worried we were gonna drift off the road. When he spoke, his voice was low, a secret meant just for me. "We bomb the clouds."

"Bomb the clouds?"

He grinned and finally returned his attention to the road. A lone drop of sweat dripped from his nose. "A war on weather, if you will."

I scooted closer to the door, peeling sticky legs from the ripped seats. I'd've jumped if I hadn't thought it would kill me. "You are completely crackers."

He neighed again. "Not crackers at all, little lady. Why,

just last week, I opened up the clouds in Council Grove. Sent my special mixture up into the sky and boom! Within the hour, an inch of rain had fallen."

I leaned against the seat, staring ahead. There were no clouds in the sky. Patches of asphalt shimmered in the heat, melting into dust that swirled around our tires. Even with the windows rolled up, I could smell the brittleness of the grass. All these miles and I still hadn't seen a drop of water yet. The entire world was drying up.

I wanted to believe him. I wanted to buy what he was selling. Rain. Sweet, blessed rain. We could sew clothes. We could plant food. We could build houses. But not one of us could make it rain. And especially not an idiot like Frank Fleming.

"If you honestly think dynamite can make it rain, then you ain't crackers—you're just a plain old dip."

Though traces of a smile remained on his lips, Frank's body deflated. He removed his hat and smoothed down the greasy strings underneath. "Suit yourself. But soon enough you'll be singing a different tune. The good folks of Pratt took up a collection and hired me to make it rain. And that's just what I'm gonna do. You stick around. You'll see."

"And what if you can't?" It was a stupid question. He wasn't going to make it rain. And I hated him for making me think even for a second he was. "Aren't you scared of what the town will do to you if it don't work?"

For the first time since I'd gotten into the car, something changed in Frank Fleming's eyes. They seemed darker, more uneasy and fatigued. His gaze floated across the dry prairie and to the pile of dynamite in his back seat. "Darling, the only thing that scares me these days is a lighted match."

* * *

The town of Pratt, Kansas, looked just like Boise City. Houses chipped down to gray wood. Dunes pushed against stores all the way up to the windows. Sand plowed off the streets like snow and dumped in piles off the main drag. The air even smelled like home—stale and thirsty. Only I was very aware that it wasn't home.

Frank told me to wait on a bench while he went inside the headquarters of the *Pratt County Press*, promising me a sandwich if I did. Seeing as how I wasn't keen to sit in a car full of dynamite, and a sandwich was a sandwich even if it came from a crazy person, I did as he said. I counted cars as they rumbled down the dusty street and, when I got tired of that, studied the blue-and-red marquee of the Barron Theater across the street. *Star of Midnight* was playing tonight at 7 p.m. Ginger Rogers and William Powell. Melissa had loved *Flying Down to Rio*. I wondered if Henry would take her to see this one. Probably not. Only Technicolor films for the Mayfields. Not that the Palace Theater in Boise City got many of those.

"Hey," Frank said, interrupting my thoughts. "You actually stayed put."

"You promised me a sandwich."

He blew a short burst of air out of his nose. "So I did." He shoved a wad of cash into his breast pocket and, noticing me staring, winked. "Money now, rain later."

I pressed my lips together. "Just get me my sandwich."

He replaced his hat. "As you wish. Follow me."

I didn't realize how hungry I was until the bread hit my tongue. This was real food. Not jackrabbit stew. Not water gravy. Not hard wheat bread and dry wheat cereal and grainy wheat macaroni. No. This was soft, fluffy, and covered in butter. And there was chicken! Chicken, dripping with grease. Back home, our hens were for eggs alone; we couldn't afford to slaughter them. But here, with Frank Fleming, I feasted. And I feasted well.

He watched with a curled lip as I licked the last of the crumbs from my fingers. "Better?"

I downed the last of my Coca-Cola and burped, pinching my nose at the burn. "Yep."

"Good. Because now we work."

Gone was the sensation of contented fullness. The chicken turned in my stomach. "'Scuse me?"

Frank stretched his arms behind his head, revealing perfect circles of sweat beneath his armpits. "I'm a nice guy, but I ain't that nice. I gave you a ride and a meal. Least you can do is give me a couple hours of work."

"Now hold on just a minute. I didn't ask you for nothing. You offered."

He laughed that stupid, obnoxious laugh again. "So I did." He leaned toward me, pressing his jacket against his plate. "To tell you the truth, you hurt my pride, Miss Baile."

His breath smelled like tuna. In fact, there was still a piece of it stuck in his mustache.

"I did no such thing."

"Come on, now. Give me a chance to prove my science."

"I gotta go find my pa."

He leaned back. A line of grease ran across the front of his coat. "And then what?"

"And then we'll go on to Indianapolis. Like I said."

Frank Fleming took a cigarette from his pocket and lit it slowly, savoring. He had all the time in the world, it seemed. "And whatchu gonna do in Indianapolis? Outrun the drought?"

He looked at me like he was expecting an answer. I didn't have one. Not that I was going to tell him that.

He took another drag from his smoke and shook it at me, dropping ash onto the table. "That's the problem with you folks. Everybody's running. Let me tell you something, Miss Kathryn Baile. There ain't no escaping this drought. The whole country's gonna be covered in dust soon. You mark my words. There ain't no running from this one."

"I ain't running." I fiddled with my napkin, pulling it across my mouth like I hadn't licked every drop of grease from my lips already. This man was a fool. Plain and simple. Looked like one, talked like one; I swear I could even hear his empty head rattle when he moved. And yet I'd traveled for days only to find everything around me still dead. What if there really was no end to it? No water anywhere?

I drew my arms in against my sides, staring at my hands. In that moment, I'd have given anything to see Melissa, hear her whispering those words of faith, even if I didn't believe them. Being with her, seeing her, feeling her—it would have been enough.

But Melissa was hundreds of miles away; her faith felt even farther. Instead, there was only Frank Fleming. Frank, who watched me with eyes half-hidden behind a cloud of smoke. "Well, I ain't running. I'm gonna fix it." He smashed his cigarette into his plate. "Are you gonna help me or ain't you?"

All I wanted to do was go. I wanted to find Pa, go to Indianapolis, get my stupid foot fixed, and go home. But more than all those other things, I wanted it to rain. Without rain, none of that other stuff would matter.

"Can we at least find my pa first?"

Frank dropped a bill on the table and polished off the last of his coffee. "Trust me, kid. If your pa's still in town, he'll be there tonight. Ain't no one gonna wanna miss it."

And that's how I found myself that evening carrying boxes of dynamite into an open field on the outskirts of Pratt, Kansas. Despite the setting sun, it was still hot, and the explosives were heavier than I imagined they'd be. My hands were sweaty, and my foot had swollen quickly during the heat and activity. I tripped, dropping the explosives—and luckily catching them before they hit the ground.

After that, Frank assigned me to unpacking the boxes instead. It wasn't long before he was proven right on one count—people started to gather. Families in the back of pickup trucks, couples on blankets, stragglers with their cigarettes and overalls. People brought food. The whole town had come out for the party. Because maybe, just maybe, tonight we would witness a miracle.

As Frank tinkered with his rockets, I scanned the crowd

for signs of Pa. From this distance, everyone looked the same. Dirty. Tired. Hopeful. Just like the people in Boise City. But not one of them resembled my father.

Despite my disappointment, I could feel electricity in the air. And it wasn't from an incoming duster. It was coming from the crowd. From their eleventh-hour faith. Women twirled umbrellas. Kids stomped around in rain boots. Because this was going to work. It had to work. If hope alone could bring rain from the clouds, Pratt, Kansas, would be flooded. But since it couldn't, we could only pray that Frank Fleming's rockets would.

And so help me, I found myself praying right along with them.

"Alright," Frank huffed, stepping back from his work. Sticks and canisters wrapped around rockets and balloons. It looked dangerous. And exciting. "Stand back. We're gonna aim for that cloud there." He pointed into the orange sky.

A lone, tiny cloud—the only one for miles—sat directly over our heads. It was shaped like a poppy.

He crouched on the ground, arranging and rearranging his TNT. He set a bucket at my feet, water sloshing onto my shoes. "I need you to be on the lookout for embers."

"Embers?"

He threw his hands in the air. "Sam Hill, girl. Yes. Sparks. I know how to shoot these here to get 'em high enough into the sky, but this entire county is a tinderbox. All it would take is one spark and the whole place'll go up in flames." He pointed one finger in the air. "I'll keep my eye on the sky. You keep yours on the ground."

"Now you wait one minute. I didn't sign up to be putting out no fires. Didn't you—?" I stopped.

Frank grunted as he shifted another box. "Didn't I what?"

He was going to make me say it. Didn't he see my foot? I couldn't move quick enough to put out no sparks. But he didn't say it. And neither did I. Because at just that moment, the first rocket shot into the sky. The entire town sucked in its breath.

The thing burst on target, right in the middle of the rapidly dissipating cloud, casting a white glow in the fading daylight. The explosion rumbled through the soles of my feet. The crowd oohed in excitement.

A second rocket went off.

As the boom faded and the ringing in my ears quieted, a stillness fell over the field, the sound of a hundred people, palms held upward, holding their breath. I was one of them. And yet no rain fell.

At my feet, Frank scrambled, repositioning and lighting more rockets.

"What—?"

"It don't happen on the first try," he snapped.

Four more rockets went into the sky. Then six more. Night began to fall. Rain did not.

Frank fiddled with matches and dynamite and a funny-looking gadget he called a barometer. I watched him for several minutes before remembering I was supposed to be keeping an eye out for fires. Not that I would have been able to move if there had been one. Frank's anxiety pinned me to the ground like an anchor. It was like watching pigs root around in dried-up slop. Didn't matter how hungry they were. Wasn't nothing in that trough gonna satisfy.

As more and more rockets exploded and the earth still remained dry, the hopefulness of the crowd melted into the darkness. What started as impatient grumbling swelled into angry shouts. Curses and bottles were thrown in our direction. It was hard to see the masses through the haze of smoke, but I didn't need to. You could *feel* their disappointment and fury. If it didn't rain soon, the drought wouldn't matter anymore. Because we'd both be dead.

"Frank?"

He didn't hear me. Or couldn't. He kept lighting. Feverishly. Wordlessly.

"Frank?"

Sweat rolled down his forehead and collected in his mustache. He adjusted wires and tied strings with the urgency of a surgeon. The sun was completely gone now, the only light from the rockets he refused to stop firing. The white glow made him look like a spook. A twitchy, agitated spook. But unlike me, he didn't seem the least bit concerned with the crowd. His only worry was failure.

I scratched at my arms, swallowing an ache in my throat, surprised by unexpected sympathy. Rocket after rocket fizzled, and still Frank tried. Because the world needed fixing, and he honestly believed he could do it. In his mind, he was a savior, his life's purpose born out of desperation and delusion. Frank Fleming was no crook. He was a poor, pitiful sap. Just like the rest of us.

I wanted to hate him. I should've hated him. His science

was wrong, his optimism absurd. And I had been stupid enough to believe him. Just for a minute, but nevertheless I had believed. There was no magic cure. There would be no end to this drought. The ground at my feet was withering while the sky above me collapsed under the weight of our hope.

Frank didn't even notice as I walked away. I hobbled into the dispersing crowd, trying to be heard over their aggravated mutterings.

"Excuse me, do you know James Baile? . . . Have you heard of a James Baile? I'm looking for him."

Downcast faces, miserable shrugs.

"Have you seen any travelers from Oklahoma coming through this way? A man and a woman, maybe?"

People pushed past me without answer, just averted eyes and weary shakes of the head. Umbrellas were folded once more, rain boots still covered in dust. Who had the energy for compassion when yet another dream had been shattered?

I slumped next to a fence post, pulling at my hair in frustration and misery. This was just another dead end in more ways than one.

The crowd thinned, disappointment filling the gaps between stragglers. But near the back, two black masses separated themselves from the assembly and moved toward the open field. No, not masses. Groups of men. Large men. Heading right for Frank.

"Hey!" I shouted, scrambling to my feet.

Three large explosions muted their approach. Frank remained hunched over his science experiment, barely visible in the orange glow.

"Frank!"

Too late. One of the men grabbed Frank's arms, yanking him upward.

"No, please," I heard him whimper. "Sometimes it can take a couple days. I have to get the conditions—"

His words were cut off by a punch to the stomach.

"Hey!" I yelled again. My foot was stiff as I tripped my way across the lumpy ground.

The sky went dark. The noise of the rockets stopped, the thud of fist against bone carrying across the field. *Crack. Thump. Squish.* One after another after another.

And then silence. So thick it felt perverse, the stench of sulfur and ashes mixing with smoke in the air. My brace squeaked as I rushed forward, dry grass crunching beneath my feet. In front of me, Frank's body dropped to the ground and was still.

Apparently satisfied, the men abandoned their prey and moved toward me. In too much pain to flee, I stopped and held up my fists. *Do it,* I screamed inside my head. I was no match for them. But I was angry enough to fight anyway. Not for Frank. But for myself.

They passed me without a second glance. The smell of alcohol lingered in their wake.

I stared after them, my relief only lasting a few seconds before turning into rage. "Hey!"

They continued to walk.

"Hey!" Angry tears streamed down my cheeks. I was too slow to catch up. Always too slow. *"Hey!"*

I didn't want them to turn around. I needed them to

turn around. I would not be left behind, invisible to these monsters, too.

The men climbed into Frank's car, laughing. By the time I reached the street, the taillights had faded into blackness. I kicked at the dusty ground and screamed. My clubfoot throbbed inside my boot. I kicked harder.

I made my way over to Frank. His jacket was ripped. Blood crusted his face. But his chest rose and fell. I lay down next to him, curling my knees to my chest. From my pocket, I took Melissa's handkerchief and held it next to my face, holding back tears determined to fall. "I want to go home," I whispered. "Please, God, I just want to go home." I prayed harder than I'd ever prayed before, twisting Melissa's handkerchief around my fingers. I prayed until I ran out of prayers and then started over again. "Please, I'm sorry. I just want to go home."

When I opened my eyes, I thought for a moment it had worked. Miles of dirt and dead grass stretched out all around me. Oklahoma. I was back in Oklahoma. Then, at my feet, Frank Fleming moaned and stirred.

Before giving myself over to sobs, I prayed one more time. To a God I wasn't sure was listening, that I was even less sure cared. But as I'd done a million other times before, I prayed for rain. Only this time, not for it to end the drought, but to come and wash me away.

CHAPTER TEN

MELISSA

The town of Boise City would not let drought or dusters keep it from hosting the county fair. Forget that most of the population had little money to spend on such foolishness. Forget that the sunbaked earth was so hard the tents were nearly impossible to pitch. Forget that there was nothing really to celebrate. The summer carnival was tradition, and tradition was all the people of Boise City had left.

When she was small, Kathryn loved the carnival. The noise, the smell, the excitement. It was as if we weren't in the middle of nowhere Oklahoma but instead in some city somewhere, with all its buzz and energy and life. People traveled for miles to see it. For a few days, Boise City was the center of the world. Or at least it felt that way. Vendors lined the streets, selling popcorn and candy and small wooden toys. Ring toss and strongman games sat on every corner. A local band played on a makeshift stage, banjo and six-string knitting a melody that rained over the crowd like confetti.

Here in this place, I was twelve years old again, Kathryn at my side, sweaty hand in mine. Hundreds of people flocked onto Main Street, swallowing the two Baile girls, here without their pa again. He hadn't been seen much since that Barrett woman came into town. But Pa's absence was the last thing on our mind. I'd heard a rumor about a new sweet coming to the carnival, something called "cotton candy." Betty Purcell had bragged about it in school, saying she'd already had some at the fair down in Dalhart. I didn't believe her. How could sugar turn into string? Betty was a fibber. But if she *was* telling the truth, I didn't want to be the only one to miss out. I was going to find it, and I was going to find it first.

"Look, Em!" Kathryn pulled my hand, forcing me to stumble. She was barely six, her brace still too big for her scrawny leg, but her arms were stronger than an ox.

We were close. I could smell a sweetness in the air. Why was she stopping now? "What?" I snapped, spinning around.

My sister's cheeks were red from exertion, and sweat dampened the hair around her face. Her clubfoot twisted inward despite her brace, a trick Kathryn learned early on would ease a nasty cramp. I'd been pulling her too hard. All because I wanted candy. I leaned down to her level, my voice softer. "What is it, Kathryn?"

She wasn't even looking at me. Her eyes were skyward, the lights above us reflecting in them like fire. "It's the road of yellow brick."

Hundreds of small bulbs hung above us, connecting building to building and turning the street at our feet a pale shade of yellow. There were no bricks in sight. Only miles of hardened dirt. But for that moment, I saw Boise City through Kathryn's eyes. Somehow the road was glittering. For the Baile sisters, it was no longer just Main Street. It was magical. And so were we.

I squeezed my sister's hand and smiled. The cotton candy was forgotten as we walked, just the two of us in a sea of people, on the road to the City of Emeralds.

Tonight, though, the lights seemed dimmer. And they didn't make anything glitter. They just made it hotter. The sun had set behind the western hills, but instead of a blissful respite, the evening air remained stagnant. One of my arms was wrapped tightly around Henry's; the other wiped sweat from my brow. It wasn't ladylike, I knew. I should dab with my handkerchief. Not that I had one.

"Mr. and Mrs. Mayfield! Hello!"

"How's your father? Missed him at the chamber meeting Tuesday evening."

"Rain in Dallas last night. We're next! I can feel it!"

"Price of wheat fell again. I swear the government is trying to kill us faster than this drought."

Hands shaken, cigarettes exchanged, voices raised to be heard over the music and by everyone else. *I'm talking to Henry Mayfield. Henry Mayfield is talking to me.* We were Boise City royalty and this was our victory parade.

As Henry led me into the center tent, its red-and-white canopy flapping gently in the breeze, the crowds parted before us. On the stage, the horns silenced, a montage of

Bing Crosby's latest cut short. My heels echoed on the dirt as
Henry pulled me to the middle of the dance floor, a hundred
interrupted revelers crowding the edges. Not one of them
dared say a word.

Shivers crept up my spine even as sweat dripped from my
neck. "Henry. Henry, what—?"

He cut off my question by spinning me once, quickly,
sending my maroon dress twirling.

I let out a surprised giggle, gripping his arm to steady
myself.

He held me close as the band started up again, the first
strains of a familiar tune. "Moonglow." The first song we'd
danced to at our wedding.

"For you," he whispered, his freshly shaved cheek smooth
against my own. "For us."

I pulled away slightly, running my hands through the
wisps of hair at the back of his neck as I looked into his eyes.
Those eyes. "I love you."

He winked and kissed my forehead before drawing my
body close once more. His hand traveled down my back a
little lower than what was proper. I let it.

Feet shuffled and the crowd returned to the dance floor.
Bodies bumped and mixed around us, but Henry and I
remained undisturbed. In our bubble. The Mayfield bubble,
a space reserved just for us no matter how many others
wanted to join.

Faces swirled around us. A few I recognized. Like Mrs.
Bonnifeld, winking at me over the shoulder of her husband,
her dress a deep green, not a single frayed thread or patched

hem. Her husband was clothed in a gray suit, probably from his own department store, pressed and crisp, his tie a shade of emerald to match his wife. And there, behind them, Pastor and Mrs. Brownstone, their clothes not quite so new, not nearly as polished, but still clean and modern. Cotton, perhaps. At the very least, not made out of flour sacks.

And then there were the others. The blur of gray faces at the edge of the crowd. Watching.

"You're so beautiful," Henry breathed. "Look at how they're all staring. At you. My wife."

Heat rose in my cheeks. "Henry."

But they were. They were staring. All around us, eyes pierced my skin. But what my husband mistook for adoration, I understood to be bitterness. Desperation. Beneath multicolored lights and joyful music, the people of Boise City looked tired, the forced happiness empty. Weary smiles painted across defeated faces. Feet waltzing across dead earth. Earth that had broken some, driven many more away . . . and left Henry Mayfield untouched. Resentful of circumstance but powerless to change it, the entire lifeless population of Boise City was here tonight, dancing on ground that was killing them because there was simply nothing else to do. Not when the sky stubbornly refused to fall.

And in every single dirty face, I saw Annie Gale. I saw myself.

I kept my eyes closed for the rest of the dance.

On the drive home, the Oklahoma countryside lay barren before our headlights. One of Henry's hands draped lazily across the steering wheel. The other wrapped around my shoulder and stroked my hair. I stole a sideways glance at my husband. If I'd not married Henry Mayfield, would I be like the rest of them? Like Annie? In her eyes, I had seen what my future could have been. Should have been. Why was I lucky, and she was not? What had I done to deserve this? What had she?

Later that night, after performing my wifely duty, I lay staring at the ceiling while Henry snored beside me. Our lovemaking was no longer painful. It was still rough, urgent, and nightly, but I'd grown used to it. Submitting was a small price to pay for what I knew was out there. My mind drifted to Annie, then wandered further—to my mother. I'd been so young when she passed, and the memories of her were hazy, little snippets of time that were more feelings than actual events. I remembered waiting by the window, anxiety growing as the sudden rain poured harder, wondering why our neighbor couldn't have just harvested her garden herself, broken arm and all, and the feeling of elation when Ma finally burst through the door, soaked, tired . . . smiling. I remembered my protests upon spotting her favorite blue dress now on the thin frame of the widow Granger at church, and Ma's firm hand on my arm, eyes speaking the truth of a world I didn't yet understand.

A world in need of a faith like hers. A faith of sacrifice, of service, of loving others before self, no matter the cost.

I remembered her prayers, every morning, every evening, short, quiet . . . and powerful. She never left those prayers sitting on her Bible; they went with her all through the day, draped over her like a shawl, opening her eyes to things others couldn't see, giving her strength to charge forward when others shrank away.

I prayed now, fingering the cross at my neck, trying to match the memories of my mother's passion. *I need vision like hers,* I pleaded silently, *so I can figure out how all these pieces are supposed to fit together.* Another set of choices—if Henry had merely looked the other way that first day or if I'd chosen to stay home instead of ride into town for a new book from the library—and I would never have ended up here, in this house and in this bed. Maybe I would have married Lucas McCarty, spending my days chasing away the centipedes and trying to stretch last summer's cabbage into thin soup.

Perhaps I wouldn't have been miserable. After all, I would never have known what life was like here, on the other side. And yet, now that I knew, I couldn't unknow. Now that it had me, the truth of our world would never let me go. I traced Henry's brow lightly with my finger. I had been spared. God's plan for my life, though inexplicable, had brought me here, blessed me. And perhaps, like Esther, my blessing came "for such a time as this."

I told my husband so the next morning over breakfast.

He glanced up from the paper, a piece of scrambled egg hanging from his lip. "What did you say, honey?"

"I said the Lord has blessed us." I wiped the food from his mouth with a smile. "And we should bless others."

"Isn't that what you do at your meetings?"

"Well, yes," I said, untying my apron and sitting beside him. "But that's more the church blessing people. I want *us* to help people. Me and you. We have no children and—"

"Yet."

"Yet." I gave him a small smile as I rested my hand on his arm. "Soon, I'm sure. But right now, we have so much to give. And the Bible says, 'He that hath pity upon the poor lendeth unto the Lord; and that which he hath given will he pay him again.'"

Henry scowled. "Don't quote Scripture at me, Melissa. I was raised in the church, same as you. I know what it says."

"I didn't mean—"

"It also says in the book of Luke, 'Blessed be ye poor: for yours is the kingdom of God.'"

"I don't think—"

"And God helps those who help themselves."

I bit my tongue so hard it hurt. I was positive *that* wasn't in the Bible anywhere. But I knew better than to say so. This was not going how it was supposed to.

"Henry, I just feel like God wants us to—"

"Oh, are you speaking for God now? A divine revelation just plopped inside that pretty little head of yours?"

My face flushed, as hot and tingly as if I'd been slapped.

Henry sighed, folded his paper. "I'm sorry. I didn't mean that, okay? I'm just tired and I have a headache and . . ." He rubbed the back of his neck with a grimace. "Look. I get it. I know you used to be poor. I know you still have friends who are poor."

Another punch. I drew my arms back toward my stomach. He sounded detached and matter-of-fact, speaking about my old life as if it were some common disease.

"But that's not who you are anymore, Melissa." He pushed

the chair back with a rude squeak. "You're a good person, and it's a nice thought. But that's what the church is for. If we were to start handing out charity to every person who needed it, there'd be nothing left for us." He squatted in front of me and took my hands in his. "We have to take care of ourselves first. You, me, and all those little ones who will come along soon. Don't you want to make sure they're taken care of?"

"Of course I do. I just wanted . . ." I wanted to tell him this was about more than me. It was about finally understanding God's plan, about fulfilling the role He had led me here to play. It was about the faith of my mother, about all the good she'd done in her life and the things left unfinished the day she'd gone home. It was about Pa, Kathryn, all those who'd done nothing wrong but still failed. It was about proving there was something here worth saving . . . and showing myself that there was still a reason for them to come back.

All of these reasons . . . and yet not one I could bring myself to speak.

"And it's not just us, Melissa. Think of all the people who depend on us. If our family suffers, what will our tenants do? What would happen to them?"

My eyes examined his, searching for any hint of irony. There was none. "But I'm not asking for charity. I want to hire her."

"Her? Her who?"

"There's this widow in town who cleans houses. Hiring her would help her and help me. She comes very highly—"

"We have a cleaning lady. At the front house. I thought you said you didn't want help."

I knew he'd bring that up. "I was . . . I was wrong." I tucked a loose strand of hair behind my ear. "And anyways I don't think we need to borrow from your father's staff. I think we deserve our own." The words sounded ridiculous coming from my lips.

Henry must have thought so too because he smiled and let out a small laugh. "Is that so?"

I stuck out my chin. "Yes. And Annie Gale comes very highly recom—"

"Gale? Jeremiah Gale's wife?"

"Yes, I assume so. Annie Gale."

Henry recoiled from me as if I'd spoken blasphemy. "No, Melissa. No way."

"But why?"

He wrinkled his nose and pushed his tongue against his teeth. "That guy was worthless. Way behind on his payments when he died. And you know why? It wasn't because we're blessed and he wasn't." He gave me a pointed look. "It was because he was lazy. I don't think there was a time I visited him when I didn't find him sitting on that front porch of his, smoking a cigarette instead of doing some actual work. All while those thirty squalling kids of his crawled around in the dirt."

I pulled my hands into my lap. I didn't know anything about Annie's husband. Maybe he had been idle and fruitless. Or maybe he'd been a ruined farmer with nothing to do. Either way, it didn't matter. He was dead, and his wife and children were not. "But that's not Annie's fault."

"Annie? Shoot, that woman was mean as a hornet and

ungrateful as a mule on Sunday. Cussing and spitting when I came to collect. It took two of my men just to hold her back." He chuckled, but there was nothing funny in it. "Didn't even say thank you. Dead or alive, that man still owed me several hundred dollars in back pay. But I was feeling generous. Took back the farm and called it even. All I got for my trouble was a scratch across my arm and a string of curse words that would have made a sailor blush." He shook his head. "No, Melissa. We won't be giving no charity, and we darn sure won't be giving it to Annie Gale."

I picked at the fabric on my dress, any protests turning to ash in my mouth.

"Melissa."

It wasn't a question, but I knew he was requesting an answer. I gave him a slight nod.

He smiled, satisfied. Victorious. "Well, I have to get going. I gotta run to Dalhart today. Doc says there's some medicine there might get Dad back up on his feet. Break that stubborn fever."

I frowned, Annie momentarily pushed to the back of my mind. William Mayfield had been battling the flu for several weeks now, but this was the first time Henry had been sent out of town for reinforcements. "Should I go see him? Maybe there's something I could bring? Cheer him up a bit?"

"Nah, he's got the help. He's fine. Don't need you catching whatever he's got." He pressed my palm to his cheek before kissing it. "Your allowance is on the counter. Go on into town today and get some groceries instead." He pulled an extra bill from his wallet. "And buy something nice for yourself while you're at it. You've been working so hard, you deserve it." He winked.

I managed a small smile in return.

He grabbed his hat from the hook by the door, turning to me as he reached for the doorknob. "We'll find you a cleaning lady if you want one, Melissa. But it won't be Annie Gale. Okay?"

I listened to the echo of his boots against the hardwood. To the door shutting, to the roar of his engine, to the crunching of tires on gravel. I waited until silence filled our big empty house again before moving. As I stood to clear the table, the sight of our plates stopped me. Mine was empty. A slice of bacon and several forkfuls of eggs still lay on his, already attracting flies and ready to be fed to the dogs.

*   *   *

I hadn't allowed myself to go to the dugout since they left. Each time I ventured out, I took the long way into town on purpose just so I wouldn't be tempted.

But not today.

Today I needed to see it. To smell it. To go inside and be in a place where the world had been poor and dirty but still made sense.

The long, rutted drive was covered with dunes. Parking my bicycle next to a half-covered fence post, I crested the hill on foot, the late-morning sun searing my dress onto my skin. There was no more grass here; it was as if it had given up the moment Kathryn left. Strands of brown and yellow drooped in clumps, brittle blades scratching against one another in mourning. At the top of the hill, a tree, twisted and barren. There hadn't been figs in years.

And there, just over the crest. There it was. Home. Or rather, what used to be home.

In the distance, under the dying maple, sat mounds of broken earth. Probably Henry, checking up on our land like he promised, testing the water pump and monitoring the underground spring, one of the few things that had kept our crops afloat while all our neighbors' had wasted away. It was the only sign of life on the entire property.

A large dune pushed against the west side, nearly to the roof. On the front, black tar paper wilted, revealing the sun-bleached boards beneath. One of the windows Helen had worked so hard to keep clean was cracked. On the doorstep, a jackrabbit stood frozen, watching me with accusing eyes, as if I were the intruder. And the garden—Kathryn's garden, the one chore she never minded—was nothing but a mess of dead leaves and tangled wire.

I didn't need to go inside. Even from here, the truth curled around my heart like tendrils. My home was gone.

Bile rose in my throat as I fled back down the hill, tears blurring my vision. I'd thought coming here would give me peace, but there was no peace anywhere anymore. The whole world had gone mad. I had a beautiful home, fancy clothes, a full stomach . . . and still the rain refused to fall. My sister was still gone. Boise City was still dying.

And I was supposed to close my eyes, concentrate only on myself, and pretend like the world around me wasn't blowing away beneath my feet.

* * *

"And a right good day to you!"

I slammed on my brakes at the sound of yelling, harsh words floating across the otherwise-quiet street. I was only a few blocks from the market, and though my tears had dried quickly after leaving the remains of our dugout, my heart still felt empty. All I wanted to do was get my groceries and get home. I was in no mood to play Mrs. Mayfield today.

Just ahead of me lay St. Paul's and, beside it, the squat brown building of the parsonage. The yelling, it seemed, was coming from there.

"Outrageous, it is!"

Sure enough, the door to the parsonage flew open and a brown shape emerged, arms thrown in the air and legs stomping as if trying to put out a fire. The woman—for that's what the shape was—strode down the walk, curses spewing from her mouth.

I shrank back, horrified. Annie. The woman was Annie Gale.

"Jesus never turned anyone away!"

I hopped from my bicycle and pulled it into the grass, pressing myself against a tree. It was ridiculous, hoping to blend in with the remaining bark, but still I tried, letting out a breath only when I realized she had turned, heading west on Main, away from my pathetic hiding spot. Her muttered swears lingered behind her like a fog.

I waited several moments before emerging just in case she changed her mind. When I was sure the coast was clear,

I mounted my bike and made to turn north—the long way to the market but, at least for now, the safer one.

"Mrs. Mayfield!"

Mrs. Brownstone came out of the parsonage, her mouth pressed into a frown, her thin arms waving.

My fingers squeezed my handgrips. I was caught.

"Mrs. Mayfield!" Mrs. Brownstone reached my side, her chest rising and falling rapidly. "My dear, what are you doing here?"

"I was just passing by," I said, looking at the top of her graying hair. Very deliberately avoiding her eyes. "On my way to the market."

She nodded, turning her head to look behind her. The way Annie Gale had just gone. "Yes. Yes." Apparently satisfied the woman wasn't coming back, she returned her attention to me. "Well, I'm so sorry you had to see that. To *hear* that." She tsk-tsked with her tongue.

I shook my head quickly. "No, it's fine. I didn't—"

"She doesn't understand that we're doing the best we can. I sent extras over with you a few weeks ago, out of the goodness of my heart, but I can't be handing out food willy-nilly. She's gotta learn to make it last."

My mouth felt dry. I swallowed, noisily.

Mrs. Brownstone gave me a half smile. "We're doing the best we can," she repeated. "Once a month simply has to be enough. There's too much need all around."

Somehow I nodded, though everything in me was screaming no. No, once a month was not enough, precisely *because* of all the need. I'd seen Annie's children—one of them, at least—and I knew that food wasn't being wasted. And it wasn't as if Annie failed to ration it. There simply wasn't enough. I'd felt hunger, remembering well the enormity of that want. It wasn't something I'd ever forget, no matter the richness of my current diet.

Shame burned through me as I thought back to the carnival, to all the faces in the crowd, to the dresses. The ridiculous *dresses*. Mrs. Bonnifeld's dress. Mrs. Brownstone's dress. *My* dress.

No, we weren't doing the best we could. None of us.

It wasn't a conscious decision to go to Annie Gale's house. Or maybe it was. All I knew was that something came over me as I stood talking to Mrs. Brownstone. Something like tranquility in the midst of grief, like being led by something other than myself for once. I didn't look back when I finally left her, promising my presence at the next Auxiliary meeting, and I didn't stop pedaling until I reached the market. I knew what I was doing when I grabbed an extra loaf of bread. When I told the butcher to halve the meat and package it separately. When I grabbed a few pieces of penny candy near the register. When I turned left outside the market instead of right, a mixture of both serenity and dread swirling inside my stomach. But I was still surprised to find myself on her front porch, knocking on her door, staring into one of the dirty faces that had haunted my dreams for weeks.

"Is your momma home?"

The child stared at me shyly, dust caked in the creases of her mouth. She was once again shirtless, ribs visible beneath her tan skin.

"Sweetie, is your momma home? Can you go get her for me?"

In lieu of an answer, Annie's face appeared around the corner. She wore the same faded dress, the same hard expression. "I asked them to send someone else."

"I'm not here on Auxiliary business."

"Then you ain't got no business bein' here at all." She moved to close the door.

"Wait!" I didn't recognize the sound of my own voice. "I'm not here from the church but I . . . I have some things for you." I held out the bag of groceries.

Her eyes flickered but she didn't move.

"It's nothing, really. Well, not nothing. It's bread, meat, canned goods. Just a few things I thought you might nee—" I stopped myself. "Want." I rummaged through the bag. "And I brought some candy. For the little ones." I leaned down and smiled hopefully at the child wrapped around her leg. I couldn't remember her name.

She smiled back and moved to grab the sweet.

"Mary Beth, don't you dare."

The child shrank back immediately, wounded but obedient.

"What are you trying to do?" Annie snapped.

I straightened. "Nothing. I—"

"You think you can just waltz over here in your Margaret Sullavan dress whenever you want?"

Margaret Sullavan? I'd dressed down today in a pale-purple button-up dress and brown flats. Nice but plain. Simple. Nothing movie star about it.

"A piece of candy and a few groceries is supposed to make everything better, huh? Never mind you stole our home right out from under us."

"I never—"

"Not like you ain't got a hundred more acres of your own. Gotta take back those five from a widow. Don't want her to get too big for her britches. She might be able to afford some candy of her own if we're not careful. Then where we would be? How could we possibly keep her in her place then?"

Hot tears filled my eyes. I willed them down, embarrassed, and shoved the candy back into the bag. "This was a mistake. I'm sorry." I stumbled over a broken board as I retreated down her porch, the splintered wood slicing my ankle.

"Maybe if I'd let Henry Mayfield under my skirt, I coulda kept our land too."

I stopped in my tracks. Blood dripped onto my shoe. It seeped into the fabric, blossoming out like a flower. It was ruined. I'd never get that stain out. Of my shoe or my name. Heat flushed through my body. I spun around and marched back up her sagging steps, ignoring the pain searing with each step. "I beg your pardon?"

For the first time since I'd met her, Annie Gale's expression changed. Although still hard, her eyes danced between amusement and surprise. It made me even angrier.

All the stares had said it. All the whispers and side-eyes since our wedding day. But she said it out loud. She made it real. "I married Henry Mayfield because I love him. And he loves me. And any notion floating around suggesting otherwise is just ugliness." I stuck out my wobbly chin. "Now, I'm sorry about whatever business there was with your farm, but that had nothing to do with me. I'm a Mayfield by name, but a Baile by blood, and I know poverty and dirt and death as well as any person in this town. I'm no saint, but I ain't no she-devil either, no matter what you think about me, Annie Gale. I'm a good Christian woman just trying to do right by the Lord." I stamped my foot in frustration. "And darn it all if you won't swallow your pride and let me!"

I dropped the bag on the porch and stormed away, pretending not to notice the drops of blood trailing behind me. I grabbed my bicycle, swearing under my breath as the kickstand brushed against my wound. I made it to the end of the street before I started to cry. Jumping from the seat, I steadied myself against a tree, sucking in a breath and sobbing from a hurt that had nothing to do with my leg.

It took several minutes to calm myself enough to get back on my bicycle. I needed to get home and clean myself up before Henry got there.

Swinging my leg over the side, I glanced back at Annie's house. The bag I'd left on the front porch was gone.

CHAPTER ELEVEN

KATHRYN

I shoulda left him there. I don't know why I didn't.

Maybe it was because Frank Fleming was the only person I knew in two hundred miles. Maybe it was because all Melissa's preaching about taking care of others finally stuck. But I think the most likely reason was because I had no other option. I didn't have anywhere else to go. Home was dying. Indianapolis was a dream. And Frank's broken hope was a bigger handicap than my clubfoot. How could one cripple abandon another?

I didn't sleep. Instead, I sat with him until he finally stirred, groaning and spitting clots of blood onto the cracked earth. His right eye was swollen shut, glistening and scarlet, with dried spittle crusting the mustache above his busted lip. Looking at him made my head hurt.

He said nothing as he stood. Just swayed a few times and then vomited, wiping his mouth with his ripped sleeve. Then, as if nothing had happened, he began loading his supplies back into boxes.

Did he even see me? Maybe those thugs had punched him blind. Or maybe he didn't remember who I was. Pa told me once about a cousin of his who got kicked in the head by a horse so hard he forgot how to go to the bathroom. Had to wear diapers again. I felt sorry for Frank, but I sure as anything wouldn't be changing his diapers.

"Frank?"

He said nothing.

Blind or stupid, I guess it didn't really matter. Not like I had anything else to do with myself. I grabbed a handful of matches and threw them into the box.

"Easy," he croaked, grabbing my wrist. His good eye washed over me, causing me to shiver. It was bloodshot and glassy, pupil dilated.

Well, he wasn't blind or stupid, that was for sure. But his gaze . . . it was as vacant as a corpse's. Surprisingly, I wished for the old Frank. Creepy was better than dead.

"If you're gonna help, do it proper now."

I nodded, and he released my hand.

We worked silently until all the debris was cleared from the field. It didn't take long. Everything he had left fit into one small box. Above us, the sky was pale and sickly. All that dynamite had done nothing. Not even a wisp of a cloud. The only thing hanging over our heads was the stink of old gunpowder.

When we finished, Frank straightened his back with a loud pop and looked across the field to where his car once sat. His car with all his belongings and remaining dynamite. It wasn't there.

Placing his crushed hat atop his head, he retrieved his box, spat another wad of blood onto the ground, and turned toward the open prairie. His feet crunched loudly as he limped away. I watched him, unsure whether to follow. Or if I even wanted to.

Suddenly the crunching stopped. "You coming?" He didn't look at me.

I found that I was. And so we hobbled, two cripples headed east, neither of us quite sure why or where to go.

* * *

"Look."

No way I was looking. It would take too much energy.

"Come on, look." Frank nudged my foot.

I yanked it away, cursing. I still did not open my eyes. "If it ain't the next town, I don't care. Ain't nothing to see but brown grass." We had stopped under a shriveled walnut tree. A full day of walking with nothing to show for it but dry mouths, rumbling stomachs, and sore feet. We'd managed to pilfer some water from a well at an abandoned farmhouse the day before last, filling a small jug we discovered in the nearly empty barn before we continued our journey. But our pathetic attempts at rationing hadn't held and that water was long gone. We'd seen nothing but parched fields and arid creek beds since.

"It's not the next town."

'Course it wasn't. There was no next town. He'd been wrong about the rockets. He was wrong about this, too. But my foot hurt too much to argue.

Leaves rustled beside me. "But it's not just grass, either."

I cracked open one eye. The sun had nearly set. All I could make out was Frank's silhouette. He was right, though. There wasn't just brown grass anymore. There was the deep purple of twilight. And in the distance, orange. A glowing orange ball. A campfire.

"We should go over there," he whispered.

"Dry up."

"Already did."

If I'd had the strength, I would have rolled my eyes. He'd lost his dignity but not his terrible sense of humor.

"They might have food. Water."

"And guns."

"I'll protect you."

"No thanks. I've seen you fight."

He scowled, reopening his split lip. "Fine. Stay here and die of thirst. I'm going over there."

I watched his head bob in the darkness for a few minutes, one pathetic box of rockets under his arm, before settling back against the hard ground, fuming. He was going to get himself killed. We were in the middle of nowhere. Anyone out here was out here for a reason, and not a respectable one. The fire was more than likely a criminal's campout. Or a group of Indians. Either way, they wouldn't take kindly to a stranger, especially not one like Frank Fleming, who looked like he'd seen the wrong side of an angry mob.

"Good riddance."

Frank's footsteps grew faint. Behind me, the grass whispered. The branches above my head groaned in a sudden gust of wind. Only there was no gust of wind. And what was that noise? Pa said rattlesnakes were getting bolder on account of the drought. And so were the coyotes.

More movement. Behind me now.

I scrambled to my feet, glad I'd kept my brace on despite the pain. What was that story Big Dumb Harry and his cronies told when they were trying to scare Alice Mitchell on the playground? She'd told us her family was fixin' to move to Kansas, and Big Dumb Harry'd told her to watch out for the spook who roams the Kansas roads. Long white beard and a staff. Always looking for traveling companions. Walking Will. That was his name.

And now I was in Kansas. Alone.

The darkness was thick. Even the sun had hidden. Try as I did, all I saw was nothing. I stilled myself, trying to hear, but the night pressed in against me, muffling its secrets. A fallen limb cracked to my right.

I limped away swiftly, heading for the campfire. Frank must have arrived by now, and I'd heard no sounds of trouble. But if there were, I'd be able to explain things. Perhaps traveling with a girl might make him seem less a danger. He needed me. And it was the right thing to do, looking out for him. Melissa would have wanted me to do the right thing. I left the night noises behind me and focused on the orange glow ahead, proud of my selflessness.

I tried to be quiet as I approached, but my swollen foot

fell heavy. More than likely, Frank heard me coming the moment I stepped away from the tree.

Sure enough, I found him smiling smugly, one large hand wrapped around a tin cup, a crust of bread in the other. "Well, lookee who decided to join us. Mr. Hickory, this here is Kathryn Baile. The girl I was telling you about."

The fire blinded me against the surrounding darkness. For a moment, I thought Frank was going crazy. But then, ever so faintly, the outline of a man appeared on the other side of the flames. He rose and walked toward me.

I shrank back. The man was thick as a barrel and near seven feet tall, with arms and legs like a spider's. A weathered cowboy hat sat atop his head, adding to his height and rendering him faceless.

Had it not been for Frank, I would have run. Or tried to. But there wasn't no way I was letting *that* man look braver than me. Summoning a courage I did not feel, I extended my hand. "Mr. Hickory. Pleased to meet you."

His face remained a shadow, and he did not accept my hand. He did, however, offer another tin cup and hunk of dry bread.

The water was dirty and tasted of sand and metal. It was the best I'd ever had. I drank greedily, nearly choking but refusing to stop, feeling every drop as it traveled through my body.

Without speaking, Mr. Hickory refilled the cup from a large canteen and handed it back to me. I still couldn't see his face.

After my second cup, Mr. Hickory lit a cigarette and

retreated, a slight shuffle in his step. The water sloshed in my stomach, making me nauseous, and I wobbled toward Frank slowly, afraid I'd lose the precious gift I'd just been given.

Frank stretched his legs out in front of him. "So as I was saying, Mr. Hickory, the science behind it goes back hundreds of years. We all know that rain falls when drops of water inside the clouds get too heavy. And they get too heavy by bumping into each other and forming bigger drops, right?"

Mr. Hickory did not answer.

Frank didn't care. His body was a wreck but his inner showman was alive and kicking. "Well, what my explosives do is force the water droplets together. The blast discombobulates the air molecules, shaking the rain right out of the sky. Why, it's a proven fact that . . ."

After everything that had happened in Pratt, Frank was still preaching. But that didn't mean I had to listen to it. I busied myself with small bites of bread, my tender stomach the only thing keeping me from eating it all at once, and sneaking glances at our new companion instead. Flames finally penetrated the darkness beneath his hat. He looked familiar, but it was a familiarity I couldn't place. Leathery skin beneath a layer of silver stubble. His hooked nose was made longer by his sunken cheeks and eyes that looked like they hadn't slept in weeks. In the light of the fire, they were the color of steel . . . and they were watching me watch him.

I wasn't as sneaky as I thought.

And still Frank talked. "The problem is that dynamite is expensive. And those hooligans stole my money and my whole lot, save for that there." He gestured to the box that was, thankfully, placed away from the fire. "I'm hoping the next town will give me a loan so I can continue my work. I gotta have some more money." He gave a high-pitched bray as his eyes flitted around the campsite. "I gotta keep going. I mean, we're all in this together, right? And I don't see anyone else stepping up to fix this drought."

Mr. Hickory was no longer looking at me. He was looking at Frank. "We should get some sleep," he said quietly.

So quietly Frank finally stopped talking. "Huh? Oh. Yes. Right. Long day tomorrow."

The fire between us popped, sending embers into the sky. Mr. Hickory lay down where he sat, placing his hat over his eyes.

Shrugging at me, Frank did the same.

Swallowing the last of my meal, I laid my head against the hard ground. The sky was moonless and quiet. Nothing but the soft crackle of the fire and the chirruping of crickets. Almost peaceful. Until Frank fell asleep.

A high-pitched whining leaked from his nostrils with each breath, like too much air being squeezed from a pin-pricked tire. He'd never whistled in his sleep before. Or maybe he had. Maybe I'd just been too consumed by my own thirst to notice.

Teeth clenched, I rolled onto my side and draped my arm over my ears. It didn't help. I lifted myself up on my elbows and glared at him, even though he couldn't see. Frank shifted and let out a hacking cough before stilling.

Finally. Silence. I lay back and closed my eyes.

A snort and the whistling began again in earnest.

I let out an irritated sigh and glanced across the fire at Mr. Hickory. His breathing was slow and quiet, hat still covering his face. How was he sleeping through all this racket?

Wheeze, whistle, grunt. Wheeze, whistle, grunt.

Inching closer to Frank, I balled up my fist and jammed it into his rib cage.

He sat up with a yelp, gooey eyes struggling to focus. "Wha—?"

"Shut up," I hissed.

He rubbed his side. "What did I—?"

I scrunched up my face and scooted away from him, turning my back to his whines. It was colder on the edge of the fire circle. Behind me, Frank coughed and shuffled. I squeezed my eyes shut, waiting for the noises to start again. They didn't. Satisfied, I curled my knees to my stomach and closed my eyes.

But in their absence, the sound of silence buried me. Even the insects had fallen into a hush. It mixed with my sudden loneliness, the distance between me and Melissa, me and Pa, me and anything normal and comforting and familiar, magnified in the dark, pushing in from all sides. I stretched out, trying to shake it away, but it simply moved with me, like the winter quilts that seemed to pin you against the scratchy mattress. I covered my face with my arms, trying to muffle the quiet with my own ragged breaths.

It took me a very long time to fall asleep.

I dreamt of Helen. Of the first night she spent in our dugout. I'd curled up with Melissa as usual, but there was nothing usual about it. There was a woman in our house who didn't belong there. She'd cooked weird food and made the place smell like a whorehouse. And now she was whispering. Loudly.

"I'm just saying there are other, better places for her, James. Institutions with people trained for her condition."

Melissa snorted softly and rolled over, taking the sheet with her. I waited until her breathing steadied before inching closer to the edge of the mattress. I strained my ears in the darkness.

"Ain't no better place than here." Pa's voice.

"But you can't go on like this. How long do you think you can care for her? She needs more, James. More than you can give her."

Pa's voice again. Too soft to make out.

"I know she's just a child, but what happens in a few more years when she's not? She won't ever be able to take care of herself, and you'll wear yourself ragged trying to do it for her."

"She's my daughter, Helen."

"And I'm your wife now. I just want what's best for her. And for you." More words, softer. The rustling of sheets.

The next words were Pa's, low but firm. "I love you."

"I love you, too."

My chest ached. But not only from the dream. Because, for some reason, my ribs hurt too.

My eyes fluttered open. Something was on top of me. And it was no longer just the darkness. I thrashed against the pressure, and a hand clamped across my mouth.

"Shhh. Shhh. Shhh. It's me." In the dying firelight came Frank Fleming's face. His eyes were bloodshot. Pus oozed from the corners.

My mind woke slower than my body. Frank. He was on

top of me, his weight against my torso, his knees pinning my arms to the ground. He was smiling, but it wasn't friendly. Fresh blood dripped from his cut lip.

I tried to scream.

His hand pushed down harder on my mouth. "Shh. Shh. Just be still. This will only take a minute." With his free hand, he reached under my dress.

I froze. No one had ever touched me under my clothes. I did not want Frank to be the first. I twisted and pushed, trying to free myself.

His body tensed, trapping me. "Stop it," he hissed. "It's not what you think. Stop it!"

I would not.

His hand went down my leg, away from what I most feared. But it didn't make me feel any less scared. "I'm sorry," he breathed in my ear. "I'm sorry. I have to do this. I need this. I ain't got nothing else. It's for us. For all of us."

I wriggled beneath him, panicked. His belt buckle scratched my stomach.

"You'll be fine. You've got Mr. Hickory now. You'll be fine." His breath was acidic, coppery. "I'm sorry, Kathryn Baile. It's the only way."

The smell of tobacco and old sweat. I couldn't breathe. His weight crushed my lungs. Dots swam in front of my eyes. There was no use fighting. He would win. The world would always win against someone like me. *Just let it end, Kathryn. Better for everyone. Let it . . .*

And suddenly the weight lifted. Too much air rushed in at once, and I rolled over, gagging. A scuffle, the crunch of grass growing faint. I opened my eyes to see not Frank, but Mr. Hickory standing over me, a pistol in his hand. He aimed it east, breaking the night with a single shot.

It echoed for miles. But I heard no thud. No scream. The wind carried nothing but Frank Fleming's footsteps across the prairie as he fled.

My arms ached; my body shivered despite the heat. I felt naked and exposed. And not just because of his abrupt departure. I rubbed at the spot where his sweaty hand had touched me, feeling his desperation where something else should have been. My brace was gone.

CHAPTER TWELVE

MELISSA

"Is this it?"

Henry's lunch plate slipped from my hand, landing with a splash in the sink. I gasped—a little too loudly—as water splashed on my apron. I'd prepared the whole way home, and still my fear threatened to give me away. The peace I'd felt about following the Spirit's nudges evaporated at the reality of what I'd done—and the reckoning that was sure to follow should I give myself away. I bit the inside of my cheek and turned, wiping my hands on a towel. "Is what *what*, honey?"

"The groceries." Henry picked up a small bag of flour from the counter. "This is all you got?"

"I got everything on the list. Beans, peanut butter, sugar—"

"There's no fruit. And the meat cuts are small."

Because it was all I could afford shopping for two families. I touched my fingertips to my lips. "They were . . . they were out of fruit. Well, oranges and bananas. I know those are your favorites. And George has raised his meat prices again. I couldn't even—"

"Raised his prices?"

"I know! Isn't it just the goldarnedest thing? Says he's bein' as fair as he can, but he's gotta make ends meet too. It's outrageous if you ask me."

Henry leaned back and crossed his arms. He didn't believe me. Of course he didn't believe me. I was talking too fast, too high, too much.

I dipped my chin and held up my hands. "Okay, you caught me. I . . . I bought some chocolate."

"You . . . bought some chocolate?"

"I was going to surprise you with a cake."

"A cake."

It was the truth. *A* truth. Sure, I'd only planned the cake to cover for the fact that half of our grocery money was now sitting in Annie Gale's kitchen cabinets, but I *was* going to make him a cake. "You told me to buy something nice for myself . . . but I wanted to do something nice for you instead. And now you've gone and ruined the surprise." I stuck out my lip in a mock pout.

"Well, well, well." Henry's eyes sparkled. Goodness, those *eyes*. "Look at you." He crossed the kitchen and wrapped me in a hug. "Someone's really getting the hang of this 'wife' thing. What could I have possibly done to deserve a woman like you? You spoil me." He kissed me, running his hands over my hips. "You know what I'd like better than cake, though?"

I let out a shaky laugh. I'd done it. I'd actually done it. The groceries were forgotten.

He kissed me again, running his fingers through my hair. Who cared about Annie Gale when he kissed me like that? Let that pigheaded old witch make a soup out of her stubbornness for all I cared. Jesus can only knock, right? A person has to be willing to open the door . . . and not swear at the knocker, for pete's sake.

Henry pulled away, leaving my lips tingling "But that, my dear, is for later. I have to get back to work." He nibbled at my neck playfully. "You sure do make it hard to leave."

I giggled and turned back to the dishes. The thin layer of soap on top of the water broke as I plunged my hand back into the sink. "What do you have to do this afternoon?"

"Got some business with the boys; then I gotta finish clearing some land. Doggone soil ain't worth what it would take to make something grow on it. And the water . . ." He cleared his throat, started again. "If we clear some of the old wheat, tear down the houses, maybe we can sell it for other things."

A sudden panic spread through my chest and I spun back around, sending droplets onto Henry's shirt and boots. "But Pa's land . . ." The words slipped out before I could stop them.

He flicked a spot of water from his pocket but didn't meet my gaze. "No, not that land."

They were meant to be reassuring. But his choice of words did not escape my notice. *That* land. Not *their* land.

I turned my back, willing myself to believe him anyway, to understand that my own guilt was projecting suspicion where it didn't belong. Willing my breath to return. "You do what you need to do," I said thickly. "I'll get started on the cake." I picked up my dishcloth and scrubbed a cup, waiting to hear the door slam shut. It never did. I turned around to find Henry still standing there, mouth curled up slightly at the corners. "What?" I asked uneasily.

"Come with me."

"What?"

"Come with me. I want you with me today."

The smile on my face froze. Henry never asked me to come do any sort of work with him. "That's sweet, honey, but don't be silly. I've got work of my own to do. And I need to get started on that cake."

"The cake can wait." He came up behind me and grabbed my arm. "I want you with me today."

My body tensed beneath his touch. He knew. Somehow he knew what I had done.

And then he pulled me in for a kiss. Slowly. Tenderly. A million moments of want inside those fifteen seconds.

Surely he wouldn't kiss me like that if all were not well.

I touched his cheek and smiled. "Well, if you insist. Just let me get my hat."

To my relief, Henry turned not toward Boise City and the direction of George's Sundry and Supply, but away into the open prairie. My breathing slowed as I watched the hills rise and fall gently. All around me, the earth was brown, dead, ugly. But the heavens above remained beautiful. Blue and cloudless. Looking up, you could almost forget the wasteland beneath our tires. I closed my eyes and breathed in deeply. The air flowing through the open windows smelled of hay.

"You know what's funny?"

"Hmm?"

"I stopped by Alice McDowell's this morning hoping to catch her husband. He wasn't home, but she insisted I stay for a cup of coffee. And you know, sitting there on her kitchen table was a bowl full of oranges and bananas."

My eyes jerked open.

Henry's gaze remained fixed ahead, one hand drooped over the steering wheel, the other hanging out of the open window. "Said she'd just been to George's and planned on making some banana bread this afternoon. It was a shame I hadn't come by later or I could've had some straight from the oven."

I dug my fingernails into my palms. *Don't look at him. Don't you look at him.*

"Isn't that funny, Melissa?"

The countryside rushed past us unaware the world had stopped. An eternity passed before I finally spoke.

"She must have bought George out," I squeaked. "Explains why there weren't any left for me."

Henry drummed the steering wheel, his wedding ring letting out a dull thump with each tap. "Yes," he said finally. "That explains it."

The crunch of tires on dirt was deafening. Every jut in

the road rattled the dash and sent tremors through my teeth. Even the gentle breeze coming through the windows now seemed to scream. Never had silence been so obscene.

"Where are we going?" I wasn't even sure I said it out loud.

"You'll see."

Ten minutes later, we turned off the main road. A fence post to our left, half-buried in blown soil, was the only marker. And yet the path was recently plowed. The remains of dunes spilled onto the ground, where fresh tire marks crisscrossed the dirt. There had been recent traffic here. Lots of it.

"Henry?"

His eyes remained ahead. "Almost there."

The truck shuddered as we bounced along, breaking clods of dirt in our tracks. I clutched the sides of the seat with sweaty palms. And then, as suddenly as they'd started, the ruts stopped and the road smoothed. We crested one final hill and continued to the valley below, where a weathered barn sat in the middle of a barren field, a dozen trucks surrounding it like sentries.

"What is this?" I whispered, not really wanting an answer.

Henry said nothing. Instead, he exited the truck with a bang and pulled me from my seat, gripping my hand tightly as he led me to the barn. Inside, I could hear raised voices.

"It's time to fight back!" someone yelled. "God gave us dominion over this land, and I'll die before I let a bunch of critters take what little dignity I have left!"

Roars of approval.

I blinked my eyes several times to adjust to the darkness.

A hundred men milled inside a space way too small for their number. The air was unbreathable, choked by the smell of manure and sweat; the mood, agitated.

"Gentlemen, gentlemen!"

The crowd hushed. The voice came from beside me. Henry.

Like a ray of light in a dark cloud, he parted the crowd as he led me to the center of the group, where a beet-faced man in ripped overalls stood fuming.

"Nice of you to finally join us, Mr. Mayfield," the man said gruffly, removing his dusty hat.

Henry tipped his head in a way that seemed part apology, part reprimand. "Al."

That was all it took. Al melted back into the group.

"Thank you all for coming out." Henry's voice was even. He would not lower himself to shouting above the rabble. The smell of corn whiskey was strong. The men watched him as though jealousy and awe battled within; unsure which would win, I shrank behind him, careful not to let go of his hand. Henry scared me. These men—angry, ruined, and mostly drunk—scared me more.

"Gentlemen, as you may have noticed, we are under attack. But this time, our scourge comes not from above, from the dusters and never-ending drought. No, my friends, this time the plague comes from those we should have mastered long ago. From those with whom we'd be happy to share if only we had something *to* share. I'm talking, of course, about the good-for-nothing jackrabbits."

A murmur of consent rippled through the audience. A

hundred angry eyes bored into my skin, each face the same. Filthy. Hungry. Exhausted. And while I knew each one had a name, a family, a life, they *were* the same—for they all had the same story.

But not Henry. Beside me, he beamed, his greased hair slicked into place, his white shirt the brightest thing in the room. "This drought has taken our land, our homes, and most of our crops. We cannot let the vermin take the rest. Not when our very survival depends on it. This is our land! It's time we start acting like it!"

Howls of approval shook the crumbling walls, scattering a few pigeons from the rafters.

"I know many of you have heard about the roundups in Dalhart and Guymon. It's time for Boise City to do the same. I've talked to old John McCarty down there, and he assured me . . ."

Henry's mouth continued to move, but I couldn't hear him. Blood filled my ears. After that, everything moved in slow motion. The fist pumps and muted shouts of agreement. The crowd spilling from the barn and into the sunshine. The gathering of bats, clubs, and guns. Henry's kiss and mouthed assurances to wait, it would be worth it. The sudden, stifling stillness as the men disappeared.

I wanted to flee but sat in the back of Henry's truck, unable to move, the ache in my heart stopping my breath. The beautiful morning had morphed into an ugly, airless day. The blue of the sky felt cruel, the landscape harsh. The Oklahoma I'd known my entire life did not feel dead until this moment, waiting for the nightmare to return.

The wind kicked up suddenly, pressing my dress against my stomach. There was an ominousness to it. This was no passing breeze. With it came the sound of screaming. Squinting my eyes against the gray, I saw the horde appear on the horizon. Hundreds of fast-moving blurs, growing larger as they approached, kicking up dust in their wake. On their heels, the men. Spread out in a line, herding them toward me. Bats in the air, drunken curses echoing across the plain. Shots fired. I crumpled to my knees, clapping my hands over my ears.

It wasn't long before the rabbits reached me. Their mass shook the truck, filling the air with panic. Confused and scared, they fell right into the trap and headed for the open barn door. I wanted to scream for them to stop, but my voice choked on dust and dread.

A hand grabbed my arm. "Come on!" Henry shouted.

I shook my head.

"You need to see this!"

I shook my head again, yanking my arm free.

Henry's eyes flashed at my act of open defiance, unblinking despite the burning sand. The wind whipped my hair, stinging my face. But I didn't dare look away. In the darkness of his gaze, I saw it. He knew I'd lied. There was no hiding from Henry Mayfield. This was his way of making sure I knew that. My lip quivered slightly before I was able to stop it.

A smile crept across his face. He didn't press for the truth. He didn't need it. Exposing my weakness—and his strength—was enough.

He pushed away from the side of the truck with a smirk, blowing me a kiss with two fingers as he retreated. On his way into the barn, he crushed three rabbits with one swing of his club, never breaking his stride.

The sound from that barn would haunt me for years to come. The dull clunk of wood against bone. The whoops and hollers. The thump of bodies being thrown against the closed door, desperate for escape. The wails and cries from animals slaughtered for just trying to survive. But above it all, I would never forget how far away God seemed in that time and that place, how alone I felt in the face of such reckless and pronounced evil. It would echo in my soul for days, as loudly as the sound of those screams.

CHAPTER THIRTEEN

KATHRYN

"So just where was it you were fixin' to go with that scoundrel?"

They were the first words Mr. Hickory had spoken to me since Frank Fleming's sudden departure. If that's what you wanted to call it. We'd given up on sleep, but the cowboy wasn't exactly a conversationalist. Not that I was in the mood to talk anyway.

My arms burned where Frank had held me down. I tucked my foot under my knee. I didn't want to look at it. Even though it was still in my shoe, it was naked now. Uglier, somehow.

I'd wished that brace gone every single day of my life. But for it to be disassembled and sold for parts—all to fund

Frank's stupid, empty lies—was worse than being crippled. I was a part of it all now. Somehow I'd gone and made bad worse. Like I always did.

"What's it matter?" I spat, kicking a rock with my good leg. "I ain't getting there."

Mr. Hickory stared at me over the flames, cup of coffee clutched in his hands. "Alright."

I wished he'd stop looking at me. I took a swig from my mug. The coffee was bitter and turned my already-irritated stomach. I kept drinking it anyway. Maybe sickness in my stomach would keep it away from my heart. "I was tryin' to get to Indianapolis. I just ain't meant to get there, I guess."

He spat a wad of tobacco into the flames, causing them to flare. "Whatcha gonna do in Indianapolis?"

"What do you care?"

Eyebrows raised, he rolled his shoulders and took another sip.

I hated that I was being so ugly. He hadn't attacked me. Stolen from me. Darkened my life with another shade of just how repulsive the world really was. No, that person was probably halfway to Wichita by now.

But it wasn't just Frank. Oh, I hated him, sure. And I was angry at him—angrier than I'd ever been at anyone in my whole life, even Helen, which is saying something. But when it came down to it, the one I was most angry with was God.

If all Melissa's preaching about how good He was, how much He loved me, how He'd made me special, was true, then why did He pick on me so much? He'd twisted my foot, made me kill my mother, brought Helen to my doorstep, and dried up the land beneath my feet. He'd forced us from our home, taken Melissa away, separated me from my pa, and—because I hadn't been punished enough—sent Frank Fleming my way to steal my brace and leave me abandoned in the middle of nowhere.

No, Melissa might have thought He was a loving God—and maybe He was, to her—but He didn't love me. I wasn't sure that anyone did.

Not that I blamed them. I didn't love me either.

I sighed. "I was going to see the Wizard."

"'Scuse me?"

"I said I was going to see the Wizard."

Mr. Hickory ran his tongue over his teeth and poked it into the side of his cheek. He didn't say a word.

"What? Ain't you never read *The Wonderful Wizard of Oz*?"

"Ain't much for reading."

"'Course you ain't." I rubbed my temples with my fists. I had a headache.

The sun finally broke free of the hills. The first time I'd ever wished it away. The orange light stole all the shadows. I couldn't hide my foot anymore. It was there in all its twisted glory. Mocking me. Challenging me.

"You need the train outta Kansas City."

"What?"

He drained his coffee cup, spitting the dregs into the embers. "Train outta Kansas City goes straight to Indianapolis."

"And how far is Kansas City?"

"About one hundred fifty miles as the crow flies."

I threw my hands up in the air. "Well, too bad I ain't a doggone crow. I ain't even barely a person, if you hadn't noticed. One hundred fifty miles might as well be a million."

Mr. Hickory poked at the ashes with a stick, releasing a cloud of sparks into the sky.

I pushed myself off the ground with balled fists, feeling the coffee slosh in my empty stomach. Straightening my dress, I noticed Frank had ripped my sleeve. Perfect. But it didn't matter. Nothing mattered anymore. I was done with all this. With traveling, with strangers, with this world outside Boise City that didn't make no sense. I was going home. Whatever was left of home. Even a sister who was not my own and brittle land that was now owned by the Mayfields was better than this.

"Well, thanks for the coffee. But I best be on my way. So . . . bye, I guess." I tried to turn my crippled foot forward. It did not cooperate. I commanded it to straighten. It didn't listen.

Mr. Hickory spread the ashes at his feet, pretending not to watch me.

A lump rose in my throat, hot tears stinging the corners of my eyes. *Don't,* I screamed inside my head. *Not here. Not in front of him.*

Gritting my teeth, I took a step, landing awkwardly on the side of my foot. Pain shot through my calf, seizing my thigh. I teetered on my good leg, grasping at the air for balance. It did not hold me. I fell to the ground with a thud.

Cheeks hot, I gripped my knees with sweaty hands. *Don't you look at him, Kathryn. Don't you dare.*

Instead, I looked at the fire. It was dead now, nothing more than a pile of smoldering sticks. Sticks! Tightening my fists, I pushed myself up, and careful not to put much weight on my throbbing foot, I took a step. Dragging my other leg behind me wasn't the classiest move, but it worked well enough to get me where I needed to go. I grabbed the largest stick from the ashes and held it up to the light.

Charred but not completely destroyed. I put the tip on the ground and leaned against it. It bowed slightly but held. It would have to do. Satisfied, I nodded at Mr. Hickory. "Well, goodbye again."

Still he said nothing.

Leaning heavily on my makeshift crutch, I took another step forward. The pain was excruciating. Like every muscle in my leg ripping in two. But I didn't feel like I was going to fall over anymore, and that was something. I took two more steps, my skin chilling instantly as I left the fire circle. An unexpected shiver ran down my spine.

One step. Two steps. Three—*crack!* The stick splintered under my weight.

I didn't even have time to curse. I simply collapsed, banging my elbow on the hard ground.

"Indianapolis is that way."

I spun on my butt, holding my wounded arm. "What?"

"You're going the wrong way. Indianapolis is thataway." He gave a slight jerk of his thumb.

I puffed out my chest and raised my chin, willing the tears

back into my eyes. "I know that. I changed my mind. I ain't going to Indianapolis. I'm going home."

He shrugged. "Alright."

I turned my eyes west once again. "Get up," I whispered to myself. "Just get up." But I couldn't do it. Both my legs ached. My foot cramped inside my boot, curling itself into a ball. And now my elbow hurt, too.

A joke Melissa used to tell when we were little suddenly popped into my head. When Pa would tell us to do some chore she didn't feel like doing, like cleaning the chicken coop or clearing the tumbleweeds, she'd get all dramatic, putting her hands over her face. *The spirit is willing but the body is weak,* she'd say.

My body was weak alright. But now my spirit was too. There was nothing in the world going to get me up off this dry ground.

"Well, if you're going, you might need these."

I turned just in time for something soft to hit me in the face. Socks. It was a pair of Mr. Hickory's smelly, rolled-up socks. Making a face, I heaved it back toward him. "I got no need for your laundry."

The cowboy caught my toss easily and threw it right back toward me. It landed by my leg noiselessly. I did not pick it up.

"They ain't for you to wash. Stuff 'em in your shoe. It'll help cushion your foot so's you can walk."

I glared at him, unmoving.

Finally he sighed. "Suit yourself." He turned around, busying himself packing up his campsite.

I scowled. Who did he think he was? He wasn't no doctor, that was for sure. Telling me all I needed was a pair of rolled-up socks to be able to walk. Ha! I unlaced my boot and shoved the socks inside. I'd show him. I wasn't going to be the only one feeling stupid today.

I stood on rubbery legs. I could feel my heartbeat inside my foot. But pain was worth knocking the self-righteousness from Mr. Hickory's face. Taking a deep breath, I stepped forward. It hurt . . . but not nearly as much. I took another step. There was no ache crawling up my leg. No loss of balance. Another step. I could walk.

Doggone it. I could walk.

I glanced over to where Mr. Hickory stood. He still was not looking. With a huff, I took off toward the road. I was not going to say thank you this time.

"I'da taken you to Kansas City."

I spun around, furious. "What?"

"I'da taken you. Heading that way anyway." He gestured behind him. Tied to a pathetic scraggle of a tree was a horse. How had I missed *that* last night?

I opened my mouth and then closed it. Then opened and closed it again. I didn't know this man. I didn't need this man. And the last time I'd trusted a stranger . . .

"No."

Mr. Hickory shrugged again, his mugs clinking in his bag, then turned and walked toward his horse. His body leaned heavily to one side each time he stepped, but he mounted the beast with ease.

I'd made up my mind. I was going back to Boise City. I

was. But . . . there weren't no doc in Boise City these days. It could be months before I got a new brace. Months of hobbling. Or worse, crawling. How Melissa would fawn over me. Treat me like a baby. In front of the Mayfields. Because she was a Mayfield now too.

And then there was God. God Himself who seemed to be pushing me back, telling me I couldn't do this, throwing everything He could against this journey. Against *me*. My anger at Him alone was enough to push me forward out of spite.

I didn't like how Mr. Hickory looked at me. I didn't like how he talked to me. Or rather, didn't talk. But if I was going to do this, a horse would get me to Kansas City in just a few days rather than the few weeks it would take me on my own. I might even catch up to Pa.

"Wait!"

Mr. Hickory pulled on the reins, turning his horse in my direction.

"I'll . . . I'll go with ya. But I ain't looking to be friends, you hear? We're just . . . traveling companions. Like in the Old West."

The horse trotted toward me, Mr. Hickory's boots jingling with each step. When he reached my side, he held out his hand. I hesitated for a moment before letting him pull me into the saddle. I tensed against his body, the memory of Frank's weight still fresh in my mind.

But he didn't linger. Instead, he hopped down and grabbed the reins, turning the animal toward the rising sun. "No need to worry about that, kid," he muttered. "I ain't got no friends. And I sure ain't looking to get one now."

* * *

Mr. Hickory's horse was barely a horse at all. Ribs stuck out from under the saddle at all angles, and his hide was so thin, I worried it would fall off if I touched it. His fur was gray and patchy, with hair matted into greasy clumps. His worst features, however, were milky eyes soured with a look of permanent annoyance.

The spittin' image of his master.

I rode for a while with Mr. Hickory walking beside, but it was slow going that way. The hobble in the cowboy's step became a full-up limp the longer he walked. Eventually he hopped up and rode behind me. I didn't like him being so close. But seeing as how it was his horse and I wasn't in any fit shape to be walking, I let him sit behind me without too much of a fuss. I kept my back straight and my body tensed, ready to flee just in case. Mr. Hickory, though, kept his hands on the reins and his eyes on the horizon. As if I wasn't there at all.

But being invisible was hard work. I felt like I should talk to him, be polite and make conversation, but I also felt like I shouldn't. In the end, boredom won out.

"So, the horse. He got a name?"

"Chelee."

"Huh?"

"Chelee."

"What kind of a name is that?"

Mr. Hickory grunted.

"It mean something?"

I couldn't see him. Turning around in the saddle was impossible, and even if I could, Chelee's back probably would have broken from the strain. But I could *feel* Mr. Hickory's irritation.

"Apache."

"Apache for what?"

"Horse."

The horse's name was Horse. There was nothing I could do with that answer. We fell back into an awkward quiet, the slow clip-clop of Chelee's hooves on dirt carrying for miles.

The sun beat down on us without mercy, not a single cloud daring to intervene. Sweat soaked through Mr. Hickory's shirt and onto my dress. It wasn't like I could scoot farther away. My throat swelled, raw and dry and itchy, but I didn't dare ask for a drink. What little water he had was now divided between us and the horse. But try as I did, I couldn't make myself not be hot or thirsty or crippled.

After two days, I knew he regretted asking me to tag along. And Kansas City was still nowhere in sight.

"How much farther?" It was the third night. We were camped under a cottonwood tree, the sky moonless.

Mr. Hickory lay on the hard ground next to me, his hat over his eyes. "Two days. Maybe three. We need to rest."

I poked at the fire with a dead branch, watching sparks float up and disappear into nothing. "I'm tired of resting. I want to get there."

"You're welcome to go on ahead. Chelee and I need rest."

Every moment we weren't moving put a bigger distance between me and Pa. Made catching up to him seem even more unlikely. And worse, made the journey take even longer. We needed to keep moving if we ever wanted to get to Kansas City. If we ever wanted to be able to go our separate ways again.

"We could have made it a little farther today," I said pointedly.

"Could have. Chelee could have stumbled in a dune or tripped over some rocks in the dark and broken his leg, too. I ain't too keen on walking to Kansas City. Don't think you are neither."

I wrinkled my nose. "You don't seem in an awful big hurry to get where we're going."

"I am and I ain't."

"What's that supposed to mean?"

"It means what it means."

He couldn't see me, but I stuck out my tongue anyways and threw my stick into the fire, causing a loud pop. Chelee neighed irritably.

Mr. Hickory sighed beneath his hat. "You talk too much."

"You don't talk at all."

"Where I come from, you don't talk unless you got something to say."

"And where I come from, it's rude to ignore someone sitting right next to you."

Mr. Hickory finally moved his hat, revealing tired eyes. In this light, his skin looked as gray as his hair. When he spoke, however, there was nothing weary about him. "I don't want to go and I don't want to stay. But I had to make a choice, and I made it. So that's that. I ain't turning back but it don't mean I gotta run with my tail between my legs. You just settle your britches. I said I'd getcha there, and I'll getcha there, alright?"

Gone was the ghost I'd been riding with. His words dripped with so much anger, sadness, and ruin, it struck me dumb. All I could do was nod.

Mr. Hickory replaced his hat over his face, coughed, and was still.

I stared at his body, now dead again on the ground. His beat-up boots. His ripped jeans. The bruised and scarred fingers intertwined across his chest, moving up and down with his breathing. I finally realized where I'd seen him before. Not him exactly but men just like him. I'd seen him in the eyes of my pa. I'd seen him all over Boise City. Men with no more hope. Those men who decided it was never going to rain again. That God had cursed us worse than Job and there was no atonement that would satisfy. The war with Mother Nature was lost.

Mr. Hickory was a defeated man. And that was even scarier than Frank Fleming.

CHAPTER FOURTEEN

MELISSA

"You again." Words as bitter as thistles. "I told you I don't need your charity."

"I'm not here to give you any."

Annie Gale glared at me through her ripped screen, face twitching. Her dress was the same as last time. So was her expression. "Well, whatcha want then? I got work to do."

What I wanted was to get on my bicycle and ride away from here, pretend she didn't exist, hide myself in my house and repeat my name in the mirror—*Melissa Mayfield, Melissa Mayfield, Melissa Mayfield*—over and over again until the events of the last few weeks faded and I no longer felt sick.

"I, um, I . . ." I fiddled with a thread on my skirt. Henry didn't know I was here. Henry wouldn't like it that I was here.

But it was Monday, and on Mondays Henry drove down to Dalhart to discuss business with John McCarty, editor of the *Texan*. *Business* meaning tobacco and whiskey, with a bit of real estate or oil gossip thrown in the mix. But it also meant he was gone all day and so Mondays were the days I was the most courageous. Or stupid.

"I heard you clean houses."

Behind her, Mary Beth peeked around a door. Her face was shiny, her stringy hair matted against her forehead. She gave me a shy smile before retreating. Annie, however, did not notice her daughter. She was too busy scowling at me. "So?"

"So I was wondering if you'd like to come clean mine?"

I'd come prepared for many reactions. In a perfect world, acceptance. More than likely, refusal. I was even ready for her to slam the door in my face. I was not prepared, however, for Annie Gale to laugh.

Her face contorted in a way that was the opposite of beautiful, her laughter that of a wounded jackal. I preferred her scowl.

"And why would I go and do something like that?"

I straightened my back, biting my trembling lip. "Because I am in need of a cleaning lady, and I heard you're the best."

Her laughter stopped abruptly, the return of her frown almost comforting. "Go get your kicks somewhere else. I ain't in no mood to be played with."

"I'm not *playing* with you, Mrs. Gale. I'm trying to hire you. If you'll let me."

"Ain't you Mayfields got your own maid?"

"Mr. Mayfield Sr. does, yes, but Henry and I do not. And I'm afraid with the dust, the house is just much too big—" I stopped myself, embarrassed. Of course Annie knew the house was big. I didn't need to point it out, especially not when I was standing on her small, crumbling porch. "I could just use the extra help, that's all."

Annie raised her eyebrows. For a moment, I thought she was going to walk away. Or perhaps strike me. But she did neither. She simply stared, face continuing to twitch in what I assumed was an internal battle between pride and desperation. "Why me?" she said finally. "Plenty other cleanin' ladies in town."

"I heard you're the best—"

"No more lies, Mrs. Mayfield."

I started. I hadn't expected to be called out, so suddenly and so directly.

"There'd have to be a darn good reason for me to take up with a Mayfield. And I sure as anything won't be working for no liars. So you go on and tell me the truth now. Why me?"

Why her? Why her indeed? I couldn't tell her about the coldness in my house, felt despite the sweat on my brow, about the void inside those walls that was bigger than the despair I'd felt when Kathryn left, more intense than the fear I now felt toward my husband. It had started with the screams of the jackrabbits, the look on Henry's face, and turned into something much more frightening.

The horror I'd witnessed in that desolate field—from godly men, from the man who shared my bed—had shaken my faith, the only solid rock I had left from a life that was fading as fast as the crops beneath the relentless Oklahoma sun. Where was God in this place? The God of my mother, of my youth—I could no longer see Him or feel Him here. He had abandoned this place. Abandoned me. And I had never, in my entire life, felt so alone.

Kathryn was gone. Pa was gone. Henry was a stranger. God was all I had left. So I was chasing Him. Chasing Him the only way I knew how: the way my mother had done— through acts of love that sometimes seemed reckless, crazy, making no sense at all. I was chasing Him through the mirror of things that could have been.

I was chasing Him through Annie Gale.

"Because you're the best." My voice was barely above a whisper.

Annie Gale slammed the door in my face.

The force broke a single tear from my eye. I needed this just as much as she did. Maybe even more. Balling my hands into fists, I pounded on the weathered wood. "Mrs. Gale!" The door shuddered beneath my hands. "Mrs. Gale, now you listen to me! I'll pay you two times whatever you're making!"

From inside the house, silence.

"Mrs. Gale!"

Down the street, a dog began to bark, competing with my shouts. And still Annie Gale did not answer.

"Fine!" A frustrated snort escaped my nose. "You go on ahead and be that way, you stubborn old mule!" I kicked at the door, wincing as the wood dented. It only made me madder. "When you get tired of trying to feed those kids with your pride, you know where to find me!" I stomped down the steps, pretending not to notice a pair of tired eyes peering at me from behind a threadbare curtain.

* * *

Those same eyes stared at me from outside my own door the following morning.

Henry had been gone less than five minutes, with some business in town. The coon dogs howled. They *knew* she wasn't supposed to be here. Somehow they *knew*. I tried not to let my panic show as I fiddled with the latch. "Mrs. Gale. Good . . . morning?"

A bag full of cleaning supplies hung from her back. She did not smile. "Morning."

I glanced over her shoulder. No car. Of course she didn't have a car. That meant she had walked. Up the driveway. Where Henry had just driven. Oh *no*. He'd seen her. He *had* to have seen her. I twisted my hands inside my apron.

Something shifted in Annie's face. "I cut through the fields to get here," she said flatly.

I gave a weak smile, forcing myself to breathe. Henry wouldn't have seen her from the fields. I was safe. But . . . did she know? "I'm, um, I'm surprised you're here at all."

She shrugged and looked down at her shoes. The tiniest hint of a stocking poked through one of the toes. "One of my regulars done packed up and moved to California last week. So I had some free time. I should ask for triple, seein' the absurd size of your house, but I'll do it for double. *Like you promised.*"

For the first time since she arrived, Annie met my eyes. It was a challenge. I was a Mayfield, but she still had her dignity.

I nodded quickly and looked away.

She let out a grunt, satisfied. A small victory. Battle won. As it should be. Because her face said all the words she hadn't spoken: in her mind, she'd lost the war just by being here.

A squeak at our feet turned my attention downward. A small, dirty face gaped at me from behind Annie's skirt. "Oh," I said, giving a smile. "Hello."

The child disappeared behind the drab folds.

"If you want me to clean, Mary Beth is part of the deal," Annie said, an edge in her voice. "Others are at school, but she ain't big enough yet."

"Of course. It's no problem at all."

"I clean Tuesdays and Fridays, no exceptions and no substitutions. Yours ain't the only house in town."

I gave a slight nod.

Her foot tapped twice on my porch. Unlike hers, mine did not creak. "Well, are you gonna let me in?"

Was I? Henry's coon dogs glared at me from beneath the shriveled pecan tree. Henry was not in Dalhart today. He could come home at any minute. My reckless confidence from the day before melted at the reality of this woman on my front step. "Um . . ."

That was enough for Annie. She swept Mary Beth into her arms and brushed past me. No turning back now.

Her shoes left smudges on the wooden floor of the foyer. She surveyed the room with a look of wonderment and disgust. With her in it, the house felt larger. Ridiculously large.

I cleared my throat. "I tidied up yesterday, but as you can

see, the dust has already seeped back in. If you could do some touch-ups, I'd really appreciate it."

"Touch-ups." The words came out like they tasted foul.

"Yes. Please," I added.

"Touch-ups ain't really what I do, Mrs. Mayfield. I clean."

"I'll still pay you full wages."

Annie sighed. "Alright."

"You can, um, you can start in the library, if you want."

"The library?" That tone again. Every word this woman said made me feel small.

"It's right through here."

I always enjoyed the library. It was the warmest place in this big, cold house. But today, everything about it made me cringe. And somehow Annie looked even dirtier in this room. I waited with bated breath for her snide comment.

But she said nothing. Merely dropped her bag to the floor and began removing her supplies. Rags, a whisk broom, a few bottles of polish. Mary Beth settled on the rug next to her and separated the items into piles. Obviously this wasn't her first time as her momma's tagalong.

I stood there for a moment, unsure what to do. Was I supposed to sit and watch? No, that would be strange. Retreat to another part of the house and pretend someone else wasn't doing my job? That would be even stranger.

Annie straightened up, one rag in her hand, the other tucked into her belt. "I'm not gonna steal anything."

"I know that," I said, slightly irritated and even more wounded. "Do you, um, do you need any water? I can get some for you from the kitchen or—"

"I am perfectly capable of getting my own water, Mrs. Mayfield."

"I didn't mean—"

"But no, I don't need any water at the moment. I'll start with the dusting, if that's okay with you."

I nodded.

Annie looked pointedly at the door, but still I didn't move. Partly out of embarrassment and partly out of spite. After several moments, she rolled her eyes and proceeded to the fireplace, running her rag carefully over the mantel. She left no streaks.

I turned my eyes to Mary Beth. She sat on the rug cross-legged, tugging at a strand of her hair, thumb in her mouth. She looked so much like Kathryn. Right down to the dark spots on her nose, which could have been dirt or freckles . . . or both. She eyeballed the books lining the shelves.

"Do you like books?"

She looked at her lap, and I instantly felt foolish. As if her family had money to spend on such things. You couldn't eat books.

I crossed the room and grabbed a familiar gold-and-green volume from its spot on the table. "This was my sister Kathryn's favorite book. I used to read it to her every night. Somehow she never got tired of it."

My voice caught unexpectedly. Oh, how I missed my sister. I'd pushed it down so far but just mentioning her name brought it rushing back. I wondered what she was doing now. I still hadn't heard from her. Surely she'd arrived in Indianapolis by now. Was she enjoying the city so much she'd forgotten Oklahoma? Forgotten me? Not, not Kathryn. She would never. Even surrounded by the beauty of the City of Emeralds, Dorothy had longed for Kansas. There was no place like home, right?

But Kathryn had been gone a month now. A lot longer than Dorothy.

The child pulled the thumb from her lips and glanced at the cover sideways, hands fiddling with the seam of her flour sack dress.

"Would you like me to read it to you? It's got a wizard and a lion and a witch and—"

"You ain't gotta entertain her," Annie interrupted. "She may still be learning to get to the toilet on time, but she knows how to sit quietly and wait."

"I don't mind. I was going to read it anyway." It could have been the truth. "No reason I can't read it out loud."

"Well, I ain't taking a dock in my pay because you played babysitter."

I ignored her, settling instead on a couch in the corner. Mary Beth remained at her spot on the rug. "'Dorothy lived in the midst of the great Kansas prairies,'" I began, "'with Uncle Henry, who was a farmer, and Aunt Em, who was the farmer's wife. Their house was small, for the lumber to build it had to be carried by wagon many miles.'" The gentle sucking of Mary Beth's thumb slowed as she studied the back cover. "'There were four walls, a floor, and a roof, which made one room. . . .'"

By the time I'd finished page two, Mary Beth had given up pretending not to listen. By the time the cyclone arrived, she had scooted to my feet, brown eyes wide. And by the time the story reached the land of the Munchkins, she had climbed onto the couch beside me, getting as close as she could to my side without actually touching me. She stared at the words as if they were magic. When I turned the page and revealed a small black-and-white drawing of Dorothy's shoes, Mary Beth forgot all pretense and leaned forward, her small hands leaving smudges on my dress. She smelled like the outside.

During all of this Annie said nothing. She dusted and polished and swept, all the while pretending like I wasn't there. Just like I pretended not to notice the small pause of the rag above the shelf as she waited to hear if Dorothy would, indeed, follow the road of yellow brick to the City of Emeralds.

Annie finished her work by eleven. The entire downstairs— the kitchen, washroom, library, and living room—sparkled. Well, sparkled for an Oklahoma house in the middle of a drought. She took her money without making eye contact and left without saying goodbye, tugging Mary Beth behind her. The child, at least, gave me a small wave as they rounded the hill and headed back toward Boise City.

I rushed through the house, searching for any sign that might reveal my secret visitor. A forgotten rag. A stray bottle. A scrunched cushion. But all was well. Annie was nothing if not meticulous. And unpleasant.

Nevertheless, the rumble of Henry's truck in the drive still sent me into a panic. Moment of truth. There was no way he would know. I had covered my tracks, left no trace. Except he was Henry Mayfield. And Henry Mayfield knew everything.

The coon dogs howled as if tattling when his truck door slammed shut. I clutched the countertop, fingers tingling, and waited for him to come inside. The air in the room pushed against me. His thirty-second walk from the truck to the door took an eternity.

"Hey, honey, what's for lunch? I'm starving." His voice was a shout in the stillness. He threw his hat on the table with a thud and kissed me on the cheek, his boots echoing on the spotless floor.

I forced my muscles to uncoil. "I . . . I made you a sandwich." The plate slipped in my sweaty hands, but I managed to grab it before it fell to the floor.

"I can't stay long," he said, crumbs spraying from his mouth. "I've got a meeting in town this afternoon with Mr. Egan."

"Everything okay?" I scrubbed a nonexistent mark on the counter.

"Everything's fine. Nothing for you to worry your pretty little head over."

I flinched as his plate clanged into the sink.

Henry laughed. "Goodness, Melissa. Jumpy today. What's wrong?"

I invited a woman to our home to clean even though you expressly forbade it. She was here only twenty minutes ago, walking on your floor, touching your things. "I . . . I saw a black widow under the sink today." *What? Where did that come from?* "I took care of it, but you know how I feel about those things. The drought is making them worse. That's the third one already this month."

Henry chuckled and nuzzled my neck. His stubble set my skin on fire. "Oh, honey." He kissed me behind my ear. "When I get home, I'll check the house. Make sure there are no webs or eggs anywhere. Would that make you feel better?"

I nodded shakily.

"Good." He tugged gently on one of my curls and smiled.

It took every ounce of courage I had to smile back.

Henry disappeared through the swinging door, and I turned to the sink, grateful for something to do with my hands. The water was lukewarm and soothing against my knotted fingers. *Just a little bit longer,* I told myself. *A little bit longer and he'll leave and you can relax.*

"Melissa? What is this?"

The water chilled instantly. He'd found something. Annie left something and I'd missed it and Henry had found it. *Oh, God. Oh, Lord, please help me.*

"Melissa!"

I shoved my shaking hands into my apron pockets, feeling them prickle as the dry air sucked the water from my skin. I took a deep breath and pushed open the door. "Yes?"

"What is this?"

Henry stood outside the washroom, holding a green book in his hand. *The Wonderful Wizard of Oz.* Of course. I'd left it on the hallway table when I'd told Annie goodbye. "It's . . . it's a book."

"What's it doing out here?"

"I was reading it."

Henry's lips pressed into a white line. "Reading it."

I nodded.

"This morning."

I nodded again, slower this time.

"Melissa, there's too much work to do around here for you to be wasting your time reading. Especially a book like this. Witches and wizards and who knows what else." He tossed the book at me. Unable to catch it, I watched it fall to the ground with a thump. "Garbage. And definitely not suitable for my wife."

I picked it up off the ground. My heart slowed, each beat painful. "It was Kathryn's favorite book."

He rubbed his brow with his knuckles and sighed. "Of course it was."

I turned the book over in my hands, unable to look at him. This book, my family's book, was more precious than anything in this entire house. And he didn't know me well enough to understand that. No, it was more than that. He didn't *care* to know me well enough to understand that. Any part of me that didn't fit neatly into his world, any part that still whispered Baile, was dirty, something to be pruned.

He took a step toward me and pushed the book down to my side. "I know you miss them, Melissa." He lifted my chin, forcing me to meet his eyes. "So keep the book. It's fine. I want you to have it. Just, maybe, keep it in the library? And don't read it during the day, when there's so many other things you should be doing. Like making me another one of those delicious chocolate cakes like you promised?"

That afternoon, I made Henry his chocolate cake. Not because he asked me to. Not even because I said I would. But because it was one more way to win, to pretend he was in control and everything was fine. And while the cake cooled, I settled myself at the table and read another chapter in Kathryn's book.

CHAPTER FIFTEEN

KATHRYN

Chelee's hooves were what finally did it.

After several days, I had gotten used to the stench of riding two to a saddle under the glaring sun with a strange man. I'd gotten used to the sore butt and the cramp in my twisted foot as it dangled without a stirrup over the horse's bony side. I'd even gotten used to the sour taste in my mouth from the lack of water.

But the constant, never-ending *quiet*. A quiet so loud it made my ears scream. It clung to every bit of me, thickening the air, crackling through my bones, and making every sound echo. Mr. Hickory's breathing was ragged, dry, and right-on-my-neck annoying. The wind scratched dirt across the pavement beneath us like sandpaper, prickling my skin. And the constant thunk of Chelee's hooves carried across the prairie and right back into my ears, pounding through my brain.

Wheeze.

Scratch.

Clip. Clop.

Mile after mile after mile.

Wheeze.

Scratch.

Clip. Clop.

Louder. Slower. Trying even harder to drive me insane.

Wheeze.

Scratch.

Cli—

"Stop!"

Mr. Hickory jerked on the reins, causing Chelee to snort unhappily.

I didn't wait for him to help. I slid from the saddle, landing painfully on my good foot. I did not allow myself to whimper. I had to get away. From him. From the horse. From *here.*

I hobbled to the nearest tree, collapsing under its dead branches and into pitiful shade.

Mr. Hickory remained on the saddle, watching me. "You gotta pee?"

"No, I ain't gotta pee. I need a break."

"Take us longer to get there that way."

"I know that," I snapped, pulling off my shoe and wincing as the cramp flooded into full-blown pain. "I still need a break."

"Alright." He dismounted and led Chelee to a patch of dead grass, dragging one leg slightly behind the other. He gave the horse a satisfied pat and then trudged up the hill behind me.

"Where you going?"

He did not turn around. "I'm gonna take a leak, if you must know. You best try and do the same. We ain't stopping again until nightfall. I ain't . . ." His voice faded as he walked away from me, toward the nearest hill. By the time it reached my ears, it was nothing but mumbles.

I stretched out my legs, ignoring the scratch of bark at my back, and pulled Melissa's handkerchief from my pocket. I laid it across my face and closed my eyes. It stank of old sweat, but for a moment, I could pretend she was with me. Like we were taking a break from chores, watching storms roll in like we used to. Back when it used to rain. I could imagine Melissa's face, smudged with dirt, lifted to the sky. I could pretend the drops were on my skin. In my hair. Yes, I could almost feel it.

A scream interrupted my daydream.

I jumped up, ignoring the stab of pain in my leg, and spun around. The air was still. Chelee had not even looked up from his chewing. Good grief. Did even *imagining* rain make you go crazy?

Another scream cut across the prairie, then a pop. Muffled. Far away. A gunshot? I fumbled with my shoe, cursing under my breath. It was stupid to take it off in the first place. I had no idea where we were. Had we wandered into Indian territory? Was there still such a thing as Indian territory? I should have paid more attention in school. Visions of Mr. Hickory's bloody scalp played in my mind as I stumbled across the hill I'd seen him climb. They didn't do that anymore, Pa told me. Indians were our friends and would respect us if we respected them. But Mr. Hickory wasn't polite or respectful at all. Maybe peeing here was against their laws?

I quickened my pace. "Mr. Hickory!" I scrambled up the hill, scanning the ground for traces of blood or hair. "Mr. Hickory! Mr. Hick—" My body slammed into something hard, sending me backward onto a sharp rock. "Ow!" I rubbed my butt, feeling a new tear in my underwear. My only underwear.

The "something hard" turned out to be Mr. Hickory, who didn't say sorry for being in my way. He didn't offer to help me up either. He didn't even look at me.

My earlier panic faded quickly. "I was calling for you," I said, rubbing the fresh scratches on my elbows. "Why didn't you answer?"

His eyes remained fixed ahead.

"Didn't you hear those screams?"

His face was tight, a slight tremble in his bottom lip.

"What—?" My words collapsed as my eyes finally found what Mr. Hickory was seeing.

In the valley below us, a hundred cattle were grouped together. If you could still call them cattle. Bones poked out from under their dusty skin. Patches of hair were missing from their hides, and scabs covered much of their bodies. Even from a distance, you could smell disease. They moved as one, shoving and leaning, some of them too weak to stand on their own. And they were screaming.

Four men on horseback circled the herd. A pop pierced the air. Then another. Then another. Pieces of the horde began dropping off one by one like flesh from a leper.

Pop. Thud. Pop. Thud.

Too sick to run, they simply stood there, waiting to die. My mind struggled to process as another cow fell to the ground, its scream cut short. The men were shooting them. In the head. Like fish in a barrel.

Bile rose in my throat. I wanted to look away, but I couldn't. "Stop," I whispered.

More shots. More bodies.

Mr. Hickory remained beside me, unmoving, unblinking. Was he even seeing what was happening? Why wasn't he *doing* something?

"Stop," I repeated, louder. "Stop! Stop!" My screams freed my legs, and I started toward the slaughter. A pair of strong arms grabbed me from behind.

"Don't." Mr. Hickory's voice was calm but firm.

I struggled against him as he pulled me up the hill. "Stop it! Stop it!"

But the popping continued and Mr. Hickory didn't release me until we reached the tree where Chelee grazed. I scrambled to my feet. "What are you doing? We have to go back!"

"We'll be doing no such thing." He fumbled with Chelee's reins.

"But that's someone's herd! And they're *killing* them!"

"And it ain't none of our business." He reached for my hand to lift me into the saddle.

I pulled away as if burned. "That's someone's livelihood down there!"

I'd heard the stories. Desperate men slaughtering others' livestock. *"Hunger makes men do terrible things,"* Pa said. Some of our neighbors had even resorted to armed patrols. Didn't stop the thieves from coming in the night, though. Old man Ackerman just a few farms over woke up one morning to find one of his cows and two of his goats slaughtered. Picked clean. And not by no coyotes, either. Pa'd given him some of our winter meat to help out. And even though I knew it was the right thing to do, I sure did curse that charity when my supper was only half what it used to be.

I slapped the tears off my cheeks. "You go on and be a coward all you want. I ain't gonna let a bunch of criminals steal someone's food." I brushed past him, knocking into his shoulder a little harder than necessary and pretending it didn't hurt.

"Those ain't no criminals." He was up in the saddle now. He wasn't going to stop me.

"What?"

"I said those ain't no criminals. Didn't you see the badges? Those is government men. They ain't breaking no laws. You go down there and try to stop 'em, you're liable to get your-self shot."

"What are you talking about?"

"Roosevelt." He lifted his hat up slightly. "You know Roosevelt?"

I puffed out my chest. "I ain't no idiot!"

Mr. Hickory held up his hands. "I didn't say you were." He led Chelee over to where I stood. "It's Roosevelt's grand plan to get the animals off the prairie. Stabilize the market, get the grass growing again—"

"By killing them?" My voice was shrill, unrecognizable.

"Cows are dying off anyways. It's either this or let 'em starve to death."

"You're lying."

He gave a half shrug. "Fine. I'm lying."

Only he wasn't. Something in his voice told me he wasn't. I stamped my foot, suddenly angry. Where was Melissa's "good God" in all this? "That is the most disgusting thing I've ever heard."

Mr. Hickory did not disagree.

I knew nothing of government beyond one lesson I'd only half paid attention to in school and the grumbles from the men in the sundry and supply. But Pa had said Roosevelt was a good man. I wondered if I'd get the chance to tell him how wrong he was. Melissa, too. "So Roosevelt ain't nothing but a murderer."

Mr. Hickory gave a small shake of his head. "This ain't Roosevelt's fault."

"Not his fault? You just said—"

Mr. Hickory grabbed my waist and lifted me onto Chelee's back. This time I didn't fight him. "It ain't right, and it ain't wrong. It's just the way things are now." I felt his body deflate behind me as he turned the horse back east. "Roosevelt didn't do this. Wasn't even God Himself that done this. We done this to ourselves."

* * *

We rode until sunset in silence. The loud sounds from before were drowned out by the cows screaming in my head. No matter how far we traveled, I couldn't stop hearing them. Mr. Hickory was quiet. I wondered if he could hear them too.

It was a relief to stop, and not just for my aching body. The nightmare we'd seen sat between us, so big I thought I'd fall right off the saddle. I scrambled from Chelee's back the moment he stilled, but the hell of that Kansas pasture clung to me like manure.

Mr. Hickory busied himself building a fire. I walked in circles around the campsite, looking for signs of rattlers. It was a routine we'd fallen into every time we'd camped. This time, though, it felt stupid. Gross, even. Who cared if there were rattlers? The world was garbage now. Let 'em come.

"So how'd you know about Roosevelt's plan?" I didn't want to ask, but I couldn't think of anything else to say. Beans and pickled eggs lay uneaten at our feet. I was hungry, of course. I was always hungry. But I couldn't eat. Maybe talking would take the smell of death out of my nose and mouth.

"I read it in the paper."

"What paper?"

"*A* paper. In Colorado."

"Is that where you're from?"

"You ask a lot of questions."

"Fine," I said, stretching back against the rock I'd claimed as my spot. "We ain't gotta talk. If you'd rather sit here and think, that's fine with me."

Mr. Hickory spat a wad of tobacco from his mouth with a sigh. "I'm from Texas originally," he said finally. "Spent most of my life as a Texas Ranger."

Well, I'll be. Here I was, riding with a real-life Texas Ranger. Melissa would have been so jealous. We'd all heard the stories. Seen the flyers down at the post office. *Join up!* they'd said. *Protect our God-given homesteads!* A pair of them had even come into town one winter and stayed at the Boise City Inn. Trevor Callahan said he'd seen one of them shoot a pinto bean off the top of a beer bottle without even rattling the glass. Trevor Callahan was a liar, but even I believed that story a little bit.

"Did you fight the Indians?"

"Comanches, mostly. It was hell. They'd kill us; we'd kill them. I was shot twice." He patted his right leg. "Had to pull the arrows out myself. Lucky I didn't bleed to death right then and there. Leg ain't worked right since, though."

I glanced down, half-expecting to still see a wound. *Wish I had a story like that to go along with my limp.*

"Rode with them until the Comanches had enough and the job was done. Or at least I thought the job was done. Then the government gets it in their head that killing Indians wasn't enough. We had to kill their buffalo too. Had to make sure the Comanches didn't have a reason to come back, see?" He shook his head. "But that weren't right. It was just killing after killing after killing. What that does to a person's soul . . ." He scratched at his throat as if the words burned.

"So I left. Packed up and headed for Pritchett, Colorado. Ranchers there were hiring cowboys to help with the herd. Figured I'd earned me a nice, quiet life. And it was for a while. Out on the prairie, big open sky. And no more death. But then came the people. More and more and more, all thinking they was gonna make a fortune farming out here. 'Every man a landlord,' Congress was saying. Trouble is, not every man is fit to be a landlord. And not all land is fit to be lorded over."

I picked at the scab on my forearm. My family had been one of the ones who came. I'd never thought to be ashamed of it.

"I told 'em and told 'em the dust was the wrong side up. West wasn't meant to be farmed like that. It was meant to be grazed. But they just kept coming with their plows. Ripping up the grass, planting crops that ain't got no business being planted. But ain't no one gonna listen to naysayers when the rains are good and the harvest is better." He poked at the fire with a stick and let out a low, ugly laugh. "I'm through with it. They done this, and they can reap till they rot for all I care."

I dug my nails into my palms. I'd spent all this time trying to get him to talk; now I wished he'd never opened his mouth.

"I ain't got the heart for it no more. I just want to get out of here." He spoke softly, only to himself. "I can't watch it all die. Not anymore."

His words hung in the air, heavy as smoke. So thick I could hardly breathe. "Take it back."

He lifted the brim of his hat, eyes wide. "'Scuse me?"

I sat up straighter, hands on my hips. "You take it back now, you hear? My pa is a farmer. A good farmer. He didn't cause no drought."

"I didn't say he did."

"You might as well have! Whining and moaning like some yellow-livered Nancy. My pa ain't got any more to do with this drought than you do with making the sun shine. So you take it back right now."

Mr. Hickory shrugged. "He might not have stopped the rain, but his plow took the grass. And without the grass, ain't nothing to hold back the dirt when those spring winds blow."

I opened my mouth, then stopped. The grass. I'd ripped it up myself with bare hands before I was old enough to reach the curved handles of the plow. Me and Pa out in the field, turning up earth, changing the hills from green to brown. Even then, we'd watched the particles tumble and dance with the breeze.

"It was one field," I said finally, jutting out my chin. "Just one field. Not like we slashed up the entire prairie. There was still grass everywhere."

"Until your neighbors plowed up their field, too. And then their neighbors. And theirs."

I shifted where I sat, tightness spreading from my chest to my stomach. The tractors. I'd loved to watch the tractors on the way to school. More land, more wheat, more money. Faster, bigger, better. Miles and miles of crops, as far as the eye could see. It was beautiful.

Until the rains stopped.

Somehow I hadn't even noticed the change. But there weren't no grass in Cimarron County anymore. And now there weren't no wheat, either.

The lump in my throat gagged me, making my words stiff. "Take it back."

Mr. Hickory snorted and lay on the ground, covering his face with his hat. "Ain't nothing to take back."

I scrambled to my feet, ignoring the stab of discomfort. I hobbled to where he lay and stood over him, breathing heavily.

He didn't stir.

Balancing painfully on my twisted foot, I kicked him in the ribs.

He shot up, his hat tumbling to the ground. "Ouch! Whatcha do that for?"

"Take. It. Back."

He held up his hands as I lifted my foot again. "Okay, okay! Fine! Your pa didn't cause no drought." He snatched up his hat and scooted away from my reach. "You happy?"

For the moment, yes. But as I retreated to my side of the fire, back curled away from Mr. Hickory's snores, the small victory couldn't smother the tears. Or the truth in words I wished I'd never heard.

I'd killed my mother. And I'd killed Oklahoma, too.

CHAPTER SIXTEEN

MELISSA

"Should I continue?"

Annie Gale looked up from her mop. "'Scuse me?"

"I was just asking if I should continue," I repeated, closing the book's cover.

It was Friday again, the end of Annie's second week in my home. Her face was still sour, her mouth still pinched as if the stench of my house lingered long after she'd left. And she still refused to say anything more to me than absolutely necessary. But at least she'd given up the pretense of not listening to my reading of *The Wonderful Wizard of Oz*. She often paused her cleaning and stared, tongue rolling over her lips as if tasting the words. Today, however, we'd reached the part of the story where Dorothy and her friends leave the City of Emeralds for the Land of the South, and Annie had grunted.

After weeks of silence, the grunt might as well have been a shout. It demanded acknowledgment. "You made a little noise," I said. "I wondered if that meant stop."

Perched on a chair at the kitchen table, Mary Beth giggled. Several crumbs fell from her mouth, and she wasted no time rescuing them before giggling again.

Annie waved her hand. "You ain't gotta stop. She likes it."

"And you don't?" I cast a sly glance at Mary Beth. She shoved another cookie in her mouth and smiled.

"I didn't say that. I just think Dorothy's a fool."

"Oh?"

"Well, yeah. That wizard done promised to get her home, but he didn't. And all she says is 'He did his best, so I forgive him'? That's foolishness if I ever seen it. And I have." She slapped the mop on the floor as if to make a point.

"Maybe she was just kind."

"Same thing."

"So you want me to stop?"

"I didn't say that!"

Mary Beth let out another crumby giggle.

I bit down on my lip and reopened the book. "Very well. Now where were we? Ah, yes. 'In the morning they traveled on until they came to a thick wood. There was no way—'"

"And another thing!" Annie slopped her mop back into the bucket. Dirty water splashed over the sides. "What's all this nonsense about 'he was a good man, even if he was a bad Wizard'?"

I closed the book again and sighed. "It means just what it says." I was not prepared to have a literary debate. It was a good story. No, a great story. That had always been enough for Kathryn. And it was enough for me.

"He was not a good man. He was a liar and a cheat and a swindle."

"Who did good things. He built the Emerald City and fulfilled his promises to the Scarecrow, the Tin Woodman, and the Lion. He may have lied about *what* he was, but *who* he was is as plain as day. He was a good man."

Annie grunted. "You're either a good person or you ain't. No middle ground."

"Well, that's a very black-and-white view of things to take."

"This world *is* black-and-white. For us regular folks."

She gave me a look so pointed, my chest grew tight and I had to draw in my shoulders just to take a breath. I'd been lying to Henry, and I'd been lying well. Swindling my allowance to pay her, stretching the meals to conceal the difference. I was putting her and Mary Beth in danger with every step inside my home. I'd been playing Wizard. Doing wrong all in the name of doing right. It never occurred to me that someone like Annie Gale might see only one side of the moral fence.

I stared at the book in my hand, the cover blurring, before turning my attention to Mary Beth. "Well, how about you?" I asked, my voice overly cheery. "Do *you* want me to keep reading?"

The girl smiled and nodded shyly. She hadn't spoken more than five words to me in the entire time I'd known her, but she was still more polite than her mother.

"Very well then. I'll continue. The story is for the child, after all."

Annie wrinkled her nose and returned her attention to her bucket. "Sure. Fine. Makes no difference to me."

I flipped through the yellowed pages. "Now where were we? Oh yes. 'In the morning they traveled on until they came to a thick wood. There was no way of going around it, for it seemed to extend . . .'"

My heart swelled as the familiar words filled the air. These moments with Annie in my home, reading to Mary Beth, feeling her excitement and wonder as Dorothy and her friends continued their magical journey, were the happiest of my week. The only time I didn't feel alone within the walls of this big old house. Sure, my time at the Ladies Auxiliary was tolerable, sewing and mending and sorting. The women were kind, nurturing, faithful, and—above all—didn't ask questions about anything deeper than casserole recipes or sermon notes. They were genuine in their desire to do good work—important work—and being a part of it *did* make me feel good.

But still my soul struggled to find God. For me, the work was forced, the prayers empty. I was there only because I was expected to be. The need too great, the effort too little, and God's absence too resounding. Try as I did, my heart wasn't in it. Probably because my heart, for all its searching, was the most lost of all.

It was only in these moments, as I recounted the story I'd shared with my sister so many times, that I found anything resembling peace. That I ever felt, even for a fleeting moment, that things were right in my life.

Curious, because having the Gales in my house at all was, in fact, so very, very wrong.

"'So they looked for the place where it would be easiest to get into—'"

Crash!

Startled, I dropped the book, screeching as it landed in a pool of water at my feet. I snatched it up, frantically wiping away the suds as the pages began to wilt under my touch. How quickly the black ink smeared, as if the words were just waiting for a chance to escape. I recoiled, afraid of further damage.

"I'm so sorry," Annie stuttered. The bucket lay on its side below the sink, dirty water forming rivers in the space between the tiles. "My hand slipped. Doc says I got the arthritis, and my fingers just ain't what they used to be. Sometimes it—"

"Mrs. Gale, it's fine. It's fine." I put the book on the table, its pages flat. *It will dry,* I told myself. *Please, God, let it dry.* "I'll fetch us some towels."

When I returned, Annie was already on her hands and knees, wiping the water with rags from her bag. "I'm so sorry, Mrs. Mayfield. I really am."

Humility was a new look for Annie Gale. I wasn't quite sure how to take it. I dropped to my knees and ran a towel over the floor.

"You don't have to do that. Please—"

"I don't mind."

"Mrs. Mayfield."

I ignored her and continued to scrub. After several moments, she fell into line beside me. The water retreated into the towels quickly, their bright-white color soon becoming a muted brown. Much quicker than with Annie's rags. Of course. These were good towels. All the way from Oklahoma City. Only the best for the Mayfields.

We worked in silence, save for the scratch of fabric against tile. My eyes watered and my nose burned at the stench of lye. I shook my head to clear it. Lye had never bothered me before. It was a comforting smell, actually. Like home. But now it was overpowering. Suffocating. Nauseating.

Sweat broke out on my forehead. I barely made it to the sink before I retched. Over and over and over again. I vomited until nothing was left in my stomach but bile, and then I vomited that too. My knees grew weak from the force, and I sank to the ground, swallowing another wave of sickness.

Suddenly a cold washcloth pushed against my forehead. Annie hovered over me, eyebrows knit.

I tried to stand, clutching the countertop as I swayed. "I'm fine," I mumbled. "I must have . . . ate something."

Annie's lips disappeared beneath her tight frown. "Ate something?"

"Yes, I—"

The sound of a truck door interrupted me. My nausea vanished, replaced by something much worse. Henry. He wasn't supposed to be home for another two hours.

"You have to hide."

"Hide?"

I pushed against her, ignoring my stomach and guiding her toward the pantry. "Please, Mrs. Gale. Take Mary Beth. There's a closet right over here. Henry never uses it."

"Now why in the world—?"

"Please, Mrs. Gale. Please." I stared at her tired eyes, pleading, praying my own would speak all the things my mouth didn't have time to say.

She stared back. For a moment, I thought she'd yell. Or even flat-out refuse to move. But after several agonizing seconds, she scooped up Mary Beth and retreated to the closet, closing the door softly behind her.

I pushed Annie's supplies to the corner, hoping they'd pass as my own, and gathered the book in the folds of my apron, cringing at the sickening squish of the pages. If he didn't leave quickly, they'd dry together and be ruined. Although there was no possible way he could have known, it felt like he'd done it on purpose.

Henry was in the kitchen within seconds. All the air rushed out behind him, fleeing. He surveyed the mess with a curled lip. "What happened here?"

"I'm so sorry," I said, dropping to my knees. "I was mopping, and the bucket slipped. I was trying to get it cleaned up before you got home."

He stepped over my head, avoiding the spill. "Where's lunch?"

I stopped scrubbing and looked up at him. He was serious. "I . . . I was going to start that as soon as I finished cleaning."

"Start it?"

"You're home early," I said pointedly.

"Oh." He paused as if considering. "Well, make me a sandwich or something. I'm starving, and I'm in a hurry." He collapsed at the table and grabbed the crumpled newspaper he'd left unfinished this morning.

I stood up, closing my eyes as another wave of sickness swept over me.

Henry didn't notice. "Use some of that chicken from last night."

The kitchen was quiet as I prepared his sandwich. Every rustle of the newspaper, every squeak of Henry's chair was a scream. Any minute now, he was going to find an excuse to go into that closet. Or worse, Annie was going to come out. Give me away. Because we were the bad guys. What better way to stick it to me than to ruin everything. She'd gotten paid. Now was the time to cut and run. And if I got what I had coming in the process, all the better.

Pain erupted across my finger. I'd sliced it with the knife without noticing. I wrapped a rag around it before blood dripped onto the bread. One of Annie's rags. Panic seemed to make the wound bleed more. I set the plate in front of Henry with a crash.

He glanced at me from behind his paper.

I smiled. "Sorry. I, um, I cut my finger. Made me lose my grip."

"You alright?"

"I'm fine, sweetie." I gestured to his sandwich. "Dig in."

Behind us, the floor creaked. Henry turned around in his chair.

"Wind's picking up," I said quickly.

"Is it?"

"Yes. I can always tell because the house starts to pop."

I picked at my fingernails behind my back. "Hopefully we don't get another duster. That one last week was terrible. I was cleaning out the foyer for days."

Henry grunted. He hated it when I talked this much. But I needed to keep his attention. And break this awful silence.

I sat down across from him. "So, um, why are you home so early? Everything okay?"

"Dad." The word dripped with frustration and a tenderness Henry quickly tried to cover. "He needs me to come take care of the books. Ain't got the strength to do it today. Says I need to know how to just in case . . ." His voice trailed off.

My heart softened despite my fear. I knew what it was like to lose a parent. Even a heart as cold as Henry's could not be immune to that kind of pain. "Is there anything I can do?"

He smacked his palm on the table, startling me. "Don't be stupid, Melissa. Of course not. You ain't no doctor. You can't even take care of the doggone house."

I recoiled, wounded.

Seeing my face, Henry sighed. "I'm sorry. I didn't mean that. Everything's just gone to pot. The price of wheat is garbage. The land is garbage. Bank's breathing down my neck, trying to come in and take what's mine all because a bunch of useless farmers ain't been paying their rent. Like it's my fault!" He pushed his sandwich away. "And I can't even kick 'em out and rent to someone else because there ain't no one left to rent to! Ain't nobody got honor anymore? All these immigrants moving out here for a better life, and they quit the moment it gets hard. Bunch of worthless cowards—"

He stopped. He didn't say it. He didn't have to. The

damage was already done. My father was one of them. One of the ones who left.

Henry reached for my hand.

I pulled it away before I could stop myself.

Henry's face went tight. The vein in his forehead—the one usually covered by a lock of that soft, beautiful hair I'd always loved—twitched. "Watch yourself, Melissa."

I couldn't meet his gaze. And I hated myself for it.

He reached for my hand again. This time I let him take it. He squeezed my fingers just hard enough to cause me to flinch before letting go, coldness radiating through my body from the contact. Despite their throbbing, I didn't dare move them to my lap.

The chair squeaked loudly as he pushed it back. He kissed the top of my head, his hand lingering too long at the nape of my neck. "I'll be home later. Get this cleaned up."

He disappeared out the back door, but it took several minutes before his presence actually left. I sat frozen at the table, afraid to move, afraid to cry, afraid to breathe. It wasn't until Annie and Mary Beth tiptoed from their hiding place that blood returned to my body. I began to sob.

Annie stood next to me stiffly. "I . . . I guess we should go."

I nodded through tears, embarrassed. Sad. Scared. Most of all, alone. "Yes, that's probably best."

She finished cleaning the spill while I gathered her supplies. We made quick work of it, both of us wanting to be done but for very different reasons. By the time I followed her to the doorway, my tears were dry, but my shame was still fresh.

She nodded at me once before taking Mary Beth's hand

and stepping onto the porch. The coon dogs howled at our appearance, but the heaviness that hung between Annie and me muted their condemnation.

"He doesn't know," she said without looking at me. "Your husband. He doesn't know about me coming here."

I shook my head, biting away fresh tears.

She took a deep breath, lifting her chin toward the sky as I waited. I wanted her to yell at me, tell me how stupid I was, how I had no right to put her in this position. I wanted the words of God to stream from her lips, reprimand me, punish me even, if only to give a sign He still cared about this place. About me.

But she didn't. Instead, she swallowed whatever words might have been itching her tongue, shifted her bag on her shoulder, and started down the steps. Away from this place, from my lies, from me.

"Thank you," I called quietly. "For staying quiet, I mean. Not giving me away."

To my surprise, she turned and rolled her shoulders. "I wasn't doing it for you. I did it for the baby."

I instinctively put a hand over my stomach. It was too early. I hadn't told anyone yet. Not even Henry. "How did you know?"

"I've got five kids, Mrs. Mayfield. I know what morning sickness looks like."

I gave her a small smile. "Of course you do."

She placed her weather-beaten hat atop her head and gave me another nod. "Let's go, Mary Beth. We've got lots to do before the others get home."

"Will you be back?"

Annie Gale stopped, her foot hovering above the parched earth. "You want me to come back?"

I did. Desperately.

She shook her head. "Mrs. Mayfield, I don't know if that's such a good idea. No good ever came from lying to your husband, and especially from lying to a Mayfield."

"I'll triple your pay."

"Mrs. Mayfield—"

"Mrs. Gale. Please." My throat closed over my words as I fingered the cross at my neck. I knew I should let her go. It *was* dangerous. For her, for Mary Beth, for me. But as this baby grew inside me, so did a new, intense, and frantic kind of grief. Melissa Baile was dying—everything about who I once was seemed to be chaff, burned and destroyed by the fire of the Mayfields' world. And this child, this precious child, though loved, would be the final spark to fully engulf me inside the Mayfield flames.

Annie shifted, the bag of supplies clinking on her shoulder. Her eyes flickered over my face before looking skyward. "Well, alright then."

She was doing it for the money, I reminded myself. It wasn't as if she cared. But there was something in that passing glance. Something like sympathy, fear, and maybe even pity. Not all good. But not all bad, either. And coming from Annie Gale, it gave me hope.

I watched her walk down the drive, heading for the fields, until she was merely a shadow in the hazy light. Then I turned and retreated into my lonely house once more.

CHAPTER SEVENTEEN

KATHRYN

I heard Kansas City before I saw it.

The thunder was such that I thought a duster must be blowing up. Weren't nothing else I'd heard made a noise that loud. Little did I know, a duster sounds exactly like hundreds of cars itching to all get someplace at the same time. Cresting the hill and staring at the mess below, I thought maybe I'd prefer a duster. At least a duster ends.

Mr. Hickory didn't hesitate, though, leading Chelee into the city at a steady trot, the first time the horse made any effort to move quickly. It was as if he could taste freedom from having me on his back.

Or maybe he just knew better how to blend in. Because once we got inside the city proper, the cars, the people, the horses—everything moved fast. This way and that way, constant, frenzied movement. Where in the world could everyone need to go in such a hurry? It made me dizzy. I closed my eyes, but the hustle still burned into my lids.

"Hold it in and then let it out. Just breathe, Kath."

It was Melissa's voice. Coming from somewhere inside my head. Tellin' me to starve the twister again.

"Just breathe."

So I tried. I really did. But closing my eyes made the smell grab hold—exhaust and rotting food and manure. I opened them again and held my breath, but the stench didn't go away.

The buildings around us got taller the farther we went. I tried to find the top of one, but the tower swayed as I searched, like a piece of wheat in the breeze. My eyes moved with the spinning concrete, nearly causing me to slide off Chelee's back.

"Whoa," said Mr. Hickory, grabbing my arm and wrenching me back into place. "You don't wanna be falling off here. Those streetcars are liable to cut you in two and never even slow to move the pieces off the track."

His hat brushed against the back of my head as he nodded toward a red-and-yellow *something* headed our way. It wasn't a car. It wasn't a train, though it ran on rails. A metal stick jutted from its roof, connecting to wires above my head I'd been too dizzy to notice. It buzzed and clacked, causing the hair on my arms to stand on end. The passengers inside didn't even look up from their newspapers as they passed. Like it was the most normal thing in the world to be dangling from electric wires in a rolling buggy.

Sputtering cars filled in the road behind it, swerving and honking, each one more impatient than the last. People zig-zagged across the street like fire ants, all red and shouting. Every single thing in this city was trying to be heard over everything else. I stared at my hands, trying to focus only on what I could feel. The scratch of fabric on my legs. The cracked leather of the saddle horn. The sweat dripping down my back.

Suddenly the vibrations of Chelee's steps changed. We were no longer on a paved street. I glanced past the tips of my fingers to the ground below. Wooden planks. And between them, water. Lots and lots of water. We were on a bridge.

I sucked in my breath. Miles of river spread out to my left and right, muddy currents flowing right through the heart of the city. "What is that?" I whispered.

"Missouri River."

"Wow."

"What? You ain't never seen a river before?"

"Not like this."

"You wanna stop or something?"

I craned my neck to see him. His face was neutral. Unimpressed. I instantly felt foolish. "Nah. No. Let's just keep going."

We arrived on the other side. Up ahead, more buildings and cars loomed. The noise was stifled here, but it lingered on the edges. A few more steps and we'd be in it once again. To my surprise, however, Mr. Hickory tugged Chelee's reins to the right.

"Where are we—?"

I didn't have to finish. The horse maneuvered down the shallow bank until we arrived at the water's edge. Mr. Hickory hopped off and offered me his hand. I stared at him.

"Chelee needs a break."

I cocked my head to the side.

"Well, come on now," he huffed. "We ain't got all day. That horse is thirsty."

I stepped onto the bank carefully, allowing time for the blood to return to my foot. Just a few feet ahead, the river slapped against the shore, waving at me, inviting me closer.

There was so much *water*. From down here, it was all I could see. No buildings. No cars. No people. Just water that kept coming and coming. Bits of wood and leaves floated by, never stopping, for new water was coming in right behind it. Busy water, in a hurry to get somewhere. It gurgled, like Melissa used to do in her sleep when the dust got bad. It was cloudy and smelled of fish.

It was beautiful.

I reached down to touch it, hesitating only a second before plunging my hand into the brown depths. It was cold, much colder than I'd expected in the glare of the sun, sending chills down my arms as it raced over my fingertips. My skin soaked up the moisture quickly, as if it hadn't felt anything wet for years. Despite having just emptied the canteen not an hour before, I suddenly felt dry. Suffocated, even. I resisted the urge to plunge my face into the oncoming wave. Shoot, if Mr. Hickory hadn't been standing behind me, I might've stripped naked and dove right in.

With Chelee at his side, he scanned the currents with the

look only someone who's known drought can wear. "Lotta water."

"Yep."

"Funny how there can be so much nature right in the middle of something completely man-made."

I looked at him. He didn't look back.

"Now, I don't right understand city slickers. Don't want to. But these people here? They done got it right. They knew they needed the river. But they also knew they couldn't move it or tame it. They worked *with* it, not trying to change it to make it fit them." He opened his mouth like he had more to say but didn't. He simply licked his cracked lips and closed them again, never taking his eyes off the river.

He didn't have to say it. The truth was sitting there right underneath his words. We'd done it the wrong way. In Colorado, Texas, Oklahoma. All of us. We hadn't just let it be, tried to work with the land. We'd tried to make it into something it was never supposed to be. And we were paying the price. The drought, the dusters, the disease—we'd tried to fight nature. And nature would always win.

Suddenly I didn't want to look at the river no more. I stood and wiped my hands on my dress, turning the dust into streaks of mud. Climbing up toward the road, I waited with my back turned until Chelee finished his libation.

* * *

The Kansas City train yard was even darker and dirtier than the rest of the city. Everything smelled like oil. Belches of black smoke poured from impatient engines waiting to be

213

filled with impatient people, who pushed and shoved in and out of the station. I shrank into Mr. Hickory as we approached, feeling very small and very sick.

He didn't notice. Instead, he hopped from Chelee's back, tied him to the nearest post, and gave him a pat on the head. "Be right back," he said to the horse. "You coming?" he said to me.

I'd been waiting for this moment for days, but it still took every ounce of strength I could muster to get off that horse. I followed Mr. Hickory into the station on shaky legs, and not just because of my foot, which had cramped terribly during the last part of the ride. There were more people inside the station than I'd ever seen in my life, and everyone seemed to be staring at me. Or ignoring me. I couldn't tell.

Mr. Hickory made quick, deliberate strides to the nearest window. He was certainly ready to be rid of me. "You got your money?"

"Money?"

"For your ticket."

Of course. Tickets cost money. Why hadn't I thought of that before? "I never said I had money."

He stopped abruptly, causing me to crash into him. "What?"

"I ain't got no money."

He grabbed my arm roughly, making me yelp. "What do you mean you ain't got no money?" His voice was sharp enough for people to look in our direction. Noticing their stares, Mr. Hickory dropped my arm. "You told me you did," he growled.

"No, I didn't."

"You mean to tell me I brought you all the way to Kansas City, and you don't even have money to get on the train?"

His gray skin was flushed, his nostrils flared. Even his eyes, normally cold and drooping, seemed to be on fire. His fists opened and closed at his sides.

I took a step backward, my fingers fluttering against my dress.

"Hey, watch it!" An overweight man in a pin-striped suit bent down and examined his feet. "You stepped on my shoe, you little brat."

"I'm sor—" I tried to step the other way but got a face full of pink cotton instead.

"Get away!" the woman screamed, putting a gloved hand near her mouth. "I'll call the police, I will!"

"Please. No. I'm sorry." I took another step. Mr. Hickory's glaring face had long since disappeared into the crowd. Another bump. Another shove. Hundreds of bodies, all yelling at me. I closed my eyes and put my hands over my ears, hoping to become invisible. It didn't work.

"Get out of the way!"

I stumbled to the ground as something hard pushed into my back. A suitcase. Its owner never even looked back.

"No loitering!" A red-faced policeman stood over me, twirling his baton. "Ain't no place for vagrants." He nudged me with his shiny shoe. "Get a move on."

"I'm not a—"

"I said scram, kid!"

So I fled. Ignoring the pain in my foot, the cramp in my calf, I pushed. I shoved. I didn't care who I angered. I just had to get out. I ran through the lobby and out into the hot, smelly Kansas City afternoon. On instinct, I turned toward Chelee but, realizing how ridiculous that was, turned again and headed in the opposite direction.

"Kathryn!"

Oh no. Mr. Hickory. He was *following* me!

"Kathryn!"

Pa'd always said some of the worst punishments were reserved for liars and cheats. I hadn't really lied *or* cheated. But I was pretty sure Mr. Hickory wouldn't let me off on a technicality.

"Kathryn! Stop!"

I tried to speed up, but my foot reduced me to a hobble. I'd never get away from him with this foot. I had to hide. But where? There was a fence right ahead. Not just a fence. A *gate*. A gate to the train yard. If only I could reach it, I could sneak inside and hide with the trains. He'd never find me.

"Kathryn, wait!"

Almost there. I grabbed the gate with both hands and pulled. It strained under my force but didn't move. I pulled again. And again and again. Still, it didn't move. A bright, shiny padlock clung to its handle. Frustrated, I tugged at it, screaming at its silver face. The lock seemed to laugh.

"Kathryn!" He was right behind me now.

I'd never see Melissa again. Wouldn't get a chance to tell her about all the things I'd seen. I'd never get to Indianapolis, see Pa, tell him how sorry I was for being awful. And I'd never get my foot fixed. I'd lived as an ugly cripple and now I'd die as one. I just hoped he'd do it fast.

I turned to see Mr. Hickory standing with his hands on his knees, breathing hard. His face was still flushed, but at least his eyes had returned to their normal gray. "Why'd you run?" he asked between wheezes.

What a stupid question. "I ain't got no money."

"So why you'd tag along in the first place?"

I straightened my back, trying to look taller and smarter than I felt. "You offered me a ride to Kansas City. And Kansas City is whole lot closer to Indianapolis than Pratt. So I went."

"Even though you didn't know what you were gonna do when you got here."

"I'da figured it out. Eventually."

Mr. Hickory's face twisted into something I couldn't read. He slid to the ground beside me, back against the fence, cupping his hat in his hands. "And you don't think that 'eventually' should have come *before* we got to the station?"

I shrugged. So he wasn't going to kill me. Or maybe he was. Later.

"What's so important about Indianapolis anyway?"

I scooted down next to him, suddenly too tired to be scared. Inside my pocket, my fingers wrapped around Melissa's hankie. "I gotta find my pa."

"Your pa?"

With a deep sigh, I told him about Melissa, about leaving Oklahoma and getting lost in the dust storm. I felt no need to mention Helen. I told him about hitchhiking and rain merchants and Frank Fleming's failure and my own stupidity for believing him in the first place. It felt good to talk. Even if it meant Mr. Hickory would murder me when I was done. At least the words would be out of me, if not the memory of it all.

"So all this is for your pa?" he asked after I'd finished.

I nodded. "I gotta find my pa so him and me can go home where we belong. I done seen enough of this city stuff. But first . . ." I glanced sideways. "First I gotta fix my foot." It came out as a whisper.

We both glanced at it, like it could hear us gossiping.

"Does it need fixin'?"

I turned to him sharply, ready to fight, only to find nothing but honesty on his face. He wasn't making a joke.

"Yes?" I didn't mean for it to come out like a question.

"Seems to me you're getting along just fine the way it is."

I pressed my lips into a scowl. "That ain't the point."

We sat in silence for several minutes, watching the comings and goings of the city around us. Hundreds of people, always going somewhere but never being anywhere, trampling the concrete earth beneath their never-still feet. And off to the side, Mr. Hickory and I sat, the two of us alone together on the shore beside a sea of busyness and bodies.

"Well," he said finally, replacing his hat atop his head and stretching. "Let's get you to Indianapolis then."

"Huh?"

"Let's get you to your pa."

"But I told you I ain't got no money."

"Neither do I." He gave me a mischievous smile, and I saw for the first time the young, dashing Texas Ranger he used to be. "So we'll just have to find a train that don't cost no money to ride." He stood suddenly. "Wait here."

I watched with a tight chest as Mr. Hickory disappeared back into the station. After what seemed like an eternity, he reappeared. But instead of walking toward me, he continued down the fence line, hands in pockets, face shadowed beneath his hat.

I lowered my head, following him with my eyes. He kept his hat down and did not turn around.

The sharp whistle of a nearby engine startled me to my feet. Nearly a hundred feet away, beneath a sign advertising some fancy new Chrysler car, Mr. Hickory finally stopped. He gave a slight bob of his head, and I approached slowly, careful to keep my eyes to the ground.

He pretended to pick something from the heel of his boot. "Go on," he mumbled.

"Huh?"

He gestured to the fence. Using one hand hidden behind his back, he'd pulled open a flap. Behind it, there was a hole just large enough for a jackrabbit to fit through.

Surely he didn't mean . . .

"Go on," he said again. "Train's leaving in ten minutes."

At that moment, another whistle blew, making me forget to tell him that sneaking on trains was illegal. By the time I'd wriggled through the hole, my dress was ripped even worse than before, my knees were bloodied, and Mr. Hickory was standing beside me.

"How did you—?"

He picked his hat up off the ground and shrugged. "I'm a fair jumper."

Of course he was. The cowboy got to jump while I was forced to slither like a snake.

Another whistle sounded.

"Come on. It'll be over here." He took off with long strides.

I struggled to keep up, tripping over the large rocks littering the yard, not wanting to follow but more scared to be left behind.

"Come on," he hissed. "You can't be seen."

"Mr. Hickory, I don't know about—"

He grabbed my arm and pulled me behind a trembling boxcar. He put one long finger to his lips and then pointed to the rails. Squatting down, we watched two sets of legs walk past, their trousers starched and black, their shoes shiny.

"Cops?" I mouthed.

He shook his head. "Worse. Train bulls. They'll beat ya if they find ya. Mean sons of guns."

My eyes widened as my stomach dropped. This was sounding less and less like something I wanted to be doing.

"But they ain't gonna find you." Mr. Hickory grabbed my hand and pulled me down the line past several cars until we came to one that was open. "This one. This is the one. Get in."

I shook my head.

"Come on. Get in. You'll be fine."

I cursed the tears that suddenly sprang to my eyes, hot and stinging. "I don't want to. I'm . . . I'm scared." The last words those of the child I'd tried so hard to pretend I wasn't.

Mr. Hickory sighed and looked down at his feet. When he looked up again, a quivery smile sat on his lips. "Don't you say that. You ain't scared of nothing. Why, if I weren't so old and worn-out, I'd sign you up for the Texas Rangers myself."

"They don't take girls."

He let out a short chuckle. "No. No, they don't. But I'd be doggoned if you wouldn't be the first." He winked, then pressed his lips into a line. "Besides, you wanna see your pa, don't you?"

I nodded.

"Then this is how you get there, scared or not."

Up ahead, a whistle cried out, shrill and agitated. Impatient.

"You best be going." He lifted me into the mouth of the car with ease. I didn't fight him.

"Aren't you coming?" It was a stupid question. And one I already knew the answer to.

He kicked at the ground and shook his head. "And leave Chelee? Nah."

I swallowed a lump in my throat. Whether it was tears or vomit, I couldn't be sure. "What do I do?"

"You just stay quiet, hide in one of those boxes if it comes to it, but you shouldn't have to. Bulls only bother looking when it's parked, and this train won't be parking till it gets to Indianapolis. Guy inside told me so." He glanced at my face, which must have been white. Or green. "But best to stay low and stay quiet anyway," he added quickly. "No need to tempt fate."

Tempt fate. As if fate had ever been on my side.

"You keep your eyes peeled for the next big city. When you start to see it in the distance, wait until the train slows to round a curve, and jump. Don't wait until it pulls into the yard or else you're done for."

His words were foreign. "Done for? Jump? But my foot—"

The boxcar jolted, sending me flying onto my rear. I scrambled to my feet, grabbing the sides of the doors as the floor beneath me lurched forward. "Mr. Hickory!"

The old cowboy jogged beside the car. "You got this! Good luck!"

The train groaned and shook and picked up speed. Mr. Hickory lagged behind. I felt the urge to call to him but found I couldn't push the words out of my mouth. I wanted to yell at him for putting me on this stupid train, making me more scared than I'd ever been in my life. But also to tell him thanks. He hadn't quit on me. The only one in my entire life except Melissa.

But it didn't really matter. Because when I looked out the train car, Mr. Hickory was gone. I poked my head through the door.

He had stopped running, but he was waving, his figure growing smaller and smaller with each passing second. "Go find your Wizard, kiddo!"

At least that's what I think he said. The wind roared past my ears, drowning out even the rumble of train wheels. Mr. Hickory and the rail yard faded behind me, until nothing was left of either of them. Tired and terrified, I nestled myself into the farthest corner of the car, hidden by boxes, leaving nothing but a sliver as my lookout. I watched Kansas City melt into the green countryside of Missouri and finally allowed myself to cry.

CHAPTER EIGHTEEN

MELISSA

I waited for almost two hours before giving up.

Annie had said she'd come back. Maybe she didn't call me a friend, but she didn't hate me anymore . . . right? If she'd hated me, she could have ruined me last week. There had to be a good reason she didn't show today. A very good reason. At least that's what I told myself as I went into town to find her. I didn't let my mind wander to the other possibility. That she'd finally decided the risk wasn't worth it. Or worse, the risk had turned real and Henry had . . .

No, there was a perfectly logical explanation.

The sky was blue with mounds of big, fluffy clouds. Perhaps rain later? It was a wish, sure, and a far-flung one at best, but I focused on it as I passed the city limits sign and maneuvered my bicycle onto Murray Avenue.

Annie's house sat in the middle of a row of shacks just like it. If I didn't know her home, how it differed from the others because of a slight droop in the right-side eave and the cottonwood tree hanging on to life in the farthest corner of the yard, how easy it would have been to ride right past, giving no thought to the people inside. People just like Annie. Just like me, only with less money. How ridiculous money always felt in a place like this.

I leaned my bicycle against the sad-looking cottonwood and scurried up the porch steps. "Mrs. Gale!"

Silence.

I knocked again, harder. Maybe she'd overslept. But Annie did not look like a woman who overslept. She looked like a woman who didn't sleep at all.

"Mrs. Gale!"

I yanked open the screen and grabbed the knob, surprised to find it moving under my grip. The interior door swung open with a rude squeak. I took a small step forward. "Mrs. Gale?"

I covered my nose with my hand to protect it from the stench of diapers and old laundry, then quickly lowered it again, ashamed at my snobbery. I took another step, removing my wide-brimmed hat. The rug was threadbare and pale, the flowers on its surface having lost their . . . yellow? White? It was hard to tell. The walls were covered in fading wallpaper. Ivy. This house must have been beautiful at one time.

To my right, the hallway creaked, startling me. "Mrs. Gale?"

A boy of about thirteen poked his head out of the nearest

door. His forehead was smudged with dirt, his dark hair wild, but his eyes were unmistakably Annie's. He was shirtless, his ribs covered by a pair of denim overalls. "Who are you?"

Who was I? I couldn't remember.

The boy's gaze traveled the length of my dress. Pink. Glaring, eye-burning pink. "You from the church?"

I nodded. Why couldn't I speak?

"Ma's in the other room with Mary Beth. You need her or something?"

"Y-yes," I stuttered. "Please."

He gestured across the hall, bored already, then disappeared back into the doorway, my presence obviously not important enough to warrant another minute of his time.

I hesitated before knocking. Behind the closed door, I could hear murmuring. My ears suddenly felt hot. I wasn't supposed to be here. But I'd already been seen. I gave a soft rap before easing open the door. "Mrs. Gale?"

The tension in the room rushed toward me, as thick as the stench of sweat in the air. Annie sat on the edge of the bed but rose quickly when she saw me. Her eyes were puffy, her normally taut face splotchy. "Mrs. Mayfield!" She took a step toward me, then stopped, putting a hand to her mouth. "I'm so sorry. I kept the oldest one home from school to help me with things, and I meant to send him—"

"It's fine," I said gently. "Completely fine. I'm not here for that. I just wanted to make sure you were okay." *I wanted to make sure Henry hadn't gotten to you.* "Are you okay? Is . . . ?"

My words collapsed as I looked over her shoulder. Mary Beth lay on the bed, clutching a lumpy pillow. Her eyes were open but glassy, her skin the same shade of gray as her tangled sheets.

"Mary Beth!" I grabbed her small hand, flinching at its coldness. She did not squeeze me back. "What's wrong with her?"

Annie shook her head. "Been like this for two days, but this morning she was worse."

The child shuddered and coughed, sucking in air and spitting it out like poison. I put my hand on her chest, feeling it rattle through my fingertips. "Is it dust pneumonia?"

"Don't know." She looked away. Because she did know, and so did I. You don't lose a husband—half a town—and not know what dust pneumonia looks like. But saying it, admitting it, was in some ways worse than the illness itself.

"Has she been to the doctor?"

"I can't afford no doctor!" Annie spat, her anger sudden and frightening. "Boise City doc packed up a long time ago, or don't you know? The good one from Dalhart comes once a week, but only for the richies." She looked at me sideways, but I couldn't meet her gaze.

Mary Beth coughed again. She blinked several times, scanning the room through a fevered cloud. She smiled slightly. "Did you . . . ?" she started, then stopped, licking her lips. "Did you bring the book?"

I struggled not to crumble. It was so *unfair*, all of it. If I caught the dust pneumonia, if Henry did, we'd deserve it. But we'd also have every remedy modern medicine could afford on our side. Because we were Mayfields. And this innocent little girl was going to die simply because she was not. I instinctively put a hand to my belly. If I'd married someone other than Henry, would I lose a child to this drought, too?

Bile rose in my throat. I hated the drought. I hated the dusters. I hated this whole ridiculous world and its perverted, uneven cruelty.

Mary Beth's eyelids fluttered. Her smile faded. She stilled, drifting into a peaceful sleep. Or at least, that's what I pretended. I knew beneath her quiet exterior, her body was fighting like mad to stay alive.

"You have to get her to a doctor."

"I told ya I ain't got the money—"

"I'll get you the money."

"Mrs. Mayfield, you don't need to be doing that."

"And what do I need to do? Sit here and watch your daughter die?"

The word hung in the air between us. Speaking the thing we both feared made it real, urgent. It was there, in the open now. Mary Beth was going to die. Unless we did something.

"Is the doctor in town?"

Annie stared at her child, unable to speak.

"Mrs. Gale, is the doctor in town today?"

She snapped her head toward me. "I don't know! I don't know! He comes into town once or twice a week, I think. I don't know what days."

"Do you trust me?"

I tossed the question out casually, not fully understanding the weight of it until it was already out there. After everything the woman had seen, heard, done, I couldn't possibly expect her to trust me. Except in this moment, she had no choice.

She clutched her arms to her sides as if trying to hold her body together. Her chin trembled as she gave the slightest nod.

"I'll get the money. And I won't come back without the doctor, okay?"

I wasn't sure if she even heard me. It didn't matter. Standing there shouting at her wouldn't help. I rushed outside and grabbed my bike. Never had the three miles to my house seemed so long. The wind kicked up, swirling the dust at my feet and forcing one hand onto my hat. It was determined to hold me back, as if it knew what I was about to do.

Throwing my bike on the ground, I burst into the house. "Henry?"

Silence. He wasn't home. Thank God.

His office was dark and stank of old cigarettes. I never came in here. I never needed to. Henry assured me nothing in the room would interest me. Finances and deeds. Bank statements and receipts. Nothing I needed to concern my pretty little head with. But today it did concern me. Because there was a safe in the room. And today I was going to open it.

Careful not to disturb the piles of papers on his desk, I pulled open the nearest drawer. Pipes and cigarette cases and pens and more papers. But no key. Frustrated, I yanked open the next drawer. Crumpled receipts and a notebook full of numbers. Still no key. And no key in the third drawer or the fourth.

I pinched the bridge of my nose, fighting back a scream.

How stupid I was to think he'd leave the key just lying around. He didn't trust me. Not anymore. It was probably in his pocket or attached to his truck keys. I slammed the drawer shut and clicked off the light. I had to try something else.

I swept up the stairs and into our bedroom, rushing past our perfectly polished headboard and ornately decorated bedspread. I pushed aside my perfume bottles and opened my jewelry box. Before Henry and I were married, I'd owned only a single piece of jewelry. Now I needed a whole box. I pulled out a pair of earrings—gold with green stones, the ones that matched my eyes—and started to put them in my pocket. I hesitated. If he asked me to wear them, what would I say? I remembered his face when I told him about the handkerchief. How much angrier would he be over the earrings? They were much more expensive.

I placed them back in the jewelry box, feeling a tear roll down my cheek. There was only one other thing I could do. I fingered the small cross at my neck. Ma's necklace. The last piece of her I had. Henry wouldn't notice its absence. If he did, it would be met with a shrug. One more piece of the Baile problem gone. I clutched it, unable to breathe. No. No, I would not give away my mother's necklace. It was her, it was her faith, so intertwined I couldn't separate one from the other in my memory. A faith she'd given me—and one I was trying desperately not to lose.

But Mary Beth. Sweet, innocent Mary Beth. Will you really let her die, Melissa? Rob her of her future to hang on to your past? Perhaps you are more Mayfield than you thought.

Disgusted and heartbroken, I pushed myself away from

the bureau. *Sorry, Ma. I have to do this.* The necklace would be tainted forever if I didn't. I would no longer see God in it, only Mary Beth. It was the right thing to do. The only thing I could do.

I started out of the room and stopped as the sun caught the edge of something shiny on Henry's dresser. A glass dish full of cuff links. Dozens of them. I reached for one, feeling the gold warm in my sweaty hand.

Don't, Melissa, I scolded myself. *It's too dangerous.*

But there were so many. He'd never feel the loss of one. He'd never even know it was gone. And I could keep my mother's cross.

He'll find out. He always finds out.

I ran my hand through the pile of cuff links, mouth dry. They jostled against each other, crowded in such a small dish, weight pressing into my skin. Before I could change my mind, I curled my fingers around the closest pair—gold with a black stone in the center—and rushed out of the house.

By the time I arrived at the doctor's office, my dress was soaked and my hat was wilted. The sun was high overhead, humidity building. Maybe we really would get some rain later. Parking my bike, I flew up the steps and grabbed the doorknob.

Locked.

"No," I whispered. "No, no, no." The doctor *had* to be here. He *had* to be. I shook the doorknob. It didn't budge. I balled my fists and pounded. "Help!" I screamed. "Open up! I need help!"

Despite my yells, the door refused to open.

Tears streamed down my face, washing sweat into my eyes. I ignored the sting, pounding harder. "You have to be here!" I wailed. "You have to be!" I pounded until my fists were numb; then I switched to scratching. "Open the door! Open! The! Door!"

"Miss?"

I spun around.

A gentleman in his late fifties stood behind me, head cocked to one side. Round glasses perched on his nose and a silver mustache hid his upper lip. It quivered at the sight of me.

It was only upon seeing the concern in his eyes that I realized how I must look. I smoothed down my hair, feeling the frizz beneath my fingertips, and replaced my drooping hat. I wiped the tears from my cheeks, rolling the mixture of dirt and sweat beneath my palm. Smudges of mascara blackened my fingers and blood oozed from my broken fingernails. I straightened my dress, cringing at the ripped, once-pink fabric.

"Miss," the man said again, "are you okay?"

"Are you—are you the doctor?"

He shifted a briefcase from one hand to the other. "Yes, ma'am, I am."

I wanted to cry. Or hug him. Or both. "And you're here? You're really here?"

"For the moment. I was on my way back to Dalhart but realized I'd left my stethoscope in the office."

I giggled, high-pitched and awkward, relief and disbelief washing over me like the long-awaited rain. He'd forgotten his stethoscope. Pure dumb luck . . . or was God in this place after all?

The doctor cleared his throat. "So, um, if you'll excuse me." He gestured to the door behind me.

I moved aside. "Of course. Of course."

He unlocked his office and stepped inside.

I followed, uninvited. "I'm so glad you're here. There's this girl and she's very sick. You really must come at once."

"I'm afraid that's out of the question, Miss . . . ?"

"Gale," I answered without thinking—or thinking too much—and pulled my hat lower over my face.

"Miss Gale—"

"Please, my . . . niece." Another lie, only it didn't feel like it this time. "And she's very sick. Won't you please—?"

"As I told you before, I am very busy. I have patients waiting for me in Dalhart. I'm already late as it is. I really must be going." He grabbed his stethoscope and shoved it in his briefcase, snapping the latch loudly for emphasis.

"Oh, please. It won't take long. Will you just see her?"

"I'm sorry, Miss Gale. I really am. Perhaps next week."

"She'll be dead by next week."

He paused, but only for a moment, his small mouth jerking to the side as if trying to conjure another weak excuse. Instead he said nothing and moved toward the door.

I blocked his path.

He stepped back, eyes bulging behind his glasses. "Miss Gale, if you please."

He was a full head taller than me and at least twice my size. He could have easily pushed me aside. No, he could have pushed Melissa Mayfield aside. But Melissa Baile would not let him get away. I straightened my back and crossed my arms, trying to look hard.

He sighed. "Miss Gale, I'm sorry about your niece. But please understand that I am just one man, and there is more need in this area than I could ever possibly meet." He scratched his head and shrugged. "I simply must—"

"Perhaps these will change your mind." I dropped the cuff links in the doctor's waiting hand. The blood on my fingers had dried a dirty shade of scarlet.

He turned them over in his palms. "Where did you get these?"

"Does it matter?"

"Yes, it matters. I will not accept stolen property for payment."

"It's not stolen," I said, jutting out my chin. "I swear on my life they aren't stolen. But I'll thank you not to ask me again where I got them."

The doctor looked back and forth between me and the cuff links, lips pressed flat. I tried to hide behind my mask of courage, afraid he would see the truth through my watery eyes.

Finally he sighed and put the cuff links in his pocket. "Alright, Miss Gale. You win. Now where is the girl?"

CHAPTER NINETEEN

KATHRYN

I woke up to the smell of fish and kerosene.

The ground beneath me rolled and shook, and it took only a moment to remember. I was on a train.

It was dark. Night. I sat up, stifling a yell as weight shifted onto my bad foot, causing it to seize. I had no idea how long I'd been riding, but it was long enough for my foot to cramp up; that was for sure. I gripped the sides of my dress, focusing on my fingers as I waited for it to pass. They were filthy, the nails bitten down to nubs. Oh, how Helen would have thrown a fit to see them. She had a thing about me biting on my nails. She—

Wait. I craned my neck toward the opening in my box fort. Blackness raced by the open door. Yes, it was night. For sure. Not even really a moon from the looks of it. So how could I see my hands?

Someone coughed. Someone that wasn't me.

The rest of my body stiffened as the cramp finally subsided. A train bull. Here. In the car. No. No, no, no. In my mind, I saw myself getting beaten, flying from the train. All the whuppings I'd gotten from Pa were nothing. I was breaking the law this time. Not sassing the teacher or forgetting to close the door to the chicken coop. Maybe I could convince the bull to take me to jail instead. Pa'd come for me. He'd understand. Right?

Right?

I had to get out of here. But there was no way to get past him, not without being seen. I curled my shoulders and pushed my back against the side of the car. Maybe he didn't know I was here. He hadn't said nothing, and I was well hidden in my fort. If I could just stay quiet until the next stop . . .

"You're awake."

The voice was deep. Gruff. I closed my eyes and held my breath, trying to fold into myself.

"Why don't you come out of there? Can't be comfortable."

I didn't move. Maybe I could make a run for it.

A run for it? Come on, Kathryn. The train is moving fast, and you ain't even got a brace on your leg. You may be scared but this ain't the time to get stupid.

The voice gave an irritated sigh. "Or stay in there. I don't care."

I peered out from behind the boxes, but my limited view showed only the faint glow of a kerosene lamp and a set of large scuffed brown boots, the soles worn down to nothing. I leaned forward on my elbow to get a better look.

The man was a beast. Even sitting down, it was impossible to miss his size. His torso was like a drum and his arms and legs as thick as fence posts. His face was hidden by a mane of strawberry-blond hair, which melted into a great red, bushy beard. He was a beast stuffed into a tight brown jacket and tweed pants, worn at the knees.

"There you are."

Without realizing it, I'd crawled almost completely out of my hiding space. No use pretending now. I climbed to my feet and straightened, thrusting my shoulders back. I pressed my lips into a snarl, hoping I looked intimidating.

I couldn't see his eyes. They were hidden by too much hair. But I could feel his gaze travel down my body, resting longer than I wanted on my foot. I tucked it behind my other leg. So much for intimidation.

What little skin showed on his face was red, shiny. "That wasn't so hard, was it?" He leaned forward, holding out an open can of sardines. "Want one? You look like you could use 'em."

I wrinkled my nose. Fish. The worst of all the meats. Pa always said it was the Oklahoma in me that hated them. I said it was the part of me that didn't want to eat things that swam around in the same place they went to the bathroom.

And more than that, they were being offered by *him*. Another stranger in this strange, savage world outside Boise City. I'd gotten lucky with Mr. Hickory. I knew God wouldn't let it happen again.

And yet my stomach rumbled. I couldn't remember the last time I had eaten. We'd run out of bread before Kansas City, and beans before that. I hated how much I wanted those smelly dead fish. Against my better judgment, I snatched the tin from his outstretched hand and retreated to the other side of the car.

He snorted, scratching at his beard. "Well, alright. You're welcome, I suppose."

I pulled the sardines from the can. *Don't look at them,* I told myself. *Just don't look.* But that didn't stop those ugly old things from looking at me. The minute the first one reached my tongue—the salt, the grease, the overwhelming *fishiness*—instinct overpowered revulsion. I devoured them, ignoring even the crunch of their tiny bones as I swallowed. My insides churned, causing a foul-smelling burp. I was afraid I was going to lose them, but they stayed put, and after a few minutes, my stomach quieted.

"These were supposed to go with them. But I guess you can eat 'em plain." He tossed over a small brown package.

Crackers. He couldn't have offered the crackers first? They crumbled in my mouth, absorbing the fishiness, tasting like dirt and paper. I ate them anyway.

He tossed me a canteen. "What's your name?"

I drank slowly, the food settling comfortably in my stomach. No longer a beggar, I remembered where I was. On a train. Illegally. With this man who might or might not throw me from it. I tossed the water back to him, glancing toward the boxcar's open door. "Why don't you tell me yours first?"

To my surprise, the man laughed, earsplitting in this small

space. "Fair enough. You can call me Bert." He dipped his head. "Your turn."

"Kathryn."

"Alright, Kathryn. Wanna tell me what you're doing on this here train?"

"Not really."

"Now, that ain't polite."

I scowled. "You wanna tell me what *you're* doing on this here train?"

Bert's head dipped to his chest. His fingers fidgeted in his lap as he scraped one thumb against the other. "Not really."

I nodded once. "Alright then." He was no train bull. That much was clear. And that much was all I cared about. I returned my attention to the open door. "Do you know where we are?"

He shrugged, his stiff jacket scraping against the wood. "Dunno. I hopped on outside Hannibal when it slowed for another freighter. So I'm guessing Illinois somewhere."

"Illinois?" My heart leapt. I was never a real good student, but I was pretty sure Illinois was pretty close to Indianapolis. I'd gone farther on this train in a single sleep than I had in over a month of travel by car, foot, and on Chelee's back. Illegal or not, this train was a chariot. I bit down on my smile and nodded, like I didn't care. "Right, right. Illinois."

Bert watched me and scratched his head, sending ripples through his hair. It was so *clean*-looking. If I touched it, I bet it would feel like silk. Not that I would.

I smoothed down my own hair, suddenly very aware I hadn't bathed in weeks. It was oiled straw under my fingers.

"Where you headed?"

I wiped my hands on my dress. Good grief. My *dress*. It hadn't been nice on a good day. Now ripped and filthy, it probably smelled worse than those disgusting sardines. I wasn't sure why I cared. "Nowhere. Where are you headed?"

He smiled like a fox, his lips darting back and forth over his teeth. "Same as you. Nowhere."

I squinted, unsure if it was a joke. His face sure had a hard time sitting still. "Well, thank you for the food, Bert. But I suppose we'll just sit quietly until we reach our nowheres?"

He gave another slight shrug. "Alright."

The rattle of the train car roared louder in our silence. I couldn't see a thing in the darkness, but the air smelled sweet, like recent rain and marigolds. I'd almost forgotten it. It was the smell of life and happiness, of my childhood. My heart ached at the memory.

Bert pulled his jacket over his face, his giant belly rising and falling slowly. I crawled back into my fort of boxes. He knew I was here. The boxes wouldn't stop him if he was a scoundrel. They wouldn't help. But somehow they did. Listening to the noisy quietness, I drifted into a deep sleep.

* * *

"Kathryn. Kathryn, get up."

A growl. Hands on my shoulders, shaking me. My eyes struggled to focus on the shape in front of me.

"Now, Kathryn. Now, now."

Frank Fleming was standing over me. In the dim light, his bony fingers reached out, touching me. My grogginess evaporated instantly. My heart began to pound, its beat thrashing in my ears and drowning out the sound of his voice. "Get off me!" I screamed, swinging my fists wildly. "Get off me!"

"Kathryn. Kathryn!" His hands left my body, pulled in front of his face to shield it from my blows. His voice was a high-pitched whisper. "We're stopping! The train is stopping. Springfield, I think."

His words hung in the air as his face morphed before my eyes. Bert. It was just Bert. But not the Bert I'd met last night.

Instead of calm confidence, his cheeks quivered under his beard, and his eyes, bulging and watery, darted this way and that as he stuffed scraps of trash into his pocket. "The bulls will be here any minute. We have to get out of the car. Now."

I jumped to my feet, feeling the blood drain from my face. "Springfield? Mr. Hickory didn't say nothing about Springfield. It's supposed to go to Indianapolis!"

"Don't matter where it's supposed to go. This is where it is. And you won't be going anywhere if they catch you." He blinked rapidly, nostrils flaring.

I clawed at my face, surprised to find my hands shaking. "But where do we go? We can't jump! It's too late. They'll find us in the yard!"

He poked his head out the door. Sure enough, real shapes rose up around us. A city. It was the end. In more ways than one.

"There," he said, pointing. "The ladder to the top. We can hide on top of the car until they've passed."

I poked my head out beside him. The train had slowed,

but the ground was still moving. I grew dizzy and took a step back, closing my eyes to steady myself.

"We have to go now."

I shook my head. The ladder was several feet from the opening. There was no way I could make it.

Bert grabbed my shoulders again. "Kathryn, they take no mercy on stowaways. You have to jump."

"I can't!" I yelled, thrusting my foot toward him. "Are you stupid? I *can't*!"

He looked from my face to my crippled leg and back again. His lips puckered and squirmed. "You have to try! If they find you, they'll look for others, and then we'll—"

The train car lurched and shuddered. The sound of brakes.

Bert grabbed my hand, his liquid eyes pleading. "If you don't jump, you're dooming us both."

Inside my shoe, my toes curled as if into a sneer. Mocking me. "I'm sorry. I can't."

He squeezed my wrist once and then dropped it. "Well, good luck, then."

My stomach rolled as I took in the enormity of his words. "What?"

A train whistle blew, causing us both to flinch. Bert's lips formed a thin line, disappearing beneath his beard. Then he took several steps back until he was diagonal from the door, paused, and barreled through it sideways at full speed.

"Bert!" I leaned out the opening, clutching the side for support.

He was hanging off the side of the ladder, his long mane

blowing in the breeze. He didn't even look back before starting to climb.

I retreated into the car, pacing. He left me. He *left* me! Just like everyone else. I rubbed the back of my neck as I walked, grit rolling beneath my fingers. My box fort blurred in front of me as I pushed down angry tears.

There was no way I'd fit inside, not with whatever was in there to begin with. Besides, if they took the box off the train, I'd still be in trouble, just a heap of a different kind.

I looked upward, past the train car roof, past the place where Bert was probably now safely hidden away. To heaven. To God. It was never enough for Him. He couldn't ever just leave me alone. There was always something else, another way to push me down, to punish me. Another way to show me just how little He thought of me.

Always another way to hurt me.

Beneath my feet, the train car clunked, slowing.

"Oh no! The bag! My bag!"

I stopped pacing.

"Kathryn, please! My bag! I forgot my bag!"

Wiping my eyes, I poked my head out the door again and looked up. Bert's head peered over the top of the car. His hair whipped around his face, wild in the breeze.

"My bag! My bag!"

Sure enough, against the far wall was a brown leather bag. I picked it up and turned it over in my hands. This. *This* was what he fretted about leaving. Not a human being. I grabbed it and reared back, preparing to chuck it toward the ground.

Bert's voice was shriller than the whine of the train brakes. "Kathryn, please!"

Beneath my feet, a groan and a shake. Shouting in the distance.

Too late now. With only anger and spite coursing through my veins, I slung the stupid bag around my neck, checked the laces on my shoes, took several steps back . . . and leapt. My left foot landed on the ladder rung. Cold steel vibrated beneath my fingers. I'd done it! I'd made it! But as my right foot swung to connect, a sudden gust of wind slammed against me and the uneven sole slipped against the smooth metal, throwing me off-balance. My other foot slid. I thrashed my body, struggling to pull my feet back up. And then I saw it. Melissa's handkerchief, dancing away from me in the breeze, heading back westward along the track.

"No!" I shrieked, reaching one hand toward it. But the once-blue fabric was gone before the word even fell from my lips. "Please." Without the hankie, my body suddenly felt too heavy, my arms too weak to hold on. The rung slipped in my sweaty fingers. I was falling.

And then I wasn't. Strong hands grabbed me from above, pulling me back onto the ladder. My feet swung wildly until I felt the rung securely beneath me. I crawled to the top of the car just as the train jerked to a stop.

"The bag! Do you have the bag?"

Sweat beaded in the hair above Bert's lip. His eyes washed over my body, not seeing me. Looking only for the bag.

I thrust it at him, disgusted.

More shouting. Closer this time. Much closer.

There was a slight dip in the roof, barely big enough for an average-size person to lie in, let alone a beast and a cripple. Bert pulled me down, cupping his hand over my mouth, and attempted to squeeze me into it next to him. I didn't want to touch him. I wanted to run, to find Melissa's hankie. Who cared if I was caught? I needed that hankie more than I needed air—the last tangible reminder of good in the face of all this bad.

But from below us came a whistle and the steady crunch of approaching footsteps on gravel. The reality of capture flared and I let him squash me, hoping it would stop me from shaking.

The footsteps stopped. The car beneath us shook as someone climbed aboard. Heels clicked on wood as they circled the cargo inside.

"Oi!"

Bert stiffened behind me. His body was warm and sweaty, his beard scratchy against my neck.

"Cargo in twenty-seven going or staying?"

"Going!"

"Alright." More shuffling. "All clear! Checkin' eighty-four boxes movin' on to Indianapolis. All clear."

"All clear."

A loud crack as the footsteps landed once again on gravel, then an earsplitting thud. Banging on the side of the car. Each tap sent a thousand painful vibrations through my body, right into my very teeth. I wiggled against them, trying to free myself, but Bert held me tighter. I wanted to scream. He was suffocating me, pushing me into the noise. Finally, though, the owner of the footsteps moved on. We listened to the crunch of rocks and the bang of each car as he made his way slowly—much too slowly—down the line.

I struggled against Bert's body.

"Don't," he whispered. His breath was hot and wet against my neck. "Not yet. They always come back."

Sure enough, the footsteps returned several minutes later. Thankfully, the tapping did not. They paused at our car.

I held my breath. Bert tightened his grip.

The steps circled. Stalling. Waiting. Torturing. And then whistles. Something happy. Something familiar . . .

Our house. Before the dugout. Before Helen. Before the drought. Before we'd sold the radio to buy new shoes. Pa and Melissa dancing. Laughing. Twirling. And me at the table. Watching.

"Come dance," Pa said.

"I can't."

"Sure you can!"

"Look at this thing!" My brace. It was new. Well, new to me. Clunky and awkward.

"Come on, Kath," Melissa said, twirling around me like only she could do. "Dance!"

"I. Can't."

Melissa stopped smiling, her dress falling limply at her sides as her hands went to her hips. "Kathryn Baile, you stop that right now. Yes, you can. You're as stubborn as an old sow. You get your rear end off that chair right this second."

I glanced at Pa for help. He stared at the floor. But was that a smile? I stood up, as much to spite Melissa as to get her off my back. My brace creaked. I wobbled. "See? I can't—"

My words were cut short by Pa. He swooped in and twirled me across the floor, gripping my hand and waist so I wouldn't slip. Melissa clapped and squealed. I spun around. I tripped and swayed. But I did not fall.

"'Oh, there's a dark and a troubled side of life,'" Pa sang. I stepped on his foot. The smile never left his face. "'There's a bright and a sunny side too.'"

I was clumsy. I was way offbeat. I pinched Pa's toes and mangled his hand. But I danced. Oh, how I danced.

I giggled as Pa continued to sing and spin. "'But if you meet with the darkness and strife, the sunny side we also may view.'"

"'Keep on the sunny side, always on the sunny side . . .'" The words slipped out against Bert's hand.

His body tensed.

The whistling stopped.

I bit my tongue. What had I done?

The footsteps came closer. There was a sound like wood being dragged across metal.

This was it. We were caught. I struggled to remain still. We needed to run. Flee. But still Bert pressed me closer.

The car trembled beneath us. The footsteps were climbing. They were climbing! But . . . they weren't. The movement wasn't from the ladder. It was from the car itself. A lurch and a moan, and the clouds above our heads drifted west. We were moving again, out of the city, away from the bulls. Toward Indianapolis.

Warmth enveloped me. A feeling of relief. Warm, sour . . . relief?

I pulled away from Bert, recoiling. His eyes were downcast.

A wet spot darkened the front of his tweed pants. He had peed himself.

I made my way back down the ladder without looking at him. I didn't slip this time, my hands and feet steady on the quivering rungs. I landed with both feet inside the train car, barely even noticing the pain. Respite faded to grief with every passing second. Melissa's handkerchief was gone, my last thread of home now swirling somewhere along the Illinois countryside.

CHAPTER TWENTY

MELISSA

"Do you really have to stop?"

Mary Beth was alive. She was weak; she was coughing; she was still coming down from her fever. But she was alive. And she was not happy I had stopped reading.

I opened my mouth to respond, but Annie did it for me. "Yes, she does. Doc said you need rest. And I know you ain't gonna rest with Mrs. Mayfield blabbing on about Dorothy and Toto and a Wicked Witch."

Mary Beth's mouth turned down slightly. "But we're almost done."

Her room was dim and suffocating, still reeking of illness. But I was grateful to be sitting on her lumpy mattress, straw poking my legs through the thin sheet. I squeezed her hand, ignoring its clamminess. "Tomorrow. I promise."

Lowering her chin to her chest with a sigh, she allowed her eyelids to flutter and close.

I tucked the book under my arm and followed Annie out of the room. Clicking the door softly shut behind me, I smiled. "She seems to be feeling better."

"She's getting there. Doc said it could take a while, but he thinks he caught her just in time." Her voice thick, she refused to meet my gaze. "Maybe in a week I can get back to workin'. I'm sure your house is a mess."

I put my hand on her arm. The dusty, coarse fabric of her dress was different from my own and yet so familiar. She stiffened beneath my fingers and I realized it was the first time I'd ever touched her. "There's no rush. The job will still be there when Mary Beth is ready."

Annie's eyes drifted to mine. They were tired, as always, but tinged today with something like humility. "I didn't ask for any of this, you know? The job, the reading, the doctor."

"I know you didn't."

"But the money for the doc—"

I looked down. I hadn't told Annie about the cuff links. I couldn't. At first, it was because Mary Beth's health was all that mattered. And now it was because of the way she looked at me. Like maybe I wasn't a monster, like I'd finally done something good. I couldn't bear to think of what she'd say if she knew how I'd done it. "It's nothing."

My answer was incomplete. Inadequate. But Annie turned away and walked toward the back of the house anyway. I followed. Two steps into her small kitchen, I wished I hadn't. A cold sweat broke out across my forehead at the stench of simmering carrots and stewed rabbit. I covered my face, but the smell had already burned into my nose and soured my throat.

Annie stood at the stove next to a large copper pot, her wooden spoon frozen mid-stir. "Mrs. Mayfield?"

I looked around frantically, trying to swallow what would not be swallowed.

"Mrs. Mayfield?"

I burst through the back door, barely making it into her yard before releasing the contents of my stomach. I retched until my sides hurt, until I was afraid the baby was going to come right up with it. It was only after the worst passed, when I was wiping my nose and mouth with the folds of my dress, that I was aware enough of what had just happened to be embarrassed. I glanced up from my mess slowly.

Annie stood on the steps, fingers drumming on her hips. "I know you richies eat better than we do, but I didn't know my cookin' was enough to make you sick."

"Oh, Mrs. Gale, please, you know—"

"I'm teasing! Them babies let you know who's boss, even before they get here." She settled on the porch steps, her gray dress riding high over her ankles. She was not wearing stockings. "But I thank you for not doing it all over my kitchen floor."

Knees still wobbly, I stood, suppressing what I hoped was just a belch.

"You told that husband of yours yet?"

I tucked my arms in at the sides, shaking my head slightly.

"And he ain't figured it out? He think you're just puking for the fun of it?"

I sat down next to her, thankful she didn't suggest going back inside. "He hasn't been home much. Mr. Mayfield Sr. is . . . not well." I rubbed a finger over my chapped lips. I wasn't supposed to be talking about this. But I wasn't supposed to be here in the first place. Mr. Mayfield's condition was the least of my secrets. "Henry spends a lot of time in the main house with him."

It was the truth, but only half. True, I hadn't seen very much of my husband lately, but there had still been plenty of chances. I didn't want to tell Henry because that would mean accepting the baby was half his. Half Mayfield. More than half, really. Because once Henry was involved, she would know nothing else. A Mayfield to the core.

She. It was going to be a girl. There was no way to tell for sure, of course, but I knew. Somehow I just knew. Like my mother had known. And the thought of raising my daughter as a Mayfield . . . I should be grateful. Instead, I only felt sorrow.

Overhead, the wind whistled through the dead branches.

"You know," Annie said finally, "he's going to find out eventually."

A pause, loaded and heavy as the static building in the dusty air. *Not just about the baby* was what she really meant. About her. About us. We both knew this couldn't last. It was too risky. And not simply because of my husband. We had crossed a line. She was just supposed to clean my house. And yet here we sat.

The sound of her hands slapping her knees broke the moment. "Well," she said, standing. "Let's get you cleaned up. You got vomit all over your shoes and mascara running down your face. You look worse than those whores down at the train depot."

I laughed and wiped at my cheeks. My fingers came back black.

"But we need to hurry. You best be getting home. Duster's a-coming. My arthritis don't lie."

I'd barely made it out of town when the wind died suddenly. No birds chirped. No grasshoppers clogged my path. Not even a single stalk of wheat shuddered. That was always the first sign. Nature knew what was coming before we did. I pedaled harder. Sweat dripped down my chest, soiling my dress and intensifying the smell of vomit. We hadn't gotten it all. But I didn't have time to worry about that now.

I had just pulled onto the long drive when I saw it. In the distance, a black wall rose from the ground, as if from the stampede of a thousand angry horses. The first blast of wind hit me—a warning shot—pushing against my bicycle and rendering me immobile. I squeezed my eyes shut, feeling the dirt roll painfully over them. I'd never make it home before the real thing hit.

I abandoned my bike next to the nearest tree and took off on foot, blindly making my way toward the big house. It was closer but not close. Patches of dead grass slowed me, rising out of nowhere to snare my feet. But I pushed on. I could see it now. Faint lights in the distance.

The blackness screamed forward. I had only minutes.

Dust tainted my tongue, gagging my still-tender throat. My eyes were slits, burning and watering in the haze. Almost there. Almost there. Steps on wood, metal in my hand, and I pushed into the living room just as the cloud slammed into the house. The walls groaned and shifted but stood their ground. Outside, the storm raged, furious.

I collapsed on the floor, panting.

"Melissa?" Henry stood over me, blocking out the glare of the overhead light, a shadow obscuring his face.

I scrambled to my feet, trying to brush the dust from my hair. "Honey, I—"

"What are you doing here?"

Not "Are you okay?" Not "Thank goodness you're alright." No, from my husband, all that came was annoyance and suspicion. "I was returning from town and got caught in the storm." I smoothed down my dress and took a wobbly step.

Henry grabbed my arm to steady me. "Are you crazy? You could have been killed. What were you doing in town anyway?"

I swayed, feeling dizzy. "I . . . I . . ."

Henry's grip tightened. "Melissa?"

"Excuse me, Mr. Mayfield?"

He dropped my arm as a voice came from the other room. Immediately I was forgotten. For once, I was grateful to be of such little importance.

Henry disappeared, hushed voices leaking from behind the closed door, giving me time to concoct a believable excuse. It wasn't Wednesday, so Ladies Auxiliary was out. My allowance for the week was gone, so I couldn't have been shopping. The library. Yes, I'd tell him I had gone to the library. But why no books? It was closed for lunch. Yes, and

I'd been riding around town waiting for it to reopen when I saw the duster blowing up. I nodded to myself, satisfied. It would have to do.

"Melissa?"

Consumed in my own lie, I hadn't noticed the two men walk over to me. I blinked, trying to return to the present.

"Melissa, this is Dr. Goodwin. He's been seeing my father once a week."

A beefy man with a silver mustache wiped his hands on his pants before offering me one. At least I think he offered me his hand. I was too busy fighting the urge to run.

Dr. Goodwin. *The* doctor.

His sleeves were rolled to his elbows, a black stethoscope around his unbuttoned collar. "Ah, yes, Mrs. Mayfield. I've heard so much about you!" His hands were moist as he cupped mine in his. "Mr. Mayfield Sr. speaks so highly . . ." He raised his chin, voice trailing.

I withdrew my hand and looked down, cheeks burning.

"Forgive me, Mrs. Mayfield, have we met?"

I could feel Henry's eyes on me. Outside, a sudden gust of wind sent dirt against the windows, scratching like a creature trying to get in. I wished it would. "I don't think so," I whispered.

"I swear, there's something so familiar—"

"Dr. Goodwin, I'm sure you see a lot of women who look like me." I twirled my hair around my finger, careful to keep my chin down and voice low. Maybe it would pass for modesty. "Lot of Irish in these parts, after all."

The doctor tapped the side of his nose. "To be sure, yes.

But you . . ." He patted his pockets. "If I could just find my glasses . . ."

I grabbed his hand. It was as sweaty as my own. "Please. Please . . . how is Mr. Mayfield? We've all been so worried."

His shoulders relaxed, the glasses momentarily forgotten. "Not well, I'm afraid. I was just telling your husband we've reached the point of no return." He clucked his tongue softly. "If you'll forgive me for being so graphic, ma'am, there's blood in his lungs now. You can see it when he coughs. And soon it will . . ." He sighed, patting my hand. "It's only a matter of time, dear."

The roar of the wind died suddenly. All around us, the house shuddered and popped, trying to right itself after the assault, thunderous in the sudden quiet.

Dr. Goodwin squeezed my arm, causing me to jump. "Well, that's that. I must be going now. It was lovely meeting you, Mrs. Mayfield, though I do wish it were under happier circumstances."

I gave a slight smile. Yes. Happier circumstances.

He turned and shook Henry's hand. "I'll be back in a few days."

Henry nodded.

"Keep him hydrated. Water. Soup. Anything he'll take. And telegram me if he takes a turn for the worse."

"Of course. Yes. Thank you again for coming."

Dr. Goodwin shuffled to the front door, taking his hat from the rack. "And if you find my glasses anywhere . . ." He grabbed his coat and then, on second thought, rehung it and began to roll down his sleeves. When he reached the end, something fell from his cuff and hit the ground with a sound much too loud for such a small object.

Something gold.

"Here, let me help you." Henry bent over and scooped the object from the floor.

Ice wrapped around my heart. Oh no. *No, no, no.*

"Goodness," Dr. Goodwin said with a chuckle. "How clumsy of me."

Henry pushed the object around in his palm, tracing the black stone with his finger. He didn't look at me. It was somehow worse than if he did. "Beautiful," he said quietly. "I have a pair just like these. They were passed down to me, my great-grandfather's originally. Rare. Priceless, really."

All the blood drained from my body. I couldn't move. I couldn't breathe.

"Wherever did you get something so exquisite, Doctor?"

"One of my patients. Here in town, actually. Payment for a sick child. Though, perhaps if what you say is true, they quite overpaid! Thank you," he added, picking the cuff link from Henry's palm and pocketing it. "What was the name again? Gane? Gile? Gale, maybe? Is there a Gale in these parts?"

"Yes," Henry said, still not looking at me. "Yes, there is."

"Well, I'm off." The doctor pulled on his coat, oblivious to the beast he had just awoken. "I'll see you in a few days." He nodded at me once and disappeared out the front door, taking the last of the air along with him.

Henry stared at the closed door, his jaw moving slightly from side to side.

"Henry, please. I can explain."

He rushed toward me, veins straining beneath his skin, and pushed me backward with a single shove. I landed on the floor with a painful gasp. "Explain? Explain what? How you *stole* from me? Lied to me? Those cuff links were a family heirloom!"

I cowered beneath his shadow. "Please, please—"

"I knew it was a mistake to marry below me! I knew it!" He kicked at the wall, causing a dent in the baseboard.

I winced, covering my face with my hands. I was next. Only the blow never came. I peered between my fingers to find him pacing, opening and closing his fists. The muscles in his forearms flexed with each movement.

"All the guys said I was crazy, taking up with you. When my father suggested it, I laughed in his face. I really did. But you were so beautiful, Melissa. So sweet. So *good.*" He looked at me accusingly. "Innocent and perfect, despite that hole you were livin' in with that bum father and retarded sister—"

"Don't you talk about my sister like that!" It came out before I could stop myself.

Henry charged me, hand raised.

I shrank back, wishing the floor would swallow me, bracing for the pain. But once again, his violence remained suspended.

"It's the only way," he said. "The only way to get James Baile to sell."

I opened my eyes, blinking rapidly, trying in vain to form a question. What was he talking about?

"Never mind the stubborn old coot was barely making

ends meet as it was. He wasn't going to sell to anyone. Anyone, that is . . . except family."

He hovered over me, sweat dripping down his forehead. He smelled faintly of cloves, remnants of the bay rum after-shave he'd used that morning. It seemed a lifetime ago I'd found the scent alluring.

"From the moment I saw you, I had to have you. The land . . . well, the land was important, but you . . . I thought I could fix you up right by getting you out of that dugout. Make you worthy of the Mayfield name. That's what I get for thinking with my pants instead of my head."

I pulled my legs up, wrapping my body around itself as if to shield from the blow. But it was useless. This kind of cruelty tore at me from the inside, made more savage by the confusion swirling in my brain. "But why . . . ?"

Henry laughed, sprouting goose bumps on my arm despite the sweat dripping down my back. "Come on, Melissa. You can't possibly be that naive. The spring! The only freshwater spring left in the whole doggone county!"

My body trembled but it was my heart that broke. It was finally out there. The truth. The entire marriage had been a lie. The whole fairy tale I'd once believed, the illusion that I'd been lucky. That we'd fallen in love despite our differences. True love in the face of all odds.

But it had never been about love at all. It had only been about the drought. I was just a bonus.

Henry was pacing now, his hands fluttering at his sides. "We thought it would take months for him to trust us enough to sell, but we got lucky—he packed up and fled after only weeks. Dangled a few dollar bills in front of his face, and he was so desperate he took the bait—hook, line, and sinker." He laughed, though there was no humor in it. "Joke was on us, though, right, Melissa? That spring—the magical spring my father said would fix it all, would keep us afloat—it's dead. We barely got two months of irrigation before it went dry, like everywhere else in this godforsaken county." He rushed at me suddenly, his breath hot on my face. "Did you know? Did your family know it was almost dry when we got married?"

"No!" I brought my hands to my face, voice quivering. "Henry, I swear, I didn't—"

He pushed himself away from me, not hearing—or not caring about—my answer. "And now he's dying!" He flung his arms in the air, gesturing wildly toward the closed bedroom door. "And you . . . you . . ." His eyes narrowed, his breath at a pant. "You're all the same, aren't you? This whole county. A bunch of weak, lying, lazy thieves."

I pushed myself up from the floor, tears blinding my vision, covering my stomach with my arms.

"You were supposed to be the queen. You could've ruled this county with me. But you chose the other side. Was it worth risking everything to help some poor piece of gutter trash who ain't never gonna be able to give you anything back?"

I knew the answer. I didn't need to say it.

An inhuman growl escaped his lips. He punched at his legs. "Doggone it, Melissa! Answer me!"

My eyes snapped back and forth between him and the door. If I hurried, maybe I could make it. But he was faster than me out in the open. I wouldn't get far. And even if I did, where would I go?

But staying . . . staying would be worse.

"Melissa!" He was running out of words. Any minute now, he would use his fists instead.

It was now or never. I reached the door within seconds. The knob slipped in my sweaty hands, slowing me for just a moment.

But a moment was all Henry needed. He grabbed me from behind and threw me to the floor. I thrashed beneath him, but he settled his weight on my legs, silencing me. He pinned my arms easily with one hand, slapping me across the face with his other.

I cried out, feeling blood trickle from my nose.

He raised his hand to strike me again.

"I'm pregnant!" I screamed.

He grabbed my hair, pulling my face nearer to his. "What?"

"I'm pregnant!" Tears rolled down my face. "I'm pregnant!"

His fingers unfurled from my hair, sending my head crashing to the floor. He stared at me, chest heaving. For a moment, I feared he didn't believe me. He remained on top of me, his weight crushing me, his eyes revealing the struggle within. Finally he rose, his hands careful not to touch even the folds of my dress. He did not help me up. Instead, he walked out the door, slamming it shut behind him.

In the silence after his departure, I lay on the floor, hands across my face, and sobbed, tasting blood as it mixed with tears on my lips.

CHAPTER TWENTY-ONE

KATHRYN

"You want some?"

The growing darkness made it hard to see what Bert was offering, but I knew the smell immediately. Bread. And cheese. The man had *cheese*. What kind of man hopped train cars but could afford cheese? And why hadn't he offered *that* before those revolting sardines?

I wanted that cheese more than anything in the world. But even my stomach wasn't enough to make me forgive him. "Don't be acting like you care," I spat. "You left me to the bulls, you lily-livered rat."

He leaned back, stuffing a wad of bread into his big mouth. "I pulled you up."

"You pulled your bag up."

"Oh, like you're so high-and-mighty," he huffed, his fingers glistening with spit. "You're the one who almost got us caught in the first place, singing your little song. What in the world were you thinking?"

I lifted my chin and stuck my hands under my armpits.

He rolled his eyes but tossed a chunk of cheese and a lump of bread in my direction.

I snatched both before they could roll out of the car and turned my back. I would eat because it was stupid to waste food. But I wouldn't give him the satisfaction of seeing me do it.

"You're horrible, you know?"

"Yeah, well, your pants are still wet."

That shut him up for a little while.

I moved closer to the open door, allowing the last of the fading daylight to wash over me. The sky was orange with building clouds, the air damp on my skin. Rain was coming. Even in the dim light, I could see the green. They'd obviously had plenty of it. So Frank Fleming was wrong— the drought wasn't everywhere. But even that realization brought me no relief.

Bert settled across the doorway from me. I wished he wouldn't.

"So what's in Indianapolis for you?"

"Don't talk to me." Not talking to him made it easier to stay mad at him. To pretend that my foot hadn't slipped and he hadn't caught me. That he hadn't stopped me from jumping up from the roof before the danger passed. It was easier that way. Easier to just be mad at him for leaving me in the first place, for making me jump when I knew darn well I couldn't do it, for forcing me to realize I could.

He rolled his massive shoulders, eyes jerking at the corners, and turned to watch the sunset. "Well, for what it's worth, I want to say thank you for saving my bag. Because unlike you, I was taught some manners."

I scowled. "I have manners."

"Whatever you say."

"And I had to save your stupid bag. You were carrying on so much, you were gonna get us both caught. What's so important about that stupid bag anyway?"

The bag had not left his side since the incident on the train roof. Even now, it sat in his lap, its strap coiled around his neck like a snake. Bert hesitated a minute before yanking open the silver zipper, pulling a small object from its depths. "This," he said, brushing dust from its side, "is what was so important."

A camera. Black and silver and beautiful, with knobs and buttons everywhere. I'd never seen one up close before. I leaned in and then back, arms across my chest, pretending to be unimpressed. "Oh."

"I'm a photographer for the Farm Security Administration. Do you know what that is?"

I nodded, even though I didn't.

"I take pictures. Or rather, I'm supposed to take pictures. Of the dusters and the people. Show everyone how the government is fixing it." There was an edge to his voice. He reached into the bag and pulled out a few photographs, holding them out to me. The wind whipped at their corners. They were going to blow away. And he didn't seem to care.

I grabbed them, holding them tightly with clammy fingers, and scooted away from the door. It was darker back here, but I didn't need the light to know what the pictures showed. People with masks and flashlights. Cars dodging drifts in a town square. Stores and homes boarded up, barely visible beneath piles of dust. A road empty as a black blizzard rose into the sky like a monster. And a herd of cattle, dead, rotting, reduced to bones from starvation.

They were pictures of home. Of Oklahoma. Or somewhere very close to it. The new Oklahoma, the one we'd all created. Things had been bad in Boise City. I'd seen it every single day with my own eyes. I'd *lived* it. But somehow seeing it here in black-and-white made it much, much worse.

I thrust them back toward him, an ache spreading from my chest.

"I wasn't supposed to be taking these pictures. I was supposed to be showing the good stuff. 'Look how we're helping' kind of thing. Make people feel good about their tax dollars at work." He shoved the photos back in his bag with quivering fingers. "But there wasn't any good stuff to be found. Those folks in Washington, they don't have any idea how bad it is. They think it can all be fixed by throwing a little green that way. That it *has* been fixed." He snorted. "There's no amount of money in the world that can save the Plains. It's over. No matter what Roosevelt thinks."

He rubbed his temples, causing the hair on his cheeks to move up and down. "I was supposed to be back two weeks ago. But I can't turn these in. FSA'd be in a whole heap of trouble, starting with me. No, no. I can't do that." He shook his head, his long hair whipping in the wind. "I gotta come up with a plan first. Find a new job or take some new pics. But in this economy? Not likely. Maybe . . ."

But I wasn't listening. Blood pounded in my ears. The train car seemed to tilt. "What did you say?"

"Huh?" Bert's hands were in the air, his mouth frozen in midsentence.

"What did you say? About the Plains?"

He shrugged. "You saw the pictures. What's money gonna do against Mother Nature? The Plains are a lost cause. Dead."

Black spots floated in front of my eyes. Heat rushed up my spine. It was a lie. A yellow-bellied lie from a twitching Nancy scared of his own pictures.

I clenched my hands at my sides, prepared to swing, only to find my arms wouldn't work. Instead, all that rage—at Frank, at Bert, at Helen, at *God*—flowed from my eyes, pouring down as hot, angry tears.

"Kathryn, whoa. What—?"

"What about us?" The words were soft, muted by my tears and drowned by the rattle of the rushing train. And yet they echoed into the night. "Where are we supposed to go?"

"Kathryn—"

"What about *me*?" I said, louder. "What am I supposed to do?"

Everything I'd seen, everything I'd done. I'd thought fixing myself would help. Then the rains would come and make things right. But the truth was bigger than my foot. Bigger than the drought, bigger than dust. The truth was right here.

In this train car, in Bert's words, in his stupid, heartbreaking pictures. The truth was in the ruin, in the failure, in the abandonment I could never shake.

"Kathryn."

"No." I shook my head. I didn't want to hear what he had to say. My questions were not his to answer. I'd come so far, endured so much, and this man—this spineless, self-centered, pants-peeing man—would not be the one to tell me it was over. "You're just gonna run, let us all waste away because you're worried about what might happen to *you*? If you show some stupid *pictures*? But what about *me*?"

Bert shifted, tucking one leg under the other. "Now hold on just a minute. I didn't make the dusters."

My throat burned as misery morphed into full-blown fury. "No. Now *you* listen to *me*! Lots of folks are running scared of things they have every right to be scared of. But you ain't never been crippled. Ain't never been suffocated in a duster. Never gone hungry or watched people die from the ground you walk on. You ain't got any right to be scared too! You ain't got any right to say quit!"

Bert opened his mouth and then closed it again, face trembling beneath all that stupid red hair. Then he slumped back, his chin resting on his chest.

I wiped my face with the back of my hand. "You're nothing but a fat, selfish coward."

"You're an Okie, aren't you?"

"What?"

A glance. His back straightened. "You said *us*. 'What about us?' You're one of them. An Okie."

That word. Spoken just like the outsider he was. "What's it to you?"

"Are you fleeing the drought?"

Fleeing. That word was worse than *Okie.* It hit me like a punch in the gut. "I ain't *fleeing* nothing."

He clicked his tongue and wagged one thick finger. "I shoulda known. A girl your age hopping a train by herself. You aren't normal stock. I've been around enough Okies to know 'em when I see 'em. Either spitting fire as they march away with their tails tucked or else wasting taxpayer money, clinging to a land not fit to be clung to. Stubbornest darn people I ever met." The corners of his mouth curled slightly.

I glowered at him and turned my back, staring out the open door.

The last of the sun had disappeared behind the hills, and pinpricks of light were starting to peek out from the purple sky. Stars. They'd been there every night of my journey, and yet somehow I hadn't noticed them. But tonight they were brighter than ever. Breaking through the night sky, demanding to be seen. As if Pa himself were right there with me. My thoughts swirled to the last night we'd spent together before we'd been separated. To his words and my own, the ignorance and idiocy of my misdirected anger. My naiveté about a world he'd tried to protect me from, the world that had already broken him.

Despite everything, he'd tried to be a star . . . for me. And I'd pushed him away.

Every ounce of fight leeched from me like water from an Oklahoma field. I suddenly felt very, very small again.

"My pa and I got separated in a duster."

I said it to the sky, but it was Bert who answered. "So you *are* an Okie."

"I've been trying to catch up ever since." It was both an answer to his question and not. I pulled at a thread on my dress and watched as a star shot across the sky, flaring and fading within seconds. "The night before I got lost, he told me a story. He said the stars make no noise, but you still notice 'em, right? You notice 'em because they shine out in the blackness around 'em."

Bert glanced out the open door, fiddling with the zipper on his camera bag.

"You folks out east, you think it's so easy just to quit. To walk away. But you can't see the stars because you ain't never seen the dark." I leaned against the wall and scratched at a scab on my knee. "This drought, this depression . . . we're in the blackness. We can either shine in the dark or be overcome by it. Sometimes shining means staying. Other times it means going. But it never means to quit."

Out of the corner of my eye, I saw Bert's head cock to one side, trying to meet my gaze. I stared straight ahead.

"My pa done made the hard choice to leave. For Helen, for me." I choked on the words. "But it was the right choice for now. The brave choice. It was his way of not quitting." I gestured to Bert's bag, swallowing the lump in my throat. "And those people in your pictures? They're making the hard choice to stay."

I finally met Bert's stare. "Don't you see? It ain't stubbornness. It's courage. They're the stars in the night. Folks like you—" *and like me*—"are just too stupid to understand it."

I didn't want to be sitting here with him. I wanted more than anything to be with my pa. To tell him I was sorry. To tell him I understood. To tell him that I wanted to be a star, that I wanted to be brave. To thank him for being a star, even when my own blackness was trying to swallow him. "We just have to keep going," I said quietly. "No matter what."

Bert said nothing for several minutes, the steady clack of the rails the only sound in the night. "I reckon we'll be in Indiana by tomorrow afternoon," he said finally. "We better get some rest."

Rest. As if rest would ever come. For me, for any of the Okies. But for now, I'd give him sleep. Because tomorrow I'd be in Indianapolis. Tomorrow I'd see Pa. And tomorrow I'd finally get a chance to meet the doctor, fix my foot, and keep going, no matter what men like Bert said to do.

* * *

Indianapolis was a lot like Kansas City. Same big buildings. Same crowds of people. Only the smell was different. Instead of fish, it smelled like manure.

The train slowed as it entered the outskirts of the city, though not enough to make jumping seem like a good idea. Bert leapt first, rolling the way he'd told me to do, and then scrambling to his feet and jogging beside the car. "Jump, Kathryn!" he panted. "You can do it!"

I thought I'd be afraid. Maybe I should have been. The ground blurred and the car wobbled, making it impossible to steady my feet. But I'd come this far. There was no way I was slowing down—or getting caught by a train bull—now.

I closed my eyes and ran, feeling the ground give way under my shoes. For three glorious seconds, I was flying. And then Bert's massive hands were on my arms and a sharp pain shot through my leg as I slid into gravel. My eyes fluttered open just in time to see the last of the train cars rumble past.

"Alright?"

I sat up, examining a fresh gash on my leg. My butt felt like I'd been kicked by ten horses at once. But nothing was broken. And there were no train bulls in sight. "Yep."

He slung his bag around his neck, eyes skyward, stuffing his fingers into his pockets. His mouth was twitching again.

I craned my neck, trying to figure out what he was looking at. Weren't nothing but a few trees and a row of scraggly houses. Abandoned, by the look of them. But then I realized it wasn't what he was looking at. It was what he was trying to *avoid* looking at. Me.

Of course. Weren't like we were friends. Weren't like I even wanted to be. I straightened my back, wincing at fresh bruises, and turned on my good heel. "Oh. Well, be seeing you. Or not."

"Where you going?"

The tall buildings were straight east. Less than a mile by the looks of it. If Kansas City taught me anything, it's that people in cities were always near the tallest buildings. "I'm going to find my pa. I done told you that."

"By yourself?"

I spun around, surprised, then irritated. "Now you want to pretend you care about me? Didn't think twice about leaving me for the train bulls, but you're worried about what a couple big buildings will do?"

Bert's mouth jerked to the side. "It's not the buildings I'm worried about. The city is no place for a little girl on her own."

I wrinkled my nose. "Good thing I ain't a little girl, then. I'm an Okie."

"Kathryn."

I didn't wait to hear what he had to say. I spun back around and marched in the direction of the buildings. My foot ached within minutes. But I wouldn't let myself limp. Not when I was this close. And not when that fool photographer kept following me.

His footsteps echoed, even as the noise increased and the traffic became thick. I wove through the crowd as best I could despite the throbbing, trying to lose him. He didn't take the hint.

Frustrated, I stopped and jabbed one finger into his barrel chest. It hurt. "Why are you following me?"

He scratched at his beard, panting. "I'm not. I'm going this way, too."

So he was a coward *and* a liar. I let out a grunt and kept walking.

A single beat and his heavy breathing was behind me once more.

We pushed further into the city. Across a wide boulevard, the buildings seemed to sprout up suddenly, brick and concrete behemoths where before there had only been squat houses. Just like in Kansas City, hundreds of people milled beneath them, walking and chatting, going about their business as if nothing loomed over them but sky.

I strode toward one of them, trying not to drag my aching foot. "Excuse me, sir?" An elderly man. Gray suit, black cane, white mustache. Old. Safe. Surely he'd help. "I was wondering if I could bother you for—"

The man recoiled. "I don't have any spare change!" he snapped.

I frowned. "I'm not asking for money. I'm wondering if—"

But he had already scurried away, glancing over his shoulder as if I'd slither up behind him and bite.

My face felt hot, my chest tight. And there was Bert, his back against the side of a building, pretending not to be watching.

I squared my shoulders and looked away. Up ahead was a woman dressed in blue, a polka-dot hat on her head. But not just any woman, I realized as she turned to the side. A woman with a baby buggy. A mother! I limped toward her. "Excuse me, ma'am?"

The buggy squeaking with the effort, the woman quickened her pace.

Thinking she couldn't hear me, I tried to do the same. "Ma'am!"

She didn't even look in my direction. She just kept walking—no, running—toward wherever it was she was going. Toward anywhere away from me.

I stopped, breathing hard. I couldn't catch up. My foot seized, and I steadied myself against the nearest lamppost. Behind me, warm light spilled from a window. Through it,

I could see baskets of biscuits, mounds of rolls, and lines of colorful iced pastries. A bakery.

The cry from my stomach suddenly overpowered my foot. It was as if I hadn't eaten in years. And I hadn't—at least not anything like this. I glanced behind me. Bert was across the street, holding up a newspaper he very obviously was not reading. He would have money to buy something. All I would have to do is ask. But nothing in the world would convince me to ask that man for anything. Not even my howling stomach.

It wouldn't hurt to smell it, though. And seeing as how I was having no luck on the street, maybe I could finally get some directions to Helen's in the process. So stuffing my hunger as far down as I could, I entered the shop. A bell tinkled overhead.

The shop was empty.

"Excuse me?"

No answer. The aroma of freshly baking bread was enough to weaken my knees. I pushed forward, swallowing too much spit, the allure of the cakes and croissants more than I could take. I put one hand on the glass divider, imagining the sugar on my tongue.

"What do you think you're doing?"

I jumped as an aproned shopkeeper emerged from some-where in the back. His eyes were narrowed, greased mustache dusted with flour.

"I'm trying to—"

"Paying customers only!" he barked, moving his hands to his hips. "You got any money?"

"No, but I—"

"Then out! Out with you!"

I pulled my hand from the glass. I'd left a smudge. "Please, I'm just trying to get dir—"

"You deaf or just stupid? I said skedaddle!" He moved toward me, arm raised.

Flinching, I fled from the store and didn't stop until I'd retreated to the closest alley, sliding onto my butt to give my aching legs—and heart—a break. I patted my shoulder. No, I hadn't grown a second head. I was still me. My hands traveled down my arms. Past the dirt and scabs and bruises. Over my ripped flour sack dress. Down my bloodied knees and scrawny legs to my scuffed-up shoes. One normal. One stuffed with a sock but obviously twisted. Yes, I was still me. But that was not good enough for Indianapolis.

Once again, stupid tears clouded my eyes. I slapped them away, glancing up as a shadow blocked the light.

Bert slid down next to me. "I tried to tell you."

I didn't look at him.

"The people here don't understand you. The rest of the nation doesn't understand you. Okies, I mean." He tugged at his shirtsleeves. "They have no idea what it's like. What you're like. They just see a flood of people coming into their neighborhoods, begging for handouts they don't have the money to give, a problem they don't have time to fix."

The lump in my throat refused to be swallowed. I closed my eyes tightly. "I just want to see my pa."

Bert's hand hovered above mine for an uncomfortable moment before patting me once. His skin was clammy. "Where is your pa?"

"4275 Meridian Street." How I remembered it after all this time was beyond me. Probably because Helen never shut up about it. Whatever the reason, it fell off my tongue like a Bible verse.

"Stay here."

Bert's boots scratched against the gritty pavement as he left the alley. He was gone less than five minutes. When he returned, he was whistling.

It hurt my ears. "What?"

He tapped a small yellow piece of paper against his temple, a smile on his quivering lips. "Well, are you coming?"

"Where?"

He rolled his eyes, letting out a roar of laughter. "To find your pa, of course!"

My body slumped, my mouth falling slack. "How did you . . . ?" A more pressing question came to mind before I could finish. "Why?"

"Why am I helping you?"

I nodded.

He shrugged, long hair rolling off his shoulders. "I don't have any right to say quit." He winked. "At least that's what someone somewhere told me anyway."

After about thirty minutes of walking, the tall buildings died down and the honking cars grew fewer. Houses replaced stores, all of them with pretty picket fences and manicured square lawns set back from the road. Everything was so *clean*. Even the sidewalk was free from dust and weeds.

"This one," I said, stopping suddenly. "Number 4275. This has to be it."

The house was massive, easily three times the size of the Mayfields'. Two stories tall, brown brick with white trim. The arched doorway perfectly matched the rows of windows on either side, the trimmed shrubs forming a protective fence around the base of the house. The door was red—bright red—brighter than any color I'd seen in a long time. A small iron balcony curved over the top of the door toward bay windows on either side.

No wonder Helen hated our dugout so much.

"Well, go on."

I'd almost forgotten Bert was there.

"You need me to walk you to the door or something?"

I shook my head.

"Well, whatcha waiting for, then?"

"Nothing!"

"Alright, alright. If you say so." He stood beside me, staring at the house for several moments, shifting from one foot to the other, waiting for me to move.

I didn't.

"Are you sure—?"

"I'm fine!"

He rolled his massive shoulders, letting out a long sigh. "Okay. Well, if you're fine, I guess this is goodbye." He stuck out one hand.

"You're leaving?" I stared at his hand but didn't shake it, ashamed of the anxiety in my voice.

Bert smirked. "You care?"

"No."

He pulled his hand back to his side. "I got you to your

pa, didn't I? Didn't quit. But now I've got some business to take care of."

"Business?"

Bert's fingers flittered over his bag. "There's a wire service here in town. Maybe I'll go send in those pictures."

I dipped my head to the side. "Really?"

He gave a sideways smile and gestured to the sky. Daylight was fading, the sun sinking behind the concrete hills. "It's getting dark. Perhaps I can get people to notice the stars."

A truck rumbled on the street behind us, sending vibrations through the soles of my feet. It was a nice thought. And I almost believed he would do it. Almost.

He gave an awkward bow, his too-tight jacket straining with the movement. "Well, good luck, Kathryn Okie. Tell that pa of yours I said hello."

I watched him walk away, his massive body turning into a speck on the horizon. When I finally turned back toward Helen's house, the driveway had tripled in length. And I was suddenly too tired to take another step. Over a thousand miles in six weeks, and I couldn't make these last few yards. My foot seized inside my shoe, sending fire up my leg and into my spine. It had finally had enough.

By the time I arrived on the stoop, I felt as if I might faint. My mouth was dry. My stomach growled. My hands looked so dirty against that red front door, I was afraid to touch it. I gave a weak knock with my shoulder instead. It left a smudge anyway.

The door opened to reveal a gray-haired man with thick spectacles. "No soliciting," he said simply, as if he'd repeated the words a hundred times and almost couldn't bear to say them again.

"I ain't—"

"Kathryn?"

A beautiful woman appeared behind him, yellow hair coiled in a tight bun, her green dress glowing in the pale light.

"Kathryn, oh, my goodness."

Helen. The woman was Helen. She rushed toward me.

The last thing I remembered was her fingernails—clean, long, manicured—reaching for my arm and the crisp smell of lilac soap filling the air before I collapsed under the weight of my own exhaustion and filth.

CHAPTER TWENTY-TWO

MELISSA

The end of August 1935 in Boise City, Oklahoma, was a collective pause. All of Cimarron County held its breath, waiting, hoping. There were no dusters. No wind at all, really. The air was hot, still, and smelled of rot. The streets emptied; the town hesitated. Maybe this was the year. Quiet prayers, breathless and whispered so as not to jinx it. Maybe this was the year the September rains would return.

I didn't pray for rain. Like the scorched earth that no longer gave way beneath my feet, I was too far gone for rain. Rain would not save my marriage or my home. Rain would not save *me*. So I did not pray for rain. I prayed for absolution.

I made up a bed in the library, no longer wanting to lay

even my eyes on our marriage bed, and also where I could more easily listen for Henry's return. I needn't have bothered; he didn't come home that first night. A respite, though a fitful one. But by the second night, my relief had faded into worry. And by the third night, I had taken to pacing the front room, chewing the ends of my hair. His absence was more frightening than his anger. The reality of what I'd done—no matter the justification—filled our house. Henry could walk in at any moment and throw me out. I had betrayed our vows, stolen. Lied. And to the most powerful man in town. My mind wandered to Annie, to Mary Beth, to every other faceless, hopeless shape that shifted through our town like the prairie dust. Alone, destitute, hated . . . I would never survive.

No, Henry wouldn't do that. His pride would never survive the gossip. He desired control above all else. Well, almost everything else. As long as his seed was in my belly, he would not throw me out. But there was no telling what would happen the moment the child's cord was cut. He craved a son; if the baby was a girl, as I knew she'd be, perhaps he'd cast us aside anyway. Or maybe he'd keep her. Just her. The only thing that scared me more than being thrust into poverty was the thought of my daughter being ripped from my bosom and raised a Mayfield, her mother's arms nothing more than a hushed memory.

On the afternoon of the fourth day, Henry's continued absence became less of a whisper and more of a scream. Fearful or not, I had to talk to him. He was still my husband, and I was still the mother of his child. And his silence about the future was a different kind of torture from his past abuses; it was worse.

I started at the big house. It seemed the most logical place. He had to be sleeping somewhere at night, and even those houses in town whose beds were warm for a fee did not offer a full night's respite. But the big house, I discovered, was not a place of rest. Dozens of trucks crowded the front lawn. Bodies milled around the porch, their murmurs wrapped around them like a blanket.

Maybe I'd start in town instead.

But before I could retreat, Mrs. Brownstone broke free from the crowd. "Mrs. Mayfield! There you are!"

I stiffened in her embrace, the starched fabric of her dress scraping against my skin like thorns. She could feel the truth in my arms, I thought. What I'd done, what Henry had said, the lie of our union and the emptiness of my soul. She'd see it all.

But when she pulled away, her eyes were watery and soft. "We're here for you both, dear. I'm sure you know that."

I did?

"Look at me, clucking away. Please, don't let me stop you. Go, go." She pushed me gently toward the porch. "A husband needs his wife."

Not a reprimand. Not even a critique. An appeal. On rubbery legs, I took a step forward, keeping my gaze on Mrs. Brownstone, hoping for answers. But all she gave me was a small frown, sad and helpless, before stepping back into the crowd. Silence fell over the group as I turned my attention ahead. My steps echoed on the porch, the only sound for miles.

The screen door creaked shut behind me, finally breaking

the chains of their stares. But my relief was short-lived. The stillness of the house held no peace. Henry was here.

I found him kneeling in the sitting room, head drooped against his chest.

"Henry?" His name felt dusty in my mouth. The man before me was a stranger.

He didn't move.

I took a step forward. "Henry?"

He jerked his head back, eyes red and moist. He was crying. This hard, strong man was crying. Had I really hurt him so bad? He wiped tears with the back of his hand quickly, any trace of softness disappearing. "What are you doing here?"

"I—"

He stood suddenly. "I guess it's just as well. Now is not the time for a scandal."

I touched my throat. How foolish I was. His tears would never be about me.

He pushed past me to the window, fingers drumming on the sill as he surveyed anything but me. "Go back home and find something to wear. Black. I won't have you embarrassing me today of all days."

I clutched the sides of my dress. Pale blue. He had bought it for me. I remembered the day he brought it home. It felt like years ago. "Henry, what are you talking about?"

He turned, jaw clenched and skin mottled. Pain was there, just below his cold exterior. Pain I recognized all too well. Pain I experienced as a child and in a million little moments afterward.

"He's dead, Melissa. My father is dead."

* * *

It hit ninety degrees at 10 a.m. on the day of the funeral. There was a pale, cloudless sky without even a hint of a breeze. It was a day when most people would have stayed home. No good would come out of a day like that. But today was the day we would bury the senior Mr. Mayfield, so the entire town crowded into St. Paul's to pay their respects. Or gawk with morbid curiosity. Or both.

Henry was silent when he picked me up, the two of us still maintaining separate residences. He was silent during the drive. And he was silent, making last-minute notes on his eulogy, as we waited in the choir room. I should have been used to it by now. But this silence felt different.

"Are you okay?" I shouldn't have cared. But I did.

Henry's pen scratched against paper. He didn't look up.

I shifted in the squeaky wooden seat. My dress pinched my tender stomach, making me queasy. "I . . . I know what it's like to lose a parent. I don't think you ever really get over it. When I lost Ma—"

He exhaled sharply and crumpled the paper in his fist. "Melissa, I'm trying to think. Will you shut up about your dead mother? She ain't got nothing to do with this."

I curled into myself, hurt. There would be no intermission from our quarrel. No mutual grief to bind us, to soften the pain. We had become completely unraveled, and there was no knitting us back together again.

During the service, I stood next to Henry when I was supposed to stand, sat when I was supposed to sit, accepted hugs when they were offered. I knew how to play the part. But Henry never spoke to me, never touched me, never looked at me. At his father's funeral, it was I who played the ghost.

The Ladies Auxiliary organized a potluck in the church basement after the service. I wondered how many people showed up just for the food. Henry walked in front of me, shaking hands and patting shoulders. I followed. The smell of potatoes and supper casseroles roiled my still-sensitive stomach. Sweaty bodies bumped into me, murmuring condolences through stale breath.

Henry disappeared into the crowd of mourners. He never looked back, his indifference sucking the last of the air from the already-suffocating room. His spurn was louder than any slap, and yet no one else seemed to notice. Head down and hands clasped, I stole through a side door and out into the bright sunlight. The air was hot and dry and plentiful. I gave a yank on my collar, one shiny gray button breaking free and falling to the ground in silent defeat.

"Mrs. Mayfield?"

Annie peered out from behind a tree. Her hair was tied back in a tight bun, her face free from dirt for the first time since I'd known her. Her brown dress was frayed at the bottom but had recently been pressed. She'd put effort into her appearance today. And it wasn't for the sake of Mr. Mayfield. She embraced me with a sad smile, the smell of polish and cooked carrots intermingling with my perfume. It was the first time I'd allowed myself to cry in days.

After a long moment, she pulled away, her eyes searching my face. "Are you okay?"

Her words awoke truth, instantly drying my tears. "Mrs. Gale, please. Thank you. Thank you for coming. But you can't be here."

She cocked her head. "It's a funeral. Can't anyone come to pay their respects?"

"It's not that. I . . . ," I stammered, still unable to tell her what I'd done. "I did something awful," I said eventually. "And I got caught. Mrs. Gale, he knows I've been helping you. He *knows*." I shook her outstretched hands. "You can't be here. You have to—"

"Melissa."

Never had the sound of my own name been so ominous. I dropped Annie's hands and turned slowly.

Henry stood in the doorway, arms stretched to either side as if holding up the frame. Sunlight filtered down through the trees, making his blond hair glitter and shading his brow. "What are you doing out here?"

"I . . . I needed some air."

He took a step forward and extended his hand. "Mrs. Gale, how lovely of you to join us."

Annie hesitated. When she finally accepted his hand, it was with the face of one who smelled rotten flesh.

My eyes pleaded with her. *Run,* I screamed inside my head. *Run.*

"You look well," he said, his voice slipping easily into the Mayfield charm. He took a step back and eyed her dress. "Very well. Especially for a widow who cleans houses for a living."

Annie's mouth puckered. She clenched her hands into fists and put them behind her back.

Please don't. Don't take the bait. You have no idea what he can do.

Henry looked to the sky, wiping his forehead with the back of his hand. "Sure is a hot one today." He grinned. "So tell me, Mrs. Gale. How is that you're doing so well when so many others are not?"

Annie stared straight ahead. "I work hard, Mr. Mayfield."

"So does everybody else." He glanced in my direction, an ugly smile on his handsome face. "Surely there must be more to it than that."

"The Ladies Auxiliary helps me out. Bein' the hands and feet of Christ, they call it."

"Hands and feet of Christ, huh?" Henry ran his tongue over his teeth. "Right." He sighed. "Well, I must be getting back inside. Melissa, it would be in your best interest to accompany me."

I gave Annie a sideways glance before following. I prayed she could read it.

Henry stopped suddenly in front of the door, causing me to bump into him. He didn't even flinch. His attention, instead, was focused on Annie. "Oh, and one more thing, Mrs. Gale. We had a . . . *curious* . . . incident in our home the other day. Perhaps my wife told you about it. A pair of very expensive cuff links was found to be missing from my bureau. A similar pair was seen on Dr. Goodwin very soon afterward."

Annie stiffened slightly as if an invisible string had been pulled tight. But not slightly enough.

"Seems they were used as payment for some sick child's

illness. Curious, indeed." He raised his eyebrows and gave a small shake of his head. "As soon as things are settled with my father's estate, I plan on launching a full investigation. Seein' as how you're friends with my wife and all, I figured you might be able to help. I'll be sure to send the sheriff over to your place—you know Sheriff Marimen, right? Real good friend of mine." His chuckle sent goose bumps down my arm. "I'll make sure he knows to talk to you first."

The last thing I saw was Annie's pale face before the door slammed shut behind us.

The wake lasted for hours. Or at least it seemed that way. Everything moved in slow motion. I stopped trying to be a good wife. I couldn't even look at Henry. How could I, even for a moment, have felt sorry for him? Have cared about his grief? He cared for no one else's.

The colorless morning faded into a pink evening as we began our journey home. As expected, Henry did not speak to me during the car ride, but this time, his silence held no grief. Instead, it was a frightful kind of peace. All forms of pretense were gone. There would be no more pretending.

He parked the car in front of the big house and started up the steps without looking back. I knew I was expected to walk the rest of the way to the back house. But I couldn't. Not yet.

I followed him inside. The house was dark, the only light coming from beneath the office door. He was already seated at his father's desk, a glass of whiskey at his lips, by the time I caught up.

"It's late, Melissa. Go home."

"I want you to promise to leave Mrs. Gale alone."

"And why would I do that?"

I stuck out my chin, trying to stop it from trembling. "Because she had no part in it. Do what you want with me. Whatever you see fit, whatever you see as just. I won't make a scene, and I promise to keep my mouth shut. But I'm begging you, please, leave Mrs. Gale out of it. She did nothing wrong."

He twirled the amber liquid in his glass with one hand while shuffling some papers with the other. "Go to bed, Melissa."

I would not. Not until this was settled. "Henry, please—" My voice caught in my throat as my gaze landed on a now-exposed piece of paper in front of him. "What is that?"

A cold smile played across his lips. "What is what?"

I was very aware I was playing into his game. I didn't care. "Henry—"

"Oh. This?" He thrust the yellow paper toward me.

I let it float in the air between us before snatching it. My eyes washed over the black ink. It was an auction notice. This coming Saturday. For several pieces of Mayfield land. Including . . .

"I'm sure you recognize one of the addresses." His voice was cool. Cruel.

"But you promised," I whispered. "You promised you'd keep my father's land until they returned. You'd keep it in the family."

He scoffed. "Yeah, well, you promised a lot of things."

So it had come to this. He didn't want to punish me. He wanted to *destroy* me. And he knew exactly how to do it. I had taken his dignity, so he would take my hope.

I grabbed his hands. He pulled away in disgust. "Henry, please don't do this." *Please don't take them away too.* They'd never come back if they had nowhere to come back to. Not even my sister's stubbornness would sway Pa's common sense in something so black-and-white. I stared into his eyes, searching for any compassion, any of the love he might have felt at one time. There was nothing.

He took another sip of whiskey. The burning smell turned my stomach. Or maybe it was Henry himself. "Business is business, and business hasn't been good. I had to make some hard choices. Times are changing, and we have to change with them. Get rid of anything that's no longer—" his eyes flickered from my face to my stomach and back again—"useful."

A beat. A moment. That's all it took.

I shrank back as he stood. "Please, Henry. I know I wronged you. I know I did. But please don't do this. I beg you, in the name of God, for His sake, not mine—"

"God?" Henry laughed, the whiskey in his glass sloshing. "Look around, Melissa. God left this place a long time ago. Haven't you figured that out? He doesn't care about us. The only authority left in Cimarron County is me."

The dim light cast darkness across the face I'd once kissed, the features I'd once found so strong and handsome.

I stepped back, tripping over my feet and landing on my rear end in the hallway.

Henry stood in the doorframe, blocking out the light from within. From my spot on the floor, he was a shadow. "Good night, Melissa."

I rose on wobbly legs. It wasn't until I was out of the

big house that my strength returned. I raced down the drive through the moonless night, not stopping until I was inside our house with the door bolted shut behind me. Finally out of his presence, my body emptied of courage. I sank to the floor, choking on my own fear, my breath coming out in ragged waves. I clutched my stomach, fighting both tremors and nausea.

There was no mistaking his meaning. After the baby was born, Henry Mayfield was going to be rid of me. One way or another.

CHAPTER TWENTY-THREE

KATHRYN

I wasn't moving.

It was the first thing to hit me when I opened my eyes. I was still. I wasn't in a car, on a horse, on a train. I was in a bed. In a house. On a street. And I wasn't moving no more. How long had it been since I had been still?

"Kathryn."

The room was dim, and I struggled to find the source of the voice. Rustling in the corner and then a soft click. Light. Just like that, there was light. And Helen. Her hair was loose around her shoulders, her face powdered, but not with dust. Her dress was yellow with blue flowers. It looked soft. A real dress. Not a flour sack like mine.

Only I wasn't wearing a flour sack anymore. My skin

didn't itch. My fingers fluttered to my stomach, feeling the smooth material. It was the same green as new wheat. And the hands touching it . . . were they even mine? They were clean, the nails trimmed. My hands didn't look like that.

"Kathryn."

I turned my head back toward Helen, squinting. Everything about her was too bright. She was clean. Her hair was shiny. Even her teeth were glossy. It made my eyes hurt. I opened my mouth to speak and found it dry. I swallowed dust.

Helen handed me a glass of water.

A glass of clear water. Like it was the most natural thing in the world. And it should have been. But it was so heavy, I struggled to raise it to my lips. When I did, I nearly gagged. Just like her, it was too clean. And too easy.

"You've been drifting in and out for a week."

Memories swam in my vision, blurry and unfocused. Helen. Forced sips of water, spoonfuls of soup, a damp cloth on my forehead. A week of fitful, dreamless sleep. And yet exhaustion still pricked at every nerve.

"Do you want something to eat?"

I shook my head. Truth was, I was starving. And if they had clean water in the house, new clothes, a soft bed, there was no telling what kind of food was in store. Maybe even pastries from that same bakery I hadn't been good enough to stand in. But food wasn't why I was here. "Where's Pa?" I croaked.

Helen smoothed her dress. She stopped looking at me.

"Where's Pa?" I repeated, louder.

"Kathryn."

If I'd had the energy, I would have screamed. Told her to stop saying my name and answer the question. I didn't come here for her. But my throat remained closed, my lips parched.

"Kathryn," she started again. She stood suddenly, moving from her chair to the edge of the bed. She reached for my hand, stopped, then reached for it again. Her hands were ice. "Kathryn, your father, he . . . he didn't make it."

What did she mean? Did the truck break down? Was he stuck somewhere?

"My father did all he could, but by the time we got here, the trip . . . it had just . . . worn him out. The dust pneumonia was too advanced."

Her words jumbled. My brain struggled to keep up. Wait. Where was Pa?

"He passed quietly. In his sleep."

She wasn't making any sense.

"We had him cremated, like he wanted."

Cremated? Cremated is only something you do when someone dies. What was she talking about?

"I'm sorry, Kathryn. He didn't suffer. Not at the end. He was comfortable. Safe. I was with him."

Her words hit me like a kick from a horse, clearing my foggy brain. I yanked my hand from hers.

Tears welled in her eyes. "Kathryn, please."

"Shut up." They were the first words I'd spoken that had flavor. I could taste them on my tongue. I sat up, feeling an ache travel down to my foot but refusing to give it the attention it demanded.

Helen slid from the bed, backing toward the wall.

I struggled to stand on my own, gripping the bedpost for support. My foot was red, angry, bruised into a mess. My shoe. It wasn't on my foot. It wasn't on this ridiculous pink floor. She'd taken it. She'd taken *my* shoe. And Mr. Hickory's sock. And my pa. "*I* should have been with him. Not you! *I'm* his daughter."

"Kathryn—"

"Does Melissa know? Did you bother to tell her? Or was this one more way you could have him all to yourself?"

"I wrote her a letter. About you, about James. But I haven't . . . I couldn't bear to send it."

"*You* couldn't bear it?" I wanted to laugh. But not enough to actually do it. "You are so selfish, Helen. You know that? My pa couldn't see it, but I could. You only care about you. My pa had a whole other life before you. *Besides* you. And you couldn't stand it."

Helen wept openly now, covering her face with her hands.

It almost broke me. Almost. How dare she cry? Those tears were rightfully mine. But I was too angry to back down. And not just at her. "You did this to him! You brought him to this place, forced him to leave his home, lost his daughter along the way—"

"We looked everywhere for you!" Trails of black mascara rolled down her face. She looked like a fancy raccoon. "For over an hour we roamed those dunes, looking for that handkerchief."

A sudden coldness seized my gut. "Handkerchief?"

"Yes," she sniffed. "The blue-and-white one. Your pa

knew it was the brightest thing you had, that it would be the easiest thing to spot in the dirt."

I swayed, suddenly dizzy, and gripped the bedpost with numb fingers, sweat chilling my forehead. "Pa didn't know I had that hankie. It was Melissa's. She gave it to me before we left, but I didn't tell anyone."

Helen opened and closed her mouth several times. "Well, he must have seen it."

I shook my head. "No. I kept it in my pocket. Because I knew he'd make me give it back if he saw it."

She blinked, twisting her pale hands together. Beneath her flowered dress, her chest fell and rose rapidly.

I couldn't breathe. My nightgown was too tight. And sweaty. But still I was cold. Heart-pounding, shivering cold. "You saw me, didn't you?"

"Kathryn—"

"I had the handkerchief across my face, trying to keep the dust out of my nose. When I came to, it was still there." I took a wobbly step forward. "You saw me. In the ditch . . . and you left me there."

The words lingered on my lips. They had been so hard to say and yet so easy. "You left me there," I repeated, louder. "You left me there." It was out in the open. She couldn't take it back. I couldn't take it back. But I wasn't surprised. I was relieved. The game was over. We could stop pretending now.

"I had to!" Helen rushed toward me, causing me to fall backward into the bed. Her nails dug into my shoulders. "He would have made us go back!" Makeup smeared, her face was no longer perfect. It was red, splotchy, scary. "Don't you see? We'd come so far! We were so close to being free! When I saw you, I thought you were already gone. Or else very close. And if he'd found you, hurt or sick or dying, he would have made us go back." She released her grip on my arms, her body collapsing into itself. "That place was killing us, Kathryn. Killing *him*. We couldn't go back."

The air in the room, so clean and fresh, smelling of powder and honeysuckle, suddenly felt dirty. I pulled away from her and retched. Nothing came up. There was nothing *to* come up. I was empty.

"Please, Kathryn. You have to understand. I was trying to save him. I loved him. I thought if I could just get him home—"

"Home?" I exploded, finding my voice again. "Home? You took him from his home, Helen! Stole him from it!"

She collapsed on the floor, sobbing. She grabbed at my legs as I stood and stepped away, wincing as my bad foot made contact with the soft carpet.

I'd never liked Helen. I didn't like how she looked at me, how she looked at my father. I didn't like how she walked around our dugout, doing the things my mother should have done. And I certainly didn't like how . . . *Helen* she'd tried to make everything in our lives. But now even those fake bonds between us were severed. She was no longer a Baile, if she'd ever really been one at all. She was just Helen Barrett. And I hated her. I hated her for what she'd done. Hated her for who she was. But most of all, I hated her for being the only person within a thousand miles who should have cared about me . . . but didn't.

I almost cried then. Instead I looked down at the mess of a woman at my feet. "Oklahoma didn't kill him, Helen. You did."

Ignoring her wails, I stormed from the room, forcing back tears of my own. Tears for the throbbing in my foot, for the father I'd lost, for the journey I'd made, for the God I'd wanted to find but who, it turned out, wasn't worth finding at all.

Most of all, I cried for the ending— and new beginning— that suddenly wasn't.

* * *

The house was so stupidly big, it took me ten minutes to get out. Even then, I wasn't really out. I was in the yard. I guess it was a yard. The absurd, enormous, magnificent yard. Even in the fading light, the grass was bright green, like someone had painted it. There were trees with actual leaves and a tall brick wall and a garden. A lush, full garden with roses and lettuce and corn. So much color and beauty in a world without Pa didn't make sense.

I grabbed on to the nearest tree and took several large breaths. My foot was throbbing. I needed to get out of here. But I wouldn't get far without my shoes. There was no telling what she'd done with them. They were probably in the trash somewhere. Maybe if I was quiet, I could sneak back in and look for them without anyone seeing me. Without having to see Helen. I was so angry and so desperately sad, I was afraid I would hurt her. Or collapse in her arms. I wasn't sure which would be worse.

I took a step toward the house, then stopped. Even if I found my shoes, then what? I didn't have any money to get home. I didn't know how to get to the station or find the right train to hop. I didn't even know how to get out of this ridiculous house. And my foot hurt. So did my chest. So did everything.

"Good evening, Kathryn."

I jumped as a fire suddenly flared nearby. The orange glow rose and met the end of a cigarette, illuminating the silver hair of its smoker briefly before burning out and shrouding us both in darkness once again.

The man at the door. It seemed like a million years ago.

"I was wondering if you were ever going to wake up."

"I was tired."

The man laughed softly. "Yes, I imagine so." He moved toward me, a dark shadow in an even darker twilight. Then came the rustling of his jacket and the sound of flesh against metal as he patted a bench I hadn't realized was there. "Sit."

I straightened, ignoring the protest in my foot. "No thank you."

"Suit yourself." A long sigh and the tip of his cigarette flared again. "So you're my granddaughter."

No, I'm not.

"Helen talked a lot about you."

Sure she did.

"I'm glad I got the chance to finally meet you. I didn't think I would."

Because your daughter left me for dead.

Another long pause, another drag on his cigarette. "I'm sorry about your father, Kathryn."

I took a step back as if burned. "You didn't even know him."

"He was sick when he got here. The cough . . ." He cleared his throat as if just talking about it made it catching. "I'd heard physicians talk about it, those who'd been to the Dust Bowl—that's what they're calling it, you know? The Dust Bowl. I read it in the paper." He waited for me to say something, to respond, but I had nothing. Like giving our plague a name was what really mattered right now. After a few moments, he continued. "But to experience it for myself . . . I just want you to know I did my best. Did everything I could."

I wanted him to stop talking, but I didn't have the energy to yell. All that anger from before, the only thing keeping me going, pushing me past the pain, began to fizzle, leaking into my body as sadness. A sadness that threatened to drown me.

"He used to ask me to take him out here. On days he was feeling strong. He'd come out here and sit on this bench, staring up at the sky. And he'd talk. About Oklahoma, about you and your sister. But mainly you. Oh, how he loved to talk about you."

I clutched the tree at my back, focusing on the rough bark at my fingertips, the smell of wet leaves. Anything to take me away from here, from his words and his memories. Memories of my father that should have been mine.

"He told me you were a pistol. Guess he was right if you made it all the way here on your own." He chuckled. "Said you had more get-up-and-go than most able-bodied girls. Only time you ever sat still was when you were reading.

The same book over and over, he said. Your mother's. What was it again?" His mouth clicked. "Oh yes, *The Wonderful Wizard of Oz*. I used to have a copy myself around here somewhere . . ."

Stop it. Just stop it.

"He got a real funny smile on his face, talking about it. Said you were coming all this way to see the Wizard." He chuckled again. "I'm guessing that means me."

I pulled my knees together, wincing. My father went to his grave knowing me as nothing but a pigheaded, foolish little girl with notions of a Wizard. There was no Oz. There was no Scarecrow, no Tin Woodman, no Lion. And this man sitting before me was certainly no Wizard. He was just a man. And I was just a girl with a crippled foot. Alone. And a long way from home.

"I have to go."

"I beg your pardon?"

"I can't . . ." My voice cracked. I did not want this man to see me cry. "I have to go home. I ain't supposed to be here. I don't know why I came."

A scratch and the smell of sulfur as he lit another match. His face was once again illuminated. I wanted to pretend he looked wicked. But the smile on his face was kind. "You came for your pa, Kathryn. And now he's gone."

The dam burst. I couldn't hold it any longer. He'd said it with such finality, such truthfulness. I'd come for my pa. And he was gone. He was *gone*. I slid down the tree, not caring when the bark ripped at my skin. He was gone. Nothing else mattered. Not my skin. Not my foot. Not even this man staring at the ground, pretending like I wasn't wailing right next to him. I'd come all this way for a ghost.

"I'm sorry your father passed, Kathryn," he said quietly. "But that doesn't change anything."

I sniffed dry tears. "What do you know? It does! It changes everything."

A hand on my shoulder. Gentle. "You also came here for you. Don't you see? Your pa is gone, but you are here." Dr. Barrett leaned down, so close I could smell him. Tobacco and mint. "I can still help you. Isn't that what you want?"

Pa had asked me that same question before we left. And here I was a thousand miles later and still without a clear answer. What I wanted more than anything was to see my father again. To be in Oklahoma, laughing with Melissa, cussing out the jackrabbits, praying for rain. Watching the wind blow the wheat as Pa worked on his plow and Melissa swept the floor and I gathered beans in my apron. I wanted to have not killed my mother, to have not disappointed my father, to have not been a burden to my sister. I wanted all of those things very, very much. But I couldn't have any of them.

What I could have, however, was a fixed foot.

CHAPTER TWENTY-FOUR

MELISSA

I didn't sleep that night. Instead I paced the front room, every nerve in my body tensing at the slightest sound. By the time the sun finally broke over the eastern plain, my fingernails were bloody, bitten to the quick.

The way I saw it, I had two options.

The first: I could stay. Wait it out, pray to the Lord for mercy, and hope that time or—at the very least—pride would change Henry's mind. A scandal would be disastrous, especially now when Henry was working so hard to take on the Mayfield mantle. Maybe his arrogance would allow us to live, if not in peace, then at least in a stalemate. Henry could keep his dignity, and I could keep my child.

It would not be an easy life. It would be a life filled with fear, forever wondering if my next sin, no matter how small, would be my last. I would never feel safe. I would never find happiness. I would never know the love of a man.

What I wasn't willing to do, however, was live out the rest of my days as a Mayfield, in the absence of the true God, expected to worship at the feet of a man while my faith withered and died like the Oklahoma grass. And that's why my first choice was not really a choice at all.

So then there was my second option.

At ten past six, I pressed myself to the front window and watched for signs of movement at the big house. Sure enough, right on cue, a shape emerged. Henry. Many things had changed, but his schedule had not. I watched him walk down the porch and climb into his truck. From this distance, I could not make out his face. Perhaps it was lined with stress, dark circles under tired eyes. Or maybe he wore the confident smile of one who makes his own future. All I could tell from my place at the window was that there was no change in his stride. No sense of impending doom. He was the senior Mayfield now, and there was business to attend to. Dust rose from his tires as he headed down the long drive toward Boise City. He was not thinking of me. And I planned to keep it that way for as long as I could.

I forced myself to count to a hundred before stepping outside. I did not change my clothes. I did not take a bag. The coon dogs howled at my appearance, sounding the alarm, causing me to jump. Mayfield to the core, those three.

I grabbed my bike from the side of the house and then stopped. Henry had not bothered to visit our house in days, but I was sure he was keeping an eye on things. He would notice if my bicycle was missing from its usual spot. Walking would take longer. But walking it would have to be.

I stuck out my tongue at the dogs as I crossed into the barren field but did not let myself look back at the house. It was never home, no matter how much I tried, no matter how much I wished. Like the rain we'd begged so hard to fall, love had abandoned this land long before we realized it was gone. I cupped my hands around my tender middle. The *what-ifs* meant nothing; there was only the *what is*.

Sweat beaded on my skin, dripping down my chest and causing the cross at my neck to cling to my flesh. September had arrived hot, our prayers for fall rain unanswered yet again. What few rows of wheat dared to grow did not rustle as I passed. Clumps of dirt collapsed under my feet, crumbling into dust and rock. No birds soared through the sickly gray sky. No grasshoppers fluttered from dying blade to dying blade. Everything had given up.

But me.

I ran toward town. When the baby in my womb demanded I slow down, I walked. But I never stopped. The fields gave way to barren lots and, soon, abandoned stores. The fastest route would have been straight through town, but I couldn't risk Henry—or anyone else—seeing me. I crossed Main Street and kept to the alleys. The roads were quiet, most of the houses still dark. Under the cloudy sky, Boise City's usual hush felt less like a small town and more like a graveyard.

"Mrs. Mayfield! What are you doing here?"

My eyes darted over my shoulder. I wished she hadn't said

my name so loud. Even in this neighborhood, it wasn't safe. "Mrs. Gale, please, can I come in?"

I didn't breathe until the door clicked shut, the smell of coffee rushing forward to meet me. Annie took a step back, one hand clutching the front of a tattered housecoat. Her slippered feet scraped against the threadbare rug.

I suddenly remembered it wasn't yet seven in the morning. "Mrs. Gale, I'm sorry. I—"

She shook her head. "Ain't no need. No need. Just come in here. The kids ain't up yet. And I'd like to keep it that way." She led me toward the kitchen. "You want coffee? Something to eat? We ain't got much but I could—"

"No thank you."

"Well, if we're gonna bypass the pleasantries, then you wanna just tell me why you're here?"

I took a deep breath. "I'm leaving. Today."

"Whatchu mean you're leaving?"

"I'm leaving Henry. Getting out of Boise City. Today."

Her hands tightened around her chipped mug.

I cast my eyes to the floor. There was a crack in one of the wooden planks. "Mrs. Gale, I . . . I haven't been honest with you."

"Whatchu mean?"

"I was paying you from my allowance; that much is true. But Mary Beth's treatment . . ." My throat threatened to close. "I . . . I stole a pair of cuff links from Henry's dresser to pay for it. I didn't have the money to cover it, and I couldn't just let her die." I licked dry lips, still not meeting her eyes. "I thought he wouldn't notice. Thought they were just one in a dozen. But they were a family heirloom. Valuable. Really valuable."

"So that's what he was talking about at the funeral." She raised her chin, appraising. Connecting dots she should never have had to connect.

I nodded. "I told him you had no part in it. You didn't ask me to steal; you had no idea I'd done it." I picked at a hangnail until it bled, trying to shift the pain away from my chest. "I don't know if he believes me. All I know is he's angry, and I don't know what will happen to me if I stay. What will happen to her." My voice faltered as I ran my hand over my middle. I lifted my head and finally met her eyes. "I'm so sorry, Mrs. Gale. I never meant for you to get dragged into this."

She took a long sip, draining the rest of her coffee. The seconds ticked by loudly though there was no clock in sight. When at last she spoke, her voice was neutral, with no trace of anger. But no trace of forgiveness, either. "So where you going?"

I paused. "Indianapolis. That's where Kathryn and my pa went."

"It'll also be the first place he'd look for you."

My posture sagged. I already knew that, of course, but still I hated to hear her say it.

"That is," she added, "if you think he'll come looking. You really think he would?"

"Yes. He doesn't want me, but he'll want the baby."

Annie's fingers drummed against the side of her empty cup. "Even if it's a girl?"

"Even if it's a girl. It's the best way to get back at me. I . . . I took something from him. Something even more precious than his stupid cuff links. I took his pride."

Annie rose suddenly and walked to the window, staring out at her dead backyard. I could see her face reflected in the dirty glass, her lips pressed together, cheeks drawn in. Somehow, seeing her that way made me feel even more ashamed of what I'd done. Not to Henry. But to her.

"Mrs. Gale—"

"Sounds like you need a new plan."

I wrapped my arms around my body, swallowing a wave of sickness. I hadn't eaten that morning, and my daughter was not happy about it. Or perhaps the nausea had nothing to do with the baby at all. "I don't have anywhere else to go."

She turned around, chewing the inside of her cheek for a few moments. "But you do. The same place everyone in this dried-up town has gone. California."

I shook my head. "No. It's too obvious. If that's where everyone else is headed, he'd look there, too."

"And what he'd find is thousands of Okies."

"But he's Henry Mayfield. He isn't like you and me. He has friends, resources we can't even imagine. I wouldn't be surprised if he had a private investigator in his pocket. He would find me."

"Easier to hide in a crowd than it is on your own, don't you think? Easier to become someone new, too." She leaned her head to one side.

She was right. With so many migrants headed west, no one would notice me. I'd be just one more fool trying to escape the dust. The handbills promised work and land. I could start over. Me and the baby. Cut my hair, change my name. Become a nobody once more. But even then . . .

"He'd still find me."

"So you don't stay with the rest of them. All them Okies settling in the south, you go to California and head north."

"North?"

"I got a cousin lives outside Santa Rosa. She—"

"Mrs. Gale, no." My heart broke under the weight of her compassion. "I can't. I can't have you involved."

She snorted, rubbing one hand across her brow. "Mrs. Mayfield, I've been involved from the moment you knocked on my door. Ain't no turning back now."

I slumped in my seat, trying not to look at the woman in front of me. This woman with her ripped housecoat, unwashed hair, and skin weathered beyond her years. She hadn't asked to be put in the middle of any of this. And yet here she stood. Helping me. "Mrs. Gale, I really am sorry."

"I know you are. You was just trying to help. Me, the kids. And Mary Beth, she might not even . . ." She shook the words from her lips, afraid to even taste them. "You done it wrong, but you done it with a right heart. And I think . . . I think I finally understand your book now."

"My book?"

"The one you was reading to Mary Beth. About Dorothy. You read something about Oz being a good man but a bad wizard. And it didn't make no sense. Till now." She stared out the window again, speaking more to her reflection than me. "With this drought, these dusters, the world ain't so black-and-white no more. It's just all different shades of brown." She turned. "And you . . . to the Henry Mayfields of the world, you may be a bad wife, but I think you're a good woman."

I covered my face with my hands, unable to look at her.

"Mrs. Mayfield," Annie said quietly, crouching in front of me. "Mrs. May—"

"Melissa," I hiccuped. "Please. It's Melissa Baile."

She bit her bottom lip and gave a slight shake of her head. "Alright, Melissa." The tiniest of smiles played across her lips. "I'm Annie."

Fresh sobs welled up in my throat and I moved forward, needing to embrace her.

She backed away. "Mrs.—Melissa. There ain't no time for that now. You best be getting a move on. Henry . . ."

The thought of my husband dried my tears on my cheeks. "Right . . . right." I stood, pushing my chair back with a creak. "I need to leave." But my legs refused to move. And my eyes refused to leave my friend's face. "Annie, I . . . I don't know what Henry will do once he finds out I'm gone. It might not be safe for you."

She let out a short burst of air through her nostrils. "You ain't gotta worry about that. Henry won't lay a finger on me or my children."

"You don't know what he's capable of. How can you be so sure?"

"Because we're coming with you."

"What?"

She leaned back against the counter, body sagging. "This

place been killing me for a long time. Even before it took Jeremiah. No future on the horizon; nothing here but heart-ache and memories. That ain't no way to live. And maybe I don't have to no more." Her voice thickened. "Got one of those brochures from the Resettlement Administration. They want us to leave. They'll even give you money if you do. I've been saving up some of my own as best I could. Ain't got enough. Not nearly enough. But I got my cousin. And I got—"

"Annie." Pain filled my chest, choking me. I couldn't breathe. I wanted to laugh or cry or yell or all three. "But what if he finds us?"

"What if he don't?"

Her smile was tired, nowhere close to beautiful. And yet it was the most stunning thing I had ever seen. My vision blurred once more.

"No time for that! Help me get the kids ready. My hus-band's old truck is in the shed. It runs on prayers, but maybe we'll have enough to get us away from here."

I nodded, struck dumb. I not only had traveling compan-ions; I had a way to get there. This was all happening. And by golly, it just might work. There was only one loose thread. And it was a big one.

"There's something I have to do first."

Annie inhaled sharply.

"It won't take me long," I said quickly. "Get the kids ready and the truck loaded. I'll meet you at the old mill on the west side of town. You know where I'm talking about?"

"'Course I do, but—"

I grabbed her hand. "You have to promise me that if I'm not there by nine, you'll leave anyway."

"Melissa—"

"Please, Annie. Promise me."

I was being reckless. Foolish. But just in case. I had to do this just in case. Because I was willing to leave everything behind . . . except for my sister.

Annie gave me a small nod. I squeezed her hands, rough and dry inside my own, and took off before she changed her mind.

Henry's truck was still gone when I finally reached the Mayfield homestead for the last time. A good sign. The air was dense, leaving everything suspended and noiseless. Except the coon dogs, of course. They howled, hackles raised, and strained against their ropes. As if they knew I wasn't supposed to be here anymore.

I ran up the stairs, ignoring the cramp in my side, and pushed my way into the bedroom. Unexpected nostalgia stopped me in my tracks. I hadn't been in this room since our fight, and the memories woven into those blankets hit me like a brick. Our marriage bed. I'd been such a child when he'd first brought me to it.

But I wasn't a child anymore. I pulled a small green object from under the mattress and hurried down the stairs without looking back.

Fatigue settled into my muscles, but I wouldn't allow myself to stop. I burst through the back door and climbed the rusted barbed wire to the pasture. There hadn't been cows for months. It no longer even smelled like livestock, the ancient white patties crumbling into the surrounding dirt. I dodged them anyway, keeping my eyes set on the horizon.

The wind murmured life through the dead grasses, tangling them at my feet and carrying whispers across the plains. Clouds lowered, blocking the rising sun but trapping the stifling air. An unfamiliar smell drifted on the breeze, somehow both musky and sweet.

The journey seemed longer now, every step heavy. I was wasting precious time, each second increasing the risk of being found out. But then, finally, there it was. The dugout. Our dugout. Mine and Pa's and Kathryn's. And yes, even Helen's. It still looked exactly the same as it did that day I broke down on the hilltop all those weeks ago. But *I* was not the same. And this time I would not let heartache keep me from doing what I came to do.

Spiders and grasshoppers scurried beneath my feet as I stepped inside. It was dingy, darker than I remembered. But the stove where I burned dung to keep the house warm was still there. The table where I tried to teach Kathryn to write was still there. The cabinet full of dishes, most of them cracked—Kathryn's fault—was still there, too.

I moved farther in, toward the one area I cared about. The small hay mattress lay crumpled on the floor. From the looks of it, some animal had made it a home. But it remained. I swore if I looked hard enough, I could still see our footprints in the dirt. Where we'd danced and where we'd fought. Where we'd snuggled in the winter under thin blankets and listened to our stomachs rumble. Where we'd giggled and cried.

And where we'd read. Over and over and over. Every book we could get our hands on. But mainly this one. The one I'd retrieved from the Mayfield house. *The Wonderful Wizard of Oz.* My mother's book. Kathryn's book.

I could only hope Kathryn would understand. Maybe she had grown up during these past few months and forgotten childish things like Oz. Or maybe, like me, she had clung to them as a last thread of home in a world that was meaner and scarier than either of us could ever have imagined. I had no way of knowing. But when she came back—if she came back—this book would be here for her.

It was a risk. But I couldn't leave the book with Henry; he would burn it the moment he discovered my escape. And it would be months before I could write to Kathryn, if ever. I had no way of knowing how long Henry would keep up the search. Maybe the book would give her hope, as it had done for me. That I was still out there. And that somehow, someway, just as Dorothy had traveled through Oz, never ceasing in her quest to return home, I would not give up until I found my way back to her.

I tucked the book under the mattress, hoping the dugout's new animal residents would find it lacking in taste. A sudden thud at the door ripped away my attention. I pushed my back against the earthen wall, holding my breath. Another thud. And another. But not at the door.

I crept toward one of the windows and wiped away the dust and grime. There was water on the glass. Two drops, three, four. Fat, heavy, loud drops. And more on the way. I backed away and flung open the door. The smell of leaves and earth and life rushed in to meet me. Droplets from the sky released tiny dust clouds as they landed on the hard ground. Rain. It was raining.

I stepped forward. The water was surprisingly cold. It dripped down my neck and beaded on my nose. I touched the moisture on my arms, feeling the drops burst beneath my fingertips. It was real. Thunder rumbled in the distance as another wave of water dove toward the ground, harder this time. More insistent. The sweet release of a thousand prayers washed over my body. Now, of all times, God answered. I lifted my face to the heavens and laughed.

Lightning flashed, chased by thunder, closer this time, drowning out my giggles. The rain changed, falling in thick sheets, urgently, years' worth of precipitation released in one moment. No longer gentle and tender. Painful, driving, determined. Stinging my skin and burning my eyes. The rain had come home, and its return would not be a quiet one.

The water at my feet turned black as the sky from which it came. Answered prayers or not, I had to go. Now.

Squinting against the storm, I pushed forward. The rain was solid, disorienting, the landscape draped in gray. I tripped over clumps of grass and hidden fence posts. There was nothing to see but water. Water . . . and lights. Two of them.

Against the torrent, headlights.

I stumbled backward, landing on my bottom in a pool of mud. Oh no. No.

The lights raced forward, blurred but resolute. There was no mistaking them. Somehow Henry had found me.

I ran toward the dugout blindly, stopping to breathe only when I crossed the threshold. I closed the door, but the wind and water continued to roar, rattling the frame. I paced the floor, leaving droplets in my wake. He would be here in minutes. And he would find me. There was nowhere to hide in a dugout and only one way out. Already a river flowed past the doorstep, the ground having forgotten how to drink.

I shrieked as something shattered the window behind me. I was too late. But instead of Henry, a large ball of ice rolled to a stop at my feet. Hail.

From outside came what sounded like a thousand stampeding hooves. Mother Nature was in a foul mood, and she had released her full anger on Oklahoma. But even over her wrath, I could hear another sound. The slamming of a truck door. And the screaming of my name.

I ran. Henry's frame was silhouetted against the lights, his face disfigured by rain and rage. He looked massive. Monstrous. An evil I could never escape. But still I ran.

The drops pierced my skin like needles. Hail slammed the ground, putting dents in the soft earth. It battered my head and beat against my back, tearing my flesh and stealing my breath. And still I ran. What other choice did I have? There was nowhere to hide. The trees were long gone, ripped out to make room for the plows. Even the grass was missing, dusted over by storm after storm and now buried in mud. A sharp pain cramped my stomach.

"Melissa!"

His voice was close.

Keep going. Keep going.

Lightning raced across the sky, reflecting off the rain and momentarily blinding me.

"Melissa!"

Suddenly the ground beneath me gave way. I tumbled down several feet before something caught my dress, causing me to jerk forward. My face scraped against rock. The water was louder down here, echoing off the shallow walls, lapping at my fingers. A dry creek bed returned to life. I fumbled with my dress. Barbed wire, blown here in a recent storm, snagged the fabric, like fingers reaching up from the ground to hold me. I tugged frantically, biting down screams as hail pelted my head and bloodied my arms.

And then he was over me. Veins bulged from his forehead as water poured down his purple face. He reached for me, chest heaving. "Where do you think you're going?"

I let out a small cry and yanked at my dress. It ripped, but not enough. I pulled and pulled.

Henry advanced on me, ignoring the water covering his feet. There was no sneer this time, no wicked joy. Nothing at all but murder on his face.

The last of the fabric ripped free. I turned to crawl, but Henry yanked my arm upward. I yelped, choking on the rain.

"You are mine, Melissa. Did you forget that? Just like everything else in this county. Mine!"

His face was inches away, so close I could still smell breakfast on his breath.

"Nothing is going to change that. Not the dusters, not the farmers running with their tails tucked, not the bank, and certainly not some ungrateful little sneak who'd be picking out of the garbage if it wasn't for me." One hand curled around my throat.

I gasped. The pain was immediate, fiery. I swung my hands, trying to knock him away.

Another hand on my throat. Squeezing tighter and tighter. "You could have had everything, Melissa."

Spots formed in the corners of my vision. Air. I needed air.

Henry gritted his teeth. His blue eyes had never looked colder.

Hail still pelted my skin but the pain felt a million miles away. I was going to die. Right here. In this creek bed. I would never see Kathryn again. Or Pa. The baby in my womb would never draw breath. I wasn't strong enough to save us. My hands drooped; my eyelids fluttered as I collapsed into myself. It was time to let go. Finally time to let go.

Suddenly the hands released their grip, and my body fell to the ground. I sucked in a breath greedily, coughing. Feeling flooded into my hands and feet. Pain and coldness and weight. A sheet of rain crashed into the water around me, now as high as my thighs. I wiped the drops from my eyes with tingling hands.

Henry was gone.

I twisted around, light-headed. Nothing but water all around me, the roar of splashing hail muted by the blood in my ears. A muddy wave rushed forward, pushing me downstream several feet. I grasped for an anchor, but the ground below gave way beneath my hands. Another wave struck me, harder this time. Then another. I gagged as water surged over my face, then retreated, filling my mouth with grit. My arms flailed against the tide as it finally pushed me into something solid. A boulder. On the bank. I wrapped my arms around it just as another torrent rushed over me. My body jerked forward with the current, causing my fingers to slip. I held on tighter, muscles burning. I was losing my grip. I couldn't hold on.

And then, finally, it passed.

There was no time to be relieved. A wall of brown raced toward me. The next wave would be here within seconds.

Clutching the boulder with wobbly arms, I tried to pull myself up. My legs refused to move. Their weight had quadrupled, the muscles inside frozen. Leaving a hand on the boulder, I plunged the other into the water. Where my legs should be I found only earth. The water had sealed my lower half under a layer of mud and rocks as thick as concrete. I was stuck.

The wave rushed closer.

In the middle of a drought, I was going to drown.

"Melissa."

It was the eyes I saw first. The eyes I'd fallen for, dreamt about, tried to find myself in now stared at me from a spot just up the bank at the water's edge. Pale-blue eyes rimmed with red in the driving rain. A piece of hail the size of a baseball lay cracked near his forehead. Henry's face was splattered with mud, blood oozing from his temple and covering the rocks under his head. He reached one hand toward me groggily. "Melissa."

Water surged between us. To my waist now. I could no longer feel my toes.

Muddy waves lapped at Henry's mouth, then retreated. He groaned and pulled himself toward me. Inch by inch, breath by breath, those eyes never leaving my face.

The water rose, now up to Henry's chin as he slithered over the ground.

Silt covered my arms.

His hand swung at me, catching the sleeve of my dress, weakly trying to claw its way to my throat. His lip curled into a snarl before the water pushed against us, sweeping his fingers away. "You . . . are . . . mine."

With his dying breath, he was still trying to kill me.

I closed my eyes, releasing my tears and waiting for it to be over. Another rush, stronger this time, securing my body in its muddy tomb. Henry gurgled beside me, closer. I didn't bother to look. Let him come. Let the water come. Wash it all away like the Oklahoma soil.

And then, from beneath the dirt and rocks, something twisted. Something inside me. The baby. For the first time, I felt the life inside me stir. A kick, harder this time. Demanding attention, challenging my defeat. I was letting myself drown, but beneath the water, my daughter was not ready to give up.

And with that tiny little flutter, suddenly I knew. The pain and the loneliness, the drought and despair were not signs of God's absence, but His way of showing me just how big His presence truly was. God had never left me. He'd been here all along. In memories of my mother, a testament to a life lived for Someone bigger than herself. In Annie, full of grace and love I didn't deserve, yet offered to me just the same. In my daughter, a reminder of His hope in a world of brokenness and sin. And in me. For so long I'd focused on what I'd lacked, what had been taken from me—my mother, my father, my sister, even my home—while God had been trying to show me what had always and would always remain: Him.

Water rolled across my face. I tried to breathe but took in only river. Lungs burning, I thrashed against the mud. No. I would not die here. We would not die here. Not like this, suffocating in the very thing Kathryn and I—all of Boise City—had spent countless hours praying for. At long last, the heavens had parted, and the rain had returned, cleansing us of the dust, the death, the pain. Deliverance. The bad days behind us, the future ahead. All I had to do was survive.

I cried out as my arms finally broke free. With one last burst of energy, I pushed myself upward. The mud released my legs with an awful sucking sound. Water rushed in to replace them. They were purple and lifeless, buckling when I tried to stand. Clenching my teeth, I grabbed the nearest rock and pulled, attempting to drag myself up the side of the bank. It gave way under my grasp. I lunged for another rock. It too slipped from its spot and tumbled to the water below.

The river rushed forward, once again trying to cover my legs. No. No, no, no. Not like this. Not me. Not my child. Not when we were so close. And not without a fight. Screaming in frustration, I punched into the mud. The ground wrapped around my fist like a glove, holding me steady as I pulled my legs up behind me. I swung my other arm above me, letting my skin sink into the cold Oklahoma clay. My muscles burned. Sharp rocks tore into my skin. But still I crawled. Inch by inch I crept up the riverbank as the water murmured behind me, spurring me on.

At last I reached the top. Legs tingling, exhaustion flooding me, I collapsed. The rain was a drizzle up here, the wind reduced to a lazy breeze. Hailstones carpeted the ground, covering the late-summer hills with an unexpected blanket of ice. As gray clouds floated westward, I lay on my back with my eyes closed, inhaling the smell of contented earth.

Catching my breath, I pulled myself to my knees and peered over the edge. Henry lay several feet below me, arm extended upward, all but his head covered by water. His mouth opened as if to speak, then closed again as the water pushed against his lips. Instead, his gaze found my own and held it for the slightest of moments. Enough to convey the contents of his heart.

"I was never yours," I whispered. "I am His."

His eyes remained open as the waves roared forth and carried him downstream, the pale blue rolling back in his head, still swimming with hatred as they disappeared beneath the water.

CHAPTER TWENTY-FIVE

KATHRYN

Dr. Barrett's office was in the east wing of his house. Yes, east wing. He had to specify because there was more than one. It was as if the house multiplied, growing bigger with every passing day. And I was a parasite inside its belly.

He agreed to take a look at my foot once I gained back my strength. I told him I'd gain back my strength as long as he kept me away from Helen. He'd laughed at that, though I didn't know quite what was funny.

After two days, I told him I was tired but not too tired. He told me I still had to rest but I didn't have to stay in bed no more. But when I asked for my shoes, he told me they were no good. I wanted to tell him they'd gotten me this far and were just fine, thank you very much. I wasn't about to go crawling around his mansion on my hands and knees just because someone didn't like my shoes, but before I could say anything, he gave me a crutch and a new pair of socks. Cotton socks. Real soft and squishy, like pillows on my feet. So I figured that was okay.

The first few days I spent exploring the house. But I always felt like I was in the way. The Barretts had servants—servants—who were forever in a hurry. I could never be alone. No matter what room I found myself in—and there were a lot of rooms—there was someone else in it. And their stares made sure I knew I was interrupting.

Whispers followed me wherever I went. Once, I was walking through an upstairs hallway, lost as usual, and found myself unable to shake the sensation of being followed. Pausing and counting to ten, I rounded the corner and found the culprit: a maid sweeping the floor after me. I thought I was clean. She thought otherwise.

So that was the end of my exploring. I spent a lot of time in the bedroom upstairs, the one with the yellow wallpaper and lace doilies and pink carpet. And lights that came on just from a click of a switch. On and off, on and off, like magic. From the crystal-clean windows, I had a perfect view of the front lawn. Of the green grass and bright-blue sky. The orange flowers on the bushes and red-tinged brick. Nowhere in Boise City had colors like this. I wasn't sure if it was real or a trick of the glass.

But mainly, I watched the people. All day long people coming and going in suits and dresses of every color. Every evening the women click-click-clicked up the sidewalk, their hair and makeup done up like Hollywood. That first night after I'd been let out of bed, one of the servants knocked on my door and asked me to join the Barretts for supper. When I hid, Dr. Barrett himself knocked.

"Miss Baile—would you please open the door?"

Nope. I sure wouldn't. Not even with the please.

"I'd like you to join us for supper. Some colleagues of mine would like to meet you."

Sure they would. So they could stare at me.

"Kathryn, please."

It wasn't that I didn't like Dr. Barrett. But there was nothing in the world that could have gotten me to leave that room and join him and his fancy-pants friends for dinner. Especially if Helen was going to be there. Which I'm sure she was. So I ignored him. After ten minutes, he stopped. And he never asked again. A tray was left outside my door with food and clothes. I ate the food but refused to change my dress. I was finally getting the new one worn in. Seemed silly to dirty up another.

The one indulgence I did allow myself was the bath. At the Barrett house, I was drawn a bath every single day. Of my own water. It seemed so wasteful. But who was I to say no? Every night, I soaked in the huge tub until the water turned cold and my skin wrinkled. I never felt completely clean. There's some dirt you just can't get off. But it felt good to float anyway.

No one knocked on my door. No one bothered me. Helen had disappeared. And I was a shadow.

After two weeks, Dr. Barrett finally summoned me again. But not to dinner. It was time.

"Miss Baile. So nice to see you again. Please, please. Have a seat." He gestured to a long flat table in the middle of the room. "If you wouldn't mind . . ." He nodded toward my sock.

I removed it slowly, trying to hide my foot behind my other leg. But Dr. Barrett flipped on a light and pulled it closer. I looked away. I'd lived with my foot my entire life. I could never escape it. I had bathed it, cared for it, walked on it for fourteen years. But it had never looked uglier than it did under that light in this room, with all its fancy furniture and clean linens. The skin was bruised and puffy, splashed with purples and reds. The bones seemed sharper, the toes more gnarled. It was hideous. Monstrous. Embarrassing.

But Dr. Barrett never flinched. He turned it over and over in his hands, which were as soft and warm as fresh bread. "Does that hurt?"

I shook my head.

"This is a rather severe case, I'm afraid."

Of course it was. I should have known better than to even try.

"But I still think I can help." The corners of his mouth curled. "It's a simple procedure that involves cutting the tendons to allow for normal growth. What makes my method different is a cut here—" he pointed to the pad of skin beneath my toes—"and here." He ran a finger along the side of my foot, causing my skin to prickle. "This gives us a better chance to mold the foot into the correct position rather than just by cutting the Achilles."

Cut, slice, cut. Just like a piece of meat.

He stood and jotted a few notes on a yellow pad. "There

are risks involved. It's rather unfortunate, actually. If your father had elected to have surgery done as a baby, this more complicated procedure would not even be necessary."

The table shifted beneath me. "What?"

"I said, if your father had elected to have surgery done as a baby, this wouldn't be necessary. It's dangerous, of course, but all surgery is. Especially on infants. But still, usually highly successful."

He didn't look up from his pad, completely unaware I was falling on the inside.

"I will need to perform a few simple tests to ensure you're healthy enough for surgery, and we will need to . . ."

Blood pounded in my ears. Earlier surgery, he'd said. As a baby, he'd said. If my father had elected . . . The ridiculously large breakfast I'd eaten that morning lurched in my stomach. I could have had surgery as a baby. All these years, my foot could have been normal. Fixed. No one would have known I had a clubfoot. *I* wouldn't have known. My father could have saved me years of pain, years of struggle, years of want . . . and yet he "elected" not to.

"Miss Baile?"

I glanced up to find Dr. Barrett staring at me.

"Have you been listening?"

I nodded.

"Then you understand I need to take some blood?"

He had a needle in his hand, frowning under one bitten lip.

He wanted me to lie back. Roll up my sleeve. But I couldn't do it. My body was frozen.

"Miss Baile?"

"I could have had surgery as a baby?" I whispered.

Dr. Barrett cocked his head. "Yes. Yes, of course. Most clubfoot cases are treated at birth."

"But mine wasn't."

"Obviously."

I felt numb. The question I needed answered the most was not one Dr. Barrett could satisfy. Why? Why wouldn't my father have chosen to fix me when he had the chance?

"Lie back, Miss Baile. Please."

I allowed myself to be nudged backward gently onto the hard table.

"This might hurt a little bit. Have you ever had blood drawn?"

I felt my head shake.

"Best look away, then."

He turned my head for me. I felt a sharp stab in my arm, then coldness. It traveled through every part of me. Was that from the blood? Or something else?

There was no question I'd deserved the life I got. It was punishment for killing Ma. For taking away the person Pa loved most. A murderer before I knew what a murderer was. You couldn't send a baby to jail. But you could keep her in the jail she'd been born into.

Pa had relented in the end. Insisted, really, that I come get the surgery. Maybe he'd finally decided I'd done my penance. Fourteen years was enough. Maybe he'd felt guilty. Or maybe he figured surgery was the only way to get me to leave Oklahoma. To punish me in a way worse than clubfoot.

I'd never get a chance to ask him. But I guess it didn't really matter. I didn't need to know the answer. Because no matter what his excuse, no matter what his reasoning, the truth would be the same: I thought Pa loved me, and I was wrong.

The coldness spread. I couldn't even feel my foot anymore. Or my fingers. And my head—my head felt heavy and light all at the same time.

"Almost done," came a voice to my right. "Almost done."

Dr. Barrett was still here somehow. My eyes struggled to focus. A wall. A chair. A plant. A table. A table with books. Three books. Blue. Yellow. Green. Green like grass, like new wheat. Green like . . . No, it couldn't be. But it was. The gold lettering was bright, even to my blurry eyes.

"The Wizard."

"Hmm?"

"*The Wonderful Wizard* . . ."

"Oh! Yes! I knew I had a copy of that book somewhere. I found it last night. Brought it in here for your appointment. Thought it might make you feel more at ease."

I would never feel at ease again.

"There. All done. Hold this."

A pinch, a tug, and a piece of fabric tucked into the crook of my elbow. Flashes of color floated in front of my eyes. Dr. Barrett's face was swirling.

He reached over me and grabbed the volume. "Have to say I haven't read it in ages. Didn't care for it. The ending was a bit trite for my tastes." He flipped through the pages. "Ah, yes, here. '"Your Silver Shoes will carry you over the desert,"' replied Glinda. "If you had known their power you could have gone back to your Aunt Em the very first day you came to this country." Bah." He snapped the cover shut. "See? The entire book needn't have happened. Nonsense."

I closed my eyes. I was still cold. I'd never be warm again. And my head—my head would never stop spinning. I was falling deeper inside myself. Away from Dr. Barrett. Away from Indianapolis. Away from everything. From everything except the book. Because from somewhere inside the spinning came Melissa's voice. Faint at first, then deeper. Reading. Just like she'd done with me hundreds of times before.

"But then I should not have had my wonderful brains!' cried the Scarecrow. 'I might have passed my whole life in the farmer's cornfield.'

"And I should not have had my lovely heart,' said the Tin Woodman. 'I might have stood and rusted in the forest till the end of the world.'

"And I should have lived a coward forever,' declared the Lion, 'and no beast in all the forest would have had a good word to say to me.'"

From the darkness, I could see them. Not the Scarecrow and Woodman and Lion. Not even Dorothy. I could see my family. And they were smiling. Melissa smiled. Pa smiled. My mother smiled. I'd never met her, but I knew it was her. And she was smiling at me, the silver cross around her neck burning with hot, white light—the light of a star.

The reason my father hadn't allowed me to have the surgery wasn't because he didn't love me. It was because he *did*. Because Ma had loved me. Because he had just lost her and couldn't lose me, too. And because, if I'd had it, everything would have been different. Pa would have been different. Melissa would have been different. I would have been different. His choice had molded us, shaped us, defined us. If I'd had the surgery, who we were—and were supposed to be—might never have been.

I'd spent years making him feel like he'd been wrong. Like everything in life would have been better if I'd just had a better foot. And in the end, he'd given in. He'd traveled all this way to make right what was never wrong in the first place. Because he loved me.

And this journey—this journey I'd never wanted to make, that had beaten me down, stripped me bare, forced me to question everything—this journey was a part of that. A father's love.

And a Father's love.

This trip had been hard and full of grief. But all along the way there had been stars—stars I'd misunderstood but whose light now shone bright in the recesses of my mind. This whole journey was not a punishment from a mean, spiteful, distant God, a way to emphasize my weakness. Rather, it was His way of showing me my strength. Because I'd had it all along—and it came from Him and who He'd made me to be.

Not darkness. Not a mistake. *Me.* Because God wasn't bad. And neither was I.

I sat up suddenly.

"Miss Baile!"

Butterflies fluttered inside my head. I tried to stand on shaky legs, forcing down several waves of nausea. But I was warm again.

"Miss Baile, please. You need to lie back down."

"I'm sorry, Dr. Barrett. I have to go."

"Go? Go where?" He placed a hand on my forehead. "Child, you're woozy. Blood draws can do that sometimes."

I pushed his hand away gently. "I'm fine. I just have to go home. I'm not going to have the surgery."

"What?"

"This was a mistake. I . . . I thought I wanted the surgery. Thought I needed it, really. But I was wrong."

"Kathryn, don't be foolish."

"For the first time in my life, I'm not." I covered a twitch in my lip with the back of my hand. "My family kept trying to tell me there was nothing wrong with me. And I thought they were nothing but a bunch of doggone fools."

"Oh?"

"But they weren't. They were telling me the truth. This foot may be different from yours. But it's a part of who I am . . . and who I am is also bigger than this foot." I pursed my lips together and stuck out my chin as I stood, my knees no longer shaky, my twisted foot steady and strong against the cold tile floor. "Who I am is Kathryn Marie Baile from Boise City, Oklahoma. And I'd like to go home now."

Dr. Barrett's face drooped. I thought he was going to yell. Tell me how stupid I was. Maybe try to stop me even. But after several moments, he simply shook his head. "I believe you are making a mistake."

"Dr. Barrett—"

"Let me finish." He cleared his throat. "I believe you are making a mistake. But if you refuse to have the surgery, may

I at least give you a new brace? Clubfoot is entirely manageable if you have the proper equipment, and, my dear, an old pair of shoes and a wadded-up sock is most certainly not the proper equipment."

I nodded, feeling my face stretch with a smile I didn't know I had.

He walked toward the cabinet and bent to get into its dark corners, his white coat sweeping against the floor. "I thought I had . . . Ah, yes. Here." He stood suddenly and held up a new pair of pale loafers with a shiny brace attached to one.

I wanted to laugh. I was finally getting a pair of Silver Shoes.

* * *

"Kathryn."

I froze. I should have just left. Should have walked straight from Dr. Barrett's office to the front door and never looked back. But I wanted my old dress. It didn't seem right to leave it. I couldn't let it be thrown out with the trash, as I knew Helen would do as soon as I left. Not after the journey it had made.

"What are you doing?"

Helen stood in the doorway, fingers entwined in front of her chest. Her hair was curled atop her head, not a strand out of place. Her dress was blue, starched. Only her face showed signs of wear. Tired and overused. Not even the makeup could cover that.

"I'm leaving."

"Leaving? What about the surgery?"

"I ain't having it."

"What? Why?"

I shook my head until I rattled. I didn't need to explain myself to her. Not anymore. I made a move to brush past her, expecting her to move out of the way.

She didn't. "Kathryn, please don't go. I . . . I need you to stay."

My fingers curled around the dress. "You need me? *You* need *me?*" The words came out as a half chuckle, half snarl.

She stepped back like I'd hit her. Her chin trembled.

I straightened my back. My new brace made me feel taller. Or maybe it was something else. I opened my mouth, prepared to list all the ways she'd failed me, all the times she'd never cared about the things *I* needed, but realized I didn't want to say it. I would not squander one more word on this woman. And if she wasn't going to move, I'd push my way out instead. Her body gave way limply under my shove.

"I made a mistake."

I was halfway down the hall. *Keep going, Kathryn. Just keep going. Don't turn around.* Her voice was quiet. I wasn't even be sure I'd heard her. But I knew I had.

"I'm sorry, Kathryn. I know that doesn't mean much, but . . ."

Stop talking. Please stop talking.

"I was scared. I was desperate. Your father was sick. Melissa was gone. The crops were withering. And the babies . . . I didn't know what to do."

I bit my tongue. Tears sprang up in my eyes instantly.

Yes, I was crying because of my tongue. Just because of my tongue.

"All I could think about was your father, about getting out of Oklahoma before . . ."

I spun around, ready to yell. Anything to get her to stop talking. I found her still in the doorframe, her hands on her stomach. Our eyes met and she pulled hers away quickly. So quickly I might've missed it. But I hadn't. And now I couldn't unsee it.

She was pregnant.

"I had to get out of there, Kathryn. I had to go home."

The weight of her words settled on me like rain. We stood frozen, the air thick with the words she had spoken and all those left unsaid, Helen's ragged breathing the only sound in the absurdly long hallway.

Finally I took a step toward her, walking slow, hesitating before placing my hand on her arm. I'd never willingly touched her before. The fabric was soft beneath my fingers. Her perfume was fainter this time. Lilac. I stared into her face, the face that had plagued me for so many years, the face I'd hated. I wanted to remember every detail, every line, every freckle, even the flecks of brown in her green eyes. Because I knew once I left this house, I'd never see her again.

"He loved you." I could barely whisper the words.

Beneath the silky fabric, her muscles loosened. She dropped her chin to her chest as if burdened by the weight but said nothing.

"I don't know why you never loved me. Maybe it was because I was awful to you."

"Kathryn, I—"

"Or maybe it was something else. Maybe it was because cursing the land was useless and screaming up to heaven did nothing but scratch up your throat. It was easier to just blame me, a flesh-and-blood person. Someone you could hate, someone you could condemn. For everything that was wrong in the world. For everything you lost."

"Kathryn." Quieter this time.

"Because, for me, that was why I found it so hard to love you."

Helen's lips quivered, but no tears broke free. There was no need. I was only releasing the truth we'd both always known.

I pulled away from her, the feel of her dress still etched into my fingertips. "You're going to be fine."

She grabbed my hand, her palm clammy. Her head jerked forward, sending one stray curl cascading onto her forehead. She did not push it away. "Will . . . will you stay? We could try to be a family, the three of us."

I smiled slightly. I could stay. With a clubfoot, Indianapolis would be an easier life for me. A good life. I might learn to like it. There were libraries and theaters and even a racetrack. I could get used to the food and the clothes and the people. Maybe get used to the noise and buildings. And I might even figure out a way to forgive Helen. And then there was the baby. Of course I wanted to meet him or her. I hoped my brother or sister would want to meet me, too.

But this baby would grow up a Barrett, not a Baile. He or she would know the color green, the gentleness of rain, the satisfaction of a full stomach. There would be happiness here, soft beds, clean water, and dust that stayed firmly on the ground. Growing up in the City of Emeralds, the baby would never experience life on the prairie, never have a chance to get Oklahoma in his or her blood. And maybe it was better that way. Because once that child did, he or she would never be able to get it out again.

Helen knew this. Her words were spoken not out of a genuine need, but out of a want to make things right between us. To cling to what few pieces of her husband remained. She released her grip on my hand slowly, her fingers lingering on my skin. She knew my answer, too.

"Goodbye, Helen."

"Goodbye, Kathryn."

And so I left her, my old dress and Pa's ashes in a bag, a few dollars for a train ticket in my hand—put there at the insistence of Dr. Barrett—and my thoughts and my feet focused westward on home.

CHAPTER TWENTY-SIX

MELISSA

I rose, remembering to put on my shoes before letting my feet hit the floor. I'd fallen back into dugout life quickly in nearly every way except this one. The dirt floor was so cold this time of year. The stove warmed the air, sure, but it didn't touch the floor. Rugs were one of very few things I missed about the Mayfield house.

I shuffled through the dugout quietly. Dust coated the table and sink. More evidence of last night's duster. I'd have to clean again. Later. Right now, there were more important things to do. I eased open the door and pushed my way out into the early morning.

The air was cool, a taste of winter on the horizon. Soon the dust would freeze to the ground, and we'd be safe for a few months. Maybe it would even snow. But for now, a haze still hung in the sky, mainly dirt and dead wheat heads. It smelled like harvest, and we liked to pretend that it was, although the reaping was slim this year. Mother Nature claimed most of the yield. Most people in Boise City hated the smell. The dirt, the grass, the disappointment. I used to, too. But not anymore. Now it reminded me of that night. That terrible, awful night in the storm when I nearly died. No, the night Henry Mayfield tried to murder me. The night Oklahoma saved me, swelling her waters and lifting me anew from her depths. The night I'd truly understood who God was and who He always had been.

The same storm that saved me killed Henry. Dr. Goodwin said his lungs were filled with water and silt, his brain swelled under a fractured skull. A horrible tragedy. A terrible, excruciating death. He called me a miracle, though he couldn't explain the bruising around my neck. He'd never seen a thunderstorm do that. *"How did that happen, Mrs. Mayfield? Why were you both out in such weather to begin with?"*

I couldn't expose Henry without exposing myself. The stealing. The lies. The escape plan. I was the reason he was out in that weather. And exposing myself would set me up for retaliation from the Mayfield loyalists. They would never see me as a victim; I would only be an enemy, someone who wanted to scheme my way to the Mayfield fortune. We'd been clearing the dugout, I'd said, and got disoriented in the storm. An accident. I was lucky to be alive. At least that part was true.

I stopped at the garden and gathered a handful of yellow mums. The few not destroyed by rabbits or grasshoppers. I wished there were more. But I wished there were more of a lot of things.

If anyone really knew the truth about the Mayfield fortune, they'd never accuse me of trying to scheme my way into it. There was nothing left. Henry and his father had ignored the drought, squandering money on the hope that next year would be different. Even if he'd lived, by the following summer, we'd have been destitute. No better than those he'd been squeezing dry for years. There was no wheat, no cattle, no rent, no money. As the last living member of the Mayfield family, all I'd inherited was a couple hundred bucks and the land, which I promptly auctioned with the exception of a few acres. There was no way I was ever setting foot in that house again.

Because I was the sole surviving member . . . for now. The baby would come soon, and although she'd be half a Mayfield, I'd raise her as a Baile. Someday I would tell her about Henry. When she was ready.

The early morning light made it difficult to see exactly where I was going, but I knew the way by heart. The fence line behind the shed. In the beginning there had been four crosses. One for Ma and three for Helen's babies. Now there were five. Pa. Nothing but ashes, but still we buried him. Too many crosses for such a small piece of land. It should have filled me with grief. And it did, in a way. But at least they were here. In Oklahoma. With us.

I knelt and laid a flower beside each cross, tossing aside the ones that had crumbled since my last visit. Every Sunday I came. Every Sunday I wiped away the dust, replaced weeds with fresh blooms. Just because they were gone didn't mean they were forgotten. And just because it was hard to come here didn't mean I shouldn't.

Because God's there in the hard things, too.

Footsteps approached, crunching on the dead grass. They stopped just behind me, and a hand squeezed my shoulder.

"You okay?"

I looked up and nodded, Kathryn's face blurry through my tears.

She knelt down beside me and took my hand, staring at the crosses. We didn't speak. We didn't have to.

Kathryn had arrived at the hospital a few days after the storm. I'd been weak and delirious, unable to even open my eyes. I'd only heard her. The click of the door. The squeak of her brace. And I swore I had died. There was no way my sister was here in Dalhart. But her callused hand had slipped into mine, much like it was now, and I'd known the entirety of it all without her even telling me. We wept for what seemed like hours, for Pa, for us, for everything that had changed and everything that had stayed the same.

Today the sun rose completely, a perfect circle just over the edge of the prairie, before she let go of my hand. She stood and touched the top of Pa's cross gently with three fingers, as if assuring him that all was okay.

I smiled and joined her, linking my arm with hers as we made our way back toward the dugout.

"You got a letter," she said as we walked.

"Oh?"

"From Annie."

She'd kept her promise. Made it to California. Staying with her cousin, she'd written in her last letter. She'd asked me and Kathryn to join her. I'd declined, of course, citing my pregnancy. Knowing her, this letter would be more of a demand than a request. I smiled, thinking of it. I missed her. Her rudeness, her hardness, her unexpected loyalty. She'd made the right choice for her and her children. Maybe one day we'd tire of the fight and join her. But it would not be today.

"Look at that garden," Kathryn said, kicking the fence post. "We've gotta get the netting fixed if we have any hope of keeping out the critters."

I plucked a blackberry from the bush and popped it into my mouth. It was dry and sour upon my tongue. "I'll do that today after breakfast."

"And that shed needs fixin' too. Walls are starting to lean. I'll have to shovel away that dirt before the whole thing caves in." She settled on the front stoop, pushing her hair from her face. "Ain't got much time till the snows come in."

I sat down beside her, gazing out across our homestead. A breeze whistled past us, swirling the dirt at our feet.

Kathryn drew in it with her finger. In the pale light, she looked different, older. Maybe we both did. "You know," she was saying, "I was thinking that right over there might be a good spot for some grass. They say the government's handing out seeds. We could grow a patch, maybe even plant some trees. Might be good for some livestock someday. Whatcha think?"

"Perhaps."

"If it rains, of course."

I nodded, staring at the naked spot of ground, trying to imagine it covered again in long, swaying strands of green. "Of course."

Much like us, this land was changed, scarred. No one would call it beautiful. It was barren, dry, cracking beneath a sun that refused to quit and clouds that refused to open. It was a violent place, prone to wrath and cruel to those who didn't belong. But for those it called its own, there was peace. It was a peace that prevailed despite hardships, despite sorrow, despite uncertainty. A peace that encouraged us to hang on one more day, pray for one more night, and nurse the wounds of our greed, rather than abandon the land to its injuries. It was the peace of knowing that, whatever lay ahead, we were home.

And we would never be alone.

A NOTE FROM
THE AUTHOR

I was born and raised in the Midwest—rolling fields of green as far as the eye could see—but in 2014, I found myself somewhere completely unexpected: living with my husband and two small children in southern New Mexico. It was brown and dry and hot . . . and completely foreign to a Hoosier like me. But Air Force spouses are nothing if not resilient, and I was determined to make the best of it. My daughter was born just two months into our new duty station, and one afternoon as I sat rocking her, staring out a window on the upper floor of our home, I witnessed my first dust storm.

From that small seed, *If It Rains* was born.

Watching a wall of dust race across the desert floor was like nothing I had ever seen before. You could see it coming for miles, rising up from the ground and gaining speed, just like a wave right before it breaks over the beach. Only this wave was dirty, monstrous, and opaque, blocking out the sun in the middle of the day.

Always naturally curious (or nosy, depending on who you ask), I began researching dust storms: their causes, how they form, their history. I soon fell down a rabbit hole of Dust Bowl survivor stories, devouring books such as Timothy Egan's *The Worst Hard Time* and bingeing Ken Burns's *Dust Bowl* documentary in one weekend. These stories of hardship and courage, determination and grief, fascinated and inspired me. I began fleshing out the characters of Melissa and Kathryn even before the end credits started to roll.

Although *If It Rains* is a fictional story, I tried to retain a sense of authenticity by including historical facts within the text. For example, the town of Boise City was chosen as the setting because of its designation as the epicenter of the Dust Bowl. Frank Fleming's profession as a "rain merchant" was a real job during the height of the drought; when old wives' tales about hanging dead snakes belly-side up from fences didn't pan out, town leaders across the Plains turned to science. Or rather, what they thought at the time was science. Other events, such as jackrabbit roundups and government-sponsored cattle euthanasia, were also heartbreakingly real.

I believe the hallmark of any good piece of historical fiction is its ability to ignite in readers a desire to learn more about the time period and events upon which it's based. Timothy Egan's book and Ken Burns's documentary are excellent places to start, though I encourage you to seek out other resources too, including the myriad of excellent historical fiction books written about the Dirty Thirties. Rae Meadows's *I Will Send Rain* and *A Cup of Dust* by Susie Finkbeiner are two of my personal favorites.

And to those who lived through the Dust Bowl, who heard the roar of the wind and watched as the sky turned black, I will forever be in awe of your tenacity and spirit. You made hard choices, impossible choices. But whether you left or whether you stayed, you never quit. Thank you for the stories you gave and the legacy you wove of grit, resolution, and adaptation. No one could ever truly do justice to the spirit of this hardscrabble group of settlers, but I hope Melissa and Kathryn come close.

➡ TURN THE PAGE FOR A PREVIEW OF THE NEXT NOVEL FROM JENNIFER L. WRIGHT

COME DOWN SOMEWHERE

A coming-of-age story set against the backdrop
of the 1945 Trinity nuclear bomb test

COMING IN 2022
FROM TYNDALE
HOUSE PUBLISHERS

AND FOLLOW JENNIFER L. WRIGHT ON SOCIAL MEDIA:

 JenniferWrightLit   *JennWright18*   *JennWright18*

CP1697

CHAPTER ONE

The Army moved in on a Sunday.

Moved in. That's what Uncle Hershel called it. Like they'd been a happy family out house hunting and found the perfect little bungalow. Like they hadn't just walked in and taken what was ours, claiming the government needed it for the war effort. Uncle Hershel could call it anything he pleased. I called it stealing.

I was in the hayloft when they arrived. Pushing things to the side, sweeping away years of dust and bird droppings, making space for boxes of things we were no longer allowed to keep in our house. Because our house, and over 75 percent of our land, was no longer ours. It was now property of the US government.

"Olive!" Ma's voice came from outside, just below the window.

I didn't answer. Instead, I jumped over a hole in the loft floor—one more thing we didn't have the time or money to

353

fix—and tossed a bag of old grain over to the corner with a bang. Dust floated up from the impact, shimmering in the afternoon sun.

"Olive, come on down. Your brother can finish up there. I need you to help me move the last of this stuff into the casita."

I stuck my head out of the narrow opening. "Make Avery do it. I'm already up here."

Ma shielded her eyes as she looked up at me. "Avery is stronger than you. It will be easier for him to carry the boxes up the ladder. Besides—"

Her sentence was interrupted by a distant rumble. She and I turned at the same moment, searching for the source of the commotion. From my vantage point in the loft, the land spread out beneath me, shades of brown and green. Dirt and shrubs, rock and hills, miles of withered land fading in a pale sky. Ugly. Barren. *Home.* But now, in the distance, on the last hill before our house—the one with the Arizona sycamore, my initials carved in the trunk, bark worn smooth from climbing and that one branch perfect for reading . . . beside that hill, *my* hill, a large truck rolled to a stop, the words *US Army* stamped on the side.

"They're here," Ma said unnecessarily. "Avery! Hershel! They're here."

I pulled myself back from the loft window as another truck reached the barn. Tires on gravel, engines cut, and in their absence, a stifling silence. I pressed myself against the wall, unable to breathe, unwilling to move. A slamming door, muffled voices. A man. And then my mother. Laughing.

I dug my fingernails into my arm and stared at my boots,

breathing in the smell of manure and hay and memories of a place that was fading before my eyes.

And my mother was laughing.

The squeak of the barn door being shoved aside; the rush of sunlight across gray, weathered beams. "Olive?"

Uncle Hershel's gruff voice. I pushed myself further against the wall.

"I know you're up there," he hissed. "Get down here. Now." The last word cut through my resolve the way only Uncle Hershel could.

The ladder creaked as I swung my feet over the side, shuddering beneath my hands as if it too felt my apprehension. I jumped off the last rung, a small cloud of dust billowing out from my boots. I straightened my back, jutting my chin against Uncle Hershel's harsh gaze.

The buttons of his flannel shirt strained over his barrel chest as he wiped the sweat from his thinning black hair. He sneered as he placed a battered cowboy hat back atop his head. "Get out here and say hello like is proper. Ain't gonna have these men thinking we've raised a bunch of savages."

"So today we care what the Army thinks, huh? Just a few weeks ago we hated Roosevelt and the war. Then your CPUSA buddies tell you that they've changed their mind, so now we *do* support the war. I can't keep—"

"Shut your mouth, Olive."

Hershel raised his hand, prepared to strike, but I ducked out of his way. He would always be bigger than me, but now I was faster.

He scowled. "When are you going to grow up and think

about someone other than yourself? This country has made you soft and stupid, girl. When I was your age—"

But I strode from the barn before he could finish. I did not care what Hershel was like when he was my age. My bet was brooding and Russian—just like he was now.

The October sun was harsh and bright, summer refusing to give in to fall, as was often the case in this part of New Mexico. I walked with my head hung low, staring at the ground, avoiding the reality of what I knew I'd have to see eventually.

"Olive? Olive, this is Sergeant Hawthorne." My mother's tone was light, fake, grating.

"Olive, so nice to meet you."

Sergeant Hawthorne had dark hair, slick with pomade, and eyes as green as the Rio Grande valley in spring. He was tall—over six feet if I had to guess—and muscular, evident even under the drab brown of his uniform. He stared down at me with a smile that dimpled his cheeks. On a normal person, I would have found all of these traits appealing. Downright handsome.

Too bad I'd already decided to hate him.

He extended his hand. I didn't take it.

Beside me, my mother giggled and tugged at her dress. "Olive."

But still I did not shake his hand. Sergeant Hawthorne pulled his arm back to his side but kept that stupidly handsome grin on his face. "It's alright, Mrs. Alexander. I've got a daughter around her same age. I know all about teenage girls."

The two of them laughed at his joke like it was funny, my mother's giggles morphing into one of her coughing fits.

"I'm sorry," she gasped, trying to steady her breathing. "This dust. You never really get used to it." She cleared her throat and wiped a tear from the corner of her eye, gesturing toward my brother. "And this is Avery."

Tall and wiry, with a mop of jet-black hair that would never lay flat, my brother looked younger than his nineteen years, though lately he more than made up for it with his ridiculous manly posturing. He thrust his shoulders back, chin lifted, and shook Sergeant Hawthorne's hand with enough force for the both of us.

Sergeant Hawthorne's eyes widened as his arm jerked forward under the intensity of Avery's grip. He stiffened, regaining his bearing and letting out an amused laugh. "Quite a handshake there, son."

Avery gave a curt nod, lips pressed in an absurd, overly serious non-smile.

"We could use a man like you in the ranks!"

"I actually leave in two days, sir."

Sergeant Hawthorne dipped his head and grinned, completely oblivious to the effect Avery's words had on my mother. The slight shift in her stance. The almost-imperceptible intake of breath.

His initial application the year before had been rejected, though I knew nothing more about the story than Avery's return from the enlistment office with fire in his eyes and whiskey on his breath, along with a string of curse words that made even Uncle Hershel's mouth seem tame. Avery had never exactly been light, but his darkness had grown even heavier then. He spent less time in the house with us and more time in Hershel's casita, his bad temper exacerbated by our uncle's own and fueled by a steady diet of Hershel's never-ending rhetoric on this country and its problems.

Still, despite it all, I thought that was the end of it. The world would war but we would continue on, untouched. And we did . . . for a while. Then the Army sent a letter. Next thing I knew, Hershel's friends from California had shown up, their loud meetings in the casita—which now included Avery—growing louder and then markedly quieter, all manner of strange men coming and going from the ranch for days before the whole lot of them just up and disappeared. That's when Avery announced the Army had changed its mind and he was leaving soon, too.

Since then, my brother had started smiling more, my mother less and less. I kept my head down, doing my chores and trying to pretend none of it was happening.

But now here we were.

Uncle Hershel brushed past me, knocking my arm a little harder than necessary. "Sergeant Hawthorne, Hershel Alexander."

"Hershel, yes, yes, of course. I can't thank you enough for this."

I glowered at the ground. As if we had a choice.

"It's temporary, of course," Sergeant Hawthorne was saying. "Just a billet for the men while construction is ongoing. Your house will be yours again before you know it. But the land could take longer. It's all a matter of . . ." He cleared his throat, swallowing whatever he was about to say. Awkwardness seeped into the air around us.

He couldn't tell us when. He couldn't tell us why. But he knew. He knew what all of this was for, what secrets the government was hiding beneath its "war effort" label. He knew . . . and he couldn't tell. And that knowledge was a power over us no amount of smiles or small talk could ever erase.

"Let me show you around," Uncle Hershel barked, breaking the tension. "We're just about finished in the main house—a few odds and ends here and there—but let me go ahead and give you the lay of the land. Now, over here . . ." He put a hand at Sergeant Hawthorne's elbow, leading him away.

My mother sighed as she watched their retreat. The smile, the joy, the facade faded as quickly as it had appeared, her shoulders collapsing in on themselves. She pulled a cigarette from her dress pocket, lighting it with shaking hands. "Come on, Olive," she said wearily after taking a drag. "We still have work to do."

Inside the main house, Avery returned to stacking boxes in the hallway, Mama to loading dishes in the kitchen. I joined them, biting the inside of my cheek to stem tears as I folded blankets in the living room.

Pa had died seven years ago—a farming accident with a wayward bull. His brother, Hershel, had returned from California and moved into the casita not long after, sulking but dutiful, his temper and bad mood a cloud the ranch had never quite been able to shake since. I couldn't help thinking that if Pa were still alive, none of this would be happening. It wasn't true, of course—my father's presence couldn't stop the war any more than his absence—but I clung to the fantasy anyway.

"Olive, you grab that pile there and take it to the casita. Avery, that stuff goes in the barn."

Avery grunted as he lifted two boxes at once. "You sure they're okay with us storing this stuff in the barn?"

My mother lit another cigarette, inhaling deeply before answering. "The barn is still ours. At least according to the papers they gave us. 'Eminent domain' or not, we still have to make a living, and we need that barn to do it. Though heaven knows how we're going to—"

"It'll be fine, Ma." A look passed between my mother and brother, fleeting, before Avery shifted the boxes in his arms and strode from the room.

My mother stared after him, the smoke from her cigarette curling around her gaze for a long moment before she finally blinked and smiled weakly at me.

I punched at a pile of blankets, trying to force them into a ball small enough to carry in one trip, and stalked from the house. I didn't want to look at her. Or Avery. And I sure as anything didn't want to hear the words *eminent domain* again. The government kept using that term over and over. As if naming a thing made it right.

I stomped over to the casita, ignoring Uncle Hershel and Sergeant Hawthorne, who stood next to the Army truck laughing and talking like old friends. I stuck my nose in the air, not caring as the blankets began to slip and drag in the dry New Mexico dirt. Let Mama sleep in dirty blankets tonight. At least she'd still be here at our ranch. Yes, the Army would be here. The land would be smaller, the big house no longer our own. But even in the casita, she'd still fall asleep to the coyotes howling, to the smell of the sagebrush floating on the breeze. Tomorrow morning, she'd still wake up and watch the sun wash over the Jornada, the gray of night giving way to reds and browns and yellows, before stepping outside with Hershel, doing their work, playing their part, just as they'd always done.

And Avery? In a few days Avery would be shipping out, his duty finally realized, his restless anxiety now fused with purpose and a plan. With meaning.

But tomorrow morning, I'd be in Alamogordo, opening my eyes to the pale-blue wallpaper at my grandmother's house on Delaware Avenue. The one with the cracked chimney that made the whole house smell like smoke and the fenced-in front yard that wasn't even big enough to grow a row of corn. The one where the mountain view was obstructed by rows of other houses just like hers and where, instead of painted desert sunsets coloring the walls, there were portraits of Jesus in every room.

Sixty miles away but it might as well have been a million.

I should have been grateful. We all had a role to play in the war effort, all the posters said, and this was mine. We'd get our land back eventually, the Army had promised, when the war was over and the government was done. I should be proud to sacrifice in such a way.

And I was. But I didn't understand why *my* sacrifice meant moving while they got to stay. Why my work at the ranch for the war effort wasn't enough, why I was being pushed out instead, treated like an in-the-way toddler rather than the adult I practically was. Why the need for help was great . . . but not the kind I could offer.

I threw the blankets on the floor of the casita, not bothering to take them all the way to the back bedroom, and returned to the main house, my grief and anger rising with each step. The living room was empty, voices coming from the back part of the house.

No, not just the back part of the house. *My* part of the house. No. No, no, no.

I ran toward the sound, skidding to a halt in the doorway. Avery was pulling books off my shelf, tucking them into a box labeled *Alamogordo*.

My mother, perched on the corner of my bed, was the first to see me. "Now, Olive, it's the last room. We've waited as long as we could—"

I didn't bother to listen to the rest of her words. I flung myself across the room at Avery, something between a scream and a wail erupting from my throat. The book in his hands—*Treasure Island*, one of Pa's favorites—landed with a thud on the floor as he raised his arms, shielding himself from my blows.

"Get out of my room!" I screamed. My nails dug into his flesh as I swung. "Get out! Get out!"

"Olive! Olive, stop that!" My mother's voice was far away, muted inside my anger.

Blood sprouted across Avery's arm. I kept swinging anyway. It was immature, childish, as if we were kids again and he'd broken my favorite toy. But I didn't care. Surprise shone in his eyes as he wriggled and dodged, trying to both block me and escape. I moved to connect with his cheek and felt my arm jerked painfully back.

"Knock it off!" The stink of sweat and tobacco pressed into me. Uncle Hershel pinned my wrist to my spine with one hand, the other digging into my bicep. "What in Sam Hill has gotten into you?"

My mother stood to one side, hands in front of her mouth. Sergeant Hawthorne was in the doorway, that stupid smile finally gone from his face, shiny black shoes covered in dust. At the sight of him—this stranger, this intruder, standing in my bedroom as if he owned it, because he did—the blood drained from my limbs. My body deflated.

Avery wiped at the scratches on his arms and puffed out his chest, snatching the book from the ground and shoving it unceremoniously into the box, ripping the cover. He sneered, daring me to say something, to come at him again.

But instead of inciting me, that rip—that small rip in the cover of a book I hadn't read since childhood—broke me. I wrenched from Uncle Hershel's grasp, barely registering the tears on my mother's face through my own, and fled from the room. Momentarily blinded by the sun, I kept running, past the casita and the barn, past the corral, out into the open desert.

Ragged sobs choked me as the ground began to slope upward, stealing my breath but not my grief. I dodged the yuccas and prickly pears easily despite my blurry vision. The path up the mesa was as familiar to me as my own hands. I didn't stop until I came to the top, to the corner where the big boulder split, a cleft in its side shaped like lightning, opening into a secret space no one ever bothered to notice but us.

The burrow. My brother had called it that because we'd had to pretend to be small animals just to fit inside. Through the lightning-shaped crack, a hidden ledge jutted like a makeshift balcony in front of a shallow cave that was really nothing more than a crawl space. We'd outfitted it with a door made of rotted wood and stuffed the inside with old moth-eaten blankets and pillows, comic books and dime-store novels scattered over the dirt floor.

It had been our spot, Avery's and mine. Back before Pa died and Hershel moved in. When we were still friends and life was still fun. But now it was *my* spot, my safe spot, a place to escape from Mama's grief, Avery's sullenness, and Uncle Hershel's temper. A refuge and release. A remnant of child-hood I refused to let go. Because up here, among the rocks and the shrubs, the bare earth and the cloudless New Mexico sky, I could still pretend life made sense.

From this spot, I was perfectly hidden yet could still see our ranch hundreds of feet below, shimmering in the heat. In the distance rose the ragged top of Oscura Peak. Across the drabness of the desert floor, the dark stain of the ancient lava field to the east and the faint glint of the gypsum dunes to the south. I slid to my knees as a fresh wave of sorrow washed over me.

The ranch had been in our family for over half a century, before New Mexico was even New Mexico. Since my grand-parents had emigrated from the motherland with their two small boys in tow. Back then, no one wanted a piece of the

Jornada del Muerto. And why would they? The "Route of the Dead Man" was nothing but a wasteland, a ninety-mile stretch of desert between Socorro and El Paso with no water, little vegetation, and summer temperatures hot enough to boil your blood.

But the land "called" to my grandparents, or so the story went. Grandpa built the adobe walls with his bare hands, forming each brick with soil and straw gathered right here. The pitched roof, the chicken coop, the barn, the horse corral . . . everything here bore his mark. As a teenager, Hershel had fled, claiming he was going back home to fight in the revolution. Pa swore he never made it out of California, his mouth being bigger than his courage—a rumor I learned not to bring up in my uncle's presence, lest I wanted to be on the wrong end of his violent rebuttal. But my father had stayed in his adopted homeland, his Russian blood thawing in the New Mexico sun. My grandfather added the casita, attached to the house by a courtyard wall, a year after my parents' wedding, he and my grandmother planning to finish out their days there while my parents started a family of their own in the main house.

And that's what happened. Grandpa died in the casita's back bedroom and was buried in the far corner lot.

My grandmother followed soon after, and Pa took over, making the ranch his own by adding a second bedroom onto the main house for his daughter. Me. Every memory I had— of him, of my family, of my life—centered around this ranch.

New Mexico. Our home. *My* home. Only it wasn't mine anymore.

I wept for what seemed like hours, until my eyes burned and my cheeks cracked beneath dry tears. Until the sun lay only a finger length above the mountains and the shadows began to stretch, dappling the landscape with previews of the coming night. Until I heard the sound of crunching rocks and Avery's face appeared through the crack in the boulder.

I swatted at my face, wiping away the grit of evaporated grief.

"You look awful," he said, crawling through and dropping down beside me. His long legs stretched in front of him, draping over the edge of the mesa.

I scooted away, scowling. "At least my clothes match."

He let out a loud laugh, which echoed in the desert air, and glanced down at his outfit. "Mine don't?"

A pair of jeans and a faded white shirt matched well enough, but Avery had been color-blind since birth; making fun of him for it was stupid but routine. A pathetic grasp at normal when the world was anything but.

"I'm sorry about your book. It was an accident."

I scrunched my face. It was my turn to apologize; the welts on his arm looked painful, and I knew I'd landed at least one hard blow on his cheek. But I still couldn't bring myself to do it.

After a moment, he sighed. "You know, you can't hide up here forever, Olive."

"I wasn't hiding. I just wanted to be *alone*," I added pointedly.

He rubbed at his arms. I pretended not to notice the welts my nails had sprouted. "Ma's worried about you."

"Good."

"Now, stop it. That ain't no way to be."

"Ain't no way to be? You don't have any right to tell me which way to be. You're *leaving*."

"Just because I'm leaving don't mean I don't care about what happens here."

I stared at my boots. The laces were frayed, the toes scratched. Memories of a place that no longer existed. I pulled my elbows into my sides. "Why are they making me go?" I had thought my tears were spent but here they were, springing up once again. "It's not fair. Especially with you gone. I can help! They can't do this all on their own."

"Olive . . ."

"Why don't they want me here?"

Beside me, Avery shifted, his discomfort obvious. "Olive, there are some things in this world that are bigger than us. Bigger than our family, bigger than our home. I know you don't understand that yet—"

"Oh, just shut up, will you?" That was another thing Avery had started doing. Only three years older than me, but acting like it was ten. Like he was so wise and worldly, when the farthest he'd ever been was Albuquerque. "I know there's a war going on, same as you."

"I ain't talking about the war."

I turned to look at him, but his face remained forward, staring out toward the rapidly setting sun. He rubbed his temple with one hand, pushing away the dark hair matted to his forehead.

"I mean, I am talking about the war. But there's more

to it than that. There are some things . . ." He stopped and sighed deeply, chewing a moment on his lip before continuing. "There are some things even bigger than the war, Olive. I . . . I can't explain. But I hope one day you'll understand."

I scrunched my eyebrows, tilting my head to one side. "What do you mean, Avery?"

He blinked several times and shook his head, pressing his lips into a small smile before glancing at me. "Nothing, Olive. It's nothing. Just . . . just know that I do care, okay? No matter what you think, no matter what you see or hear. I do care. About you, about Ma, about this." He took my hand, pressing one finger into the dirt. Up to a point, then down again. An upside down *V*. It was the same symbol carved into the rock behind us. The one we'd sign in the air when Hershel got ugly, write on papers slid under each other's door when we'd been sent to our rooms, leave written in the dirt when Mama's incapacitating grief made the chore load overwhelming.

The three points representing the only stable things in a world of instability: me, Avery, the mesa. Home.

We hadn't used the symbol in over two years. But the weight of it now beneath our entwined fingers made the lapse evaporate, the world at large seeming to vanish at the power of our unity. I leaned against him, truly seeing my brother for the first time in months. He squeezed my shoulder and I felt his chest rise and fall in a weary sigh.

"That's why I'm going, Olive. And that's why you have to go, too."

He left after that, words hanging in the air between us,

disappearing back through the crack of the burrow with a sad, resigned smile. My shoulder was cold at the memory of his touch. Although I knew he was only going back to the ranch, it felt as if he were already a thousand miles away. Because he was; he had been for months. And no amount of childish reminiscing was going to change that.

Below me, clouds of dust rose from the desert floor as three more Army trucks made their way up our long drive. As I watched them, Avery's words hung over me like a fog. I should have felt something like pride. Camaraderie. Duty. The honor of sacrifice, of being a part of something bigger.

And I tried. Because he was right—all of that stuff was meaningful, more important. All of that stuff mattered.

The only thing that didn't matter was me.

DISCUSSION QUESTIONS

1. *The Wonderful Wizard of Oz* serves as a touchstone for both Kathryn and Melissa. In what ways does Kathryn's journey to Indianapolis parallel Dorothy's journey to Oz? What nods to that classic story (both the book and the movie) did you spot along the way?

2. When did you first begin to suspect what kind of man Henry Mayfield was? When does Melissa start to acknowledge that he's not the man she believed him to be? How does she try to hold on, to believe in his love for her?

3. Why do you think Kathryn and Helen dislike each other so much? At the start of the story, did you feel sympathy for Helen? Did your view of her change by the end?

4. Despite the drought and all the hardships they've experienced, Melissa and Kathryn both feel a deep connection to Oklahoma. Did you understand their love for the land, or would you have counseled them to leave for somewhere more hospitable? Do you have the same kind of deep roots in any particular place?

5. Like the Scarecrow, the Tin Woodman, and the Cowardly Lion, many of us find ourselves thinking we'd be better off "If I only had a _____." For Kathryn, that something is a normal foot. How does her view of her clubfoot shift over the course of the story? What did you think of her eventual decision regarding her foot? What has the longed-for something been in your own life?

6. Melissa begins the story clinging to the faith she learned from her mother, whereas Kathryn thinks God picks on her and becomes increasingly convinced that He can't be good. Which perspective did you most identify with? How does each sister's faith change by the story's end?

7. As Frank Fleming employs his method to bring rain, Kathryn watches while "rocket after rocket fizzled, and still Frank tried. Because the world needed fixing, and he honestly believed he could do it." Do you agree with her view of Frank, or did you see him as merely a charlatan? Can you think of times when you've witnessed similar desperate hope—and anger, like the crowd's, when that hope is disappointed?

8. Looking at Annie Gale, Melissa recognizes, "The woman was me. Me several years in the future. Me without this new dress and my new last name. Me in another life, another world, another twist of fate." How does identifying with Annie in this way inspire Melissa's actions? Do you believe she goes about helping Annie in the right way?

9. Kathryn tells Bert, "This drought, this depression . . . we're in the blackness. We can either shine in the dark or be overcome by it. Sometimes shining means staying. Other times it means going. But it never means to quit." How do you see characters in this story attempting to shine light in the darkness? In times of darkness, when you've felt helpless against the wrongs in the world, what has your response been—to stay or to go? To you, did that represent quitting or shining in the dark?

10. Considering the women of the church, Melissa observes, "Even these women, for all their love and faith, for all their respect within the community, were still just pawns in the game, powerless to change the rules, so intent on enforcing them instead." Have you observed this within a community—that those who can't change the rules instead work to enforce them?

11. Annie and Melissa argue over Dorothy's characterization of the Wizard: "He was a good man, even if he was a bad Wizard." What does Annie ultimately conclude about this line? Do you think this mix of good and bad is true of human nature? How do you see it reflected in characters throughout this story?

12. Both Melissa and Kathryn frequently long for the rain to fall. What do you think the rain symbolizes for each of them, besides literal relief from the drought?

ACKNOWLEDGMENTS

Writing is a solitary endeavor; publishing is not. It may be my name on the cover, but it never would have made it there without the love and support of my tribe.

First and foremost, to the God of all goodness, mercy, and sense of humor. I never set out to become a "Christian" author per se, but looking back, I can now see His gentle hand nudging me toward it the entire time. Thank You for never giving up on me and giving me this chance to combine my faith and my passion.

To Sarah Rische, Jan Stob, and the entire team at Tyndale, thank you for your enthusiasm and belief in this book. From that very first phone call (where I was struck mute with bronchitis!), I knew this team understood my vision, and I feel so blessed to have found a home for Melissa and Kathryn with people who I know love them as much as I do.

To Natalie Grazian: thank you for plucking me out of the slush pile and seeing the potential in this book when it was still only a shadow of what it would become. I learned so much working with you on this project, and I will be forever in your debt for your sheer determination to see this manuscript in print. Thank you for believing in me.

To Adria Goetz: thank you for sweeping in like the book fairy godmother you are to see this deal through and for always being there to answer my "I'm so new—help!" questions. You never batted an eye at the unexpectedness of our partnership, and your warmth and ambition put me immediately at ease. Thank you for simply being you.

To Samantha McClanahan: you are the reason this book got written. Discouraged by rejection and plagued by writer's block, I was ready to quit. Your kind emails and words of encouragement are the only reason I didn't. You were the first person outside my family who told me I could do this. Thank you for being my mentor, my beta reader, my cheerleader, and my friend.

To my parents and my sister: I never did anything the easy way, and I'm sure there were times you wondered what exactly I was doing with my life. I hope this book finally puts your minds at ease and makes you proud. Thank you for your love and support over the years and, most of all, for making it known that I always had a home to come back to.

To my in-laws and extended family: thank you for nagging me over every shelved manuscript and pushing to read my writing even when I was still hiding it from the world. You wouldn't let me give up—and I am so grateful.

To the countless friends over the years—from elementary school through adulthood—who said, "You should write a book!": I finally did. Thank you for planting seeds, watering them, and being patient as you waited for them to grow. You kept me encouraged, you kept me laughing, and you kept me writing. I wish I could name each and every one of you here, but you know who you are. Thank you.

Finally, to Jonathan, Matthew, and Meredith: none of this would mean anything if I didn't have you all standing beside me. Thank you for putting up with years of stress and heartache, small wins and big losses, and for loving me at my most unlovable. When I was sulking over my latest rejection or becoming lost inside my story (and inside my own head), it was the three of you who brought me back to earth and made me remember what was truly important. I love you all even more than books (and that's saying something).

ABOUT THE AUTHOR

Jennifer Wright has been writing since middle school, eventually earning a master's degree in journalism at Indiana University. However, it took only a few short months of covering the local news for her to realize that writing fiction is much better for the soul and definitely way more fun. A born and bred Hoosier, she was plucked from the Heartland after being swept off her feet by an Air Force pilot and has spent the past decade traveling the world and, every few years, attempting to make old curtains fit in the windows of a new home.

She currently resides in New Mexico with her husband, two children, and one rambunctious dachshund.

TYNDALE HOUSE PUBLISHERS IS CRAZY4FICTION!

Fiction that entertains and inspires

Get to know us! Become a member of the Crazy4Fiction community. Whether you read our blog, like us on Facebook, follow us on Twitter, or receive our e-newsletter, you're sure to get the latest news on the best in Christian fiction. You might even win something along the way!

JOIN IN THE FUN TODAY.

 crazy4fiction.com

 Crazy4Fiction

 crazy4fiction

 @Crazy4Fiction

By purchasing this book from Tyndale, you have

helped us meet the spiritual and physical needs of

people all around the world.

Tyndale | Trusted. For Life.